Aquamarine

Aquamarine

Marina Martindale

No part of this book may be used or reproduced or transmitted in any form or by any means, electronic or mechanical, including photocopying, recording, or by any information storage or retrieval system without written permission except in the case of brief quotations used in critical articles and reviews. Request for permissions should be addressed to the publisher:

Good Oak Press, LLC
P.O. Box 51244
Denton, Texas 76206-1244

Editor: Cynthia Roedig
Proofreader: Renate Mousseux, M.A. ED.
Cover Illustration: Wes Lowe
Cover Design: Good Oak Press, LLC
Typesetting: Good Oak Press, LLC
ISBN: ISBN: 978-0-9986105-7-3

This book is a work of fiction. The characters, corporations, and other businesses depicted in this story are all fictitious. Any and all real locations have been used fictitiously and without any intent to describe any real individuals who may be affiliated with those locations. Any resemblance to any actual persons, living or dead, is purely coincidental. The author and editors are real human beings. We do not include content generated by AI (Artificial Intelligence) software of any kind.

Acknowledgments

Thank you to the team who helped me create Aquamarine; my editor, Cynthia Roedig, my proofreader, Renate Mousseux, and Wes Lowe, for another outstanding cover illustration.

To Johnny:

∾ONE∾

TONYA CLAIBORNE SCANNED the room as she finished her guitar solo. Her college jazz ensemble was performing at a Dallas church, and so far everything had gone smoothly. She glanced at the music director, who nodded his head in approval. As the other musicians resumed playing Tonya turned her attention back to the audience. The blonde woman sitting in the front pew gave her another smile. She had been watching Tonya intently for some time. It began while Tonya was singing, "The Girl from Ipanema."

The audience members were mostly family and friends of the student musicians, along with jazz enthusiasts from the greater Dallas-Fort Worth metroplex. Tonya wondered if perhaps she had met this woman before. She appeared to be friends with the woman sitting next to her, and both appeared to be enjoying the concert. Tonya shrugged it off and refocused her attention on her music. As the chords faded, the audience once again burst into applause.

The music director returned to the microphone. Their next song would be the final one for the evening. As he stepped aside, they began playing, "Caravan." The mystery woman whispered something to her friend as she nodded toward Tonya and took another photo of her. Her actions made Tonya even more curious. Once the concert was over, she would have to find out who this woman was.

The audience rose to their feet and gave them a standing ovation once they finished. The music director thanked everyone for coming and motioned for the ensemble to stand and take a bow. As the crowd disbursed some headed for the exits while others approached the musicians. Tonya looked toward the back of the room. A young man stood from his seat in the last row and made his way towered the front of the church while the woman in the front pew, along with her friend, walked up to one of the trombone players. He greeted Tonya with a quick kiss a moment later.

"Good job," he said.

"Oh, Evan, you always say that."

"Hey, just because I'm your fiancé-to-be it doesn't mean I can't be your biggest fan too."

"I know, and I love you for it." She nodded toward the two women, who were still talking to the trombone player. "I'm wondering who the lady in the blue sweater might be."

"Which one?" He stepped back to get a better look.

"The one with the shoulder length blonde hair. She kept her eye on me for some time and she acted like she knew me. We must have crossed paths somewhere, but I can't recall when."

"Maybe she's sizing you up," Evan said jokingly. "But don't worry. I can handle her if she tries to make trouble."

"Thanks, Evan. I know I can always count on you."

As if on cue, the woman walked up to Tonya and extended her hand. "I wanted to stop by and introduce myself. My name is Melissa Atkins. I'm here tonight with a friend whose nephew is also in the band."

"Nice to meet you"

"Likewise, and at the risk of sounding too forward, I'm also with the Angela Carson Modeling Agency. The reason I was watching you so closely is because you have the perfect look to be a model. You're tall and thin and your hair is gorgeous. I snapped a few photos of you with my phone, and you're certainly photogenic. So, have you ever thought about modeling?"

Tonya brushed a strand of her long, dark hair away from her face. "Well, I'm certainly flattered, but to be honest, I've never really thought about it. I'm more focused on my music."

"I see." Melissa looked disappointed as she handed Tonya one of her business cards. "Well, you're certainly a talented musician, and you're going to a top-notch school, but we do a lot of print modeling here in Dallas, and it pays really well. If you think this is something you might be interested in doing to help with school, then please give me a call."

"Thanks. I appreciate the offer, so I'll think about it. We students can always use the extra money." Another audience member walked up to Tonya and Melissa stepped aside. Her friend soon joined her, and she gave Tonya a farewell nod as they left.

"Ready to go?" asked Evan.

"Yep. Let me get my things, and I'll tell my music director goodnight." Tonya returned a few minutes later with her gig bag, along with her coat and purse. The late winter air felt icy as they stepped outside and walked up to an older model gray sedan.

"Are you hungry?" asked Evan. "I know you didn't eat before the show."

"No, I didn't, and I'm starving."

"Me too. We're also too overdressed for fast-food, so I'll take you somewhere a little nicer."

"Thanks, I'd love it. I overheard some of the other musicians saying there's an Applebee's close by."

"Sounds perfect." Evan unlocked the passenger door and Tonya slipped inside. As they waited for the car to warm up, Tonya looked up the direction on her phone. They spotted several of her fellow musicians when they came inside the restaurant. She gave them a nod as the hostess walked them to their table. Once they were seated, she asked for a club soda with lime.

"So, what did you think of the concert?" she asked.

"It was great. I know I wasn't into jazz when I first met you, and I had no idea there was such a thing as jazz guitar, or classical guitar, but the more I hear it, the more I like it."

"Then I'm happy to know I'm making you more cultured."

After enjoying a leisurely meal together, Tonya pushed her empty plate aside. "It's been a long day," she said, "and we have a long drive back to Denton."

Evan responded with a playful look. "And here I thought you musicians were all party people and played all night long."

"Some do. However, I'm still a musician in training, and it really has been a long day. I'm ready to call it a night."

Evan dropped his credit card into the check tray, and before long they were on the freeway. Tonya took Melissa's card from her purse as she relaxed in the passenger seat.

"So, do you think this Melissa was on the level? asked Evan.

"Yep. Nothing in her body language suggested she was lying."

"You and your knack for reading people like books."

"It comes in handy. I'd be happy to teach you how to do it sometime."

"I know, but you do it naturally. Have you ever been wrong?"

"A few times, but not very often."

"I see," said Evan. "So, back to Melissa. Do you think modeling is something you'd want to do?"

"I don't know, but it's certainly something to think about."

"Really?" Evan sounded surprised.

"Yep. She said it pays well and I can always use the extra cash, so I think I'll sleep on it." Tonya stifled a yawn as she dropped Melissa's card back into her purse. "In the meantime, my focus is on my music. And graduating. And trying to get into grad school."

She leaned back in her seat and closed her eyes as Evan turned up the radio. Once they arrived in Denton, he drove to a small apartment complex near the campus and walked Tonya to her door.

"Here we are, home sweet home." Tonya flipped on the lights as they stepped inside her one-room apartment. The modest furnishings included a floor lamp, a chocolate-colored sleeper sofa, a desk, and a bistro table with two chairs. She parked her guitar in the corner while Evan took off his jacket and plopped down on the sofa.

"So, are you up for spending the night?" he asked.

"No, not tonight. I really am beat."

"Aw, c'mon. I'll be a good boy. I promise."

She sat down next to him. "Yeah, right. Tell you what. Let me get my beauty sleep tonight, and we'll hang out tomorrow night, right after I'm done practicing with my guitar group."

"But tomorrow's Sunday, and we have class Monday morning."

"Then we'll make it an early night. I should be home by five, so why don't you drop by, say around five-thirty, and you can bring a pizza."

"Of course," he said, "and I'll bring a six-pack of beer as well."

"Tsk, tsk," she said with a playful grin.

"Hey, I turned twenty-one, and so will you. Very soon."

"No doubt your roommate is relieved to no longer buy your liquor for you."

"He is." Evan smoothed a strand of hair off her face as he talked. "And then, after the pizza, we'll hang out for a while." He gave her a long kiss.

"Down boy," said Tonya once they came up for air. "But hold that thought, okay?"

"Say what?" He gave her a pouty look and Tonya burst out laughing.

"Oh c'mon. It's not the end of the world."

"I know," he said, grudgingly. Grabbing his jacket, he gave her another affectionate kiss.

"Goodnight, Evan." Her voice was firm as they walked to the door. "I'll see you tomorrow."

"Goodnight, love." After one last kiss, Evan stepped outside, and Tonya closed the door behind him.

❧TWO❧

TONYA PUT HER dustmop away and was admiring her clean apartment when her phone rang. She quickly picked it up, surprised to see her cousin calling.

"Hey, Emily. What's up?"

"I'm afraid I have bad news."

Tonya sat down on the sofa. "All right. So, what happened?"

"I just got off the phone with my dad. Grandma Barbara passed away early this morning."

Tonya was stunned. "Oh my god. Are you serious?"

"Yes, I'm afraid so."

"So, what happened?"

"I don't know all the details. All my dad said was she didn't show up for breakfast, so one of the staff went to check on her. They found her in her bed. She'd apparently died in her sleep."

"Wow." Tonya stopped for a moment to take it all in. "I know she hadn't been doing well lately."

"No, she hadn't. She's been slowly going downhill ever since she fell and broke her hip. So, I went ahead and booked us on a flight to Phoenix later today."

"When's the funeral?"

"Tuesday morning," said Emily. "It's actually a memorial service. Your mom and my dad will fill us in once we get there. She'll be cremated later this week, then my dad and your mom will scatter her ashes up in the mountains; the same place where we scattered Grandpa's. We'll fly home Tuesday afternoon, right after the service. Kyle has to get back to work, and I know you have classes."

"I sure do," said Tonya. "I'll email my professors to let them know. So what time are we leaving?"

"Four fifteen. Can Evan take you to the airport?"

"I'm sure he can."

"Good. I'll text you the flight number as soon as we're done."

"Thanks, Emily, and I'll send you the money for my ticket."

Tonya sat quietly once they ended the call. Her grandmother had been a difficult woman who never forgave her mother for marrying her father. After her father left, Tonya's well-to-do grandmother continued to punish the family by leaving Tonya and her sister to do without while their mother struggled to get by. Things finally changed when her grandmother fell and broke her hip. She was placed in an assisted living facility, and Tonya's mother and uncle took control of her finances. They also convinced her grandmother to make things right by taking care of Tonya's college expenses. While it would never make up for her impoverished childhood, Tonya was grateful to not have the worry of massive student loan debt when she graduated.

"And let's hope her estate is settled in time for the fall semester," said Tonya. She pulled up Evan's number and placed a call. While disappointed in the unexpected change of plans, Evan too thought Tonya should be with her family, and he was happy to take her to the airport.

* * *

Tonya looked at the crowd when she reached the gate and spotted a blonde-haired couple with a young boy. As she came closer, Emily greeted her with a hug.

"You okay?" Emily asked.

"I'm fine, but let me take a look at you." Tonya stepped back and looked her cousin up and down. "I see you're showing."

"I'm in my fifth month. We just found out it's a girl, and Cory's adoption will be final in a few weeks, so I'm about to become a mother twice over."

"Then congratulations, and I'm happy for all of you." Tonya gave Emily's husband, Kyle, a hug, along with a high five to his son, Cory.

"Look at you, my man," said Tonya. "You've gotten big since the last time I saw you."

"I'm nine now," Cory proudly said.

"We couldn't get four seats together," said Kyle, "so you'll be sitting with Emily, and Cory and I will be a couple rows behind you."

Tonya shook her head. "No. You sit with Emily, and I'll sit with my buddy here. We have some catching up to do."

"Are you sure?" asked Kyle as Cory's face lit up.

"Positive. I'll let the flight attendant know when we board." As they waited for their boarding call, Emily said Tonya's mother was on her way from Tucson to Phoenix.

"Is my stepdad coming with her?" asked Tonya.

"No, he has to work. My dad offered to let you and your mom stay at his place, but your mother declined, so you'll be staying at the hotel with the rest of us. It's near the church where we're having Grandma's service."

Their boarding call was soon announced, and everyone queued up at the jetway. Stepping onto the airplane, Tonya guided Cory down the aisle to their row and waited as he took his seat by the window. She sat down beside him, making sure his seat belt was securely fastened. Once the plane took off, they spent their time playing games on Cory's tablet.

"You win." Tonya felt the plane beginning its final descent.

"You wanna play again?"

"Not this time. We'll be landing in a few minutes."

Cory put his tablet in his backpack and looked out the window, eagerly pointing out some of the landmarks as the plane descended over Phoenix and made its final approach.

"My goodness, Cory," said Tonya. "You remember all of that?"

"I was six when we moved to Texas, and I remember a whole lot of stuff from back then."

Tonya burst out laughing.

"What's so funny?" he asked.

"You are."

The wheels touched down and Cory turned his attention back to the window, watching intently as they taxied up to the terminal. Once they came to a stop, Tonya guided him off the airplane. Kyle and Emily waited at the end of jetway.

"Did he give you any trouble?" asked Kyle.

"Not at all," said Tonya. "Although I must confess, I got pretty good at zapping asteroids."

It was after dark when their rental car drove up to a single-story house and parked. Emily's father had a somber look on his face when he opened the front door. A woman with long, dark hair greeted them with hugs once they stepped inside.

"You okay, Mom?" asked Tonya.

"Yeah, I'm fine. It was kind of a shock, but I'm dealing with it. Trust me, it's nothing compared to what I went through when we lost your sister."

"I know. I feel the same."

They followed Tonya's mother into the living room where they joined Emily's brother, Nick, and his family. Nick's two children were close to Cory's age, and once all the greetings were exchanged his wife took the children to the kitchen for ice cream while Tonya's mother looked at Emily's father.

"Well, Roger, do you want me to break the news? Or would you rather do it?"

"I can do it, Heather." He took a large envelope from the coffee table and gave the others a serious look.

"As you know, back when Tricia and Heather were children, your grandparents put all their assets into a living trust which stipulated that upon their deaths, everything would go to the surviving spouse, which, in this case, was your grandmother. Then, upon her death, it would go to the two daughters, who would split it fifty-fifty."

"Sounds pretty typical to me," said Nick. "So, with Mom being gone, I'm guessing her share will go to Emily and me."

"I'm afraid it's not so simple, son." Roger pulled a stack of papers from the envelope. "As you know, your grandmother had some serious issues with your aunt when she married Carlo."

"Which, in hindsight, were well founded," said Heather. "Because, as we all know, Carlo turned out to be a not so nice guy after all. But Mother being Mother, she cut me completely out of her will after your grandfather died, which would have been okay had my share gone to my two girls, but it didn't. It—"

"Are you kidding me?" asked Tonya.

"I'm afraid not," said Roger. "After your grandfather died, your grandmother changed her will and left everything to Tricia."

"Don't worry, Tonya," said Emily. "We'll make sure your mother gets her half, and Aunt Heather, you know if my mother were still here, she would have given you your half too."

"I know she would have," said Heather. "However, your grandmother had her way of doing things. A few months after Tricia died, Mother changed her will again. This time she stipulated that everything was to be sold to pay for her final expenses, and all the remaining proceeds would go to charity. "

The room suddenly went silent. Finally, Nick spoke up. "But this was years ago. We're all adults now, and Carlo's long gone as well. Surely she would have updated it since then."

"I'm afraid not." Roger handed the stack of papers to his son. "It's all in there, if you'd like to take a look. I've also put in a call to your grandmother's attorney, and your aunt Heather and I have been doing some research online. We can certainly contest the will, but it may be a long, difficult process, and there's no guarantee we'd win."

"I understand, Dad," said Nick, "but we're talking about a substantial sum of money. I have kids, Emily has kids, and no doubt Tonya will have a family of her own someday, so I don't think we're being unreasonable in wanting our inheritance so we can better provide for our own children."

"And I still have another year of college to go," said Tonya. "Grandma was helping me with my expenses. Surely there's something in there stipulating it to be continued."

"I'm sorry, Tonya," said Heather, "but her paying for your college was a verbal agreement only. It was never put in writing."

"I know, Mom, but you and Uncle Roger have been managing her finances for the past few years. Surely you can set something aside for next year's tuition."

"Which is another reason why we need to contest the will," said Nick, "and I think we're all in agreement on this."

"We are," said Tonya as Emily nodded. "And if Annette were here, she certainly would have agreed as well."

"Then I'll let the attorney know," said Roger, "but as I said before, this could be a long, drawn-out process."

"And in the meantime, it's been a long, exhausting day," said Heather. "So, if the rest of you don't mind, Tonya and I are calling it a night."

Everyone walked outside together, and Nick moved Tonya's bags into Heather's car. Once again, lingering hugs and kisses were exchanged before Heather and Tonya hopped inside, waving goodbye as they drove away.

"Well, I guess my mother got her final revenge," said Heather.

"I'm sorry, Mom, but until today I had no clue of just how much my grandmother hated my father. There are no words to describe what I'm feeling right now."

"She was something else, alright. Thankfully, Tricia and I weren't anything like her, and my father would been appalled at what she did."

"But he's not here," said Tonya. "I only have a year of college left, but I need my master's degree to become a music teacher, and I don't want to graduate with mountains of student loan debt."

"I don't want you to either, but unfortunately neither teachers, nor police detectives, make a lot of money."

"I know, Mom, and I'm not asking you and Alberto to help me. Besides, he has his own kids to think of."

"He certainly does," said Heather. "So, until we get this all sorted out, we may have to go to Plan B."

"Which is?"

"You take next year off, get a full-time job, and do whatever you have to do to establish your Texas residency and qualify for in-state tuition. Then, if worse comes to worse, and you have to get a student loan, it won't be as big of a debt, and maybe you can qualify for a grant or scholarship as well."

"Okay, I'll look into it, but what about graduate school?"

"Again, you'll have to see if you can qualify for grants or scholarships, or you may have to work and go to school part time. At lot of people do, you know. Your grandmother just threw you one hell of a curveball, and you'll have to figure out a way to work around it. In the meantime, I'm starving. Have you eaten yet?"

"No, not yet," said Tonya.

"Then let's go grab a burger."

"Sounds good, and with all we've been through today I think we've earned ourselves some hot fudge sundaes for dessert."

"Good idea, so while you're here we'll enjoy a little quality time together, and you can bring me up to date on Evan."

ॐTHREEॐ

TONYA WAS NOTICEABLY quiet as Evan drove her home from the airport. "You okay?" he finally asked.

"Yeah, I'm fine, all things considered. I'm just wondering if my family is somehow cursed."

"Cursed?" Evan sounded confused. "What do you mean by cursed?"

"My grandfather was a criminal defense attorney who excelled at helping people beat the rap, and his services were always in demand. He charged a pretty penny for his time, and he invested his money wisely. Granted, he and my grandmother were never billionaires, but they did okay. They lived in a big house in one of the ritziest neighborhoods in Phoenix, and they belonged to the country club. My mother, and her sister, went to private schools and they both went to college. They were also expected to marry well, which my aunt did, but my mother, not so much."

"Yeah, you've told me about your childhood, and how tight your grandmother was with her money."

"Tight doesn't even begin to describe it. My grandmother was nothing if not spiteful. She went out of her way to make sure my mother didn't get so much as a penny, and she made sure the rest of rest didn't get anything either."

"What do you mean?"

"She left everything to charity."

"Really?" said a surprised Evan. "Well, at least she wasn't one of those eccentric old ladies who left her millions to her cat."

"Only because she didn't have a cat."

"I see."

"When my mom and my uncle put Grandma in the retirement home, they put all her jewelry in a safe deposit box because they knew she wouldn't be wearing it anymore. So, first thing yesterday morning, Mom goes to the bank and gets it, and she brings it over to my uncle's house. She told us to pick out whatever pieces we wanted, which we did, but she didn't know my uncle had tipped us off the night before, and my cousins and I had agreed to only take one or two pieces."

"So how much jewelry are we talking about?"

"Quite a bit. My grandmother had an extensive collection. It was worth a lot of money, and we wanted the lion's share to go to my mother. For as long as I can remember, my grandmother treated my mother like dirt, and we all agreed she deserved something for her pain and suffering. You should have seen it. My mother was so overwhelmed. She just sat there and cried like a baby." Tonya's voice quivered and a tear rolled down her face. She reached into her purse for a tissue.

"So, I took a gold watch." She pulled back her sleeve and showed it to Evan.

"It's lovely, and now you have something to remember your grandmother by."

"I only took it because I need a new watch. Most of the memories I have of my grandmother are hardly pleasant."

"I'm sorry, Tonya," said Evan. "So why do you think your family's cursed?"

"We all went to lunch after the service, and we were talking about how my grandmother changed her will after Grandpa died. First, she left everything to my aunt, but then Aunt Tricia was killed in a car accident. I was pretty young when it happened, so I never had the chance to really get to know her."

"I remember you telling me about it, and I'm sorry it happened."

"It's okay. I've seen plenty of pictures of her, and of course my mother, and my cousins, often talk about her. Then there was my sister."

"Yeah, you told me all about her. It sounds like she was quite a character."

"She was adventurous alright, and she had no problem throwing caution to the wind whenever it suited her. She was only twenty-two when she died, and my aunt was in her forties. Now I know this sounds crazy, but last night we were talking about Grandpa, and how he knew most of his clients were guilty as hell, but he got them off the hook anyway, which means there was no justice for their victims. Later on, I was having trouble sleeping. I kept thinking about Annette and Aunt Tricia, and I started to wonder if our family has bad karma, or something, because of Grandpa."

"No." Evan's voice was firm. "It's not bad karma, or a curse, or anything like that, so don't even go there. Stuff happens, and there's no sense to it. What happened to your aunt was tragic. Someone was driving drunk and ran a red light. For whatever reason, it was her time."

"I suppose."

"Your sister, unfortunately, was her own undoing. She got involved with a married man. Then the guy dumped her, but later on she showed up at his home, uninvited. They argued and she fell down a flight of stairs. You told me there was no evidence of foul play, so it—"

"But I still know, in my heart of hearts, he was responsible for her taking that fall. We just couldn't prove it."

Evan's voice softened. "I know Tonya, and I honestly think he was guilty too. Unfortunately, there were no eyewitnesses, so we'll never really know for sure what happened, and mulling over it won't bring her back."

"No, it won't, but she still deserved justice, which she never got. Neither did the families of my grandfather's client's victims."

Evan's voice remained gentle. "You're connecting the wrong dots. What happened to your sister and your aunt had nothing to do with your grandfather. You need to let it go. Somehow, I doubt Annette would want you dwelling on it either. Besides, you said the guy lost everything, so there was some karmic justice, because he had no business getting involved with her either."

"No, he didn't, and you're right. It's just hard to let it go."

"And I'm sorry for what happened to both of them. I also think your grandmother's death is bringing up memories of other family members you've lost, which is perfectly understandable, but it'll get better, I promise. What you need now is a little TLC, so here's what I suggest. As soon as we get back to your place, you can take a nice hot shower. Do you still have any of the wine I brought you last week?"

"A little," said Tonya. "It's in the fridge."

"Good. So, when you get out of the shower, I'll tuck you in bed and bring you a glass of wine, but we're not going to do anything, okay? I'll just sit and let you talk until you either tell me to leave, or you fall asleep, and I promise, I'll be a perfect gentleman."

"Do you really mean it?"

"Of course, I really mean it. You're going to be my wife someday, and I'm signing up for the bad times as well as the good."

"I love you, Evan Reece."

"I love you too, Tonya Claiborne someday Reece, and don't worry. Come Friday night, we'll make up for missing last Sunday."

❧FOUR❧

THE SUN WAS SHINING when Tonya opened her eyes, but there was no empty wineglass on the bistro table. She had fallen asleep before Evan could pour it. Hopping out of the sofa bed, she took Melissa's card from her purse and looked up the Carson Agency website while she waited for her coffee to brew. The agency had been in Dallas for decades. Their models had been featured in many advertising campaigns, not only in Texas, but in national campaigns as well. They also had offices in New York and Los Angeles. She placed a call and left a message in Melissa's voicemail.

After a busy morning catching up on her missed classes, Tonya stopped at the student union for lunch. Taking her seat at an empty table, she checked her messages. Evan had sent her a text. His dad had come through. They could rent his father's friend's Airbnb for spring break. There was, however, a caveat. The house was in a quiet residential neighborhood. No parties were allowed, nor could any of their friends visit. The house was for their exclusive use only. Tonya quickly sent her reply.

"Sounds perfect. You know I'm not big on the party scene so cancel the hotel."

Checking her voicemail, she found another message. Melissa wanted to meet with her as soon as possible. Tonya quickly returned the call.

"I'm so glad you called me back," said Melissa, "because I really meant it when I said you have the right look to be a model. Is there any chance we could meet tomorrow or Friday?"

"Tomorrow would work. I only have one class, and it ends around lunchtime."

"Good. So can you come in at three?"

"Of course. Do I need to bring anything with me? Like copies of recent photos?"

"

"No, it won't be necessary. I got plenty of shots of you the other night."

"Okay. I'll see you tomorrow at three o'clock." Tonya felt relieved as she turned her attention to her lunch, but before she could take her first bite, a young woman with waist-length blonde hair approached her table.

"Mind if I join you?"

"Sure, Becca. Have a seat."

Becca set her tray down and pulled out a chair. "I saw your post on Instagram about your grandmother passing away, and I'm sorry for your loss."

"Thanks. It was sudden. She died in her sleep."

"I also saw that you went to Phoenix."

"I did, but it was only for a couple of days. Thank goodness for Evan. He took me to and from the airport. I don't know what I'd do without him." Becca winced ever so slightly, but it was enough to catch Tonya's watchful eye.

"So, are you and Evan still coming to South Padre Island for spring break?"

"We sure are."

No doubt Becca thought she was being clever, but Tonya saw through her act. Becca had set her sights on Evan, and she was fishing for information. Tonya gave her a knowing look.

"In fact, Evan just sent me a text. He's found an Airbnb off the beaten path, so it'll just be the two of us, enjoying a nice, romantic week."

Becca tried to conceal her disappointment. "Which sounds wonderful, but you guys will still be hanging out on the beach and doing the bar scene at night. Right?"

"We'll probably be at the beach during the day, but afterwards we'll be having our own little parties. Just the two of us, if you know what I mean."

Becca turned her face away and looked around the room. "That's nice, Tonya, and I know we'll all have a really good time, but I just remembered we're having a quiz in my next class. I need to go over my notes, and I see an empty table over there. You don't mind if we take a rain check, do you?"

"Of course not. I understand."

Tonya smiled to herself as Becca picked up her tray and left. "Nice try," she said under her breath, "but you need to find yourself another boyfriend. Evan is spoken for."

* * *

The butterflies roiled in Tonya's stomach when she entered the building lobby. The Angela Carson Agency was on the fifth floor. As she approached the elevators the doors opened on an empty car. Hopefully, it was a good sign. She hurried in and pushed the button for the fifth floor, but as the doors were about to close a man suddenly stepped into the doorway and motioned for his female companion to step inside.

"Thanks for waiting," said the woman.

"Of course. Which floor?"

"Nine."

Tonya pushed the button, and they gave her a nod as the doors opened on the fifth floor. Once again, her stomach fluttered when she stepped inside The Carson Agency and introduced herself to the receptionist.

"Have a seat. I'll let Melissa know you're here. Would you like some water?"

"Some water would be great, thanks." Tonya took her seat in the waiting area and looked around. The walls were covered with photos of the agency's models. Most were women, but there were some men, along with a few child models. They were of different races and ethnic groups, and each had their own distinctive look. Melissa came in and extended her hand as Tonya's water was delivered.

"Did you have any problem finding the place?" she asked.

"No, but finding a parking space was a little tricky."

"That's downtown Dallas, but don't worry. The models can use the parking garage, and we validate their tickets." Melissa told Tonya to take a seat once they stepped into her office.

"So, tell me about yourself, Tonya."

"Well, I'm originally from Arizona. My family lived in Mesa. It's just outside of Phoenix."

"I'm familiar with it. We don't have offices in Phoenix, but we've done shoots in Scottsdale, as well as in Phoenix. Sedona too. Arizona is a beautiful state, but definitely too hot for my taste in the summertime."

"I feel the same," said Tonya. "Anyway, I was in second grade when my parents split up, and my sister and I didn't see much of my father once he left, although he wrote us letters and sent us stuff for Christmas and our birthdays. He passed away a few years later. Complications from a stroke."

"I'm sorry to hear it. I lost my mother when I was twenty. It's not easy losing a parent."

"No, it isn't. My father may not have been the nicest guy around, but he was still my father, and his not being there left a big gap."

"I know the feeling. So, are you looking for part-time work while you're in school?"

"Yes. However, I'm taking next year off. I'm hoping to return the following year."

"I see. So, would you be willing to travel to New York or Los Angeles for jobs?"

"Sure, as long as I don't have to move there."

Melissa gave her a knowing smile. "I don't blame you. I love Texas too, but no, you won't have to move there. It would only be for short visits, and then you'd come home. So, would you mind standing up? I'd like to take a closer look at you."

Tonya nervously rose from her chair, feeling relieved as Melissa smiled.

"How tall are you, Tonya?"

"Five ten and a half."

"Well, you're certainly tall enough for high fashion, but unfortunately, you have too much of a bustline."

Tonya's heart sank. She wondered if Melissa was about to rescind her offer.

"However, you certainly have the right look for swimsuit and lingerie modeling, as well as glamour modeling. Swimsuit and glamour models need more of a bustline."

Finally, Tonya started to relax. "Interesting. I'm actually built like my father's mother. My grandmother. Her name was Carlotta. She was tall and thin, but she also had a generous bustline. She came from Italy, and she sort of looked like Sofia Loren. In fact, her claim to fame was being Sofia's body double in one of her early films. I don't know if it was actually true or not, but it sure was an interesting family story."

"I'll bet it was. So is your grandmother still around?"

"Unfortunately, no. After my father left, my mother really didn't want anything to do with his family, so I only saw my grandmother a few times after they divorced. I was in high school when she passed away. It happened after my father died, but my sister and I didn't have the means to travel to her funeral, which is something I'll always regret."

"I'm sorry to hear it, but I'm sure she'd be proud of you for becoming a musician."

"Thanks. I'm sure she would be as well."

"Now, I have a final question. The other night when I brought up being a model you didn't seem too interested. So, what made you change your mind?"

"Well, to be honest," said Tonya, "it really caught me off guard, but I talked to Evan, my significant other, about it on the way home. I told him I wanted to think it over, and I have. I'd love to give it a shot. It truly is a once in a lifetime opportunity, and I don't want to wonder 'what if' later on."

"Then I think you've made a wise decision. You'd be amazed at how many women come through our door, desperately wanting to become models, and while they may be attractive people, they just don't have the right look. You do, and while I can't guarantee your success, we'll do everything we possibly can to promote you to our clients, but first I need to go over a few things with you."

"Of course."

"Angela Carson was what we would call a supermodel today, but she also had a flair for business. She made the Carson agency into one of the premier modeling agencies in the country, and we're continuing her legacy into the twenty-first century."

Melissa reached into her desk and took out a card. "The first order of business is to schedule a photoshoot, and I'm sending you to Julia McCabe, although she goes by Julianna. She's one of the best photographers in the business."

"You said something before about glamour modeling. Can you tell me more about it?"

"Certainly. Glamour modeling is a specialty which includes pin-ups, posters, calendars and so forth, as well as men's magazines. It's all about making the model look as sexy as possible."

"I see." Tonya felt her cheeks turning warm.

"Nude modeling is also considered commercial work, and it pays quite handsomely, which means successful glamour models can make very good money. However, we don't work with the porn industry, nor are we a talent agency, although some of our models have gotten into acting because they were in a position to meet the right people, so you never know. While it's certainly possible for you to meet people with connections to the music industry, I'm not making any promises. I'm simply saying you have what it takes to become a successful model, and we'll do our best to make it happen for you."

"Trust me, I understand completely. There are no guarantees in the music business either."

"And I'm relieved to hear you say it, because not everyone understands. So, if this is something you want to do, then we expect you get to your assignments on time. You do everything they tell you to do, and you don't argue with them. We work with the best advertising agencies and photographers in the business. These people know their craft, but they're also working with deadlines. It's neither the time nor the place to discuss politics, your personal life, or get into any long, philosophical discussions."

"Of course."

"If something unexpected comes up and you can't do a job, you need to let us know right away. If you want to change your hairstyle, you'll need to have new photos taken. Oh, and I almost forget to ask. Do you have any tattoos?"

"No," said Tonya.

"Good, because you'll be showing a lot of skin, and please let us know if you'd feel uncomfortable wearing really sheer lingerie, or if you'd prefer to not do a job where you'd be topless, or even nude."

"Can you elaborate on that?"

"Sure. Let's say someone's doing a bodywash ad. The model will be in a shower stall. Nothing inappropriate will be showing, but for whatever reason, you can't be wearing any clothing either. Now in case you're wondering, all the photographers we work with are highly professional, and we have zero tolerance for sexual harassment. We'll also do everything we possibly can to accommodate you and make you feel safe and secure."

"I see. So, if I were to say no, I don't want to do any nude work, would it limit the number of jobs I get?"

"It may," said Melissa. "It all depends on the projects our clients are working on, but as I said, nude work pays extremely well."

Tonya stopped and thought it over. She had come from a family with limited means. As a child, she had promised herself that once she became adult, she would do whatever it took to have a better life. Now she had an opportunity to make some serious money. If she invested it wisely, she could complete her degree once she became too old to model. The only family member who would have had serious objections would have been Grandma Barbara. No doubt her mother would have some concerns as well, but Tonya was an adult and making her own decisions.

"Well," she said, "as my Italian grandmother used to say, when an opportunity comes your way, you'd better grab it fast. Otherwise, it may never come your way again. So yes, I'd love to work with you, and if someone wants to do a bodywash ad we'll go over the details and then we'll decide if it's right for me or not."

Melissa's face lit up and she extended her hand. "In that case, congratulations Tonya, and welcome aboard. Let's get started on your paperwork, and I'll call Julianna. She sometimes works on Saturdays, so I'll see if she's available this coming Saturday. If she is, I'll get you scheduled, because the sooner we can get your photos done, the better."

"What do I need?"

"I'm thinking a two-piece swimsuit, some sexy underwear, such as a matching camisole and panties, and a pair of short shorts with top to accentuate your bustline. You should be able to find what you need at Walmart or Target."

"Okay, I can stop at Walmart on my way home."

"Sounds good. I also have a job which may be a good match for you, assuming we can get everything done on time. An auto parts company is working on a new poster to promote their products in auto repair shops. They're in need of a glamour model with some cleavage to wear a pair of coveralls with their logo embroidered on the front. We've already sent a few of our models to meet with them, but so far they're still looking."

"So when would the shoot be?"

"Two weeks from Tuesday."

Tonya's heart sank. It would be the same week as spring break, but with her grandmother gone, she didn't have the luxury of turning away paying work. As she filled out her paperwork Melissa made a phone call.

"You're in luck." Melissa smiled as she set the receiver down. "Julianna can do you this coming Saturday at three o'clock. So, if all goes according to plan, you could be ready to meet with the auto parts people sometime next week, assuming the job is still open. Meantime I'll email you her address. You need to be well rested, so I suggest taking it easy and staying home Friday night."

"Of course." Tonya handed Melissa her completed paperwork. Melissa raised her brow as she looked it over.

"You're about to turn twenty-one?"

"Yes."

"Well, you certainly have a youthful look, which is certainly a plus. I had you pegged as being nineteen. And your last name is Claiborne?"

"It is, although we're not related to anyone in the fashion industry."

"Good to know. However, we'll need come up with stage name to avoid any confusion. So, what do you think of Tonya Clayton?"

"Maybe. I'm not sure."

"We can try a different name. You can also change your first name too if you'd like."

Tonya thought it over for a moment. "My sister and I had similar faces, but she wasn't as tall as me. Her hair was a little lighter than mine and it had a red undertone, and I was the plain sister when compared to her. She passed away a few years ago. Freak accident. Her middle name was Rose, so I'd like to use Tonya Rose, in honor of her."

Melissa gave Tonya a thoughtful look. "I'm very sorry for your loss, and Tonya Rose has a nice ring to it. I also think your sister would be pleased"

"I think she would be too."

"So, we'll go with Tonya Rose." Melissa took a few notes as she spoke. "We have a few more things to over, then as soon as we're done, I'm taking you down the hall and introduce you to the rest of the staff."

❧FIVE☙

EVAN TOSSED HIS notebook into his backpack as his professor announced class was dismissed. Hurrying outside, he spotted a familiar face.

"Hey, Evan. How's it going?"

"Doing all right. How 'bout you, Becca?"

"Oh, other than an assignment for yet another term paper, I'm fine, but at least this one isn't due until after spring break."

"I hear you," he said. "I'm still working on my ad campaign for my marketing class."

"Yeah, you were telling me about it, and please let me know if I can help."

"Thanks. I may have to take you up on it. So where are you heading off to?"

"The library, thanks to this new assignment." She stopped and gave him a smile. "But you know what? All of a sudden, I feel the need for caffeine, so I'm making a Starbuck's run. Would you like to join me?"

"Sorry but—" His phone vibrated before he could complete his sentence. Tonya had sent him a text message. A frown came over his face as he read it.

"Something came up. Have to cancel tomorrow so we'll do Saturday night instead. Call me later."

"What happened?" asked Becca.

"Nothing. Just a last-minute change of plans."

"Really? Hope everything's okay."

"We're good. Tonya mentioned something the other day about her guitar club. Looks like they might be having a practice session tomorrow night."

"Well, good for her," said Becca. "So if she's busy you may as well join us at Finnigan's. It's our new hangout, and we're there every Friday."

"Really? So who all's there?"

"The usual crowd. Tiffany and Bobby, Briana and Justin. Then there's me, Jacque, Rob, Jacob, Nathan and sometimes Shawn, so don't worry. It's not a date. There're always more guys than girls, and I'm sure Tonya wouldn't mind you hanging out with us for a while."

"We'll see. If it's a performance then I'll be with her. I always go to her performances to show my support."

Becca looked disappointed. "I see, but if you should change your mind, we usually get there around seven and we stay 'til late. Anyway, I gotta run. Catch you later."

Evan watched her as she disappeared into the crowd. Becca was a cute girl with a fun personality. No doubt some guy would soon find her. In the meantime, he had his own issues to deal with. He hurried off to his car and called Tonya, who quickly answered.

"What's up?" he asked.

"I called Melissa. Remember her? She was the woman at the concert who was with the Carson Agency."

"Yeah, I remember."

"She wanted to meet with me in person, and I left her office a few minutes ago. She wasn't kidding when she said I had what it takes to be a model, so I've signed on with the Carson Agency."

"Really?" said a stunned Evan.

"What's wrong? You don't sound very happy."

"Shouldn't we have discussed this first?"

"We did. The other night in the car."

"You said you were going to think about it."

"And I have." Tonya was sounding defensive. "I checked them out. They're a legit agency, and they've been around for decades."

"I understand. I'm just not sure if this was such a good idea."

"Why?"

"Because a lot of these agencies charge a hefty fee to sign up with them, and then they never find you any work."

"I didn't pay them anything," she said firmly, "and they came to me. I didn't go to them."

He realized it was pointless to argue. "Okay, you've signed on with them. So, what happens next?"

"First, I need to have some photos taken. Then they'll do whatever they can to find me some work, and if all goes well, I could make some decent money." Her voice took a more serious tone.

"Things have changed, Evan. My grandmother was taking care of my tuition and helping with my other expenses, but she's not around anymore, and she left no provision in her will to cover my costs until I graduate. You also know how I feel about taking on a lot of debt."

His tone softened. "I know, and to be honest, I wish more people thought about money the way you do."

"While I was in Phoenix my mother and I both agreed I should take next year off from school so I can establish my Texas residency. If I can qualify for in-state tuition, it'll make it easier for me to continue my education."

"I'm sorry, Tonya. I didn't realize it was this serious."

"It is. My mother and stepfather don't have the means to help me like my grandmother did, so I need to come up with a way to pay for my education without taking out a big student loan. If I can get some decent modeling work it'll help put me in a position to finish up my degree later on. Melissa has scheduled me for a photo shoot on Saturday. She said I need to be well rested, which is why I have to cancel tomorrow night, but we'll hang out Saturday night. I promise."

"Okay." Once again, there was a tone of uncertainty in his voice.

"Hey, I know it's last-minute, and I appreciate you being so understanding. I also know you're overdue for a guys' night out, so why don't you go hang with the gang tomorrow night?"

***

Tiffany greeted Evan with a warm hug. "Well, howdy stranger. It's been a while. So, how have you been?"

"I'm doing okay. Tonya had something come up at the last minute, so I'm doing a guy's night out."

"Well, good for you, and we're glad you could join us."

Evan greeted Bobby and Shawn and sat down next to Shawn. A server stopped by their table and he ordered a beer. As she stepped away, Briana and Justin came in. They, too, were happy to see Evan. Nathan, Jacob, and Rob soon arrived, and Jacob sat down next to Evan. Jacque and Becca showed up as the first pizzas were delivered. Shawn looked up and did a double take.

"I love your new haircut, Jacque," said Tiffany. "It really looks good on you."

"Thanks. It was time for a change." Jacque's long brown hair had been cut to just above her shoulders. The others complimented her as she took her seat. Becca asked Rob if he would mind switching seats so she could sit across the table from Evan.

"So, I take it Tonya has a rehearsal tonight," she said.

"Something like that," said Evan.

"Hey, we're all friends here, so don't keep us in suspense."

Evan looked at Becca and chose his words carefully. "Tonya has some personal business to attend to tomorrow, so tonight she's home catching up on her classes because she missed Monday and Tuesday. Her grandmother passed away last Sunday, and she had to fly back to Phoenix for the funeral."

"Oh my god. I'm so sorry," said a shocked Briana. "I hadn't heard anything about this. How's she taking it?"

"She's doing fine. Her grandmother passed away in her sleep, apparently from natural causes."

"Then I'm glad she didn't suffer, and please give Tonya my condolences."

"Will do. Thanks, Briana."

The conversation shifted to midterms and spring break. As the others were talking, Evan noticed Becca making eyes at him. He tried to ignore it as he focused his attention on Shawn and Rob, dropping Tonya's name into the conversation whenever he could. Becca chatted with Briana and Jacque while keeping Evan under her gaze. As he tipped his beer glass nearly vertical to wash down his last slice of pizza, he decided to take his leave, but before he could say anything, Shawn asked him if he wanted to play pool.

"Sure." He jumped up and followed Shawn to the poolroom. To his relief, there was only one table available, and what few chairs were in the room were already occupied. Shawn racked up the balls and they soon heard the others playing darts in another part of the bar. Another pool table became available an hour later, and Bobby and Nathan joined them.

"So, where are the others?" asked Evan.

"Justin and Briana are playing darts with Rob and Jacque," said Bobby. "Tiffany and Becca are sitting at the table talking while Jacob is getting acquainted with some girl he just met."

Evan nodded and took his shot, smiling with delight as his ball went into the side pocket. When the game was over, Shawn and Nathan switched places, and after a few more rounds Evan checked the time. It was after eleven o'clock.

"I think I'll call it a night. Tonya should be done studying by now."

As his friends said goodnight, Shawn nodded toward an exit in the corner and gave him a knowing look.

"You can slip out the back and I'll let the others know you left. Tell Tonya I said hello."

As Evan and Shawn were talking, Bobby ran into the other room to grab Evan's jacket. "Coast is clear, buddy," he said when he came back. "Becca went to the ladies' room, so give Tonya my best."

"Will do, and thanks." Evan threw on his jacket and hurried out the door.

❧ SIX ❧

TONYA PULLED UP TO the curb and shut down the engine. Looking up at the big, two-story house, she took a deep breath and smiled. With any luck, she was about to launch the beginning of her journey to a better life. She grabbed her duffle bag and rang the doorbell. A moment later she stood face-to-face with a woman with a gray pageboy.

"You must be Tonya," she said.

"I'm Tonya, and you must be Julianna."

"The one and only. Come on in."

"Sorry to bring such a big bag of stuff with me. I wasn't sure which outfit would work best, so I brought all of them."

"Which is exactly what you should've done. We'll go through them and pick out the ones we want, but first I want to be a good hostess and offer you something to drink. I have unsweetened iced tea and watermelon-flavored vitamin water."

"I love watermelon."

"So, watermelon it is." Julianna handed Tonya a bottle and told her to follow her upstairs. Inside one of the bedrooms was a camera mounted on a tripod in front of a gray backdrop.

"We'll take a few shots in here, and we'll use some of the other rooms too, along with the backyard. The guest bathroom is next door and you can change in there."

"Sounds good, so where would you like to start?"

"Let's start with the undies."

Tonya unzipped her bag, handing off an assortment of panties, camisoles, and teddies to Julianna, who was admiring a silky teal blue ensemble. "I love this. It's a beautiful color, and the camisole has a lovely lace trim on top."

"Are you sure? Because I also have something in red."

"We're good. The color is perfect for your skin tone, and it'll look good in black and white as well."

Tonya hurried into the bathroom, but her hands felt shaky as she changed. Once she was ready, she hurried back into the other room and gave Julianna a nervous smile. "Okay, so what do I do now?"

"You relax and let me do the work. Melissa sent me the pictures she took of you the other night. The camera loves you. I don't think I could get a bad shot of you if I tried. Just follow my lead and you'll be fine. Are you ready?"

"I think so."

"Good, so let's get started. Glamour modeling is all about looking sexy, so imagine the camera is a hot-looking guy."

Tonya burst out laughing. Julianna snapped a few shots and smiled as she looked them over. "Beautiful," she said. "Let's take a few more. Then we'll get down to business."

Tonya took a deep breath and struck the pose Julianna asked for. Before long, her nervousness wore off.

"You take direction well," said Julianna, "which is a real plus. Not everyone does."

"I played the viola in my high school orchestra, and you either did what you were told or you were out the door."

"Melissa mentioned you were a music student, so maybe you'll meet someone in the music business, but right now I need you to grab your makeup bag. We're going to go into the bathroom so I can get some shots of you in front of the mirror."

An hour later they were back in Julianna's studio. This time Tonya wore a pair of denim shorts with a red tank top and a sheer blouse.

"We've just about got it," said Julianna. "If it's okay with you, I'd like for you to take your top off so I can get a few shots of your back and shoulders, but if it makes you uncomfortable, we won't do it."

"Melissa said there may be jobs where I'd have to do this, so let's give it a shot and we'll see how I feel when we're done." Tonya took off her top, and after a few more shots Julianna turned her camera off.

"That's it. We're done."

"Really?"

"Yep. How are you feeling?"

"I'm okay." Tonya reached down and picked up her top. "It felt a little odd at first, but as you can see, I was able to handle it, and I'm sure the next time it won't feel so strange."

"That's good. Go ahead and change while I upload the photos to the computer."

Tonya grabbed her duffle bag and hurried to the bathroom. Julianna was smiling when she returned.

"Your photos have all been uploaded, and they're stunning. Ready to have a look?"

"I think so."

"Then take a seat."

"Wow." Tonya's face immediately lit up. "I had no idea they'd turn out this good."

"As I said, the camera is your best friend. Which ones do you like?"

"I don't know. There are so many to choose from."

The two women carefully went over the photos, but it was hard to decide which ones to keep. After going back and forth several times, they finally agreed on their choices, and Tonya looked at her watch.

"Whoops. I didn't realize it was so late."

"What a lovely piece of jewelry," said Julianna.

"Thanks. It belonged to my grandmother. She recently passed away."

"I'm so sorry."

"Thanks. My grandmother was, shall we say, an interesting woman. However, I'm meeting someone for dinner tonight, and I need to let him know I'm running late."

"Then I won't keep you. Grab your bag and I'll walk you out." They hurried downstairs and Julianna hugged Tonya goodbye at the front door.

"It was a real pleasure working with you, and I don't say it to everyone. You go with the flow, you don't whine, and I, for one, would love to work with you again."

"Me too." After a quick goodbye, Tonya hopped in her car and sent Evan a text message to let him know she would be a few minutes late. He quickly responded, saying he too was running late but would grab some Chinese food on his way over.

Arriving home, Tonya tossed her duffle bag on the sofa. Evan was due in less than an hour. Julianna may have nixed the red camisole and panties, but red was Evan's favorite color. She quickly fished them out of the bag and hurried into the bathroom for a hot shower. Twenty minutes later she smoothed her red tunic over her jeans. Evan arrived as she was putting on her earrings.

"You look hot tonight." He smiled as he stepped inside. "And I see you're wearing your glasses, too."

"It was time for me to take my contacts out."

He set their dinners on the bistro table and looked Tonya up and down. "You have no idea how incredibly sexy you look when you're wearing your glasses. It really turns me on." His lips pressed against hers as he ran his hand down her side and squeezed her breast.

"Not yet," said Tonya. "It's been a hectic day. I need to chill out and have a beer."

He gave her a quizzical look. "Are you sure you should be drinking beer? Don't models have to be thin?"

"They do. However, I've been thin my entire life. I have trouble gaining weight. My grandma Carlotta was the same way. Tall and skinny, and no matter how much she ate, she could never gain any weight. Apparently, I've inherited her metabolism."

"You know most girls wish they were like you."

"I'm sure they do, but being thin has its challenges too. Like trying to find clothes that fit. I have to shop at the tall girl's store, and there's not always much to choose from in the skinny sizes. So, where's my beer?"

"Coming right up." He twisted off the cap and handed her the bottle. Tonya plopped down at the bistro table, and Evan sat down next to her.

"So, tell me about your day," he said.

"It was fantastic. The photo session went really well, and the photographer told me I have what it takes to be a model. You know, this really could be my lucky break."

"I see." Evan changed the subject as he opened the take-out bag. "I got us Kung Pao chicken and beef with broccoli, along with some fried rice, egg rolls, and egg drop soup."

"Thanks. I've been so busy today I've hardly eaten anything."

"What did you wear for your photo shoot?"

"A camisole set, a swimsuit, and a pair of cutoffs."

"What?" He gave her a surprised look.

"It turns out I have too much of a bustline for high fashion, but I have the perfect body for glamour modeling. Why are you looking at me like that?"

"Because I'm still not sure this is such a good idea after all."

"Why? It's good money, and I'm not naked."

"No, but it sounds like you'll be scantily clothed."

Tonya was suddenly taken aback. "It's legit, Evan. I'll be appearing in posters at hair salons, which are frequented by women, as well as in swimsuit and lingerie ads for women's magazines, which are also aimed at women. We women buy our own swimsuits and underwear, and most men don't read women's fashion magazines."

"No, we don't. Sorry if I misunderstood."

"It's okay. It's a job, and like I said before, I could make some serious money. It's also a young woman's profession, so I may only be able to do it for a short time."

"And once I graduate and find a good paying job, we'll get married. Then you won't have to worry about any of it anymore." As they enjoyed their dinner, he filled her in on his night at Finnigan's.

"Sounds like you had a good time," said Tonya, "so I'm glad you went."

"Me too, but Becca really is getting to be a problem. Shawn and Bobby noticed it too."

"Then you need to have a serious talk with her, the sooner, the better. Spring break is coming up fast."

"I know." He reached over and touched her hand. "So, why don't we put the leftovers in the fridge? I'm ready for my dessert."

"You got it." Tonya put the food away while Evan pulled out the sofa bed and turned the covers down. Stripping down to his shorts, he sat down and patted the spot next to him.

"You are so sexy," he said.

"So, they tell me."

He gently took off her glasses. "We don't want these getting broken." He placed them on her desk, and turned on the floor lamp.

"That's better, don't you think?" He turned off the overhead light and returned to the sofa bed. Slipping out of his shorts, he kissed her and ran his hands down her chest.

"We need to get you out of this." A big smile came over his face when he pulled off her tunic and found the red camisole underneath. "What's this?"

"Oh, it's just a little something I bought for my photoshoot, but the photographer liked the blue one better."

"Really?"

"Afraid so."

"Well, I mean no disrespect to the photographer, but red makes you look super-hot." He helped her out of her jeans, and once he tossed them aside Tonya made herself comfortable on the bed.

"You have no idea how badly I want to go all the way with you."

"I know you do," said Tonya," but we both agreed we'd save it for our wedding night. Right now, we're just practicing."

"And I need all the practice I can get." He caressed her face and kissed her as his hands ran up and down her body. Tonya moaned in contentment as he slipped his hand underneath her camisole and gently caressed her breasts. Pulling down a strap, his lips covered her nipple, but when he slipped his hand into her panties, he suddenly stopped.

"What the hell?" He took her panties off and looked at her in surprise. "Tonya? What have you done to yourself?"

"It's part of doing swimsuit and lingerie modeling. Swimsuits and panties can be skimpy, so we have to take care of our bikini lines."

"Really? Well, I suppose it makes sense."

"Does it bother you?"

"No, it doesn't." He smiled as he stroked her. "Such soft, smooth skin. In fact, it's sexy as hell. So, what'd you do? Shave it off?"

"No. I used a depilatory cream."

Evan moved to the foot of the bed, and Tonya's face turned warm as he resumed stroking her skin.

"Evan? What are you doing down there?"

"Enjoying the view. I'm also your future husband, so you needn't be so shy with me."

"You're incorrigible." Tonya repositioned herself, and a warm, sweet feeling came over her as he massaged her sweet spot.

"Like it?"

She moaned in contentment.

"I'll take it as a yes, and I like it too. And because it's so sexy, I'm going to give it a little kiss."

She felt his hair brushing her inner thighs as he gently kissed her. He kissed her again, with each kiss lasting longer than the last. Tonya's pleasure grew, and she moaned even louder. Finally, he slipped his hands underneath her, massaging her with his tongue.

"Yes, yes," she said breathlessly. As her pleasure grew, her moans became louder and more vocal. Unable to hold herself back any longer, she let out a final moan as she climaxed. Evan raised up and rubbed her stomach as she came back down.

"How was it?"

Dizzy in the afterglow, Tonya groaned in contentment.

"You were amazing, and now you've got me all hot too, so I'll give you a moment to catch your breath. Then it's my turn." He laid down next to her and gave her a squeeze. "I got so excited I forgot to take your top off. You can leave it on, for now, but the panties stay off for the rest of the night."

"I think we've created a monster in you," she said with a giggle.

He smiled as he rubbed her now smooth skin once again. "What can I say? It's erotic as hell and it really turns me on, but right now, I need some good loving."

"Your wish is my command." Tonya propped herself up and gently caressed him. He moaned in pleasure, and as she worked her magic, he reached his release.

"Wow." He moaned in contentment as his body slowly relaxed. "You sure know how to please me, but I still want to make love to you."

"And I want to make love to you as well. On our wedding night. I'm going to be a virgin bride, and trust me, it'll be worth the wait."

"I know, but even if you weren't a virgin, I'd still love you and want you." He stepped away to freshen up, and when he returned, he gently stroked her hair and gave her a long, passionate kiss. As they cuddled together, he rested his head on her belly.

"I love you Tonya Claiborne, soon to be Reece."

"I love you too, Evan, so can we turn off the lamp?"

"In a little while. Right now, I'm enjoying the view."

"You're still incorrigible."

"I know."

* * *

Becca was scrolling down her phone when a server delivered their drinks. "Well, take a look at this."

"What?" asked Jacque.

"I'm on Instagram. Tonya posted something earlier today about doing a photo shoot. Apparently, she's signed up with some modeling agency in Dallas." Becca's tone tuned bitter. "Well, la ti da, Tonya."

"Let me see."

Becca handed her phone to Jacque and took a swig of beer.

"Interesting," said Jacque. "She's signed on with the Carson agency. I hear they're the best in town."

Becca's voice remained bitter. "Well, goody-goody for Tonya."

"You need to give it a rest, Becca. Last night at Finnigan's everyone noticed you have a thing for Evan, which is why he snuck out the back door. He's committed to Tonya, and they're getting married as soon as they graduate."

"Which won't be until next year, and a lot can happen in a year. Besides, he hasn't given her a ring yet."

"Maybe not, but still I wouldn't get my hopes up if I were you."

As Becca took another sip of beer, she recalled Evan telling Shawn he would be at Tonya's place tonight. She frowned as she imagined them making love.

"You okay?" asked Jacque.

"I'm fine."

"Don't worry. It'll be okay. We're here having fun, there's a good band playing, and there are lots of single guys hanging out. In fact, I see a couple of them standing next to the bar and watching us as we speak. I have a hunch they'll ask us to dance, and when they do, I'm going to dance with them, because you never know. Your future boyfriend, and mine, could be here right now, and we don't even know it."

Becca knew Jacque meant well, but her future boyfriend wasn't standing next to the bar. He was busy in another woman's bed, but if Becca had her way, he wouldn't be there much longer. Sooner or later Tonya was bound to slip up, and when she did, Becca would make her move. In the meantime, she would convince Evan she was only a casual friend and nothing more.

❧SEVEN❧

TONYA WAS STILL asleep when Evan slipped out the following morning. He soon returned with breakfast sandwiches and orange juice, and Tonya brewed a fresh pot of coffee. After enjoying a leisurely meal together, it was time for him to go. Both needed to study, and Tonya had to practice. Evan quickly tossed the food wrappers away and grabbed his jacket, giving Tonya a farewell kiss before stepping out the door.

Once he was gone, Tonya took a shower and gathered up her laundry. The laundry room was busy as usual on a Sunday morning, but with lunchtime approaching the big rush was over. As she finished loading a washer, an elderly black woman came in. She greeted Tonya with a warm smile as she set her basket down.

"I'm so glad you're here, Tonya. I was going to stop by your place later today because I have something to ask you."

"You do? So what's up, Ruby?"

"Well, I went to church this morning, like I do every Sunday morning, and the pastor's sermon was all about the evils of gossiping. Then, after the service was over, the church secretary asked me about you."

"I see. So, what did the secretary want to know?"

"One of our members is getting married, and they would like someone to sing at their wedding. Now mind you, I'm not gossiping, but I have been telling folks about you being a music student at the university, and I've even brought some of them to your school performances."

"I know you have, and I really appreciate your support. So, when's the wedding?"

"Sometime toward the end of April, but at the moment I can't seem to recall the exact date."

"No worries. Our last public performance will be in mid-April."

Ruby looked inside her purse. "If you give me a moment to find something to write on, I'll give you the church phone number."

"It's okay. If you give me the name of the church, I can look it up on my phone."

"You kids and your phones. My son gave me one of those smart phones for Christmas, and I'll be a-you-know-what if I can figure out what to do with all those apps. Facebook schmacebook. I only use it for phone calls and emails, although every once in a while, I'll send my grandkids a text message."

Tonya tapped on her phone. "They can be a little overwhelming at times, but it's nice to be able to get a weather forecast or driving directions when you need them. So, whenever you're ready, I'll look up the church."

Ruby gave her the name and address of the church. Tonya quickly punched it up and showed Ruby the photo on her screen. "Is this it?"

"Sure is," said Ruby. "The church secretary's name is Dora, and be sure to let her know I gave you her name."

"Will do, and thank you, again, Ruby."

"You're welcome. I'm always happy to help out an aspiring music student. So, how was your week?"

"Bittersweet. My grandmother passed away a week ago today."

Ruby stopped loading her washer and gave Tonya a big hug. "I'm so sorry. What happened? Was she sick?"

"No, she wasn't sick. She went to sleep and never woke up."

"Well, God bless her. At least she didn't suffer. How are you holding up?"

"Okay, I guess. My grandmother was a difficult woman, so none of us were close to her. Not because we didn't want to be, but because she wouldn't allow it."

"Yeah, some people are like that, and I'm truly sorry to hear she was that way. I can't imagine any grandparent not being close to their grandkids. Mine bring so much joy to my life."

"I can tell, and they're very lucky to have you for a grandmother."

* * *

Tonya's mother called later that afternoon, and she sounded more like herself.

"Your grandmother has been officially laid to rest. Yesterday morning your stepfather, your uncle Roger, and I drove up to Flagstaff and scattered her ashes in the forest near your grandparent's old vacation home. Now she and your grandfather will be together forever."

"Well, I'm glad it's over, Mom. Now we can all have some closure, although I'm sorry none of us grandkids could have gone with you."

"It's okay. You and your cousins have your own lives now, which brings me to the next item on the list. Your uncle and I spoke to your grandmother's attorney, and while he's sorry her will wasn't what we expected, he said she was of sound mind at the time it was written, and if she made any changes later on, he's unaware of them. He also asked about the jewelry."

"Uh-oh. So, what'd you tell him?"

"Well, I sort of told him a little white lie."

"Now, Mom." There was a chuckle in Tonya's voice.

"It wasn't a boldfaced lie. I told him we'd put her jewelry in a safe deposit box when we put her in the assisted living facility, which is true. Then I changed the timelines just a bit."

"Really? And what did you say?"

"I told him that before we put her jewelry away for safekeeping, your grandmother suggested you and your cousins go through it and pick out whatever pieces you wanted. I didn't mention how much you took. I simply said I couldn't recall who took what."

"Great. So now he'll come after us and demand we give it back."

Heather's voice was firm. "No, he won't. It would be considered a gift, so it's yours to keep. I also went through the stuff you gave me, and there were a few pieces I'll never wear, so I gave them to him and said it was all that was left. Which is also true."

"Tsk, tsk, Mom," said Tonya with a laugh.

"Hey, your grandmother isn't here to dispute it. In the meantime, your uncle Roger put in a call to his own attorney, so we're still moving forward to contest the will. I don't want you taking on any big student loan debt either."

"Well, hopefully, we'll be successful, but as you and Uncle Roger have already pointed out, there's no guarantee, so I'm planning accordingly. Remember the modeling agency I was telling your about?"

"Yes."

"I met with them last week, and I've signed on with them. Don't worry. I checked them out. They're a legitimate agency."

"I know they are," said Heather. "Your stepfather checked them out as well. So, what did they have to say?"

"They said I have the right look for swimsuit and lingerie modeling."

"I see."

"A lot of print modeling is done in Dallas, Mom."

"And I hope you do well, but you also need to look for a steady job."

"I'm hoping to be back at the music store this summer. However, there's potential for me to make some serious money doing the modeling."

"I'm sure there is, but until it happens you need to keep your options open. So is Evan okay with this?"

"I think so," said Tonya. "He was a little concerned at first, but then I told him most of the ads I'll be doing would be for women's magazines. Once he understood, he seemed to be okay with it."

"Which is good, but you need to be careful, and don't let anyone exploit you."

"I know, Mom, but like we both said, they're a legitimate agency. They won't force me to do anything I'd feel uncomfortable doing, and while they're not making any promises, I could still make some good money. They also said it's possible for me to meet people in the music industry."

"And I hope you do, but I don't want you getting your hopes up."

"I know. They made a point of saying they can't guarantee my success either. In the meantime, one of my neighbors just gave me a lead for singing at a wedding, and I'll follow up on it this week."

"Then I hope you get the gig. I also hope the modeling works out for you. You're an adult, so I'm not going to tell you how to live your life, and if there's a chance for you to make decent money then you should give it a try. I'm simply saying there's no guarantee, so you need to keep your options open. I'm also reminding you there are people out there who would have no qualms about taking advantage of you."

"I understand, but I'm also pretty good at reading people."

"I know you are, but being a police detective's wife has made me much more aware of how many unscrupulous people are out there. They can fool even the best of us, like the man who fooled your sister."

"I saw through his act, Mom."

"I know you did, but Annette didn't, and because of him, she's no longer with us. So, believe me when I tell you there are plenty of others out there who are even more devious than he was, so just be careful. Okay?"

❧EIGHT❧

SHAWN MCCOY WAS A music major at the University of North Texas. He met Tonya at the beginning of their sophomore year, and they thought of themselves as long-lost twins. They were nearly the same height and they had the same dark hair, although Shawn's was curly and it touched the top of his collar. They also had the same outlook on life. Shawn soon introduced Tonya to his roommate, Evan Reece, knowing they would be a good match.

Shawn and Tonya liked to meet for coffee on Tuesday afternoons. It was a tradition they rarely missed, and this Tuesday would be no exception. Shawn arrived first. After placing his order, he grabbed the remaining table and was booting up his laptop when Tonya came in. She grabbed his latte and sat down across the table from him.

"My expresso will be ready in a minute," she said, "so how was your week?"

"Busy, but first I want to offer my condolences about your grandmother."

"Thanks. I got your text, but I was pretty involved with family stuff, so please forgive me if I didn't respond."

"Don't worry about it. Evan brought me up to date the other night at Finnigan's."

Someone called Tonya's name and she went to get her order. Shawn looked pleased when she returned to their table.

"With all that's happened," he said, "I thought you could use some good news."

"I certainly could, so what's up?"

"Are you familiar with the Four Seasons Resort?"

"I've heard of it," said Tonya, "although I've never actually been there. It's a bit out of my budget."

"Mine too. At least for now, but while you were away, I got a lead on who to talk to for booking live entertainment, and I told him I knew someone who sings and plays jazz guitar. I also sent him links to the videos Evan shot of us performing last summer at the Hilton."

"How intriguing. So, what did he have to say?"

"He was impressed and wanted to meet with me in person, so we did. He would like to have us poolside, twice a month, starting the week after finals and going through the end of August. What do you think? Would you be interested in doing a regular summer gig there? Or would you rather be back at the Hilton?"

"Are you kidding me? Of course, I'd prefer the Four Seasons. Not that I didn't enjoy doing the Hilton, but it's a new venue."

"I feel the same, and it would be a good venue for performing your original tunes. Meantime the Sheridan has also expressed an interest, and I expect us to have a busy summer. Now, are you ready for the really big news?"

"You mean there's more?"

"You'd better believe it." He gave her a wink as he took a swig of his coffee and typed a few keys on his laptop.

"It centers on our YouTube videos. I know your mother loves them. Mine does too, and so do a lot of other people. We've had a ton of views, so I added a pitch at the end of each video asking for contributions, and we've had a good response. So, I'm pleased to announce that we now have the funds to record the album."

"Oh my god. Are you serious?"

"I'm serious." He turned his laptop so she could see the screen. Her eyes popped and he gave her a big smile.

"I know," he said. "I couldn't believe it either when I first saw it, and it's grown even more since then. So, I'm booking us a session in a recording studio in May, right after finals. I'm also hoping we'll be in a position to hire a drummer by then. I'll be on the bass, but I think adding some drums will give it more pizazz. So, what do you think? Should we do it?"

"Nah."

"What?"

Tonya burst out laughing. "You should have seen the look on your face just now. Of course, I want to do it."

He shook his head and gave her a smirky grin. "I really don't know about you sometimes. So, moving on. Evan tells me you've signed on with the Angela Carson Agency. Congratulations. That's quite an accomplishment."

"Thanks, but I wasn't looking to become a model. Someone from the agency came to my lab band performance at the church in Dallas and gave me her card. I was going to turn her down, but then my grandmother gave me and my cousins a collective, 'screw you,' in her will and left everything to charity, so I've lost my funding for school."

"Nice lady."

"Tell me about it. However, there's a chance I could make some decent money modeling, which also means with any luck, I may be able to come back and finish my degree in a year or two."

"I hope you do, and once the album is done, I'll do as much as I can to pitch it to the big record labels and see if any of them will distribute it. Maybe we'll get lucky and get a bite."

"I hope so, Shawn, I really do, for both our sakes. My biggest dream has always been to land a major recording contract."

"I know it is, but even if we don't, I'll still keep hustling gigs, and who knows? We may become an act in Vegas someday, which wouldn't be bad either."

"No, it wouldn't, and you're right. Anything's possible." Tonya grabbed her phone and tapped a few buttons. "In the meantime, the photographer emailed me my photos this morning, so tell me what you think." She handed her phone to Shawn, and he slowly looked them over.

"Wow. The photographer did a really great job, although I don't know if I should be thinking about my twin sister in this way."

"Oh, c'mon."

He gave her a look as he showed her the image of her in the camisole set. "Whoever it was made you look hotter than hell, and I'd love to have them shoot our album cover."

"Thanks. I'll let her know."

His eyes suddenly popped. "Whoa! Now you're on fire."

"Let me see."

Shawn turned the screen once again so Tonya could see the photo. It was the shot of her bare back with her head looking over her shoulder.

"Oh, yeah," said Tonya, "it was the last shot of the session."

"Has Evan seen it yet?"

"Not yet. Like I said, I just got the email this morning. Why do you ask?"

"He has some real concerns about you doing this. He knows you need the money, but he's worried about you ending up in some trashy men's magazine."

"Yeah, he's been acting a little jealous, but don't worry. I don't plan on becoming a centerfold. I told him most of the work I'll be doing will be ads for women's magazines."

"I understand. I just wanted you to be aware, and speaking of being aware, Becca is getting to be a real problem."

"I know," said Tonya. "Evan told me about what happened the other night, and thank you for whisking him out the back door."

"You're welcome and I'm sorry it happened. I feel like it's partly my fault because I'm the one who introduced her to the group when I started going out with Jacque."

"Who knew? There are lots of little vamps out there, and Becca is Jacque's best friend. And speaking of Jacque, how's it going between the two of you? Are you guys on again? Or still off?"

"We're still off. At least for now."

"Well, Shawn, all l can say is if it's meant to be it's meant to be. If not, there are still plenty of other opportunities out there."

The conversation shifted to other topics. Once again, Tonya tried to play matchmaker and introduce Shawn to some of her other friends, but he declined, as he always did. Finally, she stopped and looked at her watch.

"That's lovely," said Shawn.

"Thanks. It was my grandmother's, and while I hate to cut things short, I need to go home and put in some practice time before Evan gets there. We're going out for a burger tonight."

"Well, good for you. I have a date with a term paper myself. I'll email you the info about our album, as well as the gig at The Four Seasons."

"Thanks, Shawn. See you next week?"

"I'll be here."

❧NINE❧

MELISSA CALLED LATER that afternoon. She, too, was pleased with the photos. "I've scheduled a meeting with the ad agency for two o'clock on Thursday. I've already emailed them your photos and they liked what they saw. I'll send you the address as soon as we're done."

"So, I take it they still haven't found a model?" asked Tonya.

"Not yet."

"Do you think I'll get hired?"

"Anything's possible, so I always recommend penciling in the date of a shoot in your calendar until you hear otherwise."

"Of course."

"And be sure to call me as soon as you leave the interview."

"Will do." Tonya sighed once they ended the call. She hated the thought of telling Evan she might have work over spring break. Hopefully, he would understand.

* * *

Evan greeted her with his usual kiss when he arrived. "Ready to go?" he asked.

"In a minute." Tonya's tone turned serious. "First, I need to talk to you about something."

A concerned look came over his face. "What's wrong? Is there another family emergency?"

"No, they're all fine." Tonya grabbed her phone. After touching a few buttons she handed it to Evan. "I've got my modeling photos. So, what do you think?"

He sat down on the sofa and started scrolling. "Well, they're certainly interesting." An unexpected scowl came over his face and he showed her the image on the screen. "So, what's this?"

"It was Julianna's suggestion, and as you can see, even though I'm topless, nothing is showing. It's just my back and shoulders, and that, my dear, is as provocative as it gets."

"Okay," he said, cautiously, "but like I said before, you need to be careful. I don't want anyone taking advantage of you."

"Now you sound like my mother."

"And your mother has a point."

"I know she does, but as I've told you all before, it's a legitimate agency, and this photo is as racy as it gets. At least for me."

He seemed unconvinced as he handed back her phone. "Well, okay, I guess. Let's get going."

"In a minute." She took a deep breath looked him in the eye, hoping for the best. "As you know, everything changed after my grandmother died. Fortunately, I have some money in my savings account, so I should be able to cover my rent and groceries until the end of the semester, provided I don't splurge. I also called Mr. Loomis. He'd love to have me back at the music store this summer. Hopefully, I can stay on through the rest of the year, but until then I have to watch every penny."

"Look, if you're worried about spring break, it's not a problem. I've already taken care of our Airbnb, and we can eat in. I'm sure there are grocery stores close to where we're staying."

"Which'll help, but there's more to it." Tonya took another deep breath. "Melissa has a possible job lined up for me during spring break."

"What?"

"Evan, please, just hear me out. Yes, I'm coming to South Padre Island, but it might not be until Tuesday night, because I may have a modeling job Tuesday morning. It's a poster shoot for an auto parts company. I'm meeting with them the day after tomorrow, and they'll let me know if they want to use me or not."

"How soon will you know?"

"I'm not sure. Melissa says they usually get back with her fairly quickly, but not always. All I can tell you is they've already interviewed several other models, but so far they haven't found the right one."

"Okay, and while I don't want to sound like I'm jinxing you, if it doesn't work out, we'll still leave Friday morning, as planned."

"Hopefully, but there's no guarantee."

"If they decide they want to hire you, would you be willing to turn them down?"

Tonya shook her head. "I can't. I honestly need the money. I've also just signed on with the agency, and it's my first interview. I don't want to jeopardize them calling me for future jobs. If I get the job, I'll head straight to South Padre Island the minute I'm done. I promise."

"Unless Melissa calls you with another job."

"That's not fair!" Tonya's face flushed with anger. "I'm trying my best, Evan. I really am. I really was looking forward to us having the entire week together, and we still may, because we don't know if I'll get the job or not. I'm just saying I may have to come a few days later than planned. Either way, I should be in a much better position next year, so if I miss part of spring break this year, we can make up for it next year."

"You already told me you're taking next year off."

"To establish residency, but it doesn't mean I can't join you for spring break."

"All right, fine. You may not be there until Tuesday night, and I really am sorry you're in the mess you're in. You know I'd help you cover your expenses if I could."

"I know you would."

"C'mon, let's go grab a burger and try to enjoy the rest of the evening."

Tonya grabbed her sweater. However, Evan seemed quieter than usual, and they didn't linger afterwards as they normally did. Driving up to her apartment, Tonya gave him a sultry grin.

"I think we should kiss and make up."

"Some other time. Right now, I'm not in the mood."

"You okay?"

"Yeah. I'm just tired, and I need to finish a project."

"Well, okay, if you're sure." The disappointment resonated in her voice.

"Yeah, I'm sure. I'll text you later. Maybe this weekend we can go see a movie or something." He gave her a less than enthusiastic kiss before she hopped out of the car.

"You're sure you're okay?" she asked.

"Yeah, I'm sure. I'll text you later."

He put the car into gear and drove off, leaving an astonished Tonya standing in front of her door. Evan always made sure she was safely inside her apartment before he left. As Tonya watched him turn a corner and disappear, she tried to convince herself he was more worried about his class project than he was letting on, but a bad feeling came over her once she stepped inside her apartment. She was seeing a side of Evan she had never seen before, and she was deeply concerned about the future of their relationship.

* * *

Evan sent Tonya a text as soon as he arrived home. *"OMG! I'm so sorry. I was thinking about my advertising project and completely spaced out. Please forgive me."* He waited several anxious minutes for a response. Finally, his phone beeped. Tonya's answer was all too short.

"Okay."

"That's it?" he said out loud. Taking a deep breath, he pressed the call button. The phone rang several times before she picked up. Her voice sounded cool as she answered.

"Tonya, I really am sorry. I don't know what else to say, other than I'm seriously preoccupied with getting this project done. I know it's no excuse. I just wanted you to know I messed up, and I'm not angry or upset with you. In fact, it has nothing to do with you at all. It's my mistake, and I'm owning up to it."

Her voice remained cool. "It's okay. I understand."

"Hey, I really mean it. I'm not trying to make excuses. I'm just saying you didn't do anything wrong."

"And I accept your apology, so thank you for calling. I need to put in some practice time, and then I need do some other studying, so we'll talk later."

"Tonya, wait!" It was too late. She had already disconnected. Evan stared at his phone, unsure if he should try to call her again, or perhaps try to text her in the morning. As he thought it over, another message arrived. This one came from a different sender.

"I've emailed your files with a few suggestions in brackets. Please let me know if you need any more help."

"Becca, you're an angel," he said out loud. Becca was a marketing major who understood the creative aspects of advertising. Evan had hesitated about reaching out to her, but after becoming completely mired in the project, he felt he had no other choice but to ask for her help. To his surprise, she was happy to answer his questions without ever suggesting they meet face-to-face. No doubt she finally realized he was committed to Tonya.

"Yeah, but lately you've had a lousy way of showing your commitment to Tonya."

He sighed as he booted up his laptop. An hour later the project was nearly done. He would go over it the following morning with a fresh pair of eyes. He would also have to find a way to return the favor to Becca without giving her the wrong impression. Shutting down his computer, he ran to the kitchen to grab a cold beer and joined his roommate who was watching a pre-season baseball game. The following morning, he gave his project a final edit and emailed it to his professor. Afterwards, he took a deep breath and sent Tonya a text message.

"Morning, Sunshine. Hope you have a beautiful day and I'm very sorry about last night. Love you." He ran to the kitchen and switched on the coffeemaker before heading to shower. Her response was waiting when he returned. Once again, it was short.

"Thanks. Really busy for the rest of the week. See you this weekend."

"Well, okay, I guess," he said. It wasn't like Tonya to hold a grudge. Perhaps she was more worried about her finances than he realized. He popped some breakfast biscuits into the microwave and sent a message to Becca.

"Wish me luck. Just sent the file to my professor so thanks again."

Her reply came as he was about to walk out the door. *"My pleasure. Buy me a beer sometime and we'll call it good."*

Evan received another message from Tonya a few hours later. She and Shawn had to attend a last-minute practice session with their guitar club on Friday night. Midterms were coming up, and they needed to put in as much practice time as they could. He sent her a short reply, saying he looked forward seeing her on Saturday. To his relief, she looked forward to seeing him as well. Finally, Tonya was sounding like herself again. In the meantime, he would go back to Finnigan's and hang out with their friends on Friday. It would be the perfect opportunity to thank Becca in person.

* * *

"You again?" said Briana. "So, what brings you back this time?"

"Tonya and Shawn are rehearsing tonight, so I thought I'd hang out with you guys."

"Yeah, Shawn mentioned something about having to practice tonight," said Nathan. "So grab yourself a beer, and you can commiserate with us."

Jacque and Becca showed up a few minutes later and sat down across the table from Evan.

"I see you've been left high and dry as well," said Jacque. "Just when I thought Shawn and I might be back together in time for spring break he went poof. He and Tonya have to attend some last-minute guitar thing."

"I know, so let me buy you and Becca a beer. You because misery loves company, and Becca to thank her for helping me with my advertising project."

"Thanks, but it's really not necessary," said Becca. "I'm just happy I could help."

"And it's most appreciated. Hopefully, my professor will like it."

"I'm sure he will, so now it's onto better things. Like spring break. I don't know about the rest of you, but I can't wait."

As the conversation turned to their upcoming trip to South Padre Island, Justin said he and Briana would be going to Austin so Briana could introduce him to her family. Nathan and Rob were unable to go as well. Neither could get the time off from work. Once their pizzas arrived, Becca was more engaged with Tiffany and Bobby. Afterwards, Evan and Nathan went to the pool room for a rematch. Jacob and Rob soon joined them, while Jacque and Becca came in later and found their own table. When they finally left, Becca gave Evan a casual goodbye as she followed Jacque out the door.

❧TEN❧

EVAN TOOK TONYA to the movies the following night. Her upcoming modeling shoot was never mentioned, but both felt the tension in the air. She invited him to stay overnight, but once again he declined. Midterms were starting soon, and they both needed time to prepare.

Tonya met with the ad agency the following Tuesday. A voicemail message from Melissa was waiting for her when she got home. Tonya got the job. While disappointed about having to shorten spring break, she was nonetheless excited about her first modeling job. She held her breath as she sent Evan a text message with the news. He responded a short time later. He understood she needed the work and he offered to take her to dinner that night. Tonya breathed a sigh of relief as she read his message. Evan was over whatever issue he had with her modeling, and things were finally returning to normal.

Evan stayed at Tonya's apartment the night before he left for South Padre Island. He took her to breakfast the following morning, and after a long goodbye in the parking lot, he opened her car door and gave her a final kiss. Tonya felt a shiver go down her spine as she watched him walk away. Her bad feeling had returned. She suddenly felt as if she had kissed him goodbye for the last time.

As promised, Evan sent Tonya a text message when he arrived. He was relaxing on the beach with friends and looked forward to seeing her Tuesday night. After sending him a quick response she set her phone down with a shrug. Her mind was playing tricks with her. No doubt it was because she felt anxious about her upcoming modeling shoot.

Tuesday morning Tonya packed her bags and loaded her car. The shoot was scheduled for ten o'clock. She would leave for South Padre Island once it was over. Evan had been sending her selfies from the beach. While he was having a good time, he also missed her. She received another text as she got into her car. This time he was sending her the address for their Airbnb. He couldn't wait to see her, and he planned on taking her somewhere special for dinner.

* * *

Evan arrived at South Padre Island before sundown. The small house was spotless, and the bed felt comfortable. He quickly unloaded his car and hurried off to the beach. As expected, it was packed. South Padre Island was a popular spring break destination, attracting students from colleges and universities across the country. Walking around the beach, he soon found Jacob, with a worried look on his face.

"What's up?" asked Evan.

"I'm trying to find another place to stay. Shawn and Jacque are back on again, so she's moved into to our room. I could stay in Becca's room. It has two beds and we're hardly each other's type, but I'd prefer not to, and who needs to get the rumor mill started?"

"I agree."

"So now I'm waiting to hear back from Tyler. There's a sleeper sofa in his room which no one's using, but he has to clear it with his roommates first. If it's a no go then I may need to bunk with you until Tonya gets here."

Jacob's phone beeped before Evan could replay. "I've got good news. Tyler came through. I have a place to stay." He nodded toward a nearby seafood grill. "Tiffany and Bobby managed to snag a table, and I hear they have really good fish tacos."

"Then let's do it."

The two men had to work their way through the crowd, but once they got to the door Jacque motioned them to their table. She blushed when Jacob asked her how the honeymoon was going while Becca greeted them with a casual smile.

"Sorry Tonya couldn't make it."

"Don't worry. She'll be here Tuesday."

"So I hear, but it won't leave much time for spring break, since we're all leaving on Friday."

"Sometimes duty calls," said Shawn.

As Becca turned her attention to the menu another student approached their table and asked her to join him and his friends. She quickly excused herself and stepped away.

"Who's the new guy?" asked Evan.

"His name is Adam," said Jacque. "She met him earlier today. He goes to Texas A&M."

"Well good for her," said Shawn. "Looks like you're off the hook."

"I guess so, although I have to admit she was a big help with my ad campaign project. I don't think I could have gotten it done without her, and she certainly didn't expect anything in return. I'd say if she had a thing for me before, she's over it now."

Evan spent the next two days hanging out at the beach, but he was lonely without Tonya. On Sunday night he was drinking a beer as he watched the waves roll in. So lost in his thoughts, he hardly noticed someone sitting down next to him.

"Mind if I join you?" asked Becca.

"Hey, how's it going?" He stopped and looked around. "So where's what's his name? Alec?"

"Adam. His name is Adam, and if you don't mind my saying so, you look a little wasted. How many beers have you had?"

He shrugged his shoulders. "I don't know. Four, maybe five, but who's counting?"

"Really. How come?"

"Guess I got bored. And lonely."

"I see, and to answer your question, Adam has apparently beamed up to the mother ship."

"Come again?"

Becca sighed. "You know, I thought maybe, just maybe, I might have found someone special."

"I'm sorry. So, what happened?"

"We were hanging out. You know, just talking, and something came up about UFOS. Next thing I know, he's going on and on about Roswell and alien abductions, and government conspiracies, and how aliens are already here walking among us and it's all one big giant coverup." Becca rolled her eyes as she spoke. "I suppose anything's possible, but somehow, I doubt ET is lurking around every corner. I told him I had to go meet some other friends, and then I ran into you."

"Well, sorry to hear it, but if any aliens try to abduct you, I'll fight' em off."

"Thanks," she said, half-heartedly.

"Hey, I'm just trying to cheer you up and you really are kind of cute, so I can see why an alien might want to abduct you. So, what'd you say? Can I make up for it and buy you a beer?"

She gave him a warm smile. "Thanks, Evan. I'd love it."

Evan's body wavered as he got up. He brushed off the sand before extending his hand and helping Becca to her feet. They walked for a few blocks and found a bar which wasn't as loud as some of the others. Becca spotted an empty table while Evan walked up to the bar. She gave him a concerned look when he set their beers on the table and took his seat.

"I'm sorry you're not having such a great time either"

"It'll get better," he said. "Tonya will be here on Tuesday."

"I know. So, tell me about the modeling job."

"She's gonna be on some sort of auto parts poster. Something about wearing a pair of coveralls with their logo on 'em."

Becca raised her brow. "Really? How interesting. You know, this could be her big break, but you don't look very happy about it."

Evan sighed and took a few swigs of beer.

"Care to talk about it?" she asked.

"I dunno." He set his glass on the table with a sigh and ran his fingers through his hair.

"Well, something's obviously bothering you."

He sighed again. "Hope you don't take this the wrong way, but here goes. It's one thing when she's doing her school concerts. I mean she's a good musician and all, and people really enjoy listening to her and the other musicians play, but I'm always there in case some guy starts coming onto her, and it's not like she's ever gonna be rich and famous. She's going to be a music teacher, not a fulltime singer musician performer what have you."

"I see. So, is she planning on becoming a model instead?"

"Well, yes and no. I mean, yes, she really needs the work, and she says it pays really well, but she's apparently gonna be doing mostly lingerie and swimsuit modeling, and I don't want some guy seeing her half naked in some magazine and getting off on it. There. I said it. Hope it doesn't make me sound like a selfish bastard."

"No, it doesn't," she said, reassuringly. "I understand where you're coming from. You don't want some guy ogling at her and fantasizing about her."

"No, I don't. I know she really needs the money and all, but damn, does she really have to show off her…assets…to get it? Seriously? Then, she said something the other day about how she might get lucky and meet someone in the music industry. Really? And here I thought she was gonna be a music teacher because she likes kids." He gulped down more of his beer and looked at his nearly empty glass.

"You wanna another beer?"

"I'm good," said Becca, "but I think you've had enough. Don't you have to drive back to wherever you're staying?"

"Nah. I think I'll Uber it tonight."

"Probably a good idea." She stopped and gave him a warm smile. "Or I'd be happy to give you a ride home."

He smiled back at her and gave her a high five. "You're on. So, I'm gonna go get me another beer, and how 'bout a soda for you? Since you're driving and all."

"Sure. Thanks, Evan."

"You're welcome." He stepped away, returning a few minutes later with their drinks.

"So, where were we?" he asked.

"You were telling me how you prefer Tonya becoming a music teacher and not a supermodel."

"Damn straight. Look, I'm not saying I don't want her to be successful and do well with her career. I just don't want her becoming famous for showing off her tits and ass. It's a complication I can do without, thank you very much." He leaned back in his chair and guzzled down more beer.

"I see." Becca paused for a moment. "Evan, can I tell you something?"

"Sure. Why not?"

"Okay. You know Jacque and I have been friends for some time, and she and Shawn have been on again and off again for some time as well."

"Yeah, so what's your point?"

"My point is Shawn sometimes talks about Tonya, and he knows all about her plans to become a music teacher, but Evan, it's not her first career choice."

"It's not?"

"No, it's not. She was only going into teaching because it's a steady job and it would pay enough to live on. However, according to Shawn, what she really wants is to become the next Taylor Swift. Of course, she's realistic enough to not expect it to happen. Or at least, she was, but now, with her becoming a model, all bets are off." Becca reached across the table and touched Evan's hand.

"I hate to say it, but you can rest assured she'll use her modeling to find a way to get into showbiz. We all know the music school has many famous alumni, and Tonya would love nothing more than to add her name to the list. I'm sorry, Evan, I truly am, because I understand where you're coming from."

"No, you don't."

"Yes, I do. You're a private person. You want someone who'll come home at night and focus her attention on you instead of her fans. Nor do you want your private lives made public."

He shifted uncomfortably in his chair. "You got that right."

"Unfortunately, Tonya loves the limelight. Maybe more than she loves you, and now she has a chance of becoming famous, so she'll do whatever it takes to make it happen. And as much as I hate to be the bearer of bad news, you're going to have to seriously reconsider if she really is the right person for you. Otherwise, you'll end up being Mr. Tonya Claiborne, and you deserve better. You really do."

Evan drank his beer in silence. Finally, Becca spoke up

"Look, I didn't mean to upset you, but you deserve to know the truth. Yes, Tonya loves you. At least she does in her own way, but she also loves her career, and don't think for a moment that she won't pass up an opportunity to become a star someday. What you need is someone who'll love you unconditionally and won't try to upstage you."

Evan finished his beer in silence. Afterwards he got up to get another one.

"I think you've had enough," said Becca.

He responded with a cold stare and staggered up to the bar. This time, however, the bartender refused to serve him. Evan tried to argue, but Becca quickly intervened.

"Sorry, sir." She quickly handed the bartender her credit card. "C'mon, Evan. It's time to go."

"Leave me alone."

"It's okay. I'm taking you home, and when we get there, we can talk, okay?"

"Fine. At least I have more beer in the fridge." Evan grumbled to himself as they left the bar, but as they walked to her car the fresh air helped him sober up.

"Hey, sorry for being such a jerk in there."

"It's okay," said Becca. "You're just having a bad night. Sorry I had to bring up the things I did, but you deserve to know the truth."

Evan remained silent until they reached Becca's car and she asked where he was staying. "I don't remember the address. Just drive. I'll let you know where you need to go."

"Okay." She put the car in gear and Evan told her to turn at the next stop sign. A few minutes later they drove up to a small house on a quiet street and she shut down the engine.

"Nice place," she said.

"Yeah, I thought so too. My dad knows someone who knows someone."

"I see. Well, let's get you inside."

"Can I buy you a beer? It's the least I can do with you driving me home and all."

"Sure, but can we make it a soda instead? I have to drive back to the hotel."

"Oh, c'mon. The night is young. You could still have a beer and have enough time to sober up before you leave. So what time is it anyway?"

Becca looked at her phone. "It's a few minutes after nine."

"Oh, that's early. C'mon and have a beer with me. It's on the house."

"Okay, I think I will." She waited patiently as Evan searched for his keys and fumbled with the door. Once he finally had it open, he motioned for her to step inside.

"Cute place," she said. "I can see why you'd prefer it over the hotels near the beach."

"Yeah, it's nice, but it's a little lonely." He opened the refrigerator door, revealing a case of beer inside. He took out two bottles and invited her to take a seat on the sofa.

"So Becca, tell me about yourself."

"Well, I'm originally from San Antonio. My dad works in real estate, and my mom used to be an office manager."

Evan watched her intently as she spoke. "I already know all that stuff. I was asking you what you want to do with your life?"

"I'm majoring in marketing, and I want to work in advertising."

"But not as a print model?"

"Oh, hell no," she said with a laugh. "I plan on being the one in charge of the ad campaigns."

"Just like the one you helped me with?"

She gave him a flirtatious grin and took a sip of her beer. "Yep. Just like the one I helped you with."

"You know, I couldn't have gotten that project done without you. Damn it was hard. I'm just not a creative person."

"It's like I said before. It was my pleasure and I'm glad I was able to help you out." She looked into his eyes as she took off her ponytail scarf and shook her long hair loose. He pulled her in close and kissed her. Becca didn't resist, so he ran his hands up and down her body. She softly moaned as he squeezed her breast. Taking his cue, he stood from the sofa and extended his hand. Becca eagerly followed him into the bedroom.

∽ELEVEN∽

JACQUE WOKE UP TO people talking outside their room. Someone had slipped a sheet of paper underneath the door. She eased herself out of bed, being careful not to disturb Shawn. The paper was a letter from the hotel, reminding everyone they were being charged for the number of people included in their room reservations. If management were to find additional guests in their rooms, they would be ordered to vacate the premises immediately, and, if necessary, security would escort them off the property.

"What's that?" asked a half-awake Shawn.

"A love letter from the hotel." Jacque sat down on the bed and showed it to him. "If they catch anyone staying in a room who isn't supposed to be there, they'll kick you out."

"Then I guess it's time to bring Jacob back in, and you'll have to go back with Becca."

"Yeah, I know, but I'll miss you."

"I'll miss you too." He gave her a gentle kiss. "But we'll still hang out together during the day, and we'll make up for the rest once we get home."

"Sounds good, and it's not like I have to leave right this second."

An hour later Jacque unlocked her room door. Becca wasn't there, and her bed hadn't been slept in. No doubt she was with Adam. Jacque smiled as she unpacked her tote bag. A spring break fling would do Becca a world of good. It would help her realize there were other men out there besides Evan.

* * *

Evan woke up with a throbbing headache. The harsh glare of sunlight streaming through the blinds irritated his eyes. He groaned as he stretched, suddenly realizing he was naked and he wasn't alone. Becca slept next to him.

"Oh my god!"

Becca's eyes immediately popped open. "What happened?"

"What the hell are you doing here?"

"You invited me. Remember?"

Evan closed his eyes. He had too much to drink the night before, and Becca had given him a ride home.

"Look, Becca, I wasn't myself last night. I was drunk and acting stupid. I should have never invited you in, and you should have left before things went too far. We've made a horrible mistake. You need to go, right now, and we both need to forget this ever happened."

"But it did happen."

His response was stern. "Let it go, Becca. If you ever say anything about this, I'll deny it. You gave me a ride home and then you left. I don't know where you went after that. Got it?"

"Okay, okay. I guess I wasn't thinking clearly either. Jacque's staying in Shawn's room, so no one knows I was out all night, which means you have absolutely nothing to worry about."

"Well thank goodness for small miracles. So go get dressed, and leave."

She hopped out of bed and gathered up her clothes. "I need to go freshen up, and then I'll be gone. Like you said, we both made a mistake, but I won't mention it as long as you don't. I have my own reputation to think of too, you know."

* * *

Becca rushed into the bathroom and quickly closed the door behind her. While she had hoped Evan would wake up in a more receptive mood, it stood to reason he wasn't ready to end things with Tonya. She needed to find a way to speed up the process.

"Relax," she softly said to herself. "You've made it this far, so you'll figure something out. Just give yourself a couple of minutes."

As she washed her face and hands, she noticed the two sets of matching towels. One set looked crisp and fresh while the others were folded less neatly. No doubt the unused towels were for Tonya. Becca grabbed her t-shirt and patted the water off her face. She would have to leave some incriminating evidence of her visit behind, and what better place to hide it than underneath Tonya's bath towel? Chances were, Evan would never find it, but Tonya certainly would.

"What a brilliant idea, Becca," she said. "Too bad you left your purse in the living room. Your ponytail scarf would have been perfect."

She sighed as she put on her panties, but when she picked up her bra a big smile came over her face. It too would work. She carefully slipped it beneath Tonya's bath towel, smoothing it out once she was done. Other than a few tiny bumps, which were hardly noticeable, the towel looked fresh and unused. She quickly threw on the rest of her clothes and hurried out of the bathroom, calling out to Evan as she ran down the hallway.

"I'm outta here." She grabbed her purse and rushed out the door. Returning to her hotel room, she found Jacque's things, but no sign of Jacque herself. A piece of paper was laying on the dresser. It was a letter from the hotel, warning about unauthorized guests in the room. So, Jacque was back. Becca jumped in the shower. Once she was dressed, she hurried out the door.

* * *

Evan looked at his reflection in the bathroom mirror after Becca left. "My god," he said out loud. "What the hell have you done?"

Tonya would arrive the following night. He had to pull himself together, but for the moment he was unable to face any of his friends. If asked, he would tell the truth, or at least a half truth. He had too much to drink the night before and was nursing a bad hangover.

It was mid-afternoon when he finally punched up his Uber app and returned to the beach. For appearances sake, he needed to take a selfie to send to Tonya, and perhaps grab some fish tacos to go. So far no one had sent him an angry text message, which meant Becca was keeping her mouth shut. To his relief, he didn't see anyone he knew as he took a few quick selfies, but as he waited on his fish tacos, he saw a familiar face.

"Hey, Evan. I haven't seen you all day. How's it going?"

"So-so, Shawn. I had a hangover earlier today, but I'm finally on the mend."

"Yeah, I noticed you had a few beers last night."

"I sure did. Guess I got bored, but Tonya will be here tomorrow."

"Yes, she will. Oh, and by the way, have you seen Becca lately?"

Evan's heart skipped a beat. "No, I haven't. I just got here. Why?"

"Jacque's looking for her. The hotel is cracking down on people switching rooms, so Jacob's back in my room, and Jacque is back with Becca. However, Becca wasn't there, and her bed hadn't been slept in last night. Jacque sent her a few text messages, but so far she hasn't responded, and Jacque's getting worried."

"I'm sure Becca's fine. I know she's been hanging out with Adam and some of his friends, so she's probably with them."

"No, she isn't. Jacque ran into Adam a couple hours ago. He hasn't seen her since last night. She said she had to meet some other friends and he hasn't heard from her since."

Evan's takeout order was ready. "I'm sure she's fine. Becca's always been a social butterfly, so she probably met some new people and is hanging out with them. Meantime, I still have a headache from last night, so I'm going back to the house. I'll catch you all tomorrow."

"Of course, and you're probably right, but if you should see or hear from her, please let me know."

"Will do, and likewise."

Evan hurried out in search of his car. Thankfully, it hadn't been towed. Upon returning to the house, he searched every room. Becca hadn't left her phone behind. Two hours later he received a text message from Shawn. Becca had returned. She had made some new friends while she was out shopping and didn't realize her phone battery was dead. She also refused to say who she spent the night with. Evan sent a quick response.

"Glad she's okay and whatever she does while she's here is none of our business."

❧TWELVE❧

EVAN DESPERATELY TRIED to forget about what had happened between him and Becca. He cleaned up the room where they had their encounter and moved his belongings to the other bedroom. It too had a queen-sized bed. Once he was settled, he focused his energy on Tonya's arrival. To celebrate, he made reservations for a late dinner at an upscale restaurant. Tuesday morning, he sent her a text with a link to directions to the house. Afterwards he dusted the furniture and cleaned the bathroom. Tonya soon sent him a text saying she was on her way. Evan grabbed his keys and headed off to the beach, where he spent much of the day. So far none of his friends were acting strange and Becca was avoiding him.

Returning to the house, he showered and changed into a pair of slacks with a button-down shirt. As he anxiously waited, he gave himself yet another pep talk. No one knew about his indiscretion with Becca. If she were to say anything, he would vehemently deny her claim. Everyone knew she had been chasing after him for months, so their friends were more likely to believe him instead of her.

It was nearly eight-thirty when he saw a flash of headlights through the window and heard a car engine shut down. Tonya had arrived. His heart raced when he opened the door. Tonya rushed up to him, and he greeted her with a warm embrace and a kiss.

"How was your trip?" he asked.

"It was a long drive, but I made it." She looked around the living room and smiled in approval. "Nice place. Your dad did good."

"Thanks. I'll let him know. So, are you ready to go? Our dinner reservations are for nine o'clock."

Tonya's smile suddenly faded and she gave him a strange look. "What's wrong, Evan?"

"Nothing's wrong."

She shook her head. "No, something isn't right. I can see it in your eyes, and I can hear it in your voice."

He tried to brush it off. "Nothing's wrong. You've had a busy day and you're tired from your trip, so let's get you some food. I think you'll feel better once you've eaten."

"You're right. I am tired, and I skipped lunch too. Let me go freshen up, and then we'll unload my car."

He pointed to the bathroom and watched her as she went down the hall. She bought his excuse, at least this time, but he would have to find a way to convince her she was reading him wrong. Spotting her keys on the end table, he was about to get her bags when he heard a loud scream. He dropped the keys and raced toward the bathroom, but as he came up to the door it abruptly opened, and he found himself face-to-face with an angry Tonya. Her voice shrilled as she shoved a bra into his face.

"What the hell is this?"

"Oh my god. Where did you find that?"

Tonya's eyes were blazing. "It was hidden underneath my towel. What the hell is it doing here?"

"I swear, I have no idea. Whoever stayed here before must have left it behind."

"Bullshit!"

"Tonya, I'm telling you the truth. I never touched your towels."

"No, but someone else sure as hell did."

Evan stood by helplessly as Tonya gave the bra a closer inspection. This time her voice sounded oddly calm.

"Hmm...I see it's a size thirty-two A. Definitely not my size, that's for sure. So, who do we know who wears a size thirty-two A bra? Let's see..." Tonya shot him another angry look.

"It wouldn't be Tiffany. Her bustline is more like mine, and besides, she's with Bobby, so we can rule her out. Then there's Jacque, but she's more of an average size. I'm guessing somewhere around a C cup. Certainly not an A. I also know she and Shawn are back on again, and this time it sounds like it may be getting serious, so I think we can safely rule her out as well." She looked Evan in the eye.

"So, who does this leave? Why, it leaves Becca. She's got tiny boobs, so she'd definitely wear an A cup, and we all know she's had the hots for you for quite a while. I also caught that little flinch, just now, when I mentioned her name. Oh, by the way, your face is turning pale, and I see some tiny beads of sweat popping out on your forehead. So, is there anything you'd like to tell me, Evan? Go ahead. I'm all ears."

"Look, I can explain. It's not—"

"I'm sure you can." She pushed her way past him and hurried back to the living room. "However, I'm not in the mood to hear any more of your lies." She stuffed the bra into her purse and grabbed her keys, giving him a final look as she opened the door.

"Sayonara, Evan. We are now, officially, done. I'm going back to Denton, and please, no phone calls or text messages or emails, because I'm blocking you!"

"Tonya! Wait!" It was too late. Tonya ran out and slammed the door behind her. Evan stood in stunned disbelief as he heard her car start up and drive away.

* * *

Becca was enjoying a bowl of tomato bisque soup with her friends when Tonya came up to their table. Shawn stood and greeted her with a smile.

"I see you got my text, and I'm glad you found the place. So, where's Evan, and when did you get here?"

"I got here a few minutes ago, and I came to return something of Becca's." Tonya's face turned hard as she reached inside her purse.

"No doubt you thought you were being a clever little bitch when you left this in Evan's bathroom, but I'll bet you didn't see this coming." She hurled the bra at Becca. It landed squarely in her soup.

"What the hell?" said an astonished Jacob. He and the others stared in stunned disbelief. The white bra stood out in sharp contrast as it slowly absorbed the red soup.

"Oh my god." Jacque was horrified. She stared round-eyed at Becca. "This explains where you were Sunday night. How could you?"

An embarrassed Becca quickly fished the bra out of her soup. Big red drops dripped onto the table as she tried to wrap it in her napkin, but the soup bled through the paper. She looked around the table, but there were no extra napkins. Her voice was shaking as she spoke.

"Look, Tonya. This isn't my bra, and I have no idea what the hell you're rambling about, but I can assure you I never slept with Evan."

"Oh, please. You can stop with the lying now. He's already admitted it."

"What? That bastard! He told me he wouldn't say—"

"Outside. Now." Jacque glared at Becca. "You and I need to have a serious talk."

The color quickly drained from Becca's face. "Look, guys, I can explain. This isn't what you think."

Jacob's voice resonated with anger. "Go with Jacque, and don't bother coming back. We don't hang with skanks."

"All right, fine. You guys can all go straight to hell." An angry Becca shoved her bra into her purse and stormed off while Jacque quickly followed her out the door. Shawn wrapped his arms around Tonya, who suddenly burst into tears. A server quickly came up to their table.

"Is everything okay?"

"She's fine. She's just having a bad day." Shawn nodded toward Becca's chair. "Our other friend, with the long, blonde hair, just got called away on an unexpected emergency, and won't be coming back. If you wouldn't mind cancelling her order and clearing her spot, we'd appreciate it, and would you please set a place for this lady here? She'll be okay once she eats something."

The server grabbed Becca's soup and hurried away while Tiffany gave Tonya a hug. "Let's go to the ladies' room, and while we're there would the rest of you mind switching seats so Tonya can sit next to Shawn?"

"Thanks, guys," said Tonya, "but I'm really not hungry and I'm heading back to Denton in a few minutes. I just wanted to return Becca's bra before I left."

Shawn's voice was firm. "Not tonight you're not. You're in no condition to drive. and I don't want you driving all night by yourself. We'll chip in and buy you some dinner, and then we'll help you find a place to stay tonight."

"Come with me." Tiffany gently guided Tonya to the ladies' room. Once they were inside Tonya told her what happened.

"I knew something wasn't right the minute I came in the house, but he kept saying nothing was wrong, so I finally gave up and went to use the bathroom. Becca had hidden her bra underneath my towel. She obviously wanted me to find it."

"Wow, Tonya. I'm so sorry."

"I knew she had a thing for Evan, but I had no idea she was this conniving, and this cruel."

"Neither did I," said Tiffany, "and after tonight I don't want to have anything to do with her, and I doubt anyone else will either." She gave Tonya a closer look. "You still have a little mascara smudge. Underneath your left eye."

"Thanks, I got it."

"So, are you ready to go back to the table?"

"I don't know."

"It's okay. We're all here for you, and I'm sure Becca's long gone by now."

Tonya followed Tiffany back to their table, where they found Jacque sitting by herself. She stood and gave Tonya a hug. "Are you okay?"

"Not really. So where is everybody?"

"Shawn came out to check on me while you two were in the ladies' room. Then Evan showed up, and he and Becca got into it. I've never heard so many f-bombs in my life, so I came in and told Bobby and Jacob. They went outside, and the three of them are going to make sure Evan doesn't come in and bother you."

"Thanks. I'm so sorry you all got dragged in the middle of this." As Tonya was speaking their server arrived with a fresh glass of water.

"Are you ready to order?" she asked.

"I don't know."

"Tonight's special is baked filet of sole," said Jacque. "It's what I'm having."

Tonya nodded. "I'll have the same, with a diet soda."

"Soup or salad?"

Tonya laughed in spite of herself. "I think I'll pass on the soup. Just bring me a salad with vinegar and oil on the side please."

"You got it. Your other orders will be up soon, and I was able to cancel the grilled tilapia." She hurried away as Jacque picked up her wineglass.

"Well, Tonya, here's to both of us having better luck next time."

"Thanks, and I'm sorry, Jacque. Finding out your best friend isn't who you thought they were must be painful as well."

Tiffany grabbed her phone and punched a few buttons. "I know there were people checking out of the hotel earlier today, so I'm seeing if there are any vacant rooms where we're staying, and it looks like there are a few available. The cheapest one has two double beds, like the one you and Becca are staying in Jacque."

"Thanks, Tiff," said Tonya. "If you'll let me borrow your phone, I'll reserve it, but just for tonight. I'm pulling out first thing in the morning."

"And we'll be driving you home." Shawn had returned and sat down at the table. "Jacque rode with Becca, and I rode with Jacob, so we'll both go with you. You don't mind, do you Jacque?"

"No, I don't, and I don't want to stay with Becca tonight either."

"You can stay with me," said Tonya, "although I may be lousy company." She took out her credit card and entered it into the phone. "There. It went though. Thanks, Tiff."

"You're welcome."

An astonished Bobby returned to his seat. "Evan showed up. I'm not sure if he was looking for Tonya or Becca, but Shawn sent Jacque inside and Jacob and I went out to back him up. Evan and Becca were screaming at one another, then Becca slapped him across the face. After that it escalated pretty quickly. People started streaming it on their phones, and the three of us backed away before one of us got hurt. Someone must have called the cops, because we started hearing sirens. Becca took off, and Evan started chasing after her. Jacob said he'd stay outside a little longer, just in case either one of them comes back."

"I'm so sorry you guys," said Tonya. "I didn't mean to ruin everyone's evening."

"It's spring break," said Tiffany, "and people get drunk and do really stupid things during spring break. I'm just sorry it went so badly for you."

"I don't get it," said Tonya. "Even if he'd had too much to drink, if he really loved me, he wouldn't have cheated on me."

"It's like Tiffany said," said Shawn. "People get drunk and do stupid things. Then there are guys who like to cheat, even when they have wives and girlfriends they supposedly love. I'm really sorry this happened. I'm the one who introduced you to Evan, and I had no idea he could be this reckless."

Their server arrived with their entrees and Tonya's salad. Jacob came in after she stepped away.

"What's going on out there?" asked Shawn.

"As expected, it didn't end well," said Jacob. "Apparently, Becca got away, but the cops managed to catch Evan. They had him in hand cuffs, and it looked like they were loading him into a police car, but there was a big crowd between him and me, so I wasn't able to get a closer look."

"My god," said Tonya.

The table went quiet as they turned their attention to their meals. Tonya finished most of her plate, saying she had skipped lunch. Afterwards they all chipped in on her meal while Jacque took care of Becca's drink.

"This is the last favor I'll ever do for her," said Jacque. "At least they didn't charge me for the soup."

"Oh, I would have taken care of the soup," said Tonya, "even though I wasn't aiming for it. I was actually aiming for her face."

"It was still a memorable shot," said Jacob, "and she certainly had it coming."

Tonya soon excused herself, saying she wanted to check into her room. Shawn and Jacque rode to the hotel with her. Once Tonya was settled in her room, Jacque gave Shawn her room key and asked him to get her belongings. He returned with her bags few minutes later.

"I don't know where Becca went, but she's definitely gone," said Shawn. "Her suitcase wasn't there, and the room is now empty. No doubt she hightailed it out of here so the cops wouldn't find her."

"I'm sure she did," said Jacque, "and she and I are friends no more."

"I'm calling it a night," said Shawn. "If you two need anything let me know, and I'll be here at seven o'clock tomorrow morning. By the way, Tonya, I checked on Instagram. The cops did indeed take Evan away in a police car, so no doubt he's spending the night in jail."

❧THIRTEEN❧

SHAWN ARRIVED AT precisely seven o'clock the following morning. A yawning Jacque greeted him with a kiss when he came inside their room. Tonya looked as exhausted as she felt. She had hardly slept and had taken her contacts out, so she was wearing her glasses. All three grabbed their bags and hurried out. Once Tonya's car was loaded, Shawn offered to drive the first leg, and after a quick run through a fast-food drive-thru they were on their way.

"You know, I've been thinking a lot about my sister this morning," said Tonya.

"I didn't know you had a sister," said Jacque.

"I did, and once upon a time, and she had herself a fling with a married man."

"Really?" Jacque sounded surprised. "Did she know the guy was married?"

"She sure did. It's kind of a long story. Suffice to say she thought the married man was a friend she could confide in. Unfortunately, he took advantage of her trust, but she went along with it, and it didn't end well for either one of them. However, it wasn't until last night that I fully understood the pain they caused."

"I'm so sorry."

"Me too." Tonya leaned back in her seat and closed her eyes, but the events of the night before kept playing back in her mind. Somehow, she managed to doze off, waking up when she felt the car slowing down. They were somewhere in San Antonio. Shawn had exited the freeway and he and Jacque were deciding where to stop for lunch. As he drove into a parking lot, Jacque reached for her phone.

"Well, what do we have here? Becca posted video on Instagram about twenty minutes ago. Shall I play it?"

"Sure, why not?" said Tonya. "I'd love to hear what excuse she's come up with now."

Jacque hit the play button. An exhausted looking Becca announced that she had just arrived in Enid, Oklahoma. She was relocating there because of a family emergency. She would complete the rest of the semester online and she thanked everyone for their support.

"Sure Becca," said Jacque. "Whatever you say. She has cousins in Enid, but she hardly knows them."

"At least she's gone," said Tonya, "and I'm forever grateful she won't be coming back. I also need to block her."

"Oh look. Jacob just posted a comment." Jacque stopped for a moment to read it over. "Wow. He's calling her a skank, among other things, and he's talking about how she slept with Evan."

"Well, Becca," said Tonya, "I'd say karma has bitten you in the ass, and best of luck getting the soup stain out of your bra."

"Good job, Jacob," said Jacque. "I'm blocking her as well, so let's grab some lunch. Then we'll fill up the car, and I'll drive the next leg."

* * *

Evan posted bail the following morning and went back to the house to gather up his belongings. Before leaving, he called his father. After listening to a long lecture, his father told him he would contact an attorney, but Evan would be responsible for paying his legal bills. He also saw Becca's video about moving to Enid, but after reading his friends' comments, he realized he too had been found guilty in the court of public opinion. He quickly checked his follows list, but they were no longer there.

* * *

Tonya called her mother the day after she returned home, tearfully telling her about what had happened with Evan.

"I'm so sorry," said Heather. "If you were closer, I'd treat you to a hot fudge sundae and let you cry it out."

"Thanks, Mom. Maybe we can do it some other time."

"Of course, but I also want to talk to you about the bra incident. I know you were upset, and rightly so, but Tonya, you can't do stuff like that. It would be considered assault, and you could've spent the night in jail yourself."

"It was only a bra, Mom. It wouldn't have injured her."

"I know, but the law doesn't see it that way, and we all know what happened when Annette confronted Jesse. I've already lost one daughter. I don't want to lose another one."

"I understand, Mom, but my other friends were there, and they all had my back."

Her mother's response was stern. "I'm not going sit here and argue with you. Becca got into a physical confrontation with Evan in front of those three other boys. They could have gotten hurt, and she could've just as easily gotten into a confrontation with you as well. You need to be careful, especially if you're going into modeling. What would have happened if she'd hit you in the face, and you ended up with a big scar? You and your sister both inherited your grandmother Carlotta's temper, and it got your grandmother into trouble a time or two as well."

"I know. I remember those old family stories."

"See, there you go, and what Evan did is also disturbing. The police did the right thing when they arrested him. I'm also greatly relieved you ended it with him. I was becoming concerned when he started having issues with you becoming a model."

"I know, Mom, but it still hurts."

Heather's tone softened. "Of course it does, but you're still young. You'll find someone else. So, switching gears. Our attorney has been in touch with your grandmother's attorney. He's willing to give you, Nick, and Emily, five thousand dollars each."

"I see, and while I don't mean to sound ungrateful, it's only a drop in the bucket compared to her total net worth, and it won't be enough to cover next year's expenses."

"Your cousins felt the same. However, their kids are all young, and it's still a nice boost for their college funds. You can put your five grand in your savings account."

"I know, and while it'll certainly help, I'm still wondering if we have other options."

"We could continue contesting the will, but our attorney has advised against it. There's no guarantee the probate court will rule in our favor, and if we should lose, the fifteen grand goes off the table. Then you and your cousins end up with nothing."

Tonya let out a long sigh. "Okay, I understand, and we still have the jewelry."

"Yes, we do. I'll let the attorney know, and we'll close the book on your grandmother."

The next few weeks were hectic. Melissa called with more job prospects, and Tonya was hired for many of them. Word was getting out to the right people about how easy she was to work with. She had her first Four Season's gig with Shawn s the week after final exams. Jacque came along to live stream them on social media.

"This reminds me of last summer," said Tonya, "when Evan came along and shot videos of us at the Hilton."

"And speaking of Evan," said Shawn, "I ran into him the other day."

Tonya's mood quickly changed. "I see. So, what did he have to say for himself?"

"His attorney got the charges dropped. Yeah, he did something incredibly stupid, but I don't think he deserved a criminal record because of it."

"Neither do I."

"I think he's learned his lesson. He landed an internship with a company in Dallas, and he hopes to get on with them permanently once he graduates. And just so you know, he has a new girlfriend, and who's to say you wouldn't run into them somewhere."

Tonya felt a twinge of jealousy, even though she no longer wanted Evan back. "Please don't tell me it's Becca."

"No, it's definitely not Becca. Her name is Zoe, and she looks a lot like you. She's a sophomore and a business major, and they seem to have a lot in common."

"Thanks for letting me know. I guess I'm flattered in a way, and hopefully he won't make the same mistake twice. I also have a feeling he won't be bringing her here."

"I highly doubt it." A bright smile came over Shawn's face. "So, the week after next we start working on our album. Are you ready?"

"Are you kidding? I can't wait."

❧FOURTEEN❧

SHAWN AND TONYA'S album was a compilation of jazz standards and Tonya's original work, including the title song, *Between Us Friends*. Once it was complete, they scheduled a session with Julianna to shoot the cover photos.

"And that's a wrap." Julianna smiled as she put the lens cover back on. "I'll email both of you the proofs in a few days, so please let me know which ones you want to use. And Tonya, I'll see you next week for the calendar shoot."

"Yes, you will."

Julianna's face beamed with pride as she looked at Shawn. "She's doing well with her modeling, like I knew she would. She really has talent."

"She sure does," said Shawn, "and we'll be giving you a CD as soon as it's ready. Then you can hear her sing."

"I can't wait."

"You two are making me blush," said Tonya.

"You have a genuine talent," said Julianna, "and I mean it with all sincerity. I may not be psychic, but sometimes I can tell, early on, who's going to be successful and who isn't, and you had success written all over you the first time you walked through my door. I'm also hoping you'll get lucky and meet someone with connections to the music industry."

"You and me both." Shawn extended his hand. "Julianna, it's been a pleasure."

"Likewise." Julianna walked them to the door, and Shawn spoke up as they walked out to his car.

"Seriously, is there any chance of you meeting anyone in the recording industry?"

"Anything's possible," said Tonya. "However, it hasn't happened yet, and there's no guarantee it will."

"Maybe not, but it doesn't hurt to be optimistic and put those positive vibes out there."

"I know. I've been putting out positive vibes as well."

"I'm also looking forward to seeing how our photos turned out and getting the album cover done. With any luck, we'll have everything done by the end of summer. Then I can start promoting it. Between the two of us, one of us is bound to run into the right person with the right connections."

"As I said, anything's possible," said Tonya. "In the meantime, today's Tuesday, so let's go grab an expresso."

"You got it."

Melissa called Tonya the following day. "Well, hey? What about me? Don't I get a CD too?"

Both women laughed before Tonya responded. "Well, of course you can have a CD. I take it you've spoken with Julianna."

"I have, and she told me about your album cover shoot. How exciting for you. So, who's the young man you had with you?"

"Shawn McCoy is a fellow musician and the brother I never had. He's also producing our album. Now just so you know, we have regular gigs this summer at the Sheridan and the Four Seasons. You'll have to stop by sometime."

"Thanks for the invite and I'd love to hear you sing again. However, the reason why I brought it up is because I was concerned he might have been your old boyfriend."

"No way. Evan has left the building."

"I appreciate you letting me know, and while I don't mean to stick my nose into your personal affairs, I want to make sure you're not in any kind of danger from a jilted ex-lover."

"I'm fine, Melissa. I haven't heard from Evan since the spring break incident, but he was having issues with me being a model before it happened, so I suppose it was only a matter of time before we went our separate ways. I just wish it hadn't been because he cheated on me."

"I wish it could have ended better for you as well, but don't worry. There are plenty of other guys out there."

"I know, but to be honest, I'm not interested in having another relationship anytime soon. Right now, I just want to focus on my modeling, and my music, and putting as much money in the bank as I possibly can."

"And you know I'm doing as much as I can to help you, which is my other reason for calling. A new job just came in. One that would pay really well, but it's, shall we say, a bodywash ad."

"A what?" It took Tonya a moment to make the connection. "Oh, yeah, I get it. So, what all is involved?"

"It's a black and white print ad for a men's cologne, and it's for men's magazines. The model is nude, or at least she'll appear to be nude.

She'll be curled up on a white bearskin rug in front of a fireplace, and she'll be holding an oversized prop bottle of the cologne. Her arm will be extended out toward the camera, so the bottle will cover her boobs."

"I see," said Tonya. "So, how much does it pay?"

"More than any job you've done so far."

"How much more are we talking about?" Tonya's jaw dropped when Melissa quoted the fee.

"Are you freaking serious?"

"Yes, I'm freaking serious," said Melissa. "As I said before, nude work pays really well."

"No kidding. Do you know who the photographer is?"

"Julianna. She says the model can wear a thong or a string bikini during the shoot if it makes her feel more comfortable, and she'll airbrush it out in Photoshop, so be forewarned. The final image will look like you're in the buff, even if you actually weren't. Do you think you can handle it?"

"Julianna advised me to invest in a thong just for occasions like this, and I'll let my mother know I was wearing something when the photo was taken."

"Sounds like you're interested?"

"Yes, I'm interested. I really do need the money, but even if I didn't, I'd do the job anyway, just to spite Evan."

* * *

Emily gave birth to a baby girl a few weeks later. She and Kyle named their daughter Patricia Jeanette, after both of her grandmothers, and they nicknamed her Patty Jean. Tonya's mother flew to Dallas the following day to help Emily with the baby, and Tonya invited her for dinner the night before she returned to Tucson. She wanted to introduce her mother to Shawn and Jacque, so she invited them as well. Tonya enjoyed cooking when she had the time, so she made her grandmother Carlotta's spaghetti and meatballs. Both Shawn and Jacque raved about it, and after they left her mother helped with the cleanup.

"It's a shame you and Shawn didn't hit it off romantically," said Heather. "He'd be the perfect match for you."

"I don't know, Mom," said Tonya. "I think the reason we're such good friends is because we don't have the complications of a romance. Besides, I don't have time for a relationship." She quickly changed the subject.

"Are you sure you don't want me to take you to the airport?"

"I'm positive, but thank you again for offering. Kyle has to pick up his mother, so it makes more sense for him to take me."

"But his mother is due to arrive at eleven thirty, and your flight doesn't leave until two fifteen."

Heather handed her daughter another plate to dry. "It's okay. I'll see if I can get a seat on an earlier flight. If not, I have my tablet and charger with me. I'm taking some online courses this summer, so I have plenty to keep me busy."

Tonya suddenly felt sad. "Shawn's taking a class this summer as well, and the fall semester will be here before we know it. I'm really going to miss being in school. Many of the students I performed with will graduate this year, which means they won't be there when I go back."

"I know, and I'm sorry. For what it's worth, your grandmother often talked about how much she looked forward to your graduation, so she may have forgotten the changes she made to her will."

"Maybe, although I think she expected to be around a lot longer than she was. I guess it's one of those things we'll never know for certain."

* * *

Shawn and Tonya's album was released in August. Along with promoting it online and at their gigs, Shawn was also pitching it to the major record labels, but without much success. He planned on using his experience as a class project. Hopefully, one of his professors would have the right connections. Tonya still felt sad about missing her senior year, but Shawn and Jacque reminded her that not all of their friends had enough class credits to graduate. The week after Labor Day, Tonya got the phone call she had been hoping for.

"Would you be willing to take a short trip to Los Angeles?" asked Melissa.

"Maybe," said Tonya. "What's the job?"

"Alicorn Records is working on Mickey Lee Janson's next album. No doubt you've heard of him. He sounds like a cross between Buddy Holly and Credence Clearwater Revival."

"Of course, I've heard of him. I like his music, and my mother just adores him. She was a big Credence Clearwater fan when she was a kid."

There was a smile in Melissa's voice. "I figured you'd know who he is. Apparently, they're having trouble with the album cover. They're looking for a young woman to stand next to Mickey, and they've interviewed several different models, but so far none have had the right look. We sent the Los Angeles office your photo, and they would like to talk to you."

"Oh my god. You're joking." Tonya's hands were shaking, and her voice was trembling.

"Nope. This is the real deal. I've scheduled a video conference with the client in my office at eleven o'clock on Wednesday. If all goes well, we'll be booking you on a flight to LA next week."

"Wow. I can't believe this. Someone needs to pinch me in case I'm dreaming."

"This business is always full of twists and turns. Remember how I said it was possible for you to meet someone in the record business? Granted, there's no guarantee you'll get the job, but if you do, the same rules apply. You're there to do a modeling job. But should someone offer to buy you a cup of coffee while you're in town, well, that's a whole 'nother story."

"I'm putting it on my calendar right now. Wednesday morning, eleven o'clock, your office."

"You have two days to prepare, so get a good night's rest tomorrow night."

"Which'll be easier said than done."

"Tomorrow might be a good day to go to the gym and have a really good workout. Then afterwards you can get a massage."

"Good idea," said Tonya. "As soon as we're done here, I'll book the massage."

Tonya's hands were still shaking when they ended the call. She wanted to let Shawn know, but she didn't want to raise his hopes in case it didn't work out. It would be better to wait until she officially had the job. After booking a massage, she checked the time and realized she was due at the music store within the hour. She quickly changed clothes and hurried out the door.

The Wednesday morning traffic seemed slower than usual, but Tonya managed to arrive at Melissa's office with enough time to touch up her hair and makeup before the meeting began. Jack Dane, Alicorn Records' art director, was a balding, fifty-something man who came across as overworked and more than a little impatient. They were running out of time to complete the cover design, and Tonya answered his questions as best she could. As they talked, the scowl on his face slowly faded away.

"Well, Ms. Rose," he said. "I'll call Natalie at the Carson office here in Los Angeles, and we'll start working on your travel arrangements. Melissa will contact you with your itinerary as soon as it's ready."

"Thank you, Mr. Dane," said Tonya. "I look forward to working with you."

"As are we." His face disappeared from the screen and Tonya looked at Melissa.

"Did I just get the job?"

"Yes, you did. This could be your big break, so I'm keeping my fingers crossed."

"You and me both." Her hands fidgeted in her lap. "I guess I should start getting ready."

Tonya left her mother a voice mail as soon as she got to her car. Her mother called back about an hour later.

"I'm on my lunchbreak," said Heather, "so I thought I'd check my voicemail. I can't believe this."

"Neither can I."

"Just remember, you're there for a cover shoot, not an audition."

"I know, Mom. Melissa said the same thing, but I have a feeling something really big will happen while I'm there."

"And I hope it does, but even if it doesn't, you're going to meet Mickey Lee Janson. You know how much I love his music."

"I know you do, and while I can't make any promises, I'm hoping I'll have an opportunity to get his autograph for you."

❧FIFTEEN❧

ALICORN RECORDS WAS located in a four-story glass and steel office building in West Hollywood. Tonya's rideshare driver wished her the best of luck as she grabbed her duffle bag and stepped outside. Standing in front of the building, she stared at the large winged unicorn logo above the entrance before going inside. A security guard checked off her name and gave her a guest pass when she entered the lobby. Taking a deep breath, she sat down in the reception area and nervously waited. A young woman with shiny black hair stepped out of the elevator a few minutes later.

"I'm Sabrina Sanchez, and you must be Tonya Rose."

"Yes, I'm Tonya."

"Then come with me, and we'll get started." Sabrina took Tonya to a conference room on the third floor. A makeup mirror and curling iron had been placed on the table, with a navy-blue tank top and red shirt set off to the side.

"Have a seat," said Sabrina. "I'm going to put your hair in a long braid, and then I'll touch up a couple spots around your face with the curling iron. It shouldn't take long. Once I'm done you can touch up your makeup and change tops. They may also do a few shots with just the tank top, so I hope you remembered to bring a strapless bra."

"It's in my bag."

"Great, and don't worry about your jeans. They're shooting you from above the waist. When you're ready, I'll take you down the hall. You'll be working with Ryan Wilders. He's a commercial photographer who does a lot of our cover shoots."

"Will Mr. Dane be there as well?"

"Yes." Sabrina tried to suppress a giggle. "Jack has his moments, but most of the time he's okay, and when it comes to creating amazing album covers, no one does it better than Jack Dane. However, Ryan will be your buffer. You'll be working with him, not Jack."

Sabrina gave Tonya a final inspection once she changed tops. "You look fabulous, so let's get going. We're on a tight schedule." They hurried down the hallway and around a corner. Sabrina opened a door to a large room and motioned for Tonya to come inside.

"Good morning, Ms. Rose." Jack smiled and extended his hand. "Nice to finally meet you in person, and if you'll take a seat over there, we'll get started in a few minutes."

Ryan also greeted her with a handshake and a quick introduction while Sabrina excused herself to get Tonya a bottle of water. As Tonya made her way to the back of the room a young blond-haired man stood from his chair. He too greeted her with a warm smile and spoke with a southern accent as he extended his hand.

"So, you must be Tonya Rose."

"I am, and I already know who you are."

"Only to the public. My real name is Michael Lawrence Jablonski, and my friends all call me Mike. George Monroe came up with Mickey Lee Janson. He thought it sounded more southern."

"It kind of does. I use a stage name as well. My legal name is Tonya Claiborne."

"Nice to meet you, Ms. Claiborne."

"You too, Mike Jablonski. So, who's George Monroe?"

"George Monroe is the big cheese. The head honcho. The big kahuna." Mike had a twinkle in his eye as he spoke. "He's the president of Alicorn Records, USA."

"Okay guys," said Ryan. "We're ready to go."

Mike walked Tonya to the center of the room, where Ryan had set up a black backdrop. His female assistant handed Mike a pendant with a light blue teardrop stone.

"Mickey's new album is titled, *Aquamarine*," said Ryan. "He'll be standing behind you like he's putting the aquamarine pendant around your neck. You'll both be looking into the camera, and we'll try several different poses. Are you guys ready?"

"Ready and willing," said Mike.

"Okay, let's get started. Karen, I need you to move Tonya's braid to the front of her left shoulder."

Ryan began taking photos while Karen ran back and forth to reposition Tonya's braid and smooth out her clothing. Stepping away after another adjustment, her heel struck a slick spot on the floor, causing her to lose her balance. As she struggled to maintain her footing she collided with a light stand. It crashed with a loud bang, instantly covering the floor with chards of broken glass.

"Son of a bitch!" Jack slammed a hand against his forehead and made a frustrated sound.

"It's okay, Jack," said Ryan. "We'll sweep up the floor and I have more light bulbs in my van. Karen, are you okay?"

"I'm fine." She quickly brushed herself off and set the light pole back up. "I got a couple of bumps, but thankfully I didn't fall, and other than the light bulb, everything appears to be okay. I'll go get another bulb and see if I can find a broom and a dustpan. We'll be back in business as soon as we clean up the mess."

"I'll get the broom and dustpan," said Sabrina. She hurried out with Karen while Ryan looked at Jack.

"See? We've got it all under control. We'll be up and running in a few minutes while Mickey and Tonya take a short break. Do either of you need anything?"

"I'm good," said Mike.

"Me too," said Tonya.

Mike returned to where he was sitting and pulled up a chair for Tonya. "Well, that's a little more drama than we usually have around here. So, tell me about yourself, Tonya. How'd a nice girl like you end up becoming a model?"

"I was a music major at the University of North Texas."

Mike raised his brow. "Seriously? That's a really good school."

"It's not an easy school to get into, and once you're accepted, they work your fanny off. I'm studying jazz, and our ensemble performs on and off campus."

"Are you by chance in the One O'clock Lab Band?"

"Oh, so, you've heard of them?"

"Who hasn't? I've worked with some of their alumni."

"I'm actually in one of the other lab bands, but we're all damn good musicians and we all have the same set up. So, one night last winter someone with the Angela Carson Modeling Agency happened to be in the audience. She all but recruited me on the spot. I wasn't looking to become a model, but I needed the money, so, here I am."

"Somewhat similar story for me as well. I'm originally from Alabama, and one of those TV competition shows, *The Next Great American Rock Star,* had an audition in Birmingham. My friends dared me to audition, so I did, mostly for laughs. But then, much to my surprise, I got accepted. Made it all the way to the finals, which again, I didn't expect. I finally got voted off on the second to last show, but it was enough. The right people saw me, and I landed a recording contract with Alicorn Records. That's when Mike Jablonski became Mickey Lee Janson. So, what do you play?"

"Guitar. I also play violin and viola. However, jazz guitar is my specialty."

"Interesting. Do you also play the keyboard? I took classical piano lessons when I was a kid."

"No keyboard for me, just strings. You'd probably enjoy meeting my cousin. She's a concert pianist, and she also attended The University of North Texas."

Mike raised his brow. "Really? Sounds like you come from a musical family."

"Nope. It's just my cousin and me. My sister played the clarinet with our high school marching band, but she had no aspirations of becoming a professional. The rest of them are all regular folks." She smiled and made quote marks with her fingers as she spoke. "My mom's a schoolteacher."

Mike got up and took a guitar from a nearby stand. "They use this as a prop. It may be on the cheap side, but it doesn't sound bad." He handed it over to Tonya and sat back down while she gave it a quick test and began tuning it.

"There, I think I've got it." She began playing an instrumental.

"That's lovely," said Mike, "but I'm afraid I'm not familiar with the tune."

"Because I wrote it, but don't worry. It's on my album. And now, here's a jazz tune you probably already know. A singer named Etta James made it famous."

Tonya began singing, "At Last." The rest of the room fell silent. Everyone applauded when she finished, and she noticed another man whom she had not seen before. He wore an expensive suit and appeared to be in his early fifties with mostly gray salt and pepper hair and deep-set blue eyes.

"Holy crap," said Mike under his breath. "That's George Monroe himself. When did he sneak in here?"

"Sorry guys," said Tonya. "We were just passing time until the light got fixed."

"You have nothing whatsoever to be sorry about." George spoke with a distinct British accent. "You just took another artist's song and made it your own. So who are you?"

"I'm Tonya Rose. I'm a model with the Angela Carson Agency."

"She's the one they sent from Dallas," said Jack.

"Don't let her fool you," said Mike. "She's also a music student from The University of North Texas."

"Really?" George seemed genuinely impressed. "We've worked with some of their alumni, so as soon as you're done, I'd like to invite Ms. Rose to lunch. Assuming it's okay with you."

"Of course, it is." Tonya suddenly looked a little starstruck. "And thank you."

Ryan motioned for Mike and Tonya to come back to the black backdrop. "Okay, let's get back to it. We only have a few more shots left, so if you two will take your places we'll pick up where we left off."

As they resumed their session, Karen was more careful as she walked back and forth. Ten minutes later Ryan announced they were finished.

"Take a look, Jack. I've turned on Bluetooth, so you should start seeing the photos on your phone, right about now."

"May I have a look?" asked George. "You too, Mickey." Jack turned the phone so they all could see. One by one, the photos appeared on the screen.

"Outstanding," said George. "I think we found the right model. They're all good. Damn good." George and Mike stepped off to the side to talk to Jack while Sabrina took Tonya back to the conference room.

"Time to change back into your regular clothes. Then, if you'd like, I'll take you up to Mr. Monroe's office. It's on the fourth floor."

"I can't believe he asked me to lunch. I never expected anything like this to happen. What do I do now?"

"If it were me, I'd join him for lunch," said Sabrina. "You really are good, and you've obviously made a good impression on him."

"So, what's he like?"

"I honestly don't know him, but I'm told he's very approachable."

Tonya grabbed her duffle bag. "I've gotten into the habit of bringing a change of clothes with me whenever I do a shoot, just in case, and I'm not sure if what I had on before is nice enough for lunch with the boss."

Sabrina watched as Tonya rummaged through her bag. "Wait. What was the red thing?"

"You mean this?" Tonya pulled out her red tunic and showed it to Sabrina.

"Yeah. It's a beautiful color and it'll go good with your jeans. So why the sad face?"

"Red was my ex-boyfriend's favorite color, and he really liked this tunic. I haven't worn it since we broke up. I'm not even sure why I brought it with me."

"Maybe it was because deep down, you knew you would need it. This could be the start of something really big for you. I watched you and Mickey while we were waiting for Karen to fix the light, and I could tell he really likes you. I'm pretty good at reading people's body language."

Tonya's face lit up. "You too? I have a knack for reading people as well. He seemed to like me, but I was in such awe of meeting him I wasn't sure." A sad look suddenly came over her face. "And I just remembered. I meant to give him one of my CDs, but I forgot."

"Don't worry. If you'll give it to me, I'll make sure he gets it."

Tonya reached back into her bag. "Here you go, and thanks."

"Nice cover design, but you need to hurry up and get changed. Then, as soon as you're ready, I'll take you up to the fourth floor."

❦SIXTEEN❧

TONYA'S HEART WAS pounding when Sabrina led her through the etched glass French doors. Behind them was a plush reception area. She introduced herself, and Tonya, to the mature woman at the front desk, who greeted them with a smile.

"Please take a seat, Ms. Rose. Mr. Monroe will be with you shortly."

"Well, this is it." Sabrina gave Tonya a warm hug. "Enjoy your lunch, and maybe we'll run into one another again sometime." Sabrina stepped away while Tonya took her seat and grabbed her phone, quickly tapping out a text message.

"I'm in Hollywood doing a shoot at Alicorn Records. You'll never believe what happened. I can hardly believe it myself. Call me tonight. I'll be in my hotel room." She heard footsteps as she hit the send button. George Monroe extended his hand and greeted her with a warm smile.

"Ms. Rose, thank you so much for coming."

"Actually, I should be thanking you." Tonya had a slight tremor in her voice. "And please, call me Tonya."

"Of course. So, Tonya, if you're ready, you can leave your bag here. I promise it'll be safe." As George walked her to out the elevators, he mentioned a restaurant next door.

"They serve gourmet meals, and they even bake their own bread."

"Sounds wonderful. You lead the way."

Tonya smelled the fresh bread baking when they stepped inside. The hostess greeted George by name and took them to a quiet table in the back. The dining room had a garden theme with mauve-colored walls, lush silk plants, and a faux skylight ceiling. George pulled out a chair for Tonya, and once she was seated, he sat down across from her. A server immediately appeared, greeting them with a warm smile.

"Today the chef has prepared roasted lemon chicken and black bean burgers on a gluten-free bun. Or, if you prefer, we also have a fresh Cobb salad and lentil soup, served with fresh baked Kaiser rolls on the side."

"It all sounds wonderful," said Tonya.

"And it is wonderful," said George. "The chef worked at Wolfgang Pucks before she came here."

"I think I'll go with the Cobb salad and a diet soda."

"Excellent choice. I'll have the same." He gave Tonya a smile as their server walked away. "So, tell me more about your music. I overheard you telling Mickey something about writing your own material."

"Yes, I write my own material. I started playing when I was really young. My father had just left us, so my mother bought me a little guitar from a secondhand store, thinking it might help cheer me up." Tonya silently reprimanded herself. A man like George Monroe would hardly be interested in hearing about her impoverished childhood.

"I'm sorry to hear he left you," he said. "There are some famous musicians who tell similar stories. John Lennon comes to mind. Both of his parents abandoned him when he was quite young."

"Yes, I know. One of my professors told us about how his aunt raised him."

"She did indeed. Her name was Mimi. So, what happened after your mother gave you the guitar?"

"I started playing around with it and improvising my own tunes. When my mother realized what I was doing, she found me a guitar teacher, and I caught on quickly." Finally, Tonya was starting to relax. "By the time I started high school, I was also playing the violin and viola. I even dabbled with the cello, but I ended up playing the viola with my high school orchestra. My mother encouraged me to apply at several music schools, and I decided to go to the University of North Texas. My cousin was already going there. She'd dropped out of college a few years before, so she went there to finish her degree."

George looked intrigued. "Interesting. So, tell me more about her."

"Her name is Emily Madden, although she performs under her maiden name, Emily Olmstead. She's a concert pianist who mostly works with symphony orchestras, but at the moment she's on maternity leave. She had a baby girl this past June."

"I see. We record classical music under our Alicorn Sterling label, as well as country western under our Nashville label. The rest of our artists are mostly rock, pop, or hip hop, but not to worry. We record jazz artists too."

Tonya's heart skipped a beat. Perhaps George was about to offer her a recording contract, but before he could say anything more their server dropped off their sodas.

"So, here's to you, Tonya Rose." He raised his glass and took a sip. "I also overheard you telling Mickey something about an album."

"Yes, I recently recorded an album with a very dear friend named Shawn McCoy. He's one of my classmates at the University of North Texas. He's on the bass and he's also the producer."

"Do you by chance have a copy with you? If not, don't worry. You can send me a link and I'll download it later."

"I actually have a few CDs with me. I've gotten into the habit of throwing them in my bag. Word is getting out about my being a musician as well as a model, and I've had requests from some of the photographers I work with."

"Word of mouth is a great way to build a following. So, is your goal to be a musician, or a model? Or both?"

"Both, at least for now. We starving students can always use the extra money."

"I experienced some lean times myself when I was first getting started, but somehow, I don't think you'll be starving for much longer."

Once again Tonya held her breath, but George changed the subject. "I'm originally from Manchester, England, as I'm sure you can tell by the accent."

"I figured you were from England, or perhaps Australia."

"England," he said firmly. "Both of my parents were rock musicians, back when the Beatles and the Rolling Stones were in their heyday, and while their band auditioned for a number of record labels, they never got a contract. So, my father went out in search of the right investors, and once he found them, they started Alicorn Records. I was about a year old when it all began."

Their lunch soon arrived, and over the meal George talked more about his childhood and the early days of Alicorn Records.

"I grew up surrounded by famous people, although to me they were just friends of the family. It wasn't until I got older when I began to realize just how famous they actually were." He talked about how his father groomed him to take over the company someday, but he would have to work his way to the top. George came onboard at the age of eighteen, starting out as a janitor.

"As I said, I got to live through my own lean times. It taught me to appreciate the value of money, and that no job is beneath me. So, when Jack called me about the broken light, I came down to see if there was anything I could do to help, but by the time I arrived they had it under control. I was about to take my leave when I heard you singing. You are indeed a very talented woman, and I would like to get to know you better. So, when are you leaving for Dallas?"

Tonya looked at George more closely. His intentions appeared to be genuine. "My flight leaves at ten forty-five tomorrow morning."

"I see. So do you have any other modeling jobs coming up?"

"I'm meeting with someone about a prospective job next Wednesday."

"And what about your classes?"

Tonya glanced down at the table. "I had to take some time off from school. There was a problem with my funding, and I don't want to take on any big student loan debt, so I'm working full time until I can save up enough money to cover my tuition on my own."

George looked both shocked and sad. "I see, so would it be possible for you to stay over the weekend? I really would like for us to discuss a few things in detail."

"I suppose I could leave on Saturday, but I have to work on Sunday. I have a parttime job at a music store in Denton."

"Is there any chance you could get the day off?"

"I suppose I could ask."

"Then please do. Trust me, I'll make missing a day of work well worth your while. I have some ideas which may help you, and we'll discuss it more over dinner tomorrow night. My treat."

Tonya was completely overwhelmed. "I don't know what to say. What about my hotel room? I'm supposed to check out tomorrow morning."

"It's okay, Tonya. We're already taking care of your hotel and airfare, so we're more than happy to cover the additional nights and reschedule your flight home."

"Are you sure?"

"Yes, I'm sure. I know you're feeling nervous. Perhaps a little starstruck as well, but it's okay. We're all, as you Americans say, regular folks, just like you. I'll call you tomorrow, and I promise we'll have you on a flight home first thing Monday morning."

George asked for a CD once they returned to his office, and Tonya handed it to him with a proud smile.

"Well, it certainly looks professional."

"Thanks. The photographer is someone I met through the Carson agency. Then one of Shawn's friends, who's a graphic design major, did the cover art."

He turned it over and looked at the back. "And they certainly did a good job. I would have never guessed the artist was a student. So now, if you'll allow me, I'll walk you back out to the elevators, and I'll see you tomorrow night."

⸎SEVENTEEN⸎

SHAWN WAS COMPLETELY immersed in a practice session when he thought he heard his phone. Removing his headphones, he listened closely. The text alert repeated while Jacque called out from the other room.

"Your phone or mine?"

"Mine." He was taken aback when he read the message. "Hey, Jacque. Come take a look at this."

She quicky rushed in. "Is everything okay?"

"No, everything is not okay."

A concerned look came over her face as Shawn gave her a big grin. "Everything is fantastic. Tonya just sent me a text message. She's in LA doing a shoot for Alicorn Records, and she says I'll never believe what happened. She wants to me to call her tonight. I'm wondering if maybe she met the right person to get us an audition."

Jacque's face lit up. "Oh my god. You may be right. I'm really pulling for you guys, but I have to leave for work."

"What time will you be home?"

"I'm not sure. It depends on how busy we are. Do you want me to bring you anything?"

"Spaghetti and meatballs would be great, if they have any left."

"They should." Jacque gave him a quick goodbye kiss. "If not, I'll bring you some beef ravioli."

* * *

George smiled as he returned to his big, oak desk. Tonya Rose was everything he was looking for, a stunningly beautiful young woman with musical talent. He looked forward to listening to her CD once he got home. Setting it aside, he quickly placed a call to Natalie Martinez, who sounded deeply concerned.

"Please forgive me, but I wasn't expecting a phone call from you. Did something happen during the shoot?"

"Yes, something happened, but it's not what you think."

Her voice remained tense. "Alright, so what went wrong?"

"Nothing went wrong. At least nothing concerning Tonya Rose, although they did have a bit of a calamity. Ryan's assistant accidently knocked over a light stand, which, of course, resulted in one of Jack's famous temper tantrums, but Tonya took it in stride."

"Which is certainly a relief."

"She takes her job seriously, and she's highly professional. So, while they were cleaning up the mess, she and Mickey decided to entertain themselves with a prop guitar. I had no idea she was a musician until she serenaded Mickey. She's talented. Damn talented. The reason I'm calling is because I think I may have found the next Mandy West."

Finally, Natalie sounded relieved. "Melissa, from our Dallas office, spoke highly of her as well. She says some of their clients are now asking for Tonya by name. She also said Tonya learned how to handle difficult people when she was in high school. Apparently, her high school orchestra teacher was very demanding."

George chuckled. "I understand completely. I've dealt with a few symphony conductors myself. We need to convince her to relocate here. Would you be able to work with her?"

"Of course. Once a model signs on with the Carson agency, she can work with any of the offices."

"Then let's see what we can do. I have big plans for Ms. Rose. I'm taking her to dinner tomorrow night, and I'll do whatever it takes to convince her to relocate."

* * *

Tonya remained in a state of disbelief as she rode back to the hotel. She never expected to meet the company president, much less have him take a personal interest in her. Hopefully he would listen to her CD, and with any luck, she and Shawn would soon have the record deal they dreamed of. Her phone rang as the car inched its way through the early rush-hour traffic. Natalie Martinez was calling.

"I hear you had some excitement at Mickey Lee Janson's cover shoot."

"We sure did," said Tonya, "but please don't get the wrong idea. Mickey and I were just killing time while we waited for them to fix a broken light. I never intended to audition for anyone."

"I know, Tonya. They already told me. I was actually calling to thank you. I just got off the phone with Jack Dane. He was very pleased with your work. So was Mickey's management team, as well as Mickey himself. I also hear you had lunch with George Monroe."

"I did."

"You know, Tonya, George Monroe is someone who could really help you, as a musician, and as a model. He befriended another of our models a few years ago. Her name is Mandy West."

"The name kind of sounds familiar. I think I may have heard of her."

"You may have. Alicorn hired Mandy for a trade magazine ad. George stopped by during the shoot, and he took her under his wing. Mandy really wanted to get into acting, so he helped her find an agent, who got her some TV and film work. She also met her husband through George. His name is Stanley Klein, and he's a business manager for a number of well-known celebrities. Mandy recently did a pilot for a new television series, and we're all hoping one of the networks picks it up."

"How exciting. Sounds like she was in the right place at the right time."

"She certainly was. Melissa told me about you being an aspiring musician, so have you ever considered relocating? I know you've been doing well in Dallas, but you'd have a lot more opportunity here."

"I don't know if I can," said Tonya. "I signed on with the Dallas office because I need the money for school. I'm taking the year off to establish my Texas residency."

"I see. However, if you were to relocate here, you'd probably make more than enough money to cover your tuition, even if it were out of state."

Tonya suddenly felt overwhelmed. It would be a big move, but it could benefit her in the long run. "Well, tell you what. Let me think about it."

"Of course, and you certainly don't need to make any big decisions today. I'm simply letting you know it's an option, and should you decide to relocate here, you know we'll do everything we can to help make you a success."

Tonya still felt overwhelmed when they ended the call. So much had happened over the past few hours. Taking a deep breath, she sent her mother a text message. Ten minutes later she walked into her hotel room and changed into her sweats. Her mother called a short time later, and Tonya filled her in on the day's events.

"I'm sorry I wasn't able to get you Mickey Lee Janson's autograph. The opportunity to ask him never came up, but I was able to get you the next best thing. Sabrina will email you a photo from today's shoot. She said you can have a print made for your personal use, but you can't share the file with anyone, nor can you post it on social media."

"Of course, and thank you so much for thinking of me. I'll put it in a nice frame, and you know I'll always treasure it. Now, tell me more about George Monroe. You said he heard you play, and then he took you to lunch."

"He sure did. I still can't believe it."

"I know," said Heather, "but I don't want you getting your hopes up. No doubt there are many other musicians knocking on his door, trying to get in."

"I'm sure there are, but he spent a lot of time with me at lunch, and from what I'm seeing, his intentions are sincere. He says he wants to get to know me better, and yes, I thought about Annette, so I Googled him on my way back to the hotel. He's not married. In fact, he's been divorced for years, and he's the same age Dad would have been, if he were still alive."

"And you said he wants to take you to dinner tomorrow night."

"Yes, he does. He also wants me to stay over the weekend."

"Really?" Her mother sounded concerned.

"It's okay Mom. They're already paying for my hotel room. He also told me about how they take good care of their artists, so he may be courting me. Not for any kind of romance, but for me to sign on with him."

"It all remains to be seen. As I've said before, I don't want you getting your hopes up, nor do I want anyone taking advantage of you."

"Oh, come on, Mom. I already told you I watched him closely the entire time, and his intentions are sincere. He's a busy man. Somehow, I don't think he would've taken the time to talk with me if he didn't have a good reason."

"I heard you. I'm just saying let's wait and see what happens."

Shawn called later that night. "I hope I'm not catching you at a bad time, but you didn't say when you wanted me to call you, and I'm anxious to know what happened."

"Your timing's perfect. I'm hanging out in my hotel room, and I'm still not sure if any of this is real or not. I don't even know where to start."

"How about at the beginning?"

"All right, Mr. Smarty Pants," said Tonya. "I came to LA do a photo shoot with Mickey Lee Janson, who also happens to be a really nice guy."

"And you didn't tell me about this before?"

"I didn't want you getting your hopes up, nor am I allowed to talk about myself during a photo shoot. Agency rule."

"Gotcha. I was about to say I've seen Mickey Lee Janson interviewed on TV, and he didn't seem to be full of himself. He's also someone I'd love to work with someday. So, what else happened?"

"During the shoot someone accidentally knocked over a light pole and broke a bulb."

"Oh boy."

"Yeah, stuff happens, but that broken light bulb may have changed our lives forever. While we were waiting for them to replace it, I told Mickey I was going to the University of North Texas. He seemed really impressed, so he handed me a prop guitar and I sang for him, all the while not knowing the president of Alicorn Records had walked into the room. His name is George Monroe, and he wants to get to know me better."

"Wow." Shawn went silent for a moment.

"Are you still there?"

"Yeah, I'm still here. My head's swimming right now. You're right. This could be our lucky break, but we don't know it for certain, so let's not get our hopes up. And even if he were to offer us a contract, I'm not signing anything until I have a lawyer go over it."

"Of course," said Tonya. "Unfortunately, I don't have a lawyer."

"Don't worry. One of my professors knows someone, so we're covered, and we'll split the fee fifty-fifty. And by the way, for the record, I'm really jealous you got to perform for Mickey Lee Janson."

"I already told you. We were just passing the time until they got the light fixed."

"Uh-huh. So, you say, but seriously, I'm really proud of you, and while I'm hoping for the best for both of us, let's not expect anything big to come of this."

"I know. In the meantime, how's Jacque?"

"She's doing well," said Shawn. "I think I may have mentioned she only needs a few more credits to graduate, so this semester she's only going to school part time."

"Yeah, you mentioned it the other day."

"She's just started waiting tables at an upscale Italian restaurant in Frisco. Like you, she wants to start putting money in the bank, and she's already sending out resumes. She says she may have to support a starving musician someday."

"Now there's a keeper," said Tonya.

"We'll see, but even if I were to marry her, it wouldn't be until after I've graduated and have my business off the ground."

"Yeah, but you just said the m-word, so there you go."

"Only hypothetically."

"Doesn't matter. You put it out there and you can't take it back, and hypothetically means you're already thinking about it."

"Women!" said an exasperated Shawn.

Tonya burst out laughing. "Whatever you say. Give her my love, and I promise you'll be the first to know what George Monroe says about our album. Good or bad."

❧EIGHTEEN❧

THE FOLLOWING MORNING Tonya went through her suitcase. She only had one clean outfit left, which she had intended to wear home, as well as two extra tops, one of which she had worn to lunch the day before. It was still clean enough to wear again, but she didn't have enough clean clothing to last through the weekend, nor did she have anything suitable for dining at an upscale restaurant.

"Okay, Tonya," she said out loud. "Let's figure out a game plan." She grabbed her phone and found a department store which carried tall sizes, but it was a few miles from the hotel. An hour later her Uber driver pulled up to the hotel entrance. This time the driver was a woman, so when they stopped for a red-light, Tonya asked if she had any suggestions on what to wear to dinner.

"From what I've seen, celebrities tend to dress down when they're out in public, so whatever you'd wear out to dinner in Dallas would probably be fine. However, you may need a light sweater or jacket. Some parts of town can get a little cool at night, especially if it's near the ocean."

The light turned green. As the traffic started moving, Tonya wondered if she could adapt to living in Los Angeles. The driver turned a corner and Tonya saw the shopping mall coming up on her right. A few minutes later they stopped in front of the store entrance, and she hurried inside.

The women's clothing was on the second floor, with the tall section near the escalator. There was plenty to pick and choose from, with many items on sale. She soon found a short black skirt, a lightweight black jacket, and a bright red blouse with a red lace yolk. It would go perfectly with her black stilettos.

Satisfied with her choices, she quickly found a couple pairs of leggings and hurried to the register, but she did a double take when the clerk rang up the total. Even on sale, new clothing was expensive. While

Tonya's finances had improved, she still remained a careful shopper. Once her items were bagged, she went downstairs and picked out some new lace panties with a matching bra. This time, however, she felt sad when she handed over her credit card. It was her first time buying new underwear since she and Evan had gone their separate ways.

Someone from Alicorn Records left a voicemail message a few hours later. Mr. Monroe would meet her in the hotel lobby at six o'clock. Once she was dressed, she put on her grandmother's gold watch and snapped a selfie, sending it to Shawn and asking if he thought she picked out the right outfit. He replied a few minutes later.

"You look like a rock star. Good luck and keep us posted."

Tonya checked the time. It was nearly six o'clock. George Monroe was someone she didn't want to keep waiting. As she stepped into the elevator, a mom with two kids gave her a strange look.

"You seem really familiar to me. I know I've seen you somewhere. Are you an actress?" For the first time, someone had recognized Tonya in public, and she wasn't sure how to respond.

"No, I'm afraid I'm not an actress. You must be thinking of someone else."

The elevator stopped a moment later and the doors opened to the ground floor. The woman and her kids headed off to the pool, much to Tonya's relief. Entering the lobby, she found a small settee and took her phone from her purse, trying to look busy as she kept watch on the door. Six o'clock came and went, but there was no sign of George Monroe. At six ten she wondered if she might have been set up. As she thought about returning to her room, George rushed inside. He gave her a warm but embarrassed smile as he extended his hand and gave it a prolonged squeeze.

"Please accept my sincere apology for running late. Someone was pulled off to the side of the freeway with a flat tire, and it caused a bit of a back-up. I would have called you, but my assistant had your phone number, and she'd already left for the day."

"No worries."

"So, are you ready to go?"

"I'm ready whenever you are."

George walked her out the door. A silver Mercedes suv waited at the curb. "The doorman was kind enough to allow me to park here. I told him I'd only be a minute." He opened the passenger door and waited as Tonya hopped inside.

"By the way, I hope I'm not being too forward, but I must say you look absolutely stunning." He quickly closed the passenger door and climbed into the driver's seat.

"Now in case you're wondering, we hire limos for special events, such as the Grammy Awards. The rest of the time, however, I prefer to chauffer myself." He started up the engine and put the Mercedes into gear. "I thought I'd take you somewhere casual, so were going to a Mexican restaurant in Sherman Oaks."

"I had no idea you liked Mexican food. My friends and I love it too, although we sometimes call it Tex-Mex in Dallas. It's different from the Mexican food we had in Arizona when I was growing up."

"I didn't know you were originally from Arizona."

Once again, Tonya didn't want to reveal too much. "I am, although I plan on staying in Texas after I finish school."

"Interesting you brought it up. It's something I'd like to discuss with you later, but first things first. I listened to your CD last night."

Tonya took a deep breath. "I see. So, what did you think?"

"You and your friend have a lot of potential. Both of you are nearly ready."

Tonya felt the air escaping from her lungs. It wasn't the answer she wanted to hear, and she tried to conceal her disappointment.

"Tell me more about Shawn. Is he your boyfriend?"

"No. He's a very dear friend, but we were never an item. I think of him as a brother. He does have a girlfriend, however. Her name is Jacque. I expect them to be married in another year or two, although they don't know it yet."

"I see. And how do you know this?"

"I'm really good at reading people. I've been doing it my whole life, and I'm rarely ever wrong."

George seemed impressed. "Really? Now I'm curious. What do you see about me?"

"You're a strong leader, and people respect you."

He gave her a knowing smile. "All true. So, you told me you're taking the year off school, but what about Shawn?"

"He graduates next spring."

"Good to know. He certainly has what it takes to make it in this business."

"Are you serious?"

"Yes, I'm serious. Both of you have what it takes to get into the business. All you need is a little more time and experience."

Tonya sat for a moment and took it all in. As a child, she had dreamed of becoming a recording star, but she never expected it to actually happen. Now, suddenly, everything seemed unreal.

"Are you alright?" George finally asked.

"Yes, I'm fine."

"As I mentioned yesterday, you may be feeling a bit overwhelmed, but I really mean it, and I intend to help you as much as I possibly can."

"I am overwhelmed, and flattered too, so please don't take this the wrong way, but surely you must have people showing up at your door everyday wanting to break into the music business."

"Indeed, I do. However, they don't have what it takes. You do."

"Interesting. Melissa, with the Carson Agency in Dallas, told me the very same thing. She said there were many women out there who wanted to become models, but they didn't have what it takes, and I did."

"And look at how successful you've become in such a short period of time, and you have it in you to become even more successful. You're an extraordinarily gifted woman. People like you are rare, which is why I want to help you reach your full potential, not only as a musician, but also as a model."

Once again, Tonya was at a loss for words.

"Don't worry," he said. "I'll go over the details with you later. Right now, I'd like to simply enjoy your company and get to know you better. So, I guess a good place to start would be to show you around the neighborhood." He pointed out a few landmarks as they drove, some of which Tonya recognized.

"I've been living here for almost fifteen years. Alicorn had become a successful label in the UK, and we wanted to expand the business to America, so I was sent here to get things started. Then, once it was off the ground, we'd find someone to run the Los Angeles office, but I ended up falling in love with America. I really do want to become an American citizen someday, although it'll have to wait until I have the time."

He slowed down as they approached a white masonry building with a red roof and a vintage neon sign with a red arrow marking the entrance. The name Casa Vega stood out in big red letters on top of the roof.

"I really like this place," he said. "It's been here for decades, and it's popular with celebrities as well as the locals. We're also getting here reasonably early, so hopefully we won't have to wait too long for a table. Then, once we're seated, I want to hear your story."

It took a moment for Tonya's eyes to adjust once they stepped inside the dimly lit bar. "This reminds me of a Mexican restaurant in Arizona where my family used to go when I was a kid. Same red brick walls, and the same wonderful smell."

There were a few empty seats at the bar. George pulled out one of the red cushioned barstools and waited for Tonya to take her seat before sitting down next to her.

"I may have mentioned this place is famous for their margaritas, and by the way, I forgot to ask if you were twenty-one."

"Yes, I'm twenty-one, and I have my ID with me."

"Excellent. My favorite is the skinny margarita, and I highly recommend it."

The bartender greeted them with a smile and George placed their orders. While they waited for their drinks, a man with greased back black hair walked up to George. He wore a dark brown t-shirt with the words, "Who the Fudge?" printed on the front. A blonde woman wearing the same shirt stood nearby. She also carried a large take-out bag.

"Hey, George. I thought I recognized you," said the man.

"Well, look who's here. Rick, how are you?" George gave him a warm smile as they shook hands.

"We can only stay a minute. The kids are waiting at home. So how are things at Alicorn these days?"

"The same as usual." The two men chatted for a moment before Rick and his wife said goodnight and headed out.

"Rick was one of the first artists to sign on with Alicorn, USA," said George. "He played lead guitar with a heavy metal band called Circumference. Their first album was a huge success. Unfortunately, they split up shortly after it was released, and he quit the music business. Now he and his wife own a gourmet chocolate shop called—"

"Let me guess. It's printed on his shirt."

"It is indeed, and they sell a lot of those shirts. Coffee mugs too." The bartender delivered their margaritas, and George picked up his glass.

"So, here's to Ms. Tonya Rose, a very special lady whom I intend to make a star."

Their table was ready a few minutes later, and once they were seated George recommended the chicken fajitas. "I have them every time I'm here, and I've never been disappointed."

"Sounds good," said Tonya, "but I think I'll have the shrimp fajitas instead."

"Then you shall have them."

"Now you're making me feel like it's my birthday."

"Because it is your birthday, in a way. This is the beginning of a whole new life for you, and while we're on the subject, when is your birthday?"

"It was at the end of April, although I didn't celebrate it this year."

"Why not?"

"I'd just ended a long-term relationship. We were together for two years, but then he had a one-night stand with someone else. It happened over spring break, which was a few weeks before my birthday. Shawn and Jacque offered to take me out to celebrate, but I just wasn't in the mood." She sighed and took a sip of her margarita.

"Then I'm sorry it happened, and if you don't mind my saying so, your ex-boyfriend is a knob."

"A what?"

"A knob. A dick. What you Americans call an idiot."

Tonya laughed in spite of herself. "Yeah, you could definitely say that."

"So, you told me you're taking the year off from school."

"I am. I think I may have told you my grandmother was putting me through college."

"You mentioned something about a problem with your funding, but nothing about your grandmother."

"I see. Well, as I was saying, my grandmother was putting me through college. Unfortunately, she passed away this past winter and left everything to charity, which meant I'd lost my funding for school. However, it appears that I also have a guardian angel looking out for me, because the opportunity to become a model happened at the same time. So, for now, I need to make as much money as I possibly can so I can finish school without going into debt. At least modeling a fun job, and it pays well. I'll go back and finish my degree later on."

George held his gaze. He appeared to be in deep thought.

"Are you alright?" asked Tonya.

"I'm fine. I was just thinking about how I've never met anyone quite like you before. So many of the people I deal with love their fame and fortune, but they have no real understanding of the value of money. Some, like Mickey, are smart enough to hire a business manager. Or they're like Rick, and they have a spouse who's business savvy. The rest, however, blow it on drugs, or expensive cars, or otherwise live beyond their means. Fewer words are truer than fame is fleeting, and some of them have literally ended up on the streets."

"Believe me, I would never allow anything like that to happen. We were virtually penniless after my father left us with all of his debts, and my mother struggled for years afterwards to make ends meet. As a child, I promised myself that once I became an adult, I would do whatever it took to never be in such a position again. I also think my upbringing has given me a certain advantage."

"Which is?"

"I'm not as materialistic as other people. I don't need flashy jewelry or a luxury car to be happy. All I want is to be secure enough live in a decent neighborhood and not have to worry about where my next meal is coming from."

"Trust me, Tonya, there's no reason for you to ever have to worry about any of this. I've already told you. Your days as a starving artist are about to come to an end. That is, if you want them to, and I'd like to start by talking to you about your album. As I mentioned before, you're nearly ready, and I'm very much interested in distributing it."

Tonya's face suddenly lit up. "Oh my god. Are you serious?"

"I'm serious, so here's what I propose. First, I'd like to add a keyboard and a saxophone. Perhaps some backup singers as well, to give it more of a pop sound. I also want you out there performing as much as possible. What you need right now is hands-on experience, which you can only get performing in lounges and clubs."

"I agree. I want to get in front of an audience, as soon as I can."

"Then let's see what we can do."

Tonya sat silently for a moment. "You know I want this, and there're no words to describe how grateful I am that you're taking a personal interest in me. However, I'm just not sure as to how I could ever repay you."

He looked her in the eye and gave her a warm smile. "You don't have to worry about repaying me. I'm a businessman. I'm in the business of selling records, and I think you could be a real money maker. Therefore, I'm willing to, as you Americans say, put my money where my mouth is. Alicorn prides itself in finding artists who don't always follow the formula, and you certainly have a distinctive sound."

"Thank you. I write most of my own material."

"I know you do. You're also building a following as a model, and I want to help you build on it as well. If Natalie can keep you working, as I believe she will, then we'll find a PR firm who can make Tonya Rose a household name. Later on, when you're ready to record your first album, we'll capitalize on it. In the meantime, I'd like to use you as a backup singer for some of our other artists."

"Wow." Once again, Tonya was overwhelmed.

"And I think we've discussed enough business for now. Our fajitas should be here soon, and I'd love to hear more about what kind of music you like, and who your favorite artists are."

ைNINETEENை

TONYA SET HER FORK down and folded her napkin. "The food was excellent, but I'm afraid I overdid it. Tomorrow I'll have to spend some extra time in the hotel gym."

"I certainly don't come here every day either." George looked at his Rolex watch. "I live fairly close to here, so would you like to come over so I can discuss a few more things with you?"

"Of course, although I assumed you lived in Beverly Hills."

"No, I'm afraid not. I could if I really wanted to, but like you, I'm practical. I just couldn't see myself knocking about in a huge mansion, so I bought a home here in Sherman Oaks. A lot of well-known actors live here as well."

"Really? I had no idea."

George took care of their check, and they were soon on their way. As he drove, he talked about his home life.

"I indulge in a few luxuries. I have a personal chef and a maid who cleans twice a week, but never the same day the chef is there."

"Makes sense. You wouldn't want them squabbling in the kitchen."

"No, I wouldn't, and to be honest, at the end of a long day, I enjoy coming home to a peaceful home." He drove a little further and turned onto a side street, making his way through a quiet residential neighborhood. A few blocks later he turned into a driveway in front of a white, ranch style house with a well-manicured front yard. Pressing a button, he waited for the garage door to open.

"So, here we are. Home sweet home."

Tonya thought she had walked into a home from an architectural magazine. The kitchen had cherrywood cabinets with granite countertops. A small maple dining set sat in the breakfast nook. Next to the kitchen was a formal dining room with a walnut dining set and matching server. The living room had a built-in fireplace and was beautifully furnished with an elegant leather sectional and a matching coffee and end table. Framed gold records hung on the walls. The windows had plush treatments, including the sliding glass door, which opened to the backyard.

George turned on the outdoor lights and they stepped outside. Along with a swimming pool, the yard was nicely landscaped with trees and shrubberies, and a small flower garden.

"During the summer I enjoy taking a swim when I come home from work, and I'll often linger here until after sundown. It's a great way to relieve the stress from a busy day. I'm also a weekend gardener. We Brits love to brag about our gardens. So, can I offer you a glass of wine?"

"Maybe a soft drink, if you have one."

He brought her back to the kitchen and poured her a Sprite before showing her the rest of the house. It was larger than it appeared from the street, and one of the bedrooms had been converted into a music room.

"Sweet." Tonya took a closer look at the acoustic guitar. "You have a top-of-the-line Yamaha. I have a similar one on layaway at the music store in Denton where I work."

"Would you like to try it out?"

"Are you sure?"

"Yes, I'm sure. That's what it's here for." He handed her the guitar and sat down across from her as she tuned it.

"I'm going to play a tune which isn't on the album. It's called, "The White Rose." I wrote it for my late sister. White roses were her favorite flower." A somber expression came over her face as she sang the sad, bluesy tune.

"It's a very moving song," said George once she finished. "You have an impressive vocal range, and I can tell you loved her a lot."

"I certainly did. Unfortunately, we weren't on the best of terms when she died, so there are issues between us which can never be resolved."

"Then I'm truly sorry for your loss."

Tonya carefully set the guitar back in its stand. "As I was playing, I was thinking about the time when Annette, my sister, told me she wanted to be my manager someday. It was one of the last conversations we had."

"If you don't mind my asking, what happened between you and her?"

"She got involved with a married man, and she knew I didn't approve. After he ended it, she found out he and his wife were working things out. I told her it was a good thing. She needed to move on as well. I won't repeat what she said back to me. It isn't anything I would say in polite company." Tonya's eyes grew misty as she spoke.

"She was desperate to get him back. More so than I realized at the time, and as fate would have it, it would be the last conversation we would ever have. Sorry for putting a damper on the evening. It's just hard knowing someone you loved was angry with you when they died."

"She may have been angry in the moment, but she would have gotten over it."

"Maybe, but she was gone a few days later, so I'll never really know."

"Again, I'm sorry, and while you never get over this kind of loss, you have to go on with your life. I also think if she's anything like you, she would be very proud to see what an extraordinary person you've become. So why don't you go pull yourself together while I freshen your soda."

Tonya went into the guest bathroom and dabbed her eyes. Fortunately, her mascara wasn't running. After touching up her makeup as best she could she returned to the living room where George greeted her with a smile.

"Are you all right?"

"Yes, I'm fine. It's just one of those things." She sat down on the leather sectional and took another sip of her soda.

"After we lost my sister, my mother, and my uncle managed to convince grandmother to put me through college. However, it was too late for me to apply to the University of North Texas, so I attended a local community college my freshman year and transferred to North Texas the following year."

"Which is when you met your friend, Shawn."

"Yes. We had several classes together, and we had a lot in common. Shawn also introduced me to Evan, my now ex-boyfriend. I was immediately drawn to him, and he was drawn to me as well."

"So I take it he was your first real boyfriend?"

Tonya nodded. "He was. Back in high school my friends and I would go places as a group, but I didn't have a boyfriend per se. Just guys I was friends with. Same thing the year I went to the community college. Evan was the first guy I actually dated. We also planned on getting married after we graduated."

"Oh, so you were also engaged."

"Well, not officially engaged, but as I said, we were going to get married sometime after we graduated." A wave of sadness came over her. "Evan was my first love, and I wanted us to take our time. You know, take things really slow, and wait until our wedding night. He agreed, but then he cheated on me over spring break. Now I can't help but wonder if he was cheating on me all along. Like I said before, it's going to be a long time before I get involved in another relationship. A very long time."

"I realize you were deeply hurt, but if you let your heart grow cold, Evan wins. I'm not blaming you for what happened. Evan was responsible for the choices he made, but you need to understand that when a man's needs aren't being met at home, he may look elsewhere."

"But I—"

"Please, allow me to explain. When I was a young man, I traveled throughout Europe, and Europeans are far less sexually inhibited than Americans. To us, it's simply a part of life. Americans, however, see it as something dirty, when it isn't."

"So what are you saying?"

His tone softened. "I'm saying it would have been okay for you to have made love to the man. Again, I'm not saying you did anything wrong. I'm simply saying the next time it's okay. Intimacy is a beautiful part of any relationship, so please, for your own sake, don't shut the rest of the world out."

George looked into her eyes. "Tonya, you're a very special person in many ways. I've already said you have it in you to become a star, and I want to do everything in my power to make it happen. Natalie and I have talked it over. We both think you should relocate here so we can help you reach your full potential."

Once again, Tonya felt unsure. "I don't know. It's such a big step."

"Yes, it is a big step, so I can understand why you may be feeling hesitant. However, you can only go so far in Texas. You need to be here, where we can mentor you."

"I appreciate the offer, I really do, but I can't afford to live here. I can barely afford the dump I'm renting in Denton."

"I understand, which is why I'm also offering to let you to stay in the guest room. We'll figure out the details later, but for now I want to get you performing in front of live audiences and start introducing you to the right people. Your days as a struggling student will be over for good, and I'll introduce you to a world you could never imagine. On a more personal level, I would also like to help you mend your broken heart and make you whole again. You're an intriguing woman, and I'm very much attracted to you. I'm also fully aware that you're not looking for a serious commitment, and neither am I, so we'll just take it as it goes and enjoy it for what it is. Then, when the time is right, and you're ready to move on, I'll help you find your own place. By then you'll be more than ready to meet the man of your dreams, assuming you haven't found him already."

"And what if I were to say no?"

"I've already given you my word. I'll do what I can to help you become a successful recording artist. It's a business decision and it still stands, even if you were to say no." Once again, he looked into her eyes.

"Some people thrive in isolation, but you're not one of them. You have a zest for life. I can see it in your eyes, and I heard it in your voice when you sang for Mickey. You're not meant to cut yourself off from the rest of the world."

"Maybe not, but right now I'm completely focused on modeling and my music."

He folded his arms across his chest. "All right. So how many new songs have you written since you and Evan went your separate ways?"

His comment caught her off guard. "As I said, I've been really—"

"It's okay." His voice was gentle and soothing. "We both know the answer. Your music is suffering because you've allowed your heart to grow cold, and if you're not careful, your music will also grow cold." He looked genuinely sad as he spoke.

"Somewhere, there's a man out there for you, but if you keep your heart closed, he too will pass you by. You've also told me, quite emphatically, that you'll do whatever it takes to have a better life than the one you had when you were growing up. So if you'll allow me the opportunity to help you, then I promise you I'll do everything I possibly can to ensure that you live comfortably for the rest of your life."

Tonya went silent. George looked at her closely. "What are you thinking about?"

She took a long, deep breath and sighed. "I was thinking about how interesting life can be."

"It can be interesting indeed. So, what would you like to do now? Do you want me to take you back to the hotel? Or would you rather stay here a little while longer?"

She looked into his eyes. He stood and helped her from her seat. Tonya suddenly felt scared.

"It's okay," he said reassuringly. "I know you're nervous about this, but I promise I won't hurt you." He took her by the hand and walked her to a door at the end of the hallway. "You can still say no, and I'll take you back to your hotel right now. No hard feelings."

"I'm fine."

Like the rest of the house, the master bedroom was elegantly furnished with a king-sized bed and a carved oak dresser with matching nightstands. George dimmed the lights until the room was softly lit.

"I understand you've never done this before, so we're going to take our time, and I'm going to start by drawing you a nice warm bath, unless you'd prefer a swim instead."

"A bath would be nice."

"All right, and I forgot to ask. Are you by chance using any kind of birth control?"

Her face turned slightly pink. "I'm a lingerie model. I can't afford to turn down a job because it's the wrong time of the month, so I'm taking birth control shots."

"Good to know, and do you have anything to pin your hair up with?"

"In my purse." She took a few steps toward the door.

"No, no. Stay there. I'll get it." He hurried out, returning a minute later. "Go ahead and pin your hair up. I'll be back in a few minutes."

George stepped into the bathroom. Tonya heard the water running as she anxiously pulled her hair into a bun and pinned it into place. He returned a few minutes later in a navy-blue silk robe.

"Your bath is ready, so now we need to get you ready." He helped her out of her jacket and unbuttoned her blouse. Tossing them aside, he gently felt along her lace bra, kissing the top of her breasts as he reached back to unhook it. A big smile broke out across his face as her breasts were revealed.

"You are so beautiful. I just want to admire you for a moment." He gently massaged her breasts. As his mouth covered her nipple he squeezed her tight. Tonya liked the way it felt and she slowly became aroused. George sat her down on the bed and took her shoes off.

"How are you feeling?"

"So far I'm okay."

"Then let's not let your bathwater get cold."

She took off the rest of her clothing, feeling shy as George looked at her naked body in awe.

"You're an incredibly beautiful woman. Everything about you is perfect, and I can tell you're a lingerie model. It gives you a special kind of innocence." Tonya groaned in contentment as he gently stroked her.

"Feels good, doesn't it?"

She groaned again, and he took her by the hand. Like the rest of the house, the master bathroom was beautifully decorated and the large garden tub was filled with rose scented bubbles. Tonya felt content as she settled into the warm water.

"Would it be okay if I joined you?" he asked.

"Or course." She waited as he removed his robe. While his muscles weren't as taut as Evan's, he was nonetheless a handsome man with a nice body. As they relaxed in the water, he massaged her calves and feet.

"Well, my dear," he finally said, "are you ready to become a woman now?"

"I think so."

"Then come with me." He stepped out of the tub and extended his hand. When they returned to the bedroom, he pulled her hairpins out and gave her a warm hug.

"I don't want you to be afraid. I'm going to take my time and do this very delicately, so if anything feels uncomfortable, you'll let me know. Okay?"

She nodded her head. He gave her a long, passionate kiss as he ran his hands down her back and squeezed her rump. "Now that wasn't so bad, was it?"

"No."

He gently kissed and massaged her breasts. She softly moaned, and he eased her down on the bed. "I want you to relax and make yourself comfortable, and let me do the rest."

Once she was settled, he climbed onto the foot of the bed. Tonya moaned with delight at the warm, tingly feeling as he gently massaged her, but she was startled when he slipped his finger inside.

"Relax. I'm not going to hurt you."

"I know. I just never allowed Evan to do this." She took a deep breath and closed her eyes. It felt strange yet pleasurable at the same time.

"You're doing well," he said, "and I want you enjoy it."

Tonya moaned happily, but she grunted when he slipped in a second finger.

"I know this may feel a little uncomfortable, but you'll be fine." He massaged her sweet spot, and she moaned with pleasure.

"There you go. It feels good once you accept it." He kissed her inner thighs and touched something deep inside which made her jump. "You like that?"

"Um-hum."

"Then I think you're about ready for the next step, and we do things safely around here." He reached into the nightstand for a foil packet and a tube of lubricant. Tearing the packet open, he applied the condom and handed her the tube.

"You need to get me ready, and I'd be most pleased if you would rub some jelly on me."

"Of course." As Tonya slowly rubbed it on, George closed his eyes and moaned in contentment.

"That's lovely." he finally said. "So now I'm going to go very slowly." He massaged her for a moment longer. She moaned with pleasure, and felt him slowly enter her. It was strange and exciting at the same time.

"You're doing fine, my pet." He rubbed her sweet spot as he carefully inched his way in. Liking the way it felt, she arched her back as she groaned. He responded with a final push, and she let out a gasp.

"Are you all right?" he asked.

"I think so. I was just a little started. That's all."

"We'll no need to worry. I'm in, and it feels incredible. Umm…" As he laid his body on top of hers, she carefully wrapped her legs around him.

"Yes," he said softly.

She clamped her legs tighter. He moaned again as he thrust himself even deeper inside. As he began moving slowly she felt her pleasure growing. He kissed and sucked on her breasts. Both groaned as she squeezed him tighter and he picked up the pace. Tonya dug her fingers into his back. As she began moaning George thrust himself harder and faster. As she climaxed, he squeezed her tighter and shouted out in his own pleasure as she felt him pulsate deep inside her. He held her tight and as he came back down, he laid his head on top of her chest.

"I can hear your heart pounding," he finally said, "and you are a virgin no more. So, tell me. How are you feeling?"

"I'm not sure. I had no idea it would be so magical."

He gently stroked her face. "It is magical indeed. You also have an amazingly beautiful body. So have you ever thought about doing nude work?"

Tonya felt her face turning red. "No, not really, although I recently did a shoot for an ad where I looked nude, but I was actually wearing a thong. The photographer airbrushed it off."

"No doubt it's an amazing shot, but I'm talking about actual nude photography, and there is nothing wrong with nudity. I spent plenty of time on nude beaches when I was in Europe. It's no big deal, and it's nice to feel the sun all over you."

"I guess I'll have to take your word for it."

"For now." He gently stroked her hair. "However, if you decide to move here, our first order of business is for you to get a tan all over, and there's a spot next to the pool where the neighbors won't see you. I also want you to start feeling more comfortable with your body. It's nothing for you to feel ashamed of. Nude photography also pays extremely well."

He smiled as he gently brushed a strand of hair off her face and softly kissed her. "We'll lay here quietly for a few more moments, then I'm taking you back to your hotel. I want you to get a good night's sleep, because tomorrow morning I'm picking you up bright and early. We're going to check you out of the hotel, and then we're going on a little adventure."

"Where are we going?"

"Now, now. We don't want to spoil the surprise. Just have your bags packed and be ready to go."

᠀TWENTY᠀

TONYA RUSHED INTO her hotel room and quickly bolted the door behind her. "What the hell just happened?" she asked herself out loud.

Her world had abruptly changed forever, but it wasn't like her to be so impulsive. Maybe George was right. Maybe if she had kept Evan happy at home, he wouldn't have strayed, but because of what happened to her sister, Tonya thought taking the opposite path and remaining a virgin until marriage meant nothing bad would happen to her.

"But it did anyway." She sighed as she slowly sat down on the bed. George was also right when he warned her of the consequences of closing herself off from the rest of the world. Perhaps a short-term rebound relationship would help her learn how to trust again. George was someone who she respected and admired. He was also divorced and unattached. Neither of them would be cheating on someone else.

Feeling better, she opened the mini refrigerator and grabbed a bottle of mineral water, checking the time as she twisted off the top. Los Angeles was two hours behind Dallas. She took a deep breath and sent Shawn a text message.

"Have news on our album. Call me if you're still up. Otherwise call me in the morning." Her phone rang less than a minute later.

"So, what's up?" asked Shawn.

"I should have known you'd still be awake. I have fantastic news. He likes our album, and he wants to distribute it."

"Are you freaking serious?"

"Yes, I'm serious, although he doesn't think we're ready to distribute just yet. He says we're really close, but he'd like to add a few more tracks, and perhaps re-record parts of it."

"Wow," said an amazed Shawn. "This is exactly what I was hoping to hear. We did the best we could with what we had, but I would've liked to have done a few things differently as well. Of course, it's not a done deal until they put it in writing, and everyone has signed off on it, although I'm still remaining optimistic. You're coming home on Monday, right?"

"Yes, Monday afternoon, but whether or not I stay in Texas remains to be seen. Both he, and Natalie, want me to relocate here. They both think I'll have better opportunities."

"And they're probably right, but I'm hearing a little hesitancy in your voice. Is everything okay?"

"I'm fine," said Tonya, "although it's been kind of an emotional evening. You know, finding out the president of a major record label is interested in distributing your music and all."

"Of course. So now I have to ask if moving to California is what you really want?"

"I wouldn't want to be here for the rest of my life, but I think I could handle it for a year or two. At least until I've saved up enough money to go back to school."

"Assuming you'd even need to."

"What do you mean?"

"What it means," said Shawn, "is if you move to Los Angeles, even for the short term, you'll learn more about the music industry, hands on, then you would have had you completed your degree. Don't get me wrong. We're going to a damn good school, but you, my friend, have just been handed the golden ticket, so my advice would be to jump on it. I'll miss having you around, but once I graduate, we'll be seeing a lot more of one another. And just so you know, Rob is having roommate issues, so he may be interested in leasing your apartment."

* * *

Shawn felt mixed emotions after they ended the call. While elated at the possibility of Alicorn Records distributing their album, he also had an uneasy feeling about Tonya. He quickly launched Google and entered the name George Monroe in the search bar. Seconds later he clicked on a link.

According to Wikipedia, George Allister Monroe was fifty-one years old. His parents were former rock musicians, and his father, along with four other investors, started up Alicorn Records when George was a year old.

George lost his mother to leukemia when he was seven. His father remarried three years later. The marriage produced a second son, Lance. George came on board Alicorn when he was eighteen. At twenty-three he married Meredith Hanson, the daughter of one of his father's business partners. They had two children but divorced six years later and George never remarried. He later moved to Los Angeles and was currently in charge of Alicorn's North American division. The article ended by stating George was often seen in the company of various young singers and starlets, most notably actress Mandy West.

Shawn felt even more uneasy as he set his phone aside. Tonya may have had a knack for reading people, but she was still reeling from Evan, and he didn't want her to be taken advantage of. He took a deep breath and sighed as he headed off to bed.

"You okay?" asked Jacque.

"I'm not sure."

She rolled over and propped her head on her elbow. "What's up?"

"Tonya sent me a text message a few minutes ago, so I called her right back."

"You mentioned something about her having dinner with what's his name. George something or other. The head guy at Alicorn Records. So, what happened?"

"On the business side, it went well," he said. "According to Tonya, he's taken an interest in our album."

"Oh my god. This really could be your lucky break. So, what's bothering you? Do you think he could be leading you on?"

"Maybe, but somehow I doubt it. I'm actually worried about Tonya. George Monroe has a reputation for being a ladies' man, and I don't want her getting hurt."

"I don't want her getting hurt either, but she's a smart woman. She saw Becca for what she was long before the rest of us did, so somehow I doubt she'd allow someone like George Monroe to sweep her off her feet, unless she were a willing participant."

"Meaning?"

Jacque stifled a yawn. "It's been six months since she and Evan split up, and women have flings too, you know."

"I know. I just don't want someone using her and casting her aside."

"I don't either, but if he's expressed an interest in your album, then I highly doubt he would cast her aside. He's in business to make money, and apparently, he thinks there's money to be made with your music, so rest assured, he'll treat her right." Jacque yawned and laid back down on her pillow. "We'll have to finish this conversation in the morning. Right now, I'm beat."

❧TWENTY-ONE❧

TONYA DROPPED HER hairbrush in her bag and checked the room one last time. Nothing had been left behind. Placing her room key on the dresser, she hurried out and patiently waited in the lobby. George soon arrived and greeted her with a warm hug.

"So, how are you feeling this morning?"

"I'm good. I'm also pretending to be enjoying this really lousy cup of complimentary coffee."

"Don't worry. We'll take care of it" He dropped her Styrofoam cup in the trash and grabbed her bags. The Mercedes once again waited at the curb.

"So, where are we going?" she asked.

"We're going on a little weekend getaway."

"I know, but where?"

"You'll find out soon enough."

Once Tonya was settled in the passenger seat George put the Mercedes in gear. A few minutes later he turned into a strip mall and they went inside a mom-and-pop coffeehouse.

"Don't let this place fool you," he said. "Not only do they have the best gourmet coffee in town, their breakfast burritos are excellent. I often stop by and order one to go on my way to the office."

There was a short line inside, but by the time Tonya figured out what she wanted it was their turn to order. George grabbed their coffee and they sat down at an empty table near the window.

"Oh wow." Tonya smiled after taking her first sip. "This tastes so much better."

"I thought you might like it. So, have you put any more thought into relocating here?"

"A little. I spoke to my friend Shawn about it last night."

"And what did he have to say?"

"He said it's a golden opportunity and I should jump on it."

"I see, but what about you?"

"I told him I wouldn't want to be here for the rest of my life, but I could certainly stay for the short term."

George smiled as he picked up his cup. "I thought the same at first, but now I can't imagine living anyplace else. Yes, it's a big, crowded city. The traffic is dreadful, and we have earthquakes and brush fires from time to time, but it's also the heart and soul of the entertainment industry. You could stay in Dallas if you prefer, but as I said last night, if you're serious about your career then you really should be here."

"But what happens if—"

"Don't worry. I would never toss you out on the street. As I said before, by the time you're ready to move on, you'll be able to afford your own place."

Their burritos were ready and they quickly dug in. Soon, they were back on the road. George drove to the Burbank airport, taking a side road away from the main terminal. Driving past the hangars, he pulled into to a loading zone in front of a small building attached to a large hangar. The gold letters on the glass door read, R & K Aviation Services.

"We have arrived," he said.

"Do you mean to tell me you have your own private jet?"

"Sort of. We have a contract with a private charter service."

A young man hurried out to unload the Mercedes as George escorted Tonya inside the building. She took her seat in one of the plush leather chairs while George checked in. The young man soon returned and handed George his key fob as he sat down next to Tonya.

"My car is in the car park and our bags have been loaded onto the plane. They'll come get us when it's time to board."

"Just so you know," said Tonya, "I've only flown a few times in my life, and the hassle of getting through the airport took most of the fun out of it."

A man in a pilot's uniform approached them. George stood from his chair and introduced him to Tonya. "Captain Eddie is my favorite pilot, so I always ask for him by name."

Eddie extended his hand. "Thanks, George. I appreciate it. If you'll follow me, we're ready to board." He took them out the side door, where a small, twin-engine jet waited. The two men stepped aside as Tonya climbed up the steps, and a female pilot greeted her when she came inside. George came in behind her and greeted the female pilot with a hug.

"This is Captain Roni," said George.

"Did she tell you she's also my wife?" asked Eddie.

"She is?" asked an amazed Tonya.

"I'm afraid so," Roni said with a grin, "although we don't always fly together." She nodded toward the cabin. "So, as soon as you two take your seats, we'll get going."

George escorted Tonya into the cabin. It contained four large leather seats with pull up worktables and a small galley at the rear. "As you can see," said George, "each seat is both a window and an aisle seat. There are soft drinks and snacks in the back, and the loo is directly behind the galley."

"The what?" It took Tonya a moment to figure it out. "Oh, okay. Gotcha."

"Go ahead and pick out a seat."

"Where are you sitting?"

"I prefer the front row, such as it is, and since we Brits drive on the left side of the road, I prefer sitting on the left."

"Then I'll take the front right."

"They've nicknamed all of their jets after famous movie stars," said George as they fastened their seatbelts. "They call this one Shirley, after Shirley Temple, because it's the smallest. I fly her almost exclusively."

"Have you flown any of the others?"

"A few. The bigger ones are like luxury motorhomes, and I'll take one of them whenever I fly back to the UK because they have sleeping quarters. Most of the time, however, it's just me and perhaps one or two other passengers, so I take Shirley."

"I see. So where are we going?"

"Napa Valley."

"Are you kidding? I've always wanted to go there."

Eddie stepped inside the cabin. "Do you guys need anything before we take off?"

"We're good," said George.

"Then we'll leave as soon as we're cleared to taxi to the runway. There are a few commercial jets ahead of us, so there may be a brief wait before we take off. Once we do, the flight itself will be about forty-five minutes, so make yourselves at home."

Eddie returned to the cockpit and the plane soon began moving. Tonya took a deep breath when they stopped at the end of the runway. Seconds later they began their take-off roll. The small jet was faster than a commercial jet, so she felt the G forces push her into her seat as they raced down the runway. She watched out the window as they climbed. George stood from his seat once they leveled off.

"Do you need anything from the galley?" he asked.

"Maybe a bottle of water, if they have it. If not, I'll have a diet soda."

George returned a minute later with her water, along with a fresh apple. Tonya laughed as he handed it over to her.

"What's so funny?" he asked.

"You are. I still can't believe I'm flying on a private jet and having you for a flight attendant."

"It's like I told you last night. I'm going to introduce you to a whole new world, and this is only the beginning." They made small talk as she munched on the apple, and before long she felt the jet beginning its descent.

"We'll be landing soon," said George, "so if you need to take care of anything you should probably do it now."

"Then I guess it's my turn to be the flight attendant, so I'll take your empty soda can with me while I drop my stuff in the trash."

"Yes, ma'am."

Tonya laughed as she hurried to the back of the cabin. Returning to her seat, she leaned back and relaxed as they continued their descent and landed at the Napa County Airport. Eddie stepped into the cabin once they came to a complete stop. He opened the door and motioned for them to disembark.

"Watch your step," he said.

"Will we see you tomorrow?" asked George.

"Probably. Barring any last-minute call, Roni and I will be staying overnight as well. You said you want to leave around four o'clock tomorrow afternoon. Correct?"

"Yes. We'll be here at four, so we'll see you then."

A taxi waited nearby, and once their bags were loaded, the driver took them to a rental car agency where George had reserved an suv.

"I'm afraid they didn't have a Mercedes," said George, "so I got us a Cadillac Escalade."

Tonya hopped in and reached for her seatbelt as George fired up the engine. "My grandmother drove a Cadillac, but it was a sedan, not an Escalade."

"Tonya, can I ask you something?" said George.

"Sure."

"You've mentioned before about your grandmother being well off, yet you and your family were living paycheck to paycheck. Was she your mother's mother? Or your father's mother?"

"She was my mother's mother. However, she never liked my father, and she never forgave my mother for marrying him. So, after he left, she had no qualms about letting us starve. As far as she was concerned, we had it coming. Thankfully, my sister and I both resembled our grandfather, which was our only saving grace, although Annette looked more like him than I did."

"What about your father? Didn't he pay child support?"

"He did, whenever he could. It all depended on whether or not the next girlfriend had enough money. Fortunately, he never remarried, so there were no other children besides Annette and me. He had a severe stroke a few years after he left, and ended up dying in a nursing home. Sad ending for him, but as they say, karma's a bitch."

"Then I'm sorry for your loss. I may not have been the best father either, but I made sure my kids had a nice home and food on the table. Before I came to America, I spent as much time as I could with

Anne and Peter. They're both adults now, but I still go back to the UK a few times a year to see them."

"Sounds like you're a good dad."

"I tried, and I honestly wish I'd been able to spend more time with them, but staying here enabled me to put them through private schools, and they're both better off for it."

George had rented a small, two-story Victorian house. Inside were hardwood floors with ornate rugs and antique furniture, including a brass bed in the master bedroom. Tonya felt as if she were stepping back in time. Bringing their bags inside, George surprised her with the guitar she played the night before.

They spent the rest of the day touring some of the many wineries and learning about how wines were made. Tonya loved the scent from the wooden barrels in which the wines were aged, while George purchased several bottles to take home. Later on, he took her to dinner at an Italian restaurant popular with the locals. When they returned, they made love in the brass bed. The following day was spent relaxing while Tonya played the guitar. Finally, George looked at his watch.

"As much as I hate to say it, we need to get ready to leave."

"So soon?"

"I'm afraid so, but not to worry. We'll go on other adventures, I promise."

Tonya put the guitar back in its case and gathered up her belongings. Eddie and Roni were waiting at the airport when they arrived, and they landed in Burbank less than an hour later. George took her to dinner at another favorite restaurant and dropped her off at the airport the following morning. Upon checking in, Tonya discovered her ticket had been upgraded to first class.

⚮TWENTY-TWO⚮

SHAWN GREETED TONYA in the baggage claim area with a smile and a hug. "So how does it feel to be an up-and-coming famous recording star?"

"I have no idea," she said with a shrug. "At the moment, I'm still Tonya Claiborne, the starving music student from Arizona."

He shook his head. "No, not anymore. You're giving off a whole new vibe."

"I am?"

"You sure are. You have a happy glow, and you're more self-assured and confident, but don't worry. Underneath it all, you're still the same Tonya we know and love." The baggage carousel started turning. Shawn grabbed Tonya's bag and they were soon on their way to Denton.

"I think I told you Rob may be moving soon," said Shawn.

"You did. I'll get in touch with him later this week."

"So, tell me all about it."

"It's like I said before. I was doing the photo shoot with Mickey Lee Janson. Then a light stand gets knocked over, and—"

"I know. You already told me. I want to know what happened later."

"With George Monroe?" asked Tonya.

"Yep."

"You know, you're as bad as my mother. However, I watched him closely. He really meant it when he said we're almost ready, but we're not quite there yet."

"He's right, but we will be. Very soon."

Tonya turned her phone off airplane mode and it immediately started beeping. "I've got mail." Her brow raised as she scanned her inbox.

"Hmm…I have an email from Mike, otherwise known as Mickey Lee Janson. He says thanks for the CD, and he hopes it was okay for Sabrina to give him my email address. He's also happy to hear I may be moving to LA, and he hopes to see me sometime soon."

"Sounds to me like you made some friends while you were there."

"I guess I did, and just so you know, my friends are also your friends."

"Which I very much appreciate," said Shawn. "I take it you'll still be modeling once you move there."

"Yep. The agency says I'll get more work in there than I would in Dallas, and I'm still trying to make as much money as I possibly can."

"I know you are, but the cost of living is also higher."

"Don't worry," said Tonya. "I found a room to rent, and I don't have a lot of stuff to move. Just my clothes, laptop, two guitars, and a viola. I should be able to get it all in my car."

"What about your dishes and furniture?"

"It all came from yard sales and thrift stores, except for the sleeper sofa, which I bought new. If Rob's willing to buy it, he can have it. If not, I'll have a moving sale."

"I'd like to buy the sofa, if you don't mind. Jacque and I need a new sofa. The one we have now is falling apart. So, when do you plan on leaving?"

"Melissa scheduled a meeting with a prospective client on Wednesday. If they hire me, I do the shoot a week from Friday, and I'll leave either Saturday or Sunday. If not, I'll leave sooner. I'll give the music store my notice later today, and I need to pay off the guitar I have on layaway."

Shawn's voice sounded sad. "Sounds like you have it all figured out. We'll have to have a farewell dinner for you, either at Finnigan's, or our new hangout, Geraldo's Tex-Mex."

"Let's do the new place. I haven't been there yet."

Tonya's apartment seemed different when she stepped inside. Everything was exactly as she left it, but she was seeing it through different eyes. While she had done her best with what she had, it was still a haphazard collection of mismatched furnishings. She quickly unpacked and hurried off to the laundry room. It was empty and eerily quiet. Ruby had moved out a few weeks before, and Tonya missed their Sunday afternoon visits. She had come to think of Ruby as a surrogate grandmother. Melissa called later that afternoon.

"I hear things went really well for you in LA."

"They sure did. In fact, Natalie would like to have me there."

"I know she would. She and I had a long discussion about it. As much as I would hate to see you go, you really would be better off in Los Angeles. We'll miss having you in Dallas, so I want to take you to lunch before you leave."

"Thanks, I'd like that," said Tonya, "and I'm going to miss you too."

"Don't worry. We'll keep in touch, and if a client really wants you, we'll fly you back here for the shoot."

"I'd love it and I still have friends here, so it'll give me a good excuse to come visit."

"Meantime you still have an appointment on Wednesday afternoon."

"I know. It's on my calendar."

Tonya's phone soon rang again. This time her mother was calling. "I've downloaded the photo of Mickey Lee Janson, and I'm having a print made. So, how was your weekend?"

"Fantastic. I really needed a mini vacation."

"I see. So, what'd you do?"

Tonya didn't want to say too much. "George took me sightseeing, and we also had a long talk. Both he, and Natalie, with the Carson agency, have made the case for me moving to Los Angeles. Natalie says I'll get more work there while George is still very much interested in distributing the album. I also discussed it with Melissa, earlier today. She also said I'll have more opportunities in LA, so I'm moving there."

"When?"

"As soon as I can. I've already found a room to rent. I also found out one of my friends here in Denton is looking for a new place, and he's interested in leasing my apartment. I have to meet with a prospective client on Wednesday. Once I know if I have the job or not, I can set my moving date."

Her mother seemed upset. "But what about establishing your Texas residency? We both agreed on this."

"I know we did, but things have changed. Shawn even told me I'll get more hands-on experience with the music industry if I were to spend a year or two in LA."

Heather remained unconvinced. "What about your plans for becoming a music teacher?"

"It could still happen. I only have a year left to finish my degree, and the university will still be there."

"I know. I just wish this opportunity had come along a year from now, after you graduated. So now I have to ask if you're sure this is what you want?"

"Yes, Mom. I'm sure. I'll only be there for a year or two. Then I'm coming back to Dallas. It's where I intend to settle down."

* * *

Heather sighed loudly as she disconnected the call and gave her husband a troubled look.

"Is everything okay?" he asked.

"No, Alberto, it's not. My daughter has just informed me that she's moving to Los Angeles, and she didn't bother to discuss it with me first."

"She's an adult."

"I know she is, but it's a big move, and she should have discussed it with me first. I'm her mother. I've also lost one daughter. I don't want to lose another."

"You need to stop blaming yourself for what happened to Annette. It wasn't your fault. I've gone over every single detail in her case file."

"I know you have."

"The spring semester had just started. Annette told her boyfriend she was leaving early that morning because she wanted to add another class to her schedule. It had been over between her and Jesse for months. No one saw it coming. There wasn't anything you, or anyone else, could have done to prevent it."

"I still should have kept a closer watch on my daughter."

"How? She was no longer living under your roof."

"But I—"

"Heather, please, just hear me out. You raised her the best you could, but she made some bad choices, and, unfortunately for her, it ended tragically. I've been a homicide detective for more years than I care to admit. Annette was in the wrong place at the wrong time, just like Tricia was in the wrong place at the wrong time. There wasn't anything you could have done."

"I know, but—"

"No buts," he said firmly. "The world is a dangerous place. Bad things happen every day, and tomorrow isn't guaranteed for anyone. The only thing we can do is make the most of the time we're given. Tonya is an adult. You've taught her the difference between right and wrong. You need to let her make her own choices and live her own life."

Alberto smiled and smoothed a lock of hair away from her face. "And just so you know, you're a terrific mother and stepmother, as well as an amazing wife, and to show my appreciation, I'd like to take my beautiful wife somewhere special for dinner tonight."

～TWENTY-THREE～

GEORGE WHISTLED A happy tune as he stepped off the elevator and gave the receptionist a cheerful greeting. "Any calls?" he asked.

"A few." She handed him three message slips. "Shannon's manager is still clamoring about her release date. Harvey Morris is having some serious supply issues, and Mandy West said for you to call her at your convenience."

"Thanks. I'll be in my office." He hurried down the hallway and took his seat behind his desk. After tending to the usual urgent matters, he took a break to return Mandy's call, making sure his office door was securely closed. Mandy answered on the second ring.

"What's up my darling?" he asked.

"I hear there's a new girl in town."

"Word certainly gets out fast, doesn't it?"

"Someone snapped a photo of the two of you leaving Casa Vega and it's making the rounds on social media. So, who is she?"

"Now, now, my pet. There's no need for you to be jealous. She's with the Carson Agency in Dallas. She was here for a photo shoot for Mickey's new album cover."

"So why wasn't I on Mickey's album cover?"

"Because his people wanted a brunette instead of a blonde, and at the moment you have more projects than you can handle. I also specifically chose you for the *Sir Maxwell* layout."

"Okay, okay," said Mandy. "You've made your point."

"So, are you by chance free for a late lunch today?"

"I think it can be arranged."

He smiled. "Good. It's what I was hoping to hear, so meet me at the usual place, two o'clock."

"I'll be there."

George turned his attention back to his work. He would not be returning to the office after lunch, and he had a few more tasks to complete. Once the last email was sent, he shut down his computer and put on his coat.

"I'm meeting Ms. West for lunch," he said on his way out. "If anyone calls, take a message." He hurried to the elevator and went through a fast-food drive through on his way home. Once he arrived, he quickly set the kitchen table and poured two glasses of chardonnay. Mandy rang the doorbell a few minutes later. As she came inside, he greeted her with a long, passionate kiss.

"And I'm happy to see you too," she said, "but I'm also starving."

He squeezed her rump. "Umm…me too, but not for the food."

"Down boy. A girl's got to eat first."

"Then come with me." He took her to the kitchen and pulled out a chair. Once she was seated, he took the takeout bag from the refrigerator.

"I got us some salads, and I'll let you pick the one you want. One is chicken Caesar. The other is apple chicken."

"You can have the Caesar."

He handed her the apple chicken and sat down next to her. "So have any television networks shown an interest in your new pilot?"

"Not yet. I was wondering if you might know anyone who could put in a good word for me. This could really be the break I'm looking for."

"I'm sorry, but at the moment I can't think of anyone, although the other day I overheard someone talking about some new projects coming up at Cloudland Pictures."

Mandy raised her brow. "Anything specific?"

"Not really, but you may want to give your agent a call."

"I will, and thanks for the tip."

"You're welcome."

"By the way, I do the Sir Maxwell shoot next week."

"I know," he said. "I'll try to stop by, if I have the time."

"I'd like that. So, tell me about the new girl."

"Her name is Tonya Rose. She's a musician and a damn talented one. Like you, she got into modeling because she needed the money, but her dream is to become a recording star."

"Which you can make happen."

"I can and I absolutely will, when the time is right. I met her last Thursday, during Mickey's photoshoot. They had a little mishap. Nothing serious, just a broken light bulb, but Jack nearly had a meltdown."

Mandy rolled her eyes. "Sounds about right."

"So, while Tonya and Mickey waited for them to clean up the mess, she sang a tune for him on a prop guitar. She has an amazing voice, and she writes a lot of her own material. She was too good to pass up, but don't worry. She's not in competition with you. She's no more interested in becoming an actress then you are in becoming a singer."

"I couldn't carry a tune if it had handles," said Mandy. "So, did you sign her up?"

"Not yet. She needs to put in a little more time singing in clubs and lounges, but I want her here now so Natalie can start working with her. First order of business is to find her a publicist so we can start getting her name out there."

"Wow. You really are serious."

"I am. Talent like hers is hard to come by. She'll be staying here with me, just like you did. I also spoke to Natalie this morning. We'll be keeping her busy, just like we've kept you busy."

Mandy gave him a mischievous look. "So will she also be joining our exclusive club?"

"As a matter of fact, she will, and I'll eventually find her a permanent partner, just like I found Stan for you. And speaking of Stan, how is he these days?"

"Busy, as usual. So, will she become one of his clients as well?"

"Of course, she will. She's the quintessential starving student. She says she'll do whatever it takes to become successful in the music business."

"Sounds like you seized the perfect opportunity."

"It's what I do, love." He gave her a mischievous grin. "By the time I'm done with her, she won't be a starving artist, especially with your husband handling her finances."

"Which means she'll forever owe you a debt of gratitude."

"She will. The same way you forever owe me a debt of gratitude. So, tell me, are you complaining?"

"No." She gave him a sultry grin.

"Well, I should certainly hope not. Variety is the spice of life, my pet." As they finished their meal, they discussed other projects he had in mind for Mandy.

"It all sounds exciting." She set her empty bowl aside with a smile. "And now that we've talked, I'm greatly relieved in knowing nothing has changed between us."

"Nothing has, and nothing ever will. You'll always be my favorite mistress, Mandy. No matter who else comes along." George stood from his chair and placed their empty bowls on the counter.

"I'm going to do a quick tidy up, and you need to run down the hall and get undressed."

"I told my husband I'd be home by five."

"Did you now?" He gave her a knowing smile. "Stan knew there were strings attached when I introduced him to you, but don't worry. I'll return the favor to him as soon as I can, but for now, you need to go down the hall and get out of those clothes. I'll come join you in a few minutes. Then we'll take a shower together and enjoy one another's company for a while, and if we should happen run late, you'll have to send your husband a text message."

❧TWENTY-FOUR❧

TONYA TOOK THE last remaining garments from her closet and laid them in the backseat of her car while Shawn helped Rob load the sofa sleeper into the back of Rob's pickup truck.

"I got it." Rob pushed the sofa into the truck bed with a final grunt. "There. As soon as I tie it down, we'll run it over to your place."

"Thanks, I owe you one," said Shawn.

"We're good. You helped me move my bed, so we're even." As Rob secured the sofa, Shawn walked up to Tonya's car.

"Well, look at you," he said. "You managed to get it all in."

"I didn't have much," said Tonya.

"Looks like you're good to go. I just hope your car makes it."

"Hopefully, it will. I know the milage is really getting up there, but I just had it serviced."

Shawn's expression turned sad. "So, I guess this is it."

"I'm afraid so, but I'm going inside for one last look, just in case I missed anything, even though I know I didn't."

"Can I at least buy you breakfast before you leave?"

Tonya nodded toward Rob's pickup truck. "What about your sofa?"

"Oh, yeah."

"Don't worry. We'll take a raincheck, and you haven't seen the last of me. Not by a longshot."

"I know, and you can stay on the sofa sleeper whenever you're in town." He walked into her apartment with her and she took a final look inside the closet.

"See? It's empty. There's nothing left on any of the shelves, and my clothes are all loaded. So, I guess it's time for me to hit the road."

Shawn walked her out and patiently waited as she removed her key from her keyring and handed it to Rob. "It's all yours."

"Thanks, Tonya. I appreciate it. You got me out of a real jam." He hugged her goodbye and turned his attention to Shawn. "We need to get the sofa unloaded so I can get the rest of my stuff."

Shawn looked at Tonya. "Send me a text to let me know when you've arrived in Pecos."

"You're still as bad as my mother." Tonya gave him a final hug and hopped in her car. She waited for Shawn and Rob to get into Rob's truck and followed them out to the main road. Merging onto the freeway, she felt bittersweet memories washing over her, but once the Dallas-Fort Worth metroplex was in her rearview mirror, her sadness turned into anticipation. She arrived in Tucson the following afternoon, and her mother greeted her with a long hug.

"It's good to have you home."

"I know, Mom, although I've never actually lived here."

"Funny how I still miss our old house in Mesa, despite the neighborhood going bad."

"It got a little rundown," said Tonya, "but it really wasn't so bad. Besides, I grew up in that house, but by the time you and Alberto got married and moved to Tucson, I was already in Texas."

"I know, but you'll always have a home here. Alberto will be home soon, and then we're taking you to dinner. Hopefully, you still like Mexican food. There's a place up the road which is really good. It reminds me of Mi Tio's Café, back in Mesa. Similar looking red brick building, and they have a similar menu."

"Sounds like the place George took me to in Sherman Oaks. Casa Vega. It, too, has red brick walls on the inside. I'll have to take you there when you and Alberto come to visit."

"We'll see," said Heather. "We're already planning a family trip to the Grand Canyon for spring break. Robin and Dawson have never been there. Maybe you can join us."

While Tonya genuinely liked her stepfather, she didn't feel the same about her step siblings. Dawson was a bully who she wanted nothing to do with, while Robin was a constant complainer who could never be pleased.

"I appreciate the offer, Mom. However, spring break is a long way off, and Natalie says she'll be keeping me busy once I get to LA. And after what happened last spring break, I may ignore it altogether."

Heather's face fell. "I'm sorry, Tonya. I didn't mean to sound insensitive."

"It's okay. I'm doing much better, but I'm not in any hurry to find someone else. I simply don't have the time."

"It'll happen when it happens.".

"We'll see. As I said, I'm not looking."

Alberto soon arrived home, and over dinner Heather offered to find a substitute for the rest of the week.

"I'd really like for you to stay over the weekend. Robin and Dawson will be here, and we could have a nice family get-together."

"Sorry, Mom, but I need to be in Los Angeles before the weekend so I can get settled. I have a meeting with Natalie first thing Monday morning. I could, however, stay over tomorrow, but I'll have to leave first thing the following morning."

Heather looked disappointed. "I understand, and I guess we can have at least one day together, so I'll arrange for a substitute. It sounds like they're putting you to work, which is a big relief to me as well. You also mentioned something before about finding a room to rent. So, can you tell me more about it?"

"Sure. I'm renting an unused guest room at George Monroe's house. I thought I'd already told you."

Heather bristled. "No, you didn't. All you told me was it's in a house in a good neighborhood."

Tonya took a deep breath. She hated being less than truthful with her mother. "Mom, it's okay. It's a big house. He works long hours, and I'm going to be busy as well, so we'll probably be like ships in the night. Besides, he's the same age Dad would have been if he were still alive."

"I know. You already told me. I'm just not sure I like the idea."

"It's okay, Heather," said Alberto. "It's like we discussed before. It costs a lot of money to live in Los Angeles, so Tonya would undoubtedly need a roommate, and I'd rather have her renting a room with someone she knows instead of a total stranger."

"And it's not like I'll be living there forever. I've already told you I only plan on being there for a year or two. Then I'm going back to Dallas."

❧TWENTY-FIVE❧

GEORGE GREETED TONYA with a warm hug as she stepped out of her car. "Welcome to your new home. I'm happy to see you've arrived safe and sound."

"Thanks, although I wasn't sure if I'd make it over the mountains or not. This little car has a lot of miles on it. It's been around, and then some."

"Then you've obviously taken good care of it. However, your days as a starving artist are now officially over. So, the first order of business is to find you a new car."

"I appreciate the thought, but at the moment I'm not in a position to buy a new car. At least not yet, so I'm selling this old clunker and putting the money in the bank. I'll use rideshares while I learn my way around town." Her smile instantly faded as she recalled the long ride home from South Padre Island with Shawn and Jacque.

"Are you all right?" asked George.

"Yeah, I'm fine. I was just thinking about Evan. He always came along whenever my jazz ensemble had an off-campus performance, and we always took my car because it had a bigger trunk. Funny how I still miss him at times."

"I'd be more concerned if you didn't miss him. However, he's in the past and you're about to start a brand-new life, but first we need to get you unloaded. So, if you wouldn't mind unlocking the boot—"

"The what?"

"Sorry, I forgot. You Americans call it a trunk. So, if you'll be so kind as to pop it open, we can unload your things."

Tonya scooped up her clothing from the backseat while George grabbed her viola and guitars. He led her down the hallway to a beautifully furnished guestroom with a queen-sized bed and antique dresser.

"To the rest of the world, this will be your official residence, so we'll keep your personal belongings in here."

"I'll snap a couple of photos to send to my mother as soon as we get the rest of my things. She was concerned about my living here, although I hate keeping secrets from her."

"You're not a teenager anymore. You're an adult, and you're allowed to set your own boundaries, although I'll admit it felt a little strange when my kids first became adults. But now that they have, I neither want, nor need, to know every intimate detail of their lives. So go ahead and start unpacking while I get the rest of your belongings."

George hurried out and soon returned with another load. "So did you get the Yamaha you had on layaway?"

"I sure did, and I can't wait to play it for you."

"And I look forward to hearing it." He stepped out and brought in a few more loads.

"This is the last of it," he said, "but let's be sure we have everything." They walked back to the car together. It was now completely empty. Tonya felt sad when she slammed the trunk shut.

"Are you hungry?" asked George.

"A little, but I'm afraid I'm too tired to go out. I was thinking of ordering a pizza."

"As tempting as it sounds, I have something else in mind. My personal chef was here earlier today. He's prepared a lobster bisque, along with some fresh halibut."

"Sounds delicious. I remember my grandmother serving lobster bisque one year at Christmas. It was quite tasty."

George told Tonya to finish unpacking, and she soon smelled the soup cooking. Hanging her last sweater in the closet, she put a framed photo of her sister on the dresser and followed her nose to the kitchen. George invited her to take a seat and offered her a glass of wine.

"Are you sure I can't help with anything?" she asked.

"I'm positive. The fish is in the oven, I'm heating up the soup, and the broccoli just went into the steamer. I may not be Gordon Ramsey, but I can manage the basics in the kitchen. In fact, I rather enjoy it."

"I enjoy it too, when I have the time. I made homemade spaghetti and meatballs for my mother when she was visiting Texas. Shawn and Jacque joined us, and everyone loved it. I'll have to make some while I'm here."

"Sounds wonderful. I love Italian food." As he stirred the soup, he asked her about her plans.

"I have an appointment with Natalie first thing Monday morning, so I thought I'd do a little shopping tomorrow. Some of my clothes are getting a little threadbare, and I hear there are good consignment stores around here."

"I'm sure there are."

"I also forgot to get Sabrina's card when I was here for the photoshoot, so I'll call her at Alicorn tomorrow morning. I really liked her, and I need to start making new friends."

A strange look came over George's face. "Tonya, things have changed. You're living in an entirely different world now."

"How so?"

"You're about to become a celebrity, and celebrities need to be careful about who they associate with. Once you're in the public eye, you'll find there are many people out there who make their living preying on the famous. They'll go after someone like Sabrina, looking for any inside information they may have about you. Then the next thing you know, your face is plastered all over the tabloids with some sensationalized story which is about one percent truth and ninety-nine percent fabrication. This is why we discourage our artists from fraternizing with staff."

"You're right. I hadn't thought about that."

George grabbed a ladle and filled their bowls with steaming soup. "It's okay. You still have friends like Shawn and Jacque, and Mickey was quite taken with you. And because you're on the album cover, we plan on including you in one of his music videos. They're still working on the script. Natalie will fill you in on the details later."

George set their soup bowls on the table and sat down next to her. Tonya dipped her spoon in and took a taste.

"Yum. It's even better than the lobster bisque my grandmother served. It tastes like it came from an expensive restaurant."

"It did, in a way. My personal chef has worked in many famous restaurants."

They soon finished their soup and George took the fish from the oven. It was perfectly baked, and over the meal Tonya teased him about becoming a chef if he ever tired of the music business.

"Trust me, it'll never happen. I'll be in the music business until they drag me into the old folk's home, which will be many, many years from now. My father is nearly eighty. He's still the company CEO, and he has no plans for stepping down anytime soon. I honestly think working keeps you feeling younger, and I'll be busy doing everything I possibly can to make you a success."

"For which I'll be forever grateful, but at the moment I'm beat. It's a long drive from Dallas to Los Angeles. As soon as we clean up the kitchen, I'll be ready for a nice, hot soak in the tub."

"The master bathtub is also a hot tub."

"Thanks for the offer, but I was going to use the bathroom down the hall."

"Tonya, I love how you're so humble. In fact, I find it quite refreshing. However, you're my lover, not my roommate, so as soon as we're done in here, we'll draw you a nice, hot bath, in the master bathroom."

"Okay, okay," she said laughing, "but I'll still help with the dishes." She got up to clear the table and excused herself once the dishwasher was loaded.

"Wait. Before you go, I have something for you." George quickly stepped out and returned with a beautiful gift bag. "This is a welcoming gift, from me to you."

"Thank you, but it really wasn't necessary."

"Actually, it was. I know you probably haven't had many nice things, so please, allow me to pamper you."

Tonya reached inside the bag. Her face lit up when she saw a royal blue silk robe. "It's beautiful. I don't know what to say, other than thank you."

"You're welcome, and I'm glad you like it. The rose scented bath foam is on the vanity. Please feel free to use it."

As Tonya settled in the warm bath, she thought about how she could have never imagined herself living in such a beautiful home. Even her grandmother's house hadn't been so luxurious. Turning on the jets, she leaned back and enjoyed a long soak. The blue silk robe felt sumptuous when she finally stepped out of the tub. George was relaxing in his robe when she came out of the bathroom. Switching off the TV, he helped her out of her robe and waited for her to get into bed.

"So, how are you feeling?" he asked.

"Much better. It was just what I needed."

"I'm glad." He took off his robe and laid down next to her, propping his head on his elbow and gazing at her as he rubbed her belly.

"I know I've said this before, but you have an amazing body. I still think you should show it off."

"I already do. I wear some interesting outfits in my line of work. The other day I had on a pair of black pants with suspender like straps crisscrossing my boobs. I had to move carefully to make sure nothing fell out."

He gave her a flirtatious look. "Which would have been a fun shoot to watch, and I hope I'll get to see the photo sometime." He ran his hand up and down her torso. "All jokes aside, I know you want to make as much money as you can, and as I've said before, nude work pays quite well."

"I know it does, but what if it hurts my music career later on?"

He shook his head as he continued stroking her. "I seriously doubt it would. Times have changed. You'd be surprised at how many up-and-coming stars have been featured in men's magazines. I'm not saying you have to do anything you don't feel comfortable doing. I'm just saying you need the money, so perhaps you should consider it." A big smile broke out across his face as he cupped his hand over her breast.

"And not only do they look beautiful, they feel lovely as well. If you ever want to enhance them, I know a good plastic surgeon. He did a wonderful job on Mandy."

"I thought about having plastic surgery when I was a teenager, but I wanted to make them smaller, not bigger. When I was in high school the other girls used to call me Top-Heavy Tonya."

"Because they were jealous. Now if you don't mind, I'm going to play with them for a while."

❦TWENTY-SIX❦

TONYA'S DRIVER WORKED his way through the Monday morning rush hour traffic and drove up to the entrance of a high-rise office building in West Hollywood. She hurried inside and took the elevator to the ninth floor. Like the Dallas office, photos of the Carson Agency's models were mounted on the lobby walls, and one immediately caught her eye. Julianna had taken it when Tonya first signed on with the agency. Natalie greeted her a few minutes later and escorted Tonya to her office.

"Welcome to Los Angeles," she said. "So how was your move?"

"Not bad. It was a bit of a long drive, but now that I'm here, I'm anxious to get back to work."

"Okay. So, getting down to business; you need to fill out a little paperwork, and then we'll talk about some job prospects. George may have told you there's a video in the works for Mickey Lee Janson's upcoming new single, and they want to include you in the video."

"Yes, he mentioned something about it."

"I'm waiting to hear back from the production company. They'll be shooting it in Santa Barbara, which is where Mickey lives."

"He does?" said a surprised Tonya. "I had no idea."

"Apparently, he's done quite well with Alicorn. George Monroe is famous for turning emerging artists into household names, and I know he has big plans for you as well."

"I'm still overwhelmed by all of this. I'm so grateful to have you, and George, backing me. It feels like a dream, and I'm afraid someone will wake me up."

Natalie smiled and handed her a folder. "Don't worry. You're awake."

"Tell me about it. There's nothing quite like filling out forms to verify it's real." Tonya went to work while Natalie brought her a cup of coffee. Once the last paper was signed, Natalie clicked on her computer.

"Okay, I have a few jobs which may be of interest to you. The first is from Naughty Nellie's. Have you ever heard of them?"

"I'm not sure."

"They're a mail order lingerie company. They've been around for decades, and while they now sell most of their products online, they still produce several print catalogues throughout the year. As the name implies, it's naughty lingerie. It's either ultra-sheer or all lace. Sometimes it's topless. Their products, however, are all top quality."

"May I see a sample?" asked Tonya.

"Of course." Natalie turned her monitor so Tonya could see.

"Okay, it's not as racy as I expected. It may be on the sheer side, but the styles are pretty, and I really like the teal blue teddy. It reminds me of my teal blue camisole set from my first photo shoot."

"They believe women should look feminine and pretty, as well as sexy, in the bedroom. So, would you be interested in working with them? They pay very well."

"You bet I would."

"Good. They're getting ready to start working on their next catalog, so can you meet with them on Thursday?"

"What time?"

"I'm putting you down for ten o'clock, if it works for you."

"It does."

"The other project is a TV commercial. Would you be interested?"

"Of course. I interviewed for a commercial in Dallas not too long ago, but the job went to someone with more acting experience. So would this be an issue?"

"It depends. Some ads are scripted, such as the woman asking her husband why he came home with lipstick on his collar."

"Oh, dear," said Tonya with a giggle.

"Hey, it was just off the top of my head, but yes, some may require acting skills, so they may not be a good match for you. However, for this one you'd be demonstrating a laundry detergent. You'll smile at the camera as you pour it in the washer, and then smile again as you present a stack of clean, folded clothes."

"Sure, why not."

Natalie jotted down some notes in Tonya's file. "By the way, television ads pay nicely too, and they can give you good exposure. Mickey's video will also look good on your resume. Commercials are just like any other job. If you're the right fit, they'll hire you. If not, don't worry about it. We're going to keep you plenty busy."

"It sounds like it."

"Melissa said you're a good worker, and you were building a good following in Dallas."

"I was."

"I also had some nice feedback from Jack Dane, and he's not an easy man to please. I'm always in need of models who take direction well, and who can check their egos at the door. If you keep doing what you were doing in Dallas, you should do well here."

They soon wrapped up their business and Natalie walked Tonya out to the lobby. Another woman stepped inside as Tonya opened the door. Both were about the same height, but the other woman appeared to be in her mid-twenties with shoulder length blonde hair.

"Thank you again, Tonya," said Natalie. "I'll talk to you soon."

* * *

"So, I take it that was the famous Tonya," said the blonde.

"As a matter of fact, it was." Natalie's voice sounded cool as she motioned to the other woman to follow her to her office.

"Have a seat, Mandy."

"Are you going to tell me anything about her?"

"Nope. You know the rules."

"I know. I simply wanted to know more about my competition."

Natalie's voice was stern. "You're not in competition with her. She has a different look than you, so it's highly unlikely I would ever send the two of you out for the same job, and whatever happens between you and George Monroe has nothing to do with us. So, moving on. Any bites on your TV pilot?"

Mandy looked sad. "None. Looks like it's a no sale."

"Sorry to hear it, but it happens all the time. Are you up for any other film projects?"

"None at the moment. Nothing new has come in."

"Then I'm sorry to hear that as well. However, we had great feedback on the layout you did for *Sir Maxwell*."

"Well, of course. It's a given I'd have good feedback from them."

Natalie gritted her teeth. Mandy was becoming increasingly difficult to work with. Hopefully, she would soon land a significant acting role and Natalie could finally cut her loose.

"I have some commercials coming up. Would you be interested?"

"I don't know. I need to hear more about them first."

"Okay, I have an ad for a floor cleaner, another for frozen pizzas, and the last one is for a chardonnay."

"The wine ad sounds interesting. Tell me more."

Mandy nodded as Natalie filled her in on the details. "It's definitely up my alley."

"All right. I'll set up an appointment for you on Thursday. Morning or afternoon?"

"Morning."

"Then you'll be meeting with them at nine o'clock." Natalie typed the information into her computer. "So, what about the other two?"

"I'll pass. I'm not into playing frumpy housewives, and pizza is too fattening. Is there anything else?"

"Nope. That's it, I'm afraid."

"Okay." Mandy rose from her chair. "I'll talk to them on Thursday. Hopefully, I'll get the job."

"I hope so too." Natalie stood from her chair and walked Mandy out, letting out a loud sigh as she returned to her desk. Tonya had a genuine niceness about her. Hopefully, she would remain that way.

❧TWENTY-SEVEN❧

GEORGE INVITED MANDY and her husband, Stanley Klein, for dinner the following Saturday. His personal chef prepared beef bourguignon with all the trimmings, but Mandy dominated the conversation as she talked endlessly about her acting career while quizzing Tonya.

"It's like I said before. I have no intention of becoming an actor." Tonya fought to keep the frustration in her voice down. "Sure, it might be fun doing a production of *Grease* or *Wicked* or some other musical, assuming I had the time, but it would have to be on stage. I like to feel the audience's energy."

"Well, I suppose if I'm ever cast for a film production of a Broadway musical, they could dub my voice."

George quickly jumped in. "Now, just so you know, Tonya has been cast in Mickey's music video for his song, "Aquamarine." She's on the album cover, and the video includes a scene where he puts the pendent around her neck, which is a tie in for the cover. However, it's Mickey's video. He's promoting his song, and he has nearly all the screen time."

Mandy shot Tonya a look. "Do you have your union card?"

"We're working on it."

"Tonya never set out to become a model either," said George. "She tells me she was recruited at a Dallas church."

"I sure was, and the whole experience was pretty surreal." Tonya recounted her ensemble performance and the mysterious woman seated in the front row. "I had no idea who she was, so it was kind of unnerving. Turned out it was Melissa Atkins."

"I know who she is," Mandy said bluntly.

"She gave me her card, but I wasn't going to call her. Then something unexpected came up, and I needed additional money for school. I had no intention of becoming a model, but college isn't exactly cheap, so there you have it. I'll stay with it until I'm ready to go back and finish my degree."

"Which is where Stan comes in," said George. "He's been a celebrity business manager for years and he works with many of our artists. They've all done quite well with him, so I recommended him to Mandy. It was love at first sight."

"Something like that," said Stan with a shrug.

Stan seemed ill at ease and Tonya made a mental note. With his dark wavy hair and chiseled features, he looked like a male model himself. However, there was something odd about their marriage. Neither were in love with the other, and while Mandy tried to hide her feelings, she was deeply in love with George. Stan seemed to sense it while George was completely unaware. It was something the three of them would have to work out among themselves. The conversation shifted to other topics, much to Tonya's relief, but she remained on guard until after Stan and Mandy left. Once they were gone George suggested they have a nightcap by the pool.

"So, what did you think?" he asked.

"I like Stan. He's the kind of man I could go for myself someday. He's genuine and compassionate, and he's the real deal."

"I'm glad you like him. The reason I had them over tonight was so the three of you could get to know one another. I'll have Grace set up an appointment for you to meet with him at his office next week. I know you've been putting your money in your savings account, but Stan will invest it wisely, and you'll get a much better return. So, what did you think of Mandy?"

Tonya let out a loud sigh. "Well, let's see…"

"I know. I already told her you're not in competition with her, but Mandy likes to see things for herself. You stood your ground so you've won her respect. I'm also wondering if you think the two of you could become friends?"

"I honestly don't know. We have some things in common, and while I don't dislike her, we may be like oil and water and not blend well together." Tonya chose her next words carefully.

"I know you helped her out professionally, the same way you're helping me. I can also tell she's very special to you and the two of you are close friends, so don't worry. I have no intention of interfering in your relationship."

"I appreciate it, but I as I already mentioned, you've won her respect, so I expect her to be more cordial next time. And by the way, I forgot to mention this before. They've finished the script for Mickey's music video."

"Finally. I was beginning to think they would never get it done. So, when do we start shooting?"

"Soon. Natalie will fill you in, and you'll be spending a few days in Santa Barbara."

"Which is what she said. I've never been to Santa Barbara, so I'm really looking forward to it."

* * *

"So, tonight you won the Oscar for Best Bitch in a Supporting Role."

"Very funny." Mandy shifted uncomfortably in the passenger seat. "I was scoping out my competition."

Stan's voice was firm. "She's not in competition with you. At least not professionally. And, unlike you, she struck me as being smart enough to not become emotionally attached to George Monroe. She'll only stay with him for as long as she has to. Then, she'll move on."

Mandy shook her head. "Sorry, but no. She'll stay with him until he allows her to leave, and not a minute sooner. You of all people should understand by now that once you been one of George Monroe's kept women, you'll be his mistress for as long as he wants you, and it's long after you've stopped living under his roof."

His voice remained firm. "Not always. Some of his former mistresses are also my clients. Most of them haven't seen or heard from him in years."

"Because they weren't any of his favorites."

"Maybe, maybe not, but who's to say that when he's ready to move on from Tonya, he won't make a clean break?"

"Then I guess we'll have to wait and see what happens, won't we? If he does, he does, but if he doesn't, then it'll be the same as when George introduced you to me. He'll make sure the next guy knows there are certain terms and conditions, and they'll both become members of the club."

Stan focused his attention on the road. There was something special about Tonya. She had a certain innocence about her which he found intriguing, and he looked forward to getting to know her better.

✎TWENTY-EIGHT✎

MICKEY'S VIDEO SHOOT would take place while George was England for his father's eightieth birthday celebration. Before leaving, he surprised Tonya and rented her a red Mustang convertible to take to Santa Barbara. As he brought out her last bag, he waited patiently while she rearranged a few items in the trunk.

"Do you have everything?" he asked.

"I believe so." She slammed the trunk shut and gave him a bright smile. "So, which one are you flying today?"

"Jane, for Jane Russell. I've flown her before. It's a long flight, and she's essentially a flying hotel room."

"Are you sure you don't want me to drop you off at the airport? It's Sunday, so the traffic shouldn't be as bad, and no doubt you'll be exhausted when you get back. I'm more than happy to pick you up on my way home."

"I'm positive, but thank you anyway. For some reason, the jet lag always seems worse coming back to the states, and it takes a few days for me to readjust, so enjoy the extra time in Santa Barbara" His mood turned more serious.

"Now, just so you know, Mickey was quite taken with you. I think the two of you would be good friends, so I hope you'll take the time to get to know one another better."

"I like Mickey. He was a naturally easy-going person the day of our photo shoot. However, we're both busy people, so we'll have to see what happens."

George opened the driver's side door and gave her a final kiss before she got behind the wheel. "Drive safe and have fun with Mickey. I'll see you in two weeks."

Tonya waved goodbye as she drove away. "Right turn ahead," said a mechanical voice. It guided her to the Pacific Coast Highway, where she headed north. It was a beautiful early fall day with bright, sunny skies, and crowded beaches.

The hotel entrance looked like an old Spanish mission with its white exterior and red tile roof. A valet rushed up to greet her when she drove up to the curb. After checking in, Tonya expected to find a typical hotel room. What she found instead was a luxury suite with a balcony overlooking the pool and beach beyond. She stepped out on the balcony to take in the fresh ocean air while she waited for her bags.

Tonya's only memory of the beach was a family vacation in San Diego when she was five. She had been afraid to go into the water until Annette took her by the hand and guided her in. The rest of the day was spent racing her sister in and out of the waves until their parents finally dragged both of them out. She smiled at the memory, and for a brief moment she felt Annette's presence with her, as if she too were enjoying the view.

There was a knock at the door. Tonya quickly answered, expecting to find a bellman with her luggage, but the hotel employee presented her with a dozen long-stemmed red roses. Thinking they were from George, she took the card from the envelope, but to her surprise, they came from someone else.

Roses for Ms. Rose. Love, Mike.

Tonya was about to text him a thank you note when she realized she didn't have his phone number. Laughing at herself, she set her phone down and went to get some water. Her mother called while she was filling the vase.

"Are you in Santa Barbara yet?"

"I just got here, and you won't believe the view." She launched Facetime and walked out to the balcony.

"Wow," said an amazed Heather. "It's so beautiful."

"I know, and let me show you something else." She walked back into her room and showed her mother the roses. "And you won't believe who sent them."

Heather's tone changed. "Was it George?"

"No, it wasn't George. It was Mike."

"Okay, so who's Mike?"

"Someone I've worked with before, although you know him as Mickey Lee Janson."

"Really?" Heather sounded almost giddy. "So, Mickey Lee Janson is interested in my daughter, is he?"

"Oh, I don't know about that, although George tells me I made a good impression on him, and he wants me to get to know him better."

"Well, what do you know? For once George Monroe and I agree on something."

"I'm looking forward to spending time with him as well," said Tonya, "but we're both busy people. He also lives in Santa Barbara, while I'm in Sherman Oaks."

"If there's a will, there's a way."

"Anxious to get me married off, are you?"

"Well, maybe, and I have to admit I like the idea of having Mickey Lee Janson for a son-in-law."

"Okay Mom. That's enough," said Tonya. "I'll try and get you his autograph, but again I'm not making any promises."

"I appreciate the thought, but it's really not necessary. I just wanted to say I'm proud of you."

The following morning Tonya parked the red Mustang across the street from a large beachfront house. As she stepped inside, a young black man extended his hand and greeted her with a warm smile.

"Good morning, Ms. Rose. I'm Jordon Canfield. I'm the director of this project. I also hear this is your first time on the set."

"It is," she said nervously. "I'm a model who makes no claims of being an actress."

"So I hear, but what you'll be doing today isn't much different from a photo shoot. You don't have any lines, and I'll tell you what to do for each scene." He nodded toward a woman standing off to the side.

"Rebecca will be helping with your hair and wardrobe, so go with her and I'll see you in a few minutes."

Tonya felt an unexpected jolt.

"You okay?" asked Rebecca.

"Yeah, I'm fine. I was just having a moment. I knew a Rebecca not so long ago, only she went by Becca, and she wasn't exactly a friend."

"Ugh. I hate it when anyone calls me Becca, or Becky for that matter. I go by Rebecca. So, if you don't mind my asking, what exactly did she do?"

"She slept with my fiancé."

"Well now," said a familiar voice. "There's something I could turn into a song someday." Mike greeted her with a hug and a kiss on the cheek while Rebecca shook her head.

"Save it for the video, Mickey. We're on a tight schedule, and the lady needs to get ready."

Tonya returned a few minutes later, wearing blue jeans with a low-cut black top and a pair of cowboy boots. Holding still, she waited as Rebecca inspected her outfit. "I hope I brought enough sunscreen," she said.

"Don't worry. If you run out, I have plenty more." Rebecca looked at Jordon. "She's good to go whenever you're ready."

Jordon called out to one of the crew members. "Is the horse ready?"

The other man relayed the question on his two-way radio, and quickly shouted the response back to Jordon. "I think so. The trainer is bringing it out as we speak."

Mike looked at Tonya. "Are you okay?" he asked. "All of a sudden you look a little pale."

"I've never ridden a horse in my life," said Tonya, "so I was really hoping we'd skip this scene." She stepped outside and anxiously watched the trainer lead a bay horse out to the beach.

"It's okay." Mike wrapped his arm around her shoulder and gave her a reassuring squeeze. "The horse's name is Woody, and he's really well trained."

The handler stood by as Tonya walked up to the horse. He showed her how to mount, while another production assistant stood by in case she needed help. Everyone watched closely as Tonya cautiously put her foot in the stirrup and carefully swung her other leg over.

"There you go," said the trainer. "You did it perfectly. Now hold onto the reins, like this, and when you want him to stop you gently pull back on them. I'll lead him out to the beach and stand off to the side. The director wants to get a few shots of you riding past the camera."

"I know," said Tonya. "I guess I'm ready whenever you are."

Tonya felt her body gently sway as Woody slowly walked toward the beach. Jordon instructed her to look straight ahead as she rode past him.

"So, are you ready?" he asked

"I'll give it a try."

"Okay. Action."

Tonya tapped Woody's side with her heel and the horse moved forward.

"Not bad," said Jordon, "but you look a little stiff. You're okay. He won't buck you off, so try to relax."

Tonya made another pass. This time she felt more comfortable, but Jordon wanted to get a few more shots. By the time they were finished, Tonya was enjoying the ride.

"Good job," said Jordon. "For the next shot I want you to ride up to Mickey and stop the horse. Your characters are meeting for the first time, so act friendly."

"Hey, no problem, boss," said Mike.

"Don't get cocky," said Jordan. The rest of the crew started laughing, but they got the shot in two takes. Afterwards Mike stepped to the side while a production assistant helped Tonya off the horse.

"So, how are you feeling?" asked Jordon.

"It was actually kind of fun, although I'm relieved to be back on the ground."

"I'm sure you are," said Mike, "but you may want to get a massage when you get back to your hotel. Otherwise, you may feel a little sore tomorrow."

"Enough with the chatter," said Jordon. "You both need a wardrobe change."

Tonya and Mike spent the rest of the morning shooting scenes on the beach. As they were filming a crowd began forming off to the side, but the security guards kept them behind the temporary barricades.

"It all comes with the territory." said Mike. They were waiting on the patio while the crew set up the next shot. "Trust me, there's a paparazzi out there who'll get a shot of us kissing, and they'll send it to the tabloids."

"Does it bother you?" asked Tonya.

"Not as much as it used to. They'll make all kinds of nasty innuendos, but most people don't buy into it, and those who know me know it's all bullshit. I also have a good publicist. If some over the top story ever did any real damage, she'd be on it right away, but so far it hasn't happened." He gave her a serious look. "You may want to look into getting a publicist as well, if you don't have one already."

Jordon walked up to the patio. "Okay, kids. Breaktime is over, so let's get back to work. And by the way, Tonya, you're doing really well. You definitely have it in you to become an actress."

"I still don't know about that. I'm already suffering enough as a musician."

Another assistant handed Jordon the aquamarine pendant. "Okay, we have one more scene to shoot before we break for lunch, so let's get to it."

Once the crew was ready, Mike and Tonya took their places and the camera started rolling. The stone sparkled in the sunlight as Mike placed the pendant around Tonya's neck. Three takes later they were done. The scent of freshly roasted chicken filled the air when they came back into the house. A catering company was serving lunch. Jordon and the rest of the crew sat around the large table in the dining room while Mike and Tonya made themselves comfortable in the kitchen.

"You have a beautiful home, Mike."

"If you say so." He shrugged as he tried to suppress his laughter.

"What's so funny?"

"You are. This isn't my house. It's an Airbnb they rented for the video shoot. I live in your typical middle-class neighborhood." He took his phone from his pocket.

"So, it's okay with you, I'd like to get your phone number. I did a scene with Woody for an earlier video, and I got a little saddle sore afterwards, so you're welcome to come over and use the hot tub if you'd like."

"Are you sure? I don't want to impose."

"I'm sure. We can have dinner delivered and enjoy a nice, quiet evening in the hot tub."

"Thanks, I'd love it."

He began typing a message. "I'm texting you the address as we speak, so bring your swimsuit and a change of clothes. Any preferences for dinner?"

"I'll have whatever you're having."

He grinned. "Then it's porterhouse steak for two."

Rebecca came into the kitchen a few minutes later. "You guys almost done?"

"Yeah, I think so," said Tonya.

"Good, because we need to do your hair and change your clothes."

Tonya looked down at her flip flops. "You mean I have to put some real shoes on?"

"Yes, you do, and the black pumps you brought with you will be perfect. You need a wardrobe change as well, Mickey."

"Yes, ma'am."

They shot the next scene inside, at the front door. Mike wore a shirt and tie while Tonya was in a little black dress. She took the pendant off and handed it to a sad looking Mike before running outside. In between takes everyone joked about him getting dumped. The remaining indoor scenes went quickly, and Jordon soon announced it was a wrap.

"Tonya, it was an absolute pleasure working with you." Jordon extended his hand once again. "I direct a lot of commercials, so I may ask for you."

"I'd like that."

"What about me?" asked Mike.

"You need to stick to singing." Once again, the crew burst out laughing as they started packing up. Tonya stepped away to change and Mike was waiting near the door when she returned. He offered to walk her out to her car.

"Nice wheels," he said.

"Thanks."

He smiled as he checked his watch. "So, why don't we meet at my place, say around six-thirty."

"See you then." Tonya hopped in the car and fired up the engine, waving goodbye as she drove away.

◦TWENTY-NINE◦

MIKE'S TWO DOGS, Bruno and Maize, were waiting by the door when he arrived home. They greeted him with their usual excited whimpers and wagging tails. "I know, I know," he said. "I've been gone for months and you two haven't eaten in weeks, even though there's plenty of food in your dog bowls."

He glanced around the living room and kitchen. The house had a lived-in look. Grabbing a dust rag, he quickly went to work, straightening up the coffee table as he went along. His phone beeped while he was taking out the trash. Tonya was running late and would arrive around seven. The dogs followed him out to the backyard, keeping close watch as he checked the pool and hot tub. Leaving them outside, he hurried back in and hopped in the shower.

Tonya arrived shortly after seven and greeted him with a warm smile "I see you brought your guitar with you," he said.

"Hey, it's not every day when I get the chance to jam with Mickey Lee Janson."

He looked around and gave her a cheeky grin. "Who?"

She gave him a look in return. "Oh, so you're one of those, are you?"

"Who me?" He feigned his innocence as he led her down the hallway and opened a door. Like George, Mike had converted one of the bedrooms into a music room, complete with a laptop and sound mixer.

"Welcome to my office. This is where I do most of my song writing."

"Nice."

"By the way, I listened to the CD you gave me. Both you and your friend, Shawn, have what it takes, and I'd love to work with him someday."

Tonya eagerly grabbed her phone. "He would love to work with you as well, so I'm texting you his number."

"I take it George is planning on signing you on?"

"He is." Tonya's face was glowing. "First, he wants to distribute *Between Us Friends*. Then he wants me to record other albums. Like you, I'm already working on new material."

"Good for you. I'd also like to have you sing backup on a song for the *Aquamarine* album."

"Seriously?"

He looked her in the eye. "I wouldn't have said it if I didn't mean it." Fighting the overwhelming urge to kiss her, he quickly changed the subject.

"You know, I think we've had enough shop talk for now, so let's get dinner ordered. Do you still want a steak? If not, we'll get you something else."

"I'll have whatever you're having."

He grabbed his phone and pulled up an app. "I prefer mine medium rare. How 'bout you?"

"Medium rare for me as well."

"Coming right up." He touched a few buttons and gave her a smile as he set the phone down. "It should be here in about forty-five minutes, so while we're waiting, we'll open a bottle of wine and enjoy it out on the patio."

He brought her into the kitchen and opened the wine bottle, but as they walked up to the sliding glass door, two anxious dogs waited on the other side.

"Are you okay with dogs?" he asked.

"Of course. I love dogs."

"Good. They may act big and brave, but they're really a couple of wussies." He opened the door flipped on the outdoor lights. Tonya petted the dogs as she stepped outside.

"That's enough, you two," he sternly said.

"Oh, they're fine, and you have a lovely home."

"Thanks. I bought it because it's cozy and in a quiet neighborhood. In spite of everything, I'm still a simple southern boy at heart. I don't need anything big and fancy."

"Me neither. George was kind enough to rent me a room in his home, and it's really all I need for now."

Her comment made him feel uncomfortable. "So I hear, but I have a feeling things will soon be changing for you, and you'll be able to get your own place."

"I sure hope so, although I don't plan on staying here long term. Once my first album is complete, I plan on going back to Dallas."

"Then I hope we'll get to know one another better while you're here." They sat down at the patio table and Mike once again changed the subject.

"By the way, I really didn't mean to overhear you talking about your ex-fiancé this morning, and I'm sorry he cheated on you."

"Yeah, me too." Tonya's face turned sad as she took another sip of wine.

"Hey, you don't have to talk about it if you don't want to."

"No, it's okay. Evan was Shawn's roommate. We were together for two years, and we planned on getting married once we graduated." A bittersweet smile came over her face. "At least he hadn't bought the ring yet, so I guess it's one thing I can be grateful for. We're not fighting over who gets to keep it."

"Would you have kept it?"

"I don't know. Probably not, and I now realize the relationship wouldn't have survived, even if he hadn't cheated on me. Evan had serious issues with my being a model, and I had no idea he was the jealous type. It didn't matter what I said. He didn't approve."

"Which wasn't a good sign."

"No, it wasn't. Then there was Becca. She was best friends with Shawn's girlfriend, and she'd set her sights on Evan. Unfortunately for me, my first modeling job was the same week as spring break, so I had to join him and the others after the shoot, but by the time I arrived, it was too late. He'd already had his tryst with Becca, and she made sure she left the evidence behind."

"I'm sorry it happened, but she actually did you a favor."

Tonya suddenly looked defensive. "What do you mean, she did me a favor?"

"You said it yourself. The relationship wouldn't have lasted, and she sped up the process. A jealous lover is never a good thing. You kept having to prove your innocence to him, while he had no problem cheating on you, so the sooner you got away from him, the better."

"From what I'm told, he was really drunk when it happened."

"Doesn't matter. He still had one set of rules for you, and another for himself. You don't need someone like him in your life."

"You're right." She gave him a mischievous grin. "Although I'll admit to doing a few racy modeling shoots since then."

Mike was seeing interesting images in his head. It was time to steer the conversation to a safer topic, so they talked about their music until he heard the doorbell and the dogs barking.

"Looks like dinner has arrived. So, would you like to eat out here, or inside."

"I'd love to eat out here, but I need to get my jacket first."

"Then you go get your jacket while I set the table."

Bruno and Maize sniffed loudly when Mike returned with their food. He told them to go lie down, but both dogs gave him pouty looks as they plopped themselves down. Tonya soon returned, and he topped off her wine.

"Nice jacket," he said.

"Thanks. I bought it the day after the album cover shoot. So, I've told you my story. Now I want to hear yours."

"Well, I went to audition for one of those TV music competitions, and I—"

"I know that." Her eyes sparkled as she spoke. "But I'm not talking about Mickey Lee Janson. I want to hear more about Mike Jablonski."

He couldn't resist flirting back. "You mean you want to know if I'm single and available?"

"Maybe." She gave him a coy grin as she swirled her wine around her glass.

"Well, I guess I had my own version of Evan, although it wasn't nearly as dramatic. Her name was Jodie, and we met in high school. Then, after high school, we both went to the University of Alabama in Tuscaloosa, although her parents had wanted her to go to a Christian college instead." He glanced down at Tonya's plate.

"How's the steak?"

"Delicious. Now, tell me more about Jodie."

"I wanted to make it official, and I even bought her a promise ring, but she kept saying she wasn't ready. So, after we graduated, I went to work for my dad. He owns a bar and grill in Birmingham, which is where I also learned how to cook."

"Interesting."

"I was managing the place during the day and singing and playing the guitar at night. Unfortunately, Jodie's father was a preacher who didn't want his daughter marrying a barkeeper's son, and being a musician had its perks. It was really easy for me to meet other women. Sometimes Jodie stopped by too, but whenever we tried to rekindle things, her daddy'd get wind of it and she'd disappear again. Then came the TV audition. Afterwards, I came here, while Jodie stayed in Alabama."

Tonya suddenly looked sad. "I can tell you really loved her, and I'm sorry it didn't work out. You're a good person, and her father shouldn't have been so judgmental. You should be able to marry the person you love."

"I agree, and most preachers aren't like him, but I also want a woman who understands her spouse comes first. With Jodie, I'd always be playing second fiddle to her folks."

"Because she allowed them to interfere. I love my mother very much and we have a really good relationship, but she never tried to get between me and Evan, and I've never tried to get between her and my stepdad."

"Which is the way it should be." The conversation was becoming too heavy, and he needed to break the tension.

"So, how's the rest of you feeling? Are your back and legs getting stiff?"

"Not yet. The reason I was late is because I called the spa as soon as I got back to my hotel. One of the masseuses was available, so I went and got a massage."

"Good thinking. You may still feel a little stiff tomorrow morning, but it probably won't be as bad."

They turned their attention back to their meals, and before long they pushed their plates aside.

"Well, it looks like we have plenty of leftovers," said Mike. "I make a really mean beef stew. If you're still in town tomorrow night, you'll have to come over and try some."

"Thanks, I'd love to."

"So, how long will you be here?"

"For about two weeks. George doesn't want people in the house when he's not there."

"Makes sense. Whenever he goes back to England, he's usually there for a couple weeks. Sometimes longer." Mike felt the knot building in his stomach as he asked the question he needed to ask.

"So, what exactly is the nature of your relationship with him?"

"Are you asking me if I'm in love with him?"

"Something like that."

"George is very special to me, but no, I'm not in love with him. At least not in the romantic sense. He's a dear friend and mentor, and he's certainly changed my life, but in a good way. As I said before, I'm only living in his home for the short term." She looked him in the eye.

"And to be completely honest with you, I'm so wrapped up in my own career right now I honestly don't have the time for a serious romance."

"I understand, but you're still living in his home, and he does have a reputation for being a lady's man. You can tell me to butt out if you'd like, but I consider you a friend, and I don't want to see you in a bad place."

She let out a long sigh. "I guess it's kind of complicated, isn't it? The Evan episode has left me a little gun-shy. I'm also determined to do whatever it takes to have a better life than what I had growing up. So much so that I allowed myself to become a kept woman, but only for the short term. Believe me, I'm doing everything humanly possible to get out of there, as quickly as I can."

"Then do it."

"I'm working on it, and for what it's worth, George told me I should give you a chance."

"Did he now?"

"He sure did. He said it right before he left for the airport, so maybe he's getting ready to cut me loose."

"Maybe so, but he can't hold you prisoner. You can leave anytime you want. Hell, I have an extra room. You could stay here if you'd like."

"I appreciate the offer, but what about my modeling? I'd be going back and forth between here and Los Angeles at least once or twice a week, if not more often, and at the moment I don't have a car. The convertible I'm driving is actually a rental. I'm also looking for a booking agent. I need to start performing again."

"Gotcha covered on the booking agent, and I'll see if I can set up a meeting while you're here. There are also a few spots in town with open mics that only the locals know about, and I've been known to show up from time to time. We'll figure out the rest later. Right now, we need to tidy up the kitchen, and then we'll go back to my office and have ourselves a jam session. I want to see what else you've got."

"You're on." They grabbed their plates and hurried inside. Once everything was in the refrigerator, Mike offered to refill her wine.

"I'm good for now, but I'll take some water if you have some."

"Coming right up." He grabbed two bottles of water and they hurried to the music room. He fired up the laptop and reached for a blue electric bass.

"Grab your axe. I'm pulling up the chart for the song I want you to sing background on. It's called, "My Dear Cordelia.""

"Shakespeare, huh?"

"Sort of. I wrote it for my mother, who had a difficult relationship with her father. If you'll give me a moment, I'll send it to your phone."

Tonya soon had the file. "Looks pretty straightforward to me."

"I'm going to play the latest version for you." He touched a few keys on the laptop, and they both listened to the tune.

"Nice," said Tonya. "Will this be an album track? Or do you plan on releasing it as a single?"

"It hasn't been determined, so as soon as you're ready, we'll start recording."

Tonya nodded and they counted down together. After singing and playing it back a few times, Mike smiled and put his bass back on its stand.

"There, I think we've got it for now. So, what else is on your schedule while you're here?"

"I'm doing a photo shoot on the beach next Tuesday, and I go back to Sherman Oaks the following Monday. I plan on spending the rest of my time hanging out on the beach and working on new material."

"Then I'll have my people call your people so we can make the arrangements."

"You're getting way too far ahead of me, Mike. I'm still the new kid in town. I don't have any people, other than a mysterious new booking agent."

"Who you'll soon be meeting." As he watched her put her guitar back in her gig bag, he felt an overpowering urge to scoop her up and to whisk her off to bed.

"Well," he said, "as much as I hate to say it, it's time to call it a night. My cleaning lady will be here bright and early tomorrow morning, along with my personal assistant. I'm sorry we didn't make it to the hot tub, so we'll do it tomorrow night, if it's okay with you."

"Sure, it's okay."

"I'm glad." He gave her a sweet, gentle kiss. To his relief, she didn't resist. He kissed her again, this time with a little more feeling.

"I'll send you a text as soon as everyone leaves." He waited for her to gather her things and walked her out to the car, where he kissed her goodnight and watched as she drove away. He sighed loudly when she turned a corner and disappeared. George was using her in an ugly way. He would have to find a way to get her away from him.

❧THIRTY❧

TONYA WAS EXHAUSTED when she returned to her hotel suite. The long day had finally caught up with her, and her legs and back were feeling sore. Filling the bathtub with hot water, she settled in for a long soak. Afterwards, she got ready for bed, but before turning on the TV, she took Annette's photo from her suitcase and sat down at the table.

"Well, sissy," she said, "in spite of my best efforts to not follow in your footsteps, I seem to have done so anyway. In fact, I've outdone you. I'm sleeping with a man who would have been our father's age in exchange for room and board, and a recording contract. So much for your virtuous baby sister who set out to be a virgin bride."

"I know who can get you away from George."

"Well, that was weird." Tonya looked around the room. "It's almost like I heard your voice. Must be because it's what you might have said if you were here. I also know you're looking out for me, for which I'll always be grateful." Her eyes turned misty. "I love you, Annette, and I'll always regret that things were so bad between us when you left."

She stood from her chair and grabbed the remote, but it slipped from her hand and toppled to the floor. Picking it up, she accidently turned on the TV, and a documentary about The Monkees appeared on the screen.

"I remember them," she said. "Mom liked The Monkees. Remember how she used to play their music back when we were kids?" As she watched a clip from an old, grainy looking interview with Micky Dolenz, the band's drummer, her face suddenly lit up.

"Wait a minute…Micky? Of course. Now I get it. Well, Annette, you're right. Mickey's an amazing guy, and I could fall for him. Really easily, but in spite of George encouraging me to get to know him better, I also have a feeling he won't let me go without a fight. Hopefully, I'm wrong."

Tonya felt stiff and sore the following morning, so she scheduled the earliest available appointment for another massage. Afterwards, she did a Facetime session with Shawn, who was excited to hear about her singing with Mickey Lee Janson.

"I really am proud of you. Working with a major recording star like Mickey Lee Janson is quite an accomplishment. Hopefully, once you're rich and famous, you'll think back of me fondly."

"Get out of town. If I get rich and famous, you'll be rich and famous right along with me, because you'll be included on every album I make."

* * *

Once again, Mike saw a happy face when he opened his front door. He greeted Tonya with a warm hug while Bruno and Maize wagged their tails and gave her friendly sniffs.

"Nice outfit," she said.

"What? You mean you've never seen a guy wearing a t-shirt and shorts with flip flops before? I don't always wear jeans and boots, you know."

Tonya laughed. "Of course, you don't, and I was about to say it sure smells good in here."

"I told you I make a mean beef stew."

She set her guitar down and reached into her tote bag, presenting him with a bottle of wine. "I found this in one of the hotel gift shops, and thought it might go good with the stew."

He gave it a closer look. "Nice. It's a French wine and it's perfect. So, let's take your guitar to the music room and then we'll open the wine."

He grabbed a bottle opener as soon as they came into the kitchen. Tonya stood by as he carefully removed the cork. He took a whiff and let her sniff the cork as well.

"It has a lovely bouquet," he said. "We'll let it breathe for a little while." Setting the bottle on the counter, he proudly lifted the lid off the simmering pot.

"It smells amazing," said Tonya. "Did you learn how to make stew working at your dad's place?"

"Nope. I learned this recipe from my mother, and I've added my own secret ingredient."

"How intriguing. What is it?"

He gave her a look. "Now if I told you, it wouldn't be a secret anymore, and a man's entitled to a few secrets."

"Aw, c'mon."

"Nope." He grinned as he gave it a stir and turned the burner to its lowest setting. "You'll just have to taste it and try to figure it out for yourself. Meantime, it needs to simmer a little longer, so why don't you change into your bathing suit, and we'll relax in the hot tub since we missed it last night."

"Good idea." Tonya quickly stepped out, returning a few minutes later with her hair in a bun and wearing a simple white swimsuit.

"You know, it's funny," she said. "I make good money modeling all kinds of sexy swimwear, but when it comes to my own personal wardrobe, I prefer the basics."

More interesting images went through his mind as he grabbed their beach towels. The dogs rushed out as he opened the sliding glass door. "Would you like for me to turn on the lights?"

"I'm good. There should be plenty of ambient lighting once the sun goes down, so we probably won't need them."

"You're right." The lights remained off as Mike took off his t-shirt.

The jets felt soothing as they climbed into the hot tub and settled in the bubbling water. In silence, they leaned back against the edge, eyes closed, and felt the day's worries float away. Finally, Mike spoke up.

"I'd like for us to do a studio session a week from Thursday, if it works for you."

"Well, that was certainly fast."

He grinned. "Okay, it was already booked, so I called Les, my producer, and told him I wanted you on Cordelia. You'll like Les. He's one of the best music producers in the business. He's also heard part of your CD, and he's very much interested in meeting you. Assuming it's okay with you."

"Of course it's okay with me, and thank you again for making me a part of your next album."

"You're certainly welcome, and by the way, I saw some of the rushes for the video."

"You did? How'd they look?"

"Fantastic. You looked absolutely amazing." He felt something bump against his foot. "Are you playing footsie with me, Ms. Rose?"

Tonya laughed. "I was about to ask you the same question, Mr. Janson."

"Uh-huh. That's enough shenanigans out of you." Looking into her eyes, he gently kissed her. Once again, she didn't resist, but somewhere deep down, his inner voice warned him not to move too quickly.

"I need to go check on the stew," he said, somewhat awkwardly.

"Take your time. I'm not going anywhere."

"I'll be back in a few minutes." He quickly hopped out and went straight to the kitchen. The stew was boiling, but he had gotten to it before it scorched. Giving it a good stir, he thought about how he had never met anyone like Tonya before, and he needed to take it slow. He gave it another good stir and changed into his sweats before returning to the patio.

"The stew is nearly ready," he said. "We can eat out here again if you'd like."

"I'd love it. Would it be okay if I showered off in the guest bathroom?"

"Of course, and there are extra towels in the vanity if you need them." He helped her out of the hot tub, and once she dried off, the dogs eagerly followed them to the door.

"Nope," he said in a firm voice. "You two have to wait out here." Sliding the door open, he told Tonya to hurry inside. She quickly stepped away but soon returned, once again in her street clothes.

"It's smells really good in here," she said. "I love the smell of fresh bread baking."

"Me too. I'm baking some crescent rolls, and they should be ready soon." He looked her up and down. "You know, I should have asked if you eat bread. I know models have to watch their weight."

"We do, although I have trouble gaining weight. So, can I help with anything?"

"Sure. You can set the table if you'd like."

They took their seats outside a few minutes later, and Tonya dove into the stew. "Wow, this is amazing."

"I'm a man of many talents," he said with a wink.

"I'd say so."

"You mentioned you have trouble gaining weight. Were you into sports when you were in school?"

"No, not even," Tonya said emphatically. "Of course, I had classmates who played on the varsity teams, but they were the cool kids, and I was never in their clique. I was the skinny, nerdy kid who played viola in the school orchestra."

"I think we all go through an awkward phase when we're teenagers. Even though I learned to play piano when I was younger, I really wasn't into music when I was in high school."

Tonya looked surprised. "You weren't?"

"Nope." He had a glimmer in his eye. "I was one of the cool kids who played on the varsity baseball and basketball teams, but then my junior year I had a really bad fall on the basketball court. It completely trashed my left knee."

"Ouch."

"It was a big ouch all right. They carried me off on a stretcher, and I had an MRI the following day. The damage was extensive, so I ended up having major knee surgery."

"Yikes," said Tonya. "I'll bet it wasn't fun."

"No, it wasn't. The surgery was bad enough, but the physical therapy was torture. I was done for the rest of the basketball season, and baseball season wasn't looking good either. In the meantime, my younger brother Liam had bought himself a used guitar. Turned out it wasn't his thing, so he taught me a few chords and gave it to me. The rest, as they say, is history."

"Did you take lessons?" she asked.

"Nope. I'm completely self-taught, and it was so much easier than the piano."

"Some people are musically gifted, and it sounds like you may be one of them."

"I suppose, but it was still just a fun thing I did on the side. I never took it seriously until my friends dared me to try out for *The Great American Rockstar.*"

"And I was going to be a music teacher until someone recruited me for a modeling agency, and then one fateful day, someone slipped and broke a lightbulb."

"Funny how something as mundane as a broken light bulb can change your life." He looked into her eyes and kissed her again. "You're very special to me, Ms. Tonya Rose, and I intend to take my time with you. And with that being said, I'm sending you back to your hotel right after dinner, and I'll call you tomorrow."

Tonya felt mixed emotions when she returned to the hotel. Mike's intentions were genuine. A part of her had come back to life, and she was ready to love again. She was also beginning to fully understand the repercussions of getting involved with George. He had the power to make her dreams come true, and he had used it to his advantage. Hopefully, he was getting ready to move on. Feeling more optimistic, she grabbed her phone and looked up her account on Stanley Klein's website.

"Damn," she said out loud. While she was getting a much better return on her money, she wasn't yet in a position to purchase a car or move into her own place. She would have to remain under George's roof a little while longer.

Mike sent her a text the following day. He would pick her up in front of the hotel at five-thirty that evening. She was to wear blue jeans and bring her guitar.

❧THIRTY-ONE❧

A S TONYA STEPPED OUT to the curb, a black Chevy Silverado with a club cab and tinted windows drove up to her. The passenger window rolled down and a familiar voice called her name. A valet rushed up to open the passenger door and slide her guitar behind the seats. Once inside, she strapped on her seatbelt.

"Sorry I couldn't be more of a gentleman and open the door for you," said Mike, "but it's best to avoid a potential mob whenever possible."

"I understand completely. I got recognized in the hotel elevator the day after we did the cover shoot."

"Really? So what'd you do?"

"I told her no; I wasn't an actress. She seemed to buy it, and the elevator stopped before she could question me any further."

"I've gotten used to taking service elevators, and you may want to start using them as well. The hotel staff won't hassle you. So, I bet you're wondering where we're going."

"The thought has crossed my mind."

"You may recall me mentioning there are places around here with open mics, so we're going to one of them and meeting some friends there. Then, when you're done, we're all going back to my place."

"Is there a preference for the music?"

"Most people sing soft rock, folk, or country," said Mike. "They get rappers too, and there may be some standup comedians as well."

"Then I think I'll do a Patsy Cline song, although I sing it more bluesy." Tonya reached for her phone and pulled up her music charts. As she browsed, Mike turned into a restaurant entrance and drove around to the back, parking next to the building's rear exit.

"We'll walk around to the front, but we'll leave through the back." He hopped out and opened Tonya's door, carrying her guitar for her. As they stepped inside, the hostess pointed to where they needed to go. The bar was dimly lit and two microphones had been set up on a makeshift stage. One for singing, the other for an acoustic guitar. Most of the tables were occupied, and someone waved at Mike. Two middle-aged men and an older black woman greeted them as he and Tonya walked up to their table.

"So, you must be Tonya Rose." A mustached man with curly reddish hair stood extended his hand. "I'm Kurt Porter, and I'm Mickey's manager." He nodded toward his companion, who also stood and extended his hand.

"And I'm Howie Benson, his booking agent."

The woman gave Tonya a warm smile as she extended her hand. "And I'm Mickey's publicist, Shandra Robbins."

"Well, this is quite a welcoming committee." Tonya looked at Shandra more closely. "You seem familiar to me for some reason."

"Shandra was once a recording artist herself," said Mike, "although she recorded as Shandra Steele. She had some big hits back in the seventies. Of course, it was well before my time."

"I sang disco," said Shandra, "and by the time the disco craze ended I'd met my husband and wanted out of showbiz. Then I started up a PR firm which works exclusively with musicians. I know the music industry, and I know how to promote them."

Mike looked at Howie. "Did you put her name on the list?"

"Yep. She's the first one up."

Kurt ordered a round of drinks as Mike and Tonya took their seats, and a suddenly nervous Tonya went over her music charts.

"Sorry if I'm being a little antisocial," she finally said. "I'm still figuring out what I should sing."

"Go with whatever you feel the most comfortable with," said Mike.

Tonya grabbed her gig bag and unzipped the front pocket, taking out a clear plastic bag and setting it on the table. Mike immediately perked up

"I see you have your own microphone."

"Yep. I prefer to use my own equipment whenever possible." She put on the headpiece and clipped the transmitter onto her belt before checking her watch. It was five minutes to six. A man approached their table and introduced himself as the emcee. He asked Tonya a few questions and stepped away to another table, returning a few minutes later.

"You're up." He walked back to the makeshift stage. Switching on the microphones, he gave Tonya a nod. After introducing himself, he quickly introduced Tonya. The audience politely applauded as she walked to the stage and set the house mic off to the side. Switching on her own microphone, she greeted her audience.

"Thanks. It's good to be here. I thought I'd do a little Patsy Cline. It's one of my favorites, and I hope you'll like it too." She took a deep breath, and after playing a few introductory chords she began singing,

"Crazy." The audience seemed friendly enough. She glanced at her table as she sang. Mike and the others were watching her closely. All four looked pleased. The next musician wasn't quite ready when she finished, so the emcee asked if she would mind singing another song.

"It would be my pleasure, so I'm going to shift gears and do a number by Wynonna." She played the intro and began singing, "No One Else on Earth." A big smile broke out across Mike's face as she belted out the first verse. He jumped up and grabbed the other mic, singing the chorus along with her. She gave him as big smile as the audience began clapping and cheering.

He stood off to the side as she sang the second verse, once again joining in on the chorus. Afterwards, he watched her intently as she played a guitar riff. They soon jumped back into the song and completed it as an improvised duet. Everyone stood from their seats and the bar broke out in thunderous applause. Both said a quick thank you and rushed back to their table. Kurt took Tonya's guitar and she quickly removed her headset.

"That was sensational," he said. "I'll take care of your gear because you two need to get the hell out of here right now. We'll leave as soon as they bring out the pizzas."

"See you at my place." Mike grabbed Tonya's hand and they rushed out the back door. Howie went with them and blocked the door once they were gone so they could safely exit the parking lot.

"Now that was fun." Tonya was breathless as she closed the passenger door and reached for her seatbelt.

"Yeah, but it was my blunder. I love that song, and I couldn't resist going up there and singing it with you. Hope you're not upset with me for upstaging you."

"Are you kidding? I loved having you up there with me. I like working with you, and I can't wait to sing backup on your song."

"Me too, and by the way, you've made a good impression on the right people, so tonight may be a game changer for you."

"Are you serious?"

"You bet I'm serious, and I'm keeping my fingers crossed." He grabbed her hand and give it a squeeze. "I really am proud to know you, Ms. Tonya Rose." He put the truck in gear and quickly drove out of the parking lot. Tonya touched up her makeup as soon as they returned to Mike's house. He greeted her with a smile when she stepped into the kitchen.

"You look gorgeous," he said. As they kissed, the dogs started barking from the patio. The doorbell rang a moment later.

"Next time I'm telling them to take their time making those pizzas." Mike stepped away while Tonya took a few deep breaths and tried to remain calm. Voices grew louder as they came toward the kitchen.

"Great job, and here's your guitar," said Kurt. "Mike told me you were good, but I wasn't expecting you to be this good. I'd like for the two of you to record that song as a duet on his next album."

Howie set the pizza boxes on the counter. "Way to go," he said, "that was fantastic."

"Well, Mike, you're certainly full of surprises," said Shandra. "I saw the manager snap a photo of you two performing and he's just posted it on Instagram, so it's a safe bet it'll be making the rounds on social media. Shall we handle it the usual way?"

"Yes, ma'am." Mike took a case of beer from the refrigerator and set it on the counter next to the pizzas.

"Okay, then we'll ignore it, as usual."

"I need to give you a heads up, Tonya," said Mike. "There'll be some speculation on social media, and perhaps the tabloids, about Mickey Lee Janson's mysterious new girlfriend, which means there'll be people out there saying some really stupid stuff. Our policy is to ignore it. Responding only makes it worse."

"I understand completely. My sister's death was a high-profile case, and during the investigation the media literally camped out in our front yard. My mother and I felt like prisoners in our own home."

A stunned Mike gave her a hug. "I knew you had a sister, but I didn't realize she'd passed away. I'm so sorry for your loss."

"Thanks. It happened a few years ago."

"I'm sorry for your loss as well," said Shandra. "I'm also sorry you had to experience the ugly side of the media. However, this time it shouldn't be so extreme."

"My condolences for your loss as well," said Kurt. "Mike told me rest of your story, so I know you were going to the University of North Texas. You've obviously been well trained and my ears tell me you have what it takes." He handed her one of his cards. "I want you to call my assistant and schedule a meeting as soon as you get home. I would like very much to have you for a client."

"Oh, my god." Tonya's heart skipped a beat.

"I also told Howie I want him to start getting you as many gigs as he can. We need to get you performing in front of live audiences. Mike also mentioned something about George Monroe. Has he signed you on?"

"Not officially, although he's going to. However, he doesn't think I'm quite ready yet."

"Which is all fine and good, and performing regularly will give you the polish you need. Alicorn is a good label, and Mickey's done quite well with them. However, it's not a done deal, and George isn't the only game in town."

"No, he isn't," said Mike. "Are you going to see if anyone else has an interest?"

"It all depends. I'll get in touch with George as soon as he gets back and let him know you're now my client. Mike tells me your specialty is jazz."

"It is."

"I see. However, the music business is like any other business, and the goal is to sell as many records as possible. I liked the way you did the Patsy Cline tune. It had a nice, jazzy undertone, while the Wynonna song sounded more like rock and roll. I honestly think pop would be the best genre for you. It appeals to a much broader audience, and you could certainly incorporate jazz elements into your music. You also connected nicely with the audience, even without Mickey."

Mike spoke up as the others laughed. "Well, thanks a lot," he said jokingly.

"And while Mickey's busy having his temper tantrum, I'm starving," said Shandra, "and I think our guest of honor should be the first in line."

"I don't know if I can," said Tonya. "My knees are shaking so hard right now I'm not sure I can walk."

"It's okay. I got you." Mike helped her to her chair and grabbed a plate. Opening the pizza boxes, he grabbed a few slices for Tonya and set them on the table for her. He ran back to get her a beer before going back and filling his own plate. The others were already seated when he returned, but they left an empty chair next to Tonya.

Over the meal they discussed Mike's upcoming album. It had more of a pop sound than his first album. Shandra was working on media releases and planning interviews. He would appear on all the morning network news shows as well as the late-night talk shows. He would also go on tour after the first of the year.

"Sounds like you have everything under control," said Kurt. "In the meantime, our final recording session is next week. I know you want Tonya to sing the background on "Cordelia," but if she's not available, you'll have to go with the studio vocalist as planned."

"Don't worry, I'm available," said Tonya. "My photoshoot is on a different day."

"Good to know, so tomorrow morning we'll start making the arrangements." Kurt looked at his watch. "Hate to say it, but the three of us all have long drives home, so it's time to hit the road. Shandra, good seeing you, as always."

"Likewise." She handed a card to Tonya. "Call me as soon as you get back to LA, and we'll have lunch."

"I call you tomorrow, Howie," said Kurt, "and I'll drop you off at your hotel, Tonya."

Tonya grabbed her guitar and Mike walked everyone to the door. "Call me when you get back to your room," he whispered. He hugged her goodnight as she nodded in return and walked outside with the others. Like George, Kurt drove a Mercedes SUV, although his was a different model and it was white instead of silver. Tonya waved goodbye to Mike as they drove away.

"Even though I'm not officially representing you at this time," said Kurt, "Mike filled me in on your relationship with George Monroe, and what I'm about to say stays between the two of us."

"Of course."

"George has done quite well with Alicorn Records, and he's made Mickey Lee Janson a household name."

"I know he has."

"He can make Tonya Rose a household name as well. However, I am a little concerned about a few things. While George may be an astute businessman, there've been rumors and allegations for years regarding his relationship with some of his female recording artists. Please understand, I'm not judging you. I'm simply trying to keep you from getting hurt."

"I admit it's my own fault I'm in the situation I'm in. I met George purely by accident when I did the photoshoot for Mickey's album cover."

"I know you did. Mike had already told me about it."

"George invited me to lunch and I accepted his invitation. Unfortunately, I let it slip out that I had recently lost my funding for school. He seemed genuinely concerned, so he invited me to dinner the following night. He was trying to convince me to relocate here, and during the conversation I told him I'd recently ended a long-term relationship. I also said I grew up in a family that lived paycheck to paycheck, and I was willing to do whatever it took to have a better life."

"So, he made you an offer you couldn't refuse."

"I'm afraid so," said Tonya. "My dream has always been to become a recording star, and he promised he'd make it happen."

"And I have no doubt he will. He's helped other women become famous as well. However, he's not as benevolent as he appears. There are certain favors he expects in return."

"I know there are." Tonya let out a deep sigh. "Through a strange twist of fate I met the president of a major record label who promised to make all my dreams come true, and I was completely overwhelmed. I guess I wasn't thinking clearly at the time."

"Don't go beating yourself up. He saw the perfect opportunity to take advantage of you and he seized it. You just didn't know it at the time."

"Perhaps he did. I care deeply about him as a friend, but I'm not in love with him, and in hindsight, I realize I shouldn't have gotten this involved. However, it's only a temporary living arrangement, and there are no strings attached. I'm also trying to get as much modeling work as I can, so as soon as I'm in a position to move out, I'll find a place to rent. Then, once I complete my first album, I'm going back to Texas."

"I see."

"You sound a little unsure."

"Tonya, I don't mean to worry you, but there've been all kinds of stories out there about women who tried to end things with George Monroe. Apparently, it's not so easy. Record contracts were broken due to so-called artistic differences, or because they were supposedly too difficult to work with, or because of claims about their music not selling as well as expected."

"What happened to them?"

"Most were able to sign on with other labels, but not all, and some quit the business entirely. There've also been rumors about him paying off former girlfriends, which may explain why no one has ever come forward with any claims of sexual harassment. Again, it's all rumor and speculation, and there are many other women out there who speak very highly of him."

"Like Mandy West," said Tonya.

"She's a good example."

"So what do I do now?"

"You keep modeling, and we'll keep you busy too. Sooner or later George will find someone else, and when he does, then yes, you probably should go back to Dallas, and we can certainly work with you in Texas. I'll email him and let him know I'm now managing you, and from here on out any business matters concerning you and Alicorn Records go through me."

Everything seemed surreal when Tonya returned to her hotel room. She slowly sat down on the bed, trying to take it all in when her phone suddenly rang.

"You forgot to call me," said Mike, "and I wanted to be sure you made it back to your room okay."

"I'm so sorry," said an apologetic Tonya. "What time is it anyway?"

"It's almost ten o'clock."

"Good grief. We left your place over an hour ago. I guess I must have spaced out completely."

"It's okay. You've had a big night." His voice took a more flirtatious tone. "So now you not only have people, you have the same people as me, which'll come in handy. Like when I need you to sing background."

She couldn't resist teasing him back. "Wait a minute, does this mean that from here on out, if you want to have me over for dinner, you'll call your people and have them call me?"

"Maybe."

"Okay. So, what happens if I tell them, no, I'm busy?"

"Then I'll have them call you back to tell you I'm pining away."

"Then I'll tell them to tell you that if you're really pining away then maybe you should hop in your truck and come on over. And maybe bring me something nice while you're at it, like some flowers."

"Speaking of which, how are the roses doing?"

"Blooming their heads off. I'll send you a photo when we're done, and I'm hoping they'll be good until I leave."

"Me too, but seriously, Tonya, I really am proud of you. These people don't work with just anyone, and I felt as overwhelmed as you when they signed me on. So why don't you get a good night's rest, and I'll call you tomorrow."

❧THIRTY-TWO❧

MIKE HAD NEVER ridden in a convertible before, so when he called Tonya he suggested they take a day trip together. She arrived at his house an hour later and handed him the keys to the Mustang.

"I think we can cheat a little," she said. "You seem to be a pretty good driver, and you know your way around better than I do."

"Somewhat, although I don't get out as often as I'd like. Let me grab my ballcap and sunglasses and we'll be on our way."

Mike slipped behind the wheel and fired up the engine. Turning on the radio, he gave Tonya a smile. "I see you also like to listen to classic rock and roll when you're driving."

"I sure do. I grew up listening to it, and I think it's had an influence on my music as well."

"Same here." He put the car in gear and drove north, through San Luis Obispo to the small seaside community of Morro Bay, where he stopped to take the top down. Driving further north, they made their way toward San Simeon and he pulled over to the side.

"I think we'll pass on Hearst Castle," he said. "It's best for me to avoid crowds. So, are you getting hungry?"

"A little."

"Then let's see what we can find." They turned around and headed south, making their way back to Morro Bay. After filling up on fish and chips at a local bistro, they strolled around the quiet, pristine beach. A passerby offered to take photos of them with Morro Rock in the background. They handed him their phones, and afterwards he wished them a good day.

"Wow," said Tonya. "He had no idea who you were."

"No, he didn't. No one expects to see Mickey Lee Janson in a back country place like this." They stayed on the beach for most of the afternoon, until Mike finally looked at his watch. It was time for them to start making their way back to Santa Barbara. Before leaving, Mike put the convertible top back up.

"I'm afraid I'm out of leftover stew," he said, "so what would you say about grilling burgers on the patio?"

"I say let's do it."

The two dogs pounced on Mike when they returned. He leaned down to ruff up their fur. "You're not starving," he said. "We've been over this before, so you're both going outside." The two dogs gave him sad looks when he closed the sliding glass door.

"They're probably upset because we didn't take them with us," said Tonya

"Maybe so, but we didn't need dog hair all over the backseat. It's a rental car."

She gave him a mischievous look. "Yeah, but George is paying for it. So, how did you like driving around in a topless car?"

Mike felt his face turning red as he tried to suppress his smile. "Ms. Rose, I'm trying my best to be a gentleman here. I really am, but I'm also a guy who happens to like you. A whole lot. Which is why I'm trying to be a gentleman. When you go saying stuff like that it makes things, well, even more difficult."

She couldn't resist flirting with him. "It does? Gee, I had no idea. However, I was talking about the car, and not, well, you know, other stuff. It's not my fault if your mind wanders elsewhere, now is it?"

"Now you just stop it right now. Or else."

She gave him an innocent look. "Or else what?"

"Or else this." He wrapped his arms around her and kissed her passionately. When he finally came up for air, he gently smoothed a strand of her hair away from her face and kissed her again. He ran his hands down her back, and she softly moaned as he lightly caressed her breast.

"Tonya, are you okay with this?"

"I am, but what about you?"

Mike looked her in the eye and did what he had fantasized about a few nights before. Picking her up, he carried her into his bedroom, but both started laughing when he stopped at the bed. The coverlet wasn't turned down.

"Awkward," he said. Tonya gave him a reassuring look as he gently set her down.

"Nah. It means you really are a gentleman, just like you said you were, and you didn't invite me here to seduce me."

"No, I didn't." He turned down the bed, motioning for her make herself comfortable. She kicked off her shoes, and once she was settled, he took off his boots and laid down next to her. She softly moaned as he kissed and squeezed her breasts.

"I think we can do without this." He helped her out of her top and unhooked her bra. Tossing them aside, he squeezed and kissed her breasts. Looking underneath them, he found no surgical scars.

"Well, I'll be damned," he said with delight. "They're real."

"You'd better believe they're real, because I'm the real deal."

"That you are, Ms. Rose, and you're certainly prettier than a topless car." He took off his t-shirt and tossed it on the floor next to hers. Giving her breasts a gentle nibble, he rubbed her belly and slowly worked his hand down, stopping at her waistband.

"Well, what have we here?"

Tonya laughed and shrugged her shoulders as Mike sat up.

"Hmm…it appears we're both a little overdressed for the occasion." He helped her out of her leggings, and raised his brow when he saw her fully naked body.

"Wow," he said. "You look like a Greek statue."

"I make my living modeling skimpy swimsuits and lingerie, so I have to take care of certain things."

"Which makes you look sexy as hell." He tore off the rest of his clothes and hugged her tight as he kissed her passionately. Reaching for her thigh, he pulled it aside and began stroking her. She moaned in contentment and started pleasing him. He too moaned and kissed her again as his pleasure became more intense.

"Hold that thought." He grabbed a condom from the nightstand and quickly rolled it on. As she resumed pleasing him, he massaged her again, making sure she was completely ready. She softly groaned as he climbed on top of her, gently working his way in as she wrapped her legs around him. Watching her body writhe with pleasure as he made love to her the most erotic thing he had ever seen. She pushed and squeezed her body against his, and he bit down on her breast as she cried out in pure ecstasy. Unable to hold himself back any longer, he thrust his body into hers and suddenly felt as if he were falling down a mountain. She squeezed him tight as he collapsed on top of her in total bliss. They held onto each other and neither moved for several minutes.

"What's that?" Tonya finally asked.

"What's what?" He stroked her frazzled hair away from her face and gently kissed her.

"I just heard a loud bang."

They listened closely and heard another loud bang, followed by a bark.

"Bruno's having a tantrum. I'm going to have to let them in and feed them."

"You know, I'm getting kind of hungry myself," said Tonya.

He grinned. "I guess we did have a workout, didn't we? So would you mind if I grilled the burgers inside, instead of outside?"

"Whichever works best for you is okay with me."

He reached into his dresser for a pair of sweatpants and took a red plaid shirt from the closet.

"I wear this onstage, and you look good in red."

"It's okay. I can put my clothes back on."

He gave her a funny look. "Suit yourself, but I'm not responsible for any damages which may occur when I rip them off later, because after dinner we're coming back here for dessert."

* * *

The rest of Tonya's Santa Barbara stay was magical. Her beach photoshoot went flawlessly. She had worked with the photographer before, and he remarked about her happy glow.

Kurt emailed his contract, which she forwarded to Shawn, asking him if his professor would mind looking it over. Shawn replied the following morning. Not only did his professor say it was a standard contract, she also knew Kurt Porter personally. They signed the contract at Mike's final recording session. The Aquamarine album was now complete, and Mike took her to dinner to celebrate. He had fallen hard. He had also broken down the wall Tonya built around herself after Evan's infidelity. Finally, the morning they both dreaded had arrived. George was back from England, and it was time for Tonya to return to Los Angeles.

"I don't want you to leave," said Mike after they made love. "I told you before, I have an extra room here, and we'll find you a car."

"I don't want to go either, but I don't have a choice."

"Yes, you do."

Mindful of Kurt's warning, Tonya was careful with her response. "I have to take care of some unfinished business with George so I can end things on a good note. In the meantime, you need to get busy promoting *Aquamarine*. It'll all work out, I promise. I just don't know how long it'll be."

He smoothed the hair off her face. "So, what's Texas like?"

"It's a beautiful state. The people are friendly, and I feel very much at home there. You can do pretty much do everything in Dallas you can do here, but we don't have earthquakes."

"Yeah, but you get tornados. We get them in Alabama too, and they're not fun."

"No, they're not," said Tonya, "but at least you know when a tornado is coming."

"Good point. We're still working on my tour schedule, and I've already told them I want to take a few days off after I perform in Dallas. Then you can tell what's his name you have to go back for a photo shoot."

Tonya's face instantly lit up. "I like the way you think, although chances are George will have moved on by then."

"Yeah, he usually doesn't stay with anyone longer than a few months at the most. I just hate the thought of you going back to him."

She gave him a squeeze. "Me too, but like I said, I'm going to do everything I can to get out of there as quickly as possible, but right now I'm starving. What's for breakfast?"

"I can whip up some omelets. What time do you have to check out of the hotel?"

"One o'clock. My reservation included a late check out."

Mike rolled out of bed and put on his bathrobe. "The omelets coming up. Then we can either hang out by the pool, or go for a stroll on the beach."

"We'd probably be better off by the pool, away from cell phone cameras."

* * *

Tonya asked Mike for one more favor after he loaded her bags in her car.

"Sure, what is it?"

"I need to call my mother. She's one of your biggest fans. Would you mind doing a Facetime session so she can meet you?"

"I don't see why not."

"You don't know how much this means to me." She pulled up her mother's number and waited for her to answer. After they exchanged greetings, Tonya tapped the FaceTime app.

"I'm getting ready to go back to Los Angeles, and a friend invited me over for breakfast, so I wanted to introduce you. Say hello to Mickey."

"Oh my god! Are you serious?"

"I sure am." She handed her phone to Mike and stepped off to the side.

"Nice to meet you, ma'am," said Mike.

"Likewise, and thank you for being so kind to Tonya. I really appreciate it."

"The pleasure is all mine. Your daughter is very special to me."

Heather gave him a concerned look. "Is she still with you?"

"No. Looks like she's stepped away for a moment."

"Good, because I wanted to ask you about George Monroe. I'm not at all comfortable with her living arrangements. Is he on the level?"

"As a businessman, yes. She's in very good hands. He's done a lot for me, as you know, and he'll do a lot for her as well."

"Thanks, but I'm worried about what else he sees in her."

"I understand, and one of the things we accomplished while she was here was to get her signed on with my manager. Trust me, he'll be looking out for her, as will I. We all love Tonya."

"I appreciate it, Mickey, and I'm sorry for coming across as a doting mother."

"Don't worry about it. I have a doting mother myself, and if I'm lucky enough to have kids of my own someday, I have no doubt I'll be a doting parent as well."

"I'm back," said Tonya. Mike handed her phone back and they both waved goodbye as Tonya ended the call. The time had come for them to say goodbye as well.

"I need to stop at the hotel so I can get the rest of my things, and I'm keeping the vase the roses came in."

"It'll be a nice souvenir for you."

"Yes, it will, and later on we'll put more roses in it."

"You bet." He gave her a long, lingering hug and another kiss before he opened the driver's side door.

"This was an awesome car. It was fun driving it to San Simeon and back."

"It sure was," said Tonya, "and it's a day I'll always remember."

"Me too. Maybe you'll find another red Mustang when you're able to buy a car."

"We'll see." She gave him a final hug and last kiss before she slipped behind the wheel.

"Drive safe, and let me know when you get home."

"I will." She fired up the engine and slowly drove away. Mike stood on the sidewalk and watched as she turned a corner and disappeared. Deep down, he knew he would win in the end, but he also knew George wouldn't give her up so easily. He shook it off and walked back into his now empty house. Hopefully, his instincts about George were wrong. His phone beeped an hour later. Tonya was safely home.

❦THIRTY-THREE❧

TONYA SENT MIKE A text message as soon as she arrived home. His response was brief. *"Glad you're home safe. Love you."*

"Me too," she said outload. "I just hope we're not doomed before we start." She then called Natalie, who sounded pleased. More jobs had come in, and Tonya's calendar was soon filled with job interviews for the remainder of the week. She felt relieved to be back to work, and spent the remainder of the afternoon in the music room. Taking a break to check her messages, she found a voicemail from Howie and quickly returned the call.

"I want to get you working as soon as possible," he said, "so I've got you some gigs and I'll email you the details. They're all on Friday and Saturday nights, so they shouldn't interfere with your modeling work."

"No, they shouldn't. My modeling jobs are almost always during the week."

"Then be sure to let me know if there's a conflict, and enjoy your weekend. It may be the last free one you'll have for some time to come."

"Bring it on. The more gigs I get, the sooner I'll be ready to record my first album."

"Which is exactly what I want to hear," said a cheerful British voice. George stepped in and gave her a quick kiss on the cheek.

"Sounds like George is home," said Howie.

"He is."

"Then I won't keep you. I'll send you the email in a few minutes, and be sure to let me know if there's a problem. Talk to you later."

"Well, I guess congratulations are in order," said George. "Kurt emailed me saying he'd signed you on. I also saw the photo of you and Mickey at the club in Santa Barbara."

"It was an open mic night, and his joining me on stage was purely spontaneous. He invited Kurt, Howie, and Shandra so they could see me perform."

"We'll discuss it later. Right now, you need to change into your little black dress, because I'm taking you out to celebrate your homecoming."

Thirty minutes later George drove into the entrance to The Beverly Hills Hotel and escorted Tonya to The Polo Lounge. Kurt and his wife were seated in a booth near the corner aht the two men quickly got down to business. Both agreed Tonya needed more polish, and with Howie as her booking agent they were hopeful she would be ready to record her first album after the first of the year.

"I agree," said Tonya. "I've missed performing for live audiences, and I could have easily done an entire set the other night."

"And by the way, George, Tonya is also on Mickey's upcoming album. She's the backup vocalist on, 'My Dear Cordelia.'"

George looked puzzled. "I thought you were using a session vocalist."

"We were, but then Mickey said no, he wanted Tonya, so they recorded it during his last session."

"I see." George still seemed caught off guard. "Then we'll have to be sure she gets paid and is properly credited on the album."

"Already been taken care of." The two men then discussed Mike's new album and upcoming tour. When their main course arrived, the conversation shifted to George's recent trip to England, and the music industry in general. Afterwards Tonya excused herself to go to the ladies' room. A worried looking Kurt was waiting for her when she came out.

"Mike called me after you left, and it sounded to me like the two of may be more than friends. If so, then I sincerely hope it works out for both your sakes, but I'm also deeply concerned. George can either make you or break you, so if I were you, I'd tread lightly, and remember what I told you before about those other women."

"Thanks for the warning, but as I said before, I plan on going back to Texas as soon as I complete my first album. Hopefully, he'll have cut me loose by then."

"I hope so too, but until then you need to proceed with caution. You have the potential to become a huge success, and I don't want to see your career come to an untimely end because George got jealous."

Tonya hurried back to their table and Kurt returned a short time later, saying he and his wife were calling it a night.

"I'm still readjusting to the time change as well," said George. "Are you ready, Tonya?"

"Yes." She grabbed her purse, and on the way home George told her about his father's big birthday bash and seeing his kids.

"My father may be eighty years old, but he's still in charge of Alicorn, and he still plays a mean guitar. When he's not sitting behind his desk, he doubles as a session musician."

"They say music keeps your mind sharp."

"It may indeed," said George. "It's funny how talent can skip a generation. Neither Lance nor I are musically inclined, but Pete takes after both my parents, and he records as Peter Murray."

"Really?" Tonya was genuinely surprised. "I had no idea Peter Murray was your son."

"He is, although we downplay it as much as possible. Even though he records with a different label, we still don't want the public perceiving anything as nepotism."

"Makes sense."

"We also brought Anne into the company a few years ago. She's been helping Lance run the London office for some time now."

"I've always wondered which one is the home office. London, or Los Angeles?"

"London is considered the home office, although I don't take marching orders from my daughter or my half-brother. We're actually two separate companies working under the same umbrella, and as much as I enjoy seeing my family, I'm always happy returning here. This is my home now." He pulled into the driveway a few minutes later and offered Tonya a nightcap when they came inside the house.

"I brought back a really lovely brandy, and I think you should try some." He poured her a glass, and they enjoyed it in the living room. Finally, George took her by the hand. Tonya took a deep breath as he walked her down the hallway. They stopped in her room, where he unzipped her dress and told her to join him once she changed into her robe. He greeted her with a warm hug when she arrived.

"So, how are you, my pet?" he asked.

"Tired. It's been a long day."

"Then it's time for us to go to bed, but first we'll take a nice hot shower together. It'll help you sleep better." When they returned to the bedroom, he sat down near the foot of the bed and motioned for her to lay down. Once she was settled, he rubbed her feet and shins.

"So, did you have fun with Mickey?"

"Yes. I already told you we spent a lot of time working on our music."

"I know you worked on your music, but we also have an open relationship, which means you were free to make love to him, and you should have made love to him, as long as you did it safely. And now that you're home, this is mine once again."

He pulled her knees apart and she felt his hair as it brushed her inner thighs. He began massaging her with his tongue, but she felt guilty when he climbed on top of her. After they finished, he stroked her hair and gave her a smile.

"I'm glad you had a good time with Mickey, and I certainly hope you didn't become too attached to him, because you're going to be meeting plenty of other men."

✏THIRTY-FOUR✏

AS EXPECTED, THE TABLOIDS published paparazzi photos of Mike and Tonya from the video shoot. The headlines were all about Mickey Lee Janson's mysterious new girlfriend. Inside was the photo of them performing together at the open mic night, along with a few of her more provocative modeling photos. Some articles were more salacious than others, but they all speculated about their hot new romance.

Jodie called Mike the following week. He was surprised to see her name on the caller ID. His greeting was cool, but polite.

"How have you been?" she asked. "I haven't heard from you in some time."

"I'm doing well. We've just finished recording my second album."

"I see. So, who's Tonya Rose?"

"A very dear friend."

"I guess so. The reason I'm calling is because I have some really good news. After all these years, Daddy has finally come around."

Mike's guard immediately went up. "Really?"

"Yes, he really has, and I still can't quite believe it myself. As you know, I've been very unhappy ever since you left Alabama. Sure, I've been meeting other men. Most of them go to Daddy's church, but none of them are you."

"I'm sorry, Jodie, but—"

"Please, just hear me out. As I said, none of them are you. So earlier today, Daddy and I sat down and we had a really long discussion. He now understands just how unhappy I am, and he realizes he was wrong in keeping us apart, so he's ready to give us his blessing."

Knowing there was more to the story, Mike decided to play along. "I see. So, how have you been, Jodie? Still working at the bookstore?"

"Yes. I'm now the assistant manager."

"Then congratulations on the promotion."

"Thanks. I'm still helping out at Daddy's church too. Our church building is over sixty years old, and we've been doing some renovations. You know, adding a new room to the church office, redoing the kitchen in the fellowship hall, that sort of thing."

"Uh-huh."

"Then the other day a city inspector showed up. It seems the building isn't quite up to code, so now we have to do some major repairs."

"Really? Sorry to hear it."

"It came as a shock to all of us. Never in our wildest dreams did we expect this kind of setback, and we need to get it all done before winter sets in."

"Okay, I get it. You need to raise more funds, so you'd like for me to donate some CDs, or an autographed photo, or maybe even one of my guitars for some sort of raffle. No problem. I'd be happy to."

"Well, sure. We could certainly do another raffle, but—"

"Then consider it done. I have an old guitar I which could probably part with, and I can certainly send you an autographed photo and an autographed CD of my first album, but you'll to have to wait if you want an autographed CD of my upcoming album, because it won't be out until the holidays."

There was an awkward pause before Jodie responded. "Again, it's a very generous offer, and while we're happy to accept, I'm afraid there's more to it. As you know, we're not the wealthiest congregation in Birmingham. Most of our members are lower-middle income people, and they've already contributed as much to the project as they possibly can. But now, with all the additional repairs we have to make, we're way short of what we need to complete it. And, as I already mentioned, it needs to be finished before the weather turns cold."

"So, let me guess the rest," said Mike. "If I write your daddy a big fat check, we can finally get married and live happily ever after. It's that right?"

"You know, you're making it sound kind of ugly, when it's really not like that at all. Daddy realizes he was wrong. He now understands he should have let us get married right after college, just like we wanted to, and then—"

"And then he'd have a rich son-in-law to write him big checks whenever he needed them, and how unfortunate for him that the lowly barkeeper's son would come in handy after all."

"No! That's not it at all."

"Jodie, please. I've heard enough." Mike's voice was firm but calm. "I've already said you can have the guitar and the other stuff, but they come with the following stipulations. First, you'll send my business manager a tax-deductible receipt, and we'll include the address for you to send it to."

"Sure, we can do that."

"Second, and this is the most important part. You're not to contact me again."

"What?"

"Jodie, listen to me very closely, because I'm only saying this once. Whatever we may have had between us ended a long time ago, and in hindsight, I can honestly say your turning me down when I tried to give you a ring was absolutely for the best, because marrying you would have been the biggest mistake of my life."

"Mike, please, it's—"

"Oh, and speaking of the promise ring, I took it to a pawn shop and traded it for the guitar I'm donating to the raffle, so I guess this means we've gone full circle, and I want to wish you the best of luck with your raffle. It should bring you a nice sum of money, and someone will be contacting you soon about the donation."

"But wait—"

"Have a good life, Jodie. I sincerely hope you find someone who'll truly make you happy. However, if you contact me again, I'll consider it stalking and will act accordingly."

Her voice was wavering as she tried to say something else, but Mike disconnected the call and immediately blocked her number. He leaned back in his chair and tossed the phone aside with deep sigh. Maize sensed something was wrong. Her tail was wagging as she walked up to him and licked his hand.

"You know what I wish Maize? I wish people were more like dogs. Dogs are loyal, and they love unconditionally. I truly loved that woman for a very long time, but deep down, I knew she was only playing along. I just didn't want to admit it. And do you know what else I know about dogs? Dogs trust their instincts, which is something I really need to start doing."

He looked up Kurt's number and placed a call. When his assistant answered, he told her about the donation and asked if they would mind taking care of it for him. He would stop by the office on Friday afternoon to drop off the guitar and sign the photo and CD. Tonya would be playing at a nearby hotel, and he looked forward to hearing her sing.

❧THIRTY-FIVE❧

GEORGE ROLLED OVER and relaxed for a few moments. "I have to get back to the office," he finally said, "and you need to wash the sheets before Stan gets home."

"Got it covered," said Mandy. "My cleaning lady will be here soon. So, how's Tonya these days? Did she shoot the video with Mickey?"

"She did, and yes, she got her union card, so you needn't worry about it anymore."

"Good. I figured the photos on the tabloid covers were from the video shoot."

"They were indeed. She also tells me she got along quite well with the director, so she has an interview this afternoon for a commercial he's directing."

Mandy's mood quickly changed. "You said she wasn't interested in acting."

"She's not. It's an ad for a bodywash, and again, she has no lines. It's just a few shots of her in a shower stall, using the product. She was even laughing about an inside joke between her and Melissa concerning bodywash ads."

"Really?"

George gave her a strong look as he sat up. "I keep telling you she has no desire to become an actor. Her new booking agent is also getting her gigs on the weekends. Perhaps you and Stan could stop by sometime to show your support."

"Fine. Sorry if I misunderstood. And just so you know, I got curious one day, so I downloaded a few songs from her album. She and her friend Shawn really are good."

"I'm glad you think so." He climbed out of bed and gathered up his clothes.

"I also saw the photo of her and Mickey singing in a bar in Santa Barbara. They seem to have a nice chemistry together, so why don't you give them a chance and cut her loose?"

George sat back down on the bed and gave her another stern look. "You, of all people, should understand the rules regarding my mistresses."

"Not all of them."

"She's not like any of them."

"So I take it she'll become an official member of the club."

"She certainly will."

"And what about Mickey?"

George's voice remained stern. "Absolutely not. Mickey spent several years in an on again off again relationship with a clergyman's daughter, so I somehow doubt he'd be into the swinger lifestyle. I only loaned her out to him as a reward for his hard work on his upcoming album."

"I have a funny feeling he doesn't know he only had her on loan."

George gave her a cunning smile. "You worry too much my pet. The holidays are fast approaching. He'll soon be going back to Alabama to spend time with his family. Then he starts the first leg of his tour and he'll be gone for several weeks. In the meantime, I plan on hanging onto Tonya a bit longer than originally planned. Would you believe she was still a virgin when I first met her?"

Mandy looked stunned. "What? Are you serious? I thought she was engaged before you met her."

"It was more like engaged to be engaged, and she only allowed heavy petting. They were waiting until their wedding night for him to actually penetrate her. So, I did the right thing and relieved her of her virginity the night after the album cover shoot." He smiled at the memory.

"You know, Mandy, I've never been with a virgin before, and it was an incredible experience. It was like driving a brand-new car with zero miles on the odometer, and she still has her new car smell, even after Mickey test drove her."

Mandy suddenly looked worried. "Wait a second, George. You're bonding with her."

"I'll admit to having something of a crush on her, but not to worry. You're still my favorite mistress, and you always will be. In fact, I rather enjoy our Wednesday lunches. They give a whole new meaning to the word, hump day, don't you think?"

"Yes, they do, but I'm still concerned about you and Tonya. You're jealous of her relationship with Mickey. This isn't like you. What happens if you get jealous of the other men in the club?"

"I've never been jealous. You Americans make too big of a deal of—"

"I know, I know," she said, impatiently. "You've said it all before, but you've never bonded with anyone the way you've bonded with her. This isn't good, George."

"It's only a little crush. It'll pass. You of all people should know I've never been satisfied with just one woman, and I never will be."

"I know, but I still don't think she's a suitable member for our group. Think about it. She was saving herself for her wedding night. She's not the type who'll go bed hopping."

"She certainly didn't have any problems with Mickey."

"Because they're genuinely attracted to one another. Surely you noticed the way she was looking at him in the photo. You'd have to be blind not to see it. This is Hollywood. There are plenty of women out there who'd hop into bed with you in a heartbeat." She gave him a sly smile. "And I'm number one on the list."

George smiled and stroked her hair once again. "You certainly are, you little vixen, so when did you become so sentimental?"

"I'm not being sentimental. I'm simply observing. She's in love with another man, and even if she weren't, she'd never fit in with our group."

"It all remains to be seen. In the meantime, if you don't mind, I'd like to use your shower before I go back to the office."

"Help yourself. You know where it is."

* * *

Tonya was sitting on the living room sectional playing her guitar when George arrived home. She waited until she finished before acknowledging him.

"Very nice," he said.

"Thanks. It's a new piece I'm working on, and I think I've just about got it."

George sat down next to her. "How did your meeting with the ad agency go?"

"It went well. They offered me the bodywash ad, but I haven't accepted it yet. I'm still weighing the pros and cons."

"What pros and cons?"

"They'd be shooting me in a shower stall set on a soundstage. I'd be wearing my bikini for the closeups, but they want some shots of my back, so I'd have to take the top off. They said I could wear pasties if I wanted, but you may recall what happened when I gave them a test run. The glue was really irritating."

"I remember. You were still red and itchy when you came to bed that night, and I remember you saying you thought you were allergic to it."

"I'm pretty sure I was. They also said I could go au natural if I liked, and if I did, they'd close the set. The third option, of course, would be to turn it down, but if I start turning down work, they may stop calling me. I'm still not in a position to buy a car, and I while I appreciate you taking me to my weekend gigs, I feel like I'm imposing."

"You're certainly not imposing," he said. "I have a vested interest in going with you. It's helping me determine when you'll be ready to start recording, and some of those clubs aren't in the best parts of town. I've also told you, many times, how you needn't be so uptight about your body. You have beautiful breasts, and you shouldn't be ashamed of them."

"I know, but—"

"But nothing. You need the work, and so what if they see your breasts. They've seen breasts before. They're professionals and you've done topless shots before, haven't you?"

"Yes, but only with female photographers. This time I'll be working with a male director, as well as a camera crew.

"He's the same director who did Mickey's video, and you spoke highly of him. Trust me, he won't put up with anyone gawking at you or saying anything inappropriate. They're going to be more concerned with doing their jobs than they'll be about looking at your breasts."

"I don't know. I'm still not—"

"Just do it, Tonya." There was a growl in his voice and harsh look in his eyes.

"Sorry, I didn't mean to snap at you." He wrapped his arm around her shoulder and gave her a squeeze. "You need the money, and I honestly am trying to help you. There are times when we're pushed out of our comfort zones, but it's how we grow, and if we don't grow, we don't succeed. I know it may feel a little scary, but it's really no big deal, and once it's over and done with you'll probably wonder what all the fuss was about."

"I know. We have to take the good with the bad, right?"

"Yes, we do, and as I said, they'll treat you with respect. I guarantee it."

❧THIRTY-SIX❧

TRUE TO HIS WORD, Mike dropped off his old guitar at Kurt's office and signed the photo and CD. Leaving the building, he suddenly felt free. Jodie's ghost had been exorcised once and for all, and he was ready to begin a new life with Tonya. He hurried to his truck and drove to a newly renovated hotel off the Sunset Strip.

Tonya was playing in the lounge, and all the tables were occupied. It was a good sign. Scanning the room, he saw George seated at a table near the back, along with two other people. George spotted him and motioned for him to come and join them. Making his way back to their table, he noticed another familiar face.

"What brings you into town?" asked George.

"I had to drop off a donation for a church raffle in Alabama."

"Interesting," said the blonde woman seated next to George.

"Just helping out an old friend back home, so I figured as long as I was in town, I'd stop by to see how Tonya's doing, and it looks like she's doing well."

"She is indeed," said George. "I also want to thank you for introducing her to Howie. He's keeping her busy, and as you can see, she's building a good following."

Mandy perked up as George introduced Mike to the others. "I hear she was in your music video."

"She certainly was," said Mike.

"How did she do?"

"She was great. She takes direction well, so she was a big hit with the director. I haven't seen the final version yet, but I've seen some of the rough cuts, and she looks fantastic."

"Sounds like you two are good friends."

"We are."

Unsure of Mandy's intentions, Mike turned his attention back to George. "Any plans to make it official and sign her on with Alicorn?"

"Yes, but not until she's ready. I'm thinking maybe after the first of the year."

Mike nodded toward a man seated nearby. "I wouldn't wait too long if I were you. One of Hagerman's A and R people is sitting right over there."

"And what is that?" asked Mandy.

"Artist and repertoire," said George. "They come to places like this looking for people to sign on. We're in an extremely competitive business. Everyone is looking for fresh new talent." George looked at Mike. "How do you know him?"

"Your guy wasn't the only one hanging out in the studio parking lot the night I got voted off American Rockstar. Dennis approached me about the same time as Juan, and the reason I went with you was because Juan offered me a better deal, but don't underestimate Dennis. He's definitely scoping her out, and he undoubtedly knows you're here as well."

George suddenly looked ill at ease. "Thank you for letting me know."

"You're welcome. I want her to sign on with Alicorn as much as you do, especially since we'll be doing "No Where Else on Earth" as a duet on my next album."

"So Kurt tells me, and the legal department will be working on the royalties soon."

Mandy spoke up. "I saw the photo of the two of you performing in Santa Barbara on Instagram. You guys look really great together."

"Thanks. I took her there for an open mic night so my staff could see her perform, and they all but signed her up on the spot. It's great having her work under the same management team as me."

Tonya finished her song as they were talking. "Thank you so much," she said. "I'm taking a short break, but I'll be back in a few minutes, so don't go anywhere." She had barely set her guitar on its stand when Dennis approached and handed her a business card.

"See, what'd I tell you?" said Mike. "Dennis doesn't waste any time." All four watched closely as Tonya stepped away to get a card for Dennis.

"She's telling him to call Kurt," said Mike.

"I appreciate the head's up," said George. "I'll call Kurt first thing Monday morning."

"Good idea, and Kurt would have let you know as well. However, it's up to him to determine what's in her best interests, so we'll have to see what happens."

George gave Mike a strong look. "Don't worry, Mickey. I have no intention of letting her go."

Mike heard the hidden message in George's warning. His response was equally firm. "Never underestimate your opponent." Their eyes remained locked as Dennis approached their table and extended his hand to Mike.

"Hey, Mickey. How's it going?"

"It's going great, Dennis. Thanks for asking."

"Good seeing you, George, as well. You take care, Mickey."

"Will do."

Dennis hurried out and Tonya soon came up to their table. Her face lit up as Mike stood from his chair. She wrapped her arms around him, and they held each other for a moment.

"When did you get into town?' she asked.

"A little while ago. I had to take care of something at Kurt's office, and then I came straight here."

"Well, I'm glad you did. You've just made my day." She quickly said hello to Mandy and Stan.

"I know we didn't get off to the best start," said Mandy, "but I want you to know you have a genuine talent, and I really enjoy listening to you sing."

"Thanks, Mandy. I appreciate it. So now, if you guys will excuse me, I need to take care of a few things before the next set." She looked at Mike. "How long will you be here?"

"For as long as you want, assuming I don't get recognized."

"Same here," said Mandy.

Tonya gave Mike a parting hug and hurried off while Mandy turned her attention to Mike.

"It's not easy being a celebrity, is it?" she said.

"It has it's challenges all right."

"I've been recognized in public myself. Most of the time it's just annoying, but other times it can be downright scary."

"I hear you on the annoying part," said Mike, "but so far I've not experienced anything scary, although I'm always aware of my surroundings."

"Same here." Mandy and Mike talked among themselves, but near the end of Tonya's next set they noticed a few people giving them strange looks.

"Looks like some autograph seekers may be heading our way," said Mandy.

"I'm afraid you're right," said Mike. "So, I may have to sneak out the back."

"I think we'll do the same," said Stan. "Thanks for the invite, George, and please give Tonya our best."

* * *

Tonya yawned as she stretched out in the passenger seat. "It's been a really long day. I had a photo shoot early this morning, and then a late gig tonight, so I'm glad you had Howie cut me down to one gig a week. I may spend the weekend crashed out on the coach. Still, it was good seeing Mike."

"I take it you weren't expecting him to show up."

"No, I wasn't. It was a complete surprise."

"Are you two staying in touch?"

"We are," she said.

"I see. So, what did Dennis have to say?"

"Not much. He handed me his card and told me who he was. I said he'd have to speak to my manager, and I gave him one of Kurt's cards."

George turned on the car radio. "Did you want to listen to *Coast to Coast AM?*"

"Sure. I always enjoy hearing a good ghost story, or anything else as long as it's not *The Jesse St. Claire Show.*"

"It's a shame your circumstances are what they are. He's interviewed a lot of famous musicians on his show."

"I'm sure he has, but he didn't kill any of their sisters."

"I understand how you feel, but it was never proven."

Tonya's voice was firm. "Just because they couldn't prove it doesn't mean he didn't kill her. He did something to cause her to take that fall. Annette appeared in my dreams for months afterwards, and she kept saying Jesse did it. As far as I'm concerned, the man belongs in a prison cell. And just so you know, I've already discussed the matter with Shandra."

"And what did she have to say?"

"She says I'm not to discuss Jesse publicly, like I ever would've, and if he ever talks about me on his show, she'll put a stop to it."

George sighed. "Probably the best for all concerned, and I'm sorry it happened."

"Me too. You never get over losing your sister."

* * *

George was in an upbeat mood when returned home Monday night. "I spoke to your manager today."

Tonya's face was beaming. "I know. Kurt called me. Hagerman has made me a very generous offer."

"Have you seen it?"

"Yes, I have."

"Have you accepted?"

"Of course not. I'm waiting to see what you're offering."

"You're learning how this business works," he said, "so let's take a seat at the kitchen table." As they sat down George took a folder from his briefcase. "Kurt also tells me their offer was very generous."

"It is. They think I'm ready now, and they want to start working on my first album right after the holidays."

"Do they?" George opened the folder and started taking notes. "We're wrapping up our own proposal, which we'll present to Kurt tomorrow morning. He'll go over the details with you, but it's essentially the same offer we made Mickey. However, I wanted to ask you a few questions about *Between Us Friends*."

"Okay."

"Do you still want Alicorn to distribute it?"

"Absolutely," said Tonya.

"Alright, so would you be open to making a few changes?"

"What kind of changes?"

"You've included a number of jazz standards, and while they're all wonderful classic songs, I would like for the Alicorn edition to be more contemporary so it'll appeal to a bigger audience. Would you and Shawn have any objections to replacing them with cover songs by artists such as Adele or Rihanna?"

"I certainly wouldn't object, and I doubt Shawn would either. I'll text him as soon as we're done."

"I appreciate it, and please let me know when he responds. We, of course, plan on including Shawn on the updated edition, so, assuming you accept our proposal, we'll fly him here over winter break and put him up in a hotel. You'll be in the recording studio right after New Year's, and we want to get as much done as possible before his classes start."

Tonya's face was glowing. "Actually, it's not a problem. Shawn won't mind missing a few classes."

"I see, and while I've not mentioned it before, I'm leaving for the UK on December nineteenth, and won't be back until the seventh of January, so I was already planning on putting you up in the same hotel as Shawn."

"Thank you, George. Howie says Shawn would be welcome to join me at my New Year's Eve gig if he were in town, and I've really missed playing with him."

"You're welcome, and hopefully you'll accept our proposal."

"I'm looking forward to seeing it, but regardless of who I go with, once I receive my advance, I'll be in a position to find my own place, so I plan on going back to Texas after I finish recording my first album. I appreciate everything you've done for me, but you need your house back, and I'm ready to go home."

George looked stunned. "No, I don't think it's a good idea at all. I understand if you're feeling homesick. I sometimes get homesick myself, but it's like I've told you before. Los Angeles is the heart and soul of the entertainment industry, and if you go back to Texas you'll miss out on other opportunities."

"But I'm have no desire to get into acting. That's Mandy's thing, not mine, and Elvis lived at Graceland."

"He was also Elvis," said George. "Maybe later on, when Tonya Rose is a household name, it might make sense for you to go back to Texas, but certainly not now. Once your album is released, you'll be doing the network morning news shows, and the late-night talk shows, just like Mickey's doing now."

"I know. I watch them whenever he's on, and he's appearing on another news show later this week." George winced ever so slightly as she spoke. "Okay, let's say if I were to agree to stay in here a little longer, then I'll at least be able to get my own place."

"We'll see."

Her response was firm. "George, I appreciate all you've done for me, I honestly do, but as I said, you need your home back, and I don't want to overstay my welcome. I'm getting more calls for modeling jobs, and Carson has upped my fee. So, between my modeling, and my advance, I'll be in a position to find my own place. I don't have much, so a one room apartment is all I need."

George's response was equally firm. "And as I said, we'll discuss it later. So, getting back to business. The legal department will start working on your contract once you accept our proposal. Then, when it's ready, you and Kurt can review it, but it's just a formality. Everyone has virtually the same contract I'm offering you. You'll record your first solo album next spring, and it'll be released next summer. Until then I want you to keep modeling and keep playing the clubs on weekends. We need to start getting your name out to the public."

"I appreciate it, but before I make any decisions, I want to discuss both offers in detail with Kurt, so we've scheduled a meeting for Thursday afternoon."

He gave her a smug grin. "Getting cheeky, are we? But not to worry. We'll beat anything Hagerman offers. You have my word on it. So, getting back to the public. I saw the tabloid stories about you and Mickey, and it's not the kind of publicity we want. We want the public, particularly young men, to see you as single and available, so the less you're around Mickey, the better."

"I thought you wanted me to give him a chance."

"I did, but he's going to be extremely busy over the next few months promoting *Aquamarine*, while Tonya Rose will continue being a sexy glamour model who's about to record her first album. You're also going to be meeting other men, and when the time is right, you'll have plenty to pick and choose from."

❧THIRTY-SEVEN❧

TONYA'S UBER DRIVER dropped her off at the Beverly Hills Hotel the following afternoon. She hurried to the Cabana Café, where Mike greeted her with a warm kiss.

"You certainly have a happy glow," he said.

"I have offers from two different labels."

"Let me guess. Alicorn and Hagerman."

"You got it.

"I thought so," said Mike, "which is why I took the liberty of ordering some wine to celebrate." He picked up the carafe and filled her glass. "So, may the best record company win."

"Here, here." The clanged their glasses together and took a sip.

"What about your album with Shawn? Are they both including it?"

"They are," said Tonya, "and both are willing to let us make changes on the new version. We did the best we could at the time, but we both knew it could've been better."

"And I know someone who would love to sing backup, just in case you need it."

Tonya's face lit up. "Are you serious?"

"Consider it part of your Christmas surprise. So, moving on. What's Texas like?"

"It's like I've told you before, silly. Dallas is like Los Angeles in many ways, but friendlier. We also have all four seasons. So, have you made your reservations yet?"

"Sure have. The Westin Galleria. I arrive Christmas night."

"Are you sure you don't want me to pick you up at the airport?"

"I'm positive" he said. "I'll meet you at the hotel and we'll see if we can get them to bring a bottle of champagne to the room."

"Or I can bring a bottle with me."

"Which works too, and speaking of my tour, I want to take you with me, assuming we can arrange it."

Tonya's face lit up. "Oh my god. Do you really mean it? Oh, wait. I already know the answer. You wouldn't have said it if you didn't mean it."

"You catch on quick, Ms. Rose."

"And you know I'd love nothing more, but I don't know if George will agree to it or not. You should have seen his reaction when I told him I wanted to find my own place as soon as I get my advance. Let's just say he wasn't too keen on the idea."

"Damn. I was afraid of something like that. He gave me a veiled warning the other night at your gig."

Tonya felt a shudder going down her spine. "What do I do now?"

"You stay calm, you keep working, and you let Kurt know what's going on. He's looking out for your best interests too, and if we have to, we'll come over and move you out ourselves. In the meantime, we'll keep seeing one another."

"I'm so grateful to have both of you looking out for me. So, onto happier topics. How's your family doing these days?"

"They're doing okay. I think I may have mentioned Liam took over my old job at our dad's bar, although he doesn't sing or play the guitar at night, much to everyone's relief."

"Oh, c'mon. He couldn't be that bad. Didn't you tell me he gave you his old guitar?"

"He did, and the reason was because the music gene skipped him entirely. He's practically tone deaf, but he's pretty sharp when it comes to running a business, so he's managing the place much better than I did. Meanwhile our baby brother, Marty, does have some musical talent, but he's studying to be an architect." Over the meal they shared stories of their families and talked about their music, but Mike's mood turned serious after the server picked up their plates.

"You want to know something, Ms. Rose?"

"What's that?"

"Things really are falling into place, even though it may not appear that way, and it's all going to work out. Probably sooner than you think."

"I sure hope so," said Tonya. "I just wish I'd stopped to consider the long-term consequences of accepting George's offer. I'm usually pretty good at reading people, or at least I was, but I sure missed the mark with him. Evan too. I had no idea he was the jealous type."

"Stop right there. Some people hide their darker sides better than others, and being good at reading people's body language doesn't mean you're a mind reader. Nor does it diminish the times when it steered you away from the wrong people."

"You're right. It has." A big smile broke out across her face. "And speaking of Evan, I'm shooting a body wash commercial tomorrow, and if he'd known the details, he would have lost his ever-loving mind. They want to include a shot of my back, which means I'll be topless, and even though you won't see anything on camera, some of the crew may see me, if you know what I mean. And just so you know, Jordon's the director. He asked for me personally."

"It's a job, Tonya. Even if you were buck naked, it's still a job. You need the money, so you do whatever you have to do, and with Jordon running the show I know you're in capable hands. I'm not Evan. I have no issue with it." He quickly changed the subject.

"So can I offer you a ride home?"

"I appreciate the offer, but I need to do some shopping."

"No problem. I'll drop you off wherever you need to go."

Mike drove into a Walmart parking lot a few minutes later and stopped in front of the entrance.

"What are you doing for the rest of the day?" asked Tonya.

"I'm heading straight home and making an early night of it. I have to be up before the crack of dawn tomorrow morning for a live interview on *Good Morning America*."

"Oh, the glamour of being a famous musician."

"I wouldn't laugh about it too much, Missy," he said with a smirk. "Your day is coming. Sooner than you think." He gave her a goodbye kiss and waited until she was safely out of the truck. "I'll text you later. Love you."

"I love you, too." She waved goodbye and hurried inside, in search of new clothes for her weekend gigs. Even though her finances were improving, Tonya remained a careful shopper. Waiting in the checkout line, something unexpected caught her eye. An old photo of Annette was on the lower corner of one of the tabloids, with a bold caption about Tonya Rose's tragic sister. She quickly tossed a copy in her cart. Upon arriving home, she went straight to the guestroom and started reading.

While the story of her sister's demise was reasonably accurate, the article portrayed Annette as an unscrupulous gold-digger with Jesse as an unsuspecting victim whom she had taken advantage of. The author also claimed Mickey Lee Janson's new love interest was much like her sister. Tonya's stomach turned, and for a moment she thought she might be sick. Taking a deep breath, she placed a call to Shandra, feeling relieved when she came on the line.

"What can I do for you today?" Shandra asked.

"One of the tabloids just did a hatchet job on my late sister."

"Yeah, I heard something about it, but I haven't seen the article yet."

"This isn't right. Annette isn't here to defend herself, so is there anything we can do?"

"Unfortunately, court records are public records, and you told me the story got a lot of media coverage at the time it happened. Nowadays all you have to do is Google a name, and you'll have all the old newspaper stories at your fingertips."

"I know. However, I was seventeen at the time, and the day it happened my grandmother's attorney put out the usual word to the press about respecting our privacy, along with a caveat about me being a minor and not involved in any way. They got the message. There wasn't so much as a passing reference in any news story about Annette Claiborne having a sister. I'm also known to the public as Tonya Rose, so how would they have known Tonya Rose is really Tonya Claiborne, and how would they have known I'm Annette Claiborne's sister? Unless Jesse St. Claire tipped them off."

"Maybe, but I seriously doubt it. He's always been highly professional whenever I've worked with him, nor is this the kind of publicity he would want for himself. He's worked very hard to put the incident behind him."

"I'm sure he has. So, if it wasn't Jesse, then who was it?"

"Your guess is as good as mine. It could have been anyone. Perhaps a former neighbor, or maybe even one of your high school classmates. What about your old boyfriend?"

"Evan? What would he have to gain by this?"

"Revenge perhaps? Who knows? What I can tell you is the more you become a public figure, the more people will come out of the woodwork claiming they knew you back in the day. Mickey has already told you the best thing to do is ignore it, and it'll go away by itself."

"I know, but this isn't about me. It's about Annette. Why can't they let her rest in peace?"

"They will. The story is old news, so it should fade away fairly quickly."

"I hope you're right. However, this kind of thing is especially upsetting to my mother."

"I'm sure it is. Why don't you call her and let her know? It's better if she hears it from you than from someone else, and it's okay to give her my phone number. She's your mother, so I'm happy to speak to her, mother to mother, if she'd like."

Finally, Tonya felt relieved. "I will, and thank you, Shandra."

"Anytime."

Mike called an hour later. "I just got off the phone with Shandra. She told me what happened, so I looked up the story online. Are you okay?"

"I'm fine. The one I'm concerned about is my mother. She takes things like this really hard. I've already spoken to her on the phone. She's absolutely livid and says she wants to sue, but I'm hoping she'll calm down once my stepfather gets home."

"Mothers tend to get upset. Mine's gotten upset a few times as well. You have to keep reminding them how most people won't buy into it. And by the way, your sister was a stunningly beautiful woman. You two definitely share a resemblance. She's almost as pretty as you."

"Now you're making me blush."

"No, I really mean it."

"We both took after our grandfather, who was a very handsome man, but compared to her, I was always the plain one."

"Says who?"

"My mother and grandmother," said Tonya. "Everyone, but Annette herself. She's the one who took me to the mall and taught me how to pick out the right clothes and how to do my hair and makeup. Then, later on, she started coming to me for advice, because I was the levelheaded one." A tear ran down her cheek. "I still miss her. More than you can possibly imagine."

"I'm sure you do, and I'm sorry I never had the chance to meet her. And just throw the stupid tabloid away. Nothing good will come if you keep rehashing it."

"I know." She heard the garage door opening. "Oops, I gotta go. Have a good interview tomorrow morning." Tonya put her phone away and stormed into the living room, tossing the newspaper into the fireplace. George gave her a quizzical look as he came in.

"Do we have any matches?" she asked.

"There's a box on the mantle What's the matter?"

She reached for the matches and removed one from the box. "One of the tabloids just did a hit piece on my sister, thinking it would make me look bad."

"It happens, Tonya. I'm afraid you'll have to get used to it."

"I know," she said. "I've already discussed it with Shandra. They can say whatever they want about me, but a deceased family member should be off limits."

"Yes, they should, and I'm sorry."

"Me too." She lit the corners of the paper, and it quickly ignited. George placed his hands on her shoulders and gave her a squeeze.

"I understand how you feel. The tabloids in the UK are even worse, and believe me, there've been times when family members, particularly Pete, have had unwanted press as well, but we don't respond to it. So let me go pour you a glass of wine, and we'll enjoy it out on the patio. The fresh air should help you feel better."

❦THIRTY-EIGHT❧

SHAWN CALLED TONYA the following morning. "Jacque went to the grocery store last night and saw a headline about your sister on one of the tabloids, so she brought it home."

"I know. I've already seen it. Everyone's telling me to ignore it."

"Probably the best thing to do, and while I don't mean to upset you any further, Rob tells me Evan showed up at his door, looking for you."

"You're kidding. When was this?"

"A couple weeks ago. He was surprised to find Rob living there, and then Rob slipped up and said you'd moved to California."

"I see. What else did Evan have to say?"

"He, of course, wanted more information, but Rob told him you didn't leave a forwarding address. Apparently, Evan saw the tabloid story about you and Mickey, so he asked Rob about it, and again Rob said he didn't know. Then he told Evan if he wanted to leave you a message, he would have to talk to me. Evan left and hasn't been seen or heard from since."

"What does he want from me? Doesn't he have a new girlfriend?"

"He did, but I don't know if they're still together or not. Maybe he's upset about being replaced by Mickey Lee Janson."

"I suppose anything's possible. Do you think Evan tipped off the tabloids about Annette? He knew all the details about what happened to her. There was never any mention of me in the press at the time it happened, so someone had to tell them she and I were sisters."

"He very well could've, but we don't know for certain. Do you want me to talk to him?"

"No." Tonya's voice was firm. "If it were him, he would have done it to get a reaction out of me, so the best thing to do is ignore him."

"I agree. I also wanted to let you know I got an email the other day from George Monroe. He told me about your contract and his plans for our album."

"It's not a done deal yet," said Tonya. "I haven't signed the contract, and Hagerman Records had also expressed an interest."

"Really? Wow. I never expected one person to be interested let alone two."

"And just so you know, George is genuinely interested in working with you."

"I know he is. We've scheduled a phone conference for next Tuesday. What about you and him?"

"I'm still living in his house, but as soon as I can afford my own place I'm moving out." She looked at her gold watch. "And speaking of the time, I have to run. I'm shooting a commercial today."

"Well then, congratulations, and we'll talk later."

* * *

"So, how did it go?" asked Natalie.

"Other than spending a few hours getting totally drenched, it went much better than I expected. We were on a sound stage, and the set was really interesting. The walls were moveable to allow for different camera angles, and we did the topless shot first."

"I see. And were you okay with it?"

"Yeah. It wasn't nearly as scary as I thought it would be. Jordon closed the set and looked the other way while I got into position. Then he stepped out when we were done so I could put my top on. Everything ran smoothly."

"I'm glad it went well," said Natalie.

"Me too. I also have a whole lot more respect for actors, so please tell Mandy she has nothing to worry about."

"I'll let her know, although nowadays she's mostly focused on her acting, so we don't see her very often anymore." Natalie typed something on her keyboard. "Now that you have your first topless job behind you, I have something you may be interested in."

"What is it?"

"A blue jeans ad for a men's magazine, similar to the cologne ad you did for a men's magazine a few months ago in Dallas."

"I was actually wearing a bikini, which Julianna later airbrushed out."

"You know, I've heard some really good things about her," said Natalie. "She did an amazing job."

"She was my favorite photographer in Dallas."

"This time it's a little different. The model they originally hired got into a traffic accident yesterday morning."

"Oh, no. Is she okay?"

"Other than a broken wrist she's fine, but now she's unable to do the shoot. The client, however, still has a deadline, and they would like to do the shoot as planned this coming Friday, if at all possible. Wade Harris is the photographer. You've worked with him before."

"Yes, I have. I like Wade. He's a good guy."

"You'll also be working with a male model. Carlos is a real sweetheart, and he's from Phoenix, too. You'll be holding hands, that sort of thing, but all the two of you will be wearing are the jeans. No shoes, no tops, just the jeans, or so it'll appear in the final ad. Don't worry, your nipples won't be showing. You can either wear pasties or go completely topless if you prefer."

Once again, Tonya was hesitant. "Unfortunately, I'm allergic to the glue. If it were a female photographer, or just me and Wade, I could do it, but I'm not sure I'd feel comfortable being completely topless in front of two men, especially when I've never worked with one of them before."

"You can cover your nipples with band aides if it would make you feel more comfortable. They can be easily airbrushed out, just like before. We can also send along a chaperone it you'd like."

Tonya needed the money, and she knew George would be upset if he were to find out she turned the job down. "I'll do it, but I'd also like a chaperone."

"Of course, and I'll let them know. It'll either be Jaime or the other student intern. You'll need to report to Wade's studio Friday morning, nine o'clock sharp."

"I'll be there."

"I know you're new to doing nude work, but it's a job, and if anything were to happen to make you feel unsafe or uncomfortable, you're to call me immediately."

❧THIRTY-NINE❧

KURT GREETED TONYA with a warm smile when she came into his office. "So, how have you been?" he asked.

"Busy. Ever since Mickey's video I seem to be more in demand."

"That's great. Every little bit helps. So, getting down to business. Hagerman Records wasn't happy when they lost out on Mickey. They say they'll beat whatever George offers you, and they mean it."

"While George is telling me the same."

"And I have no doubt he'll try. However, Hagerman Entertainment is a publicly owned company. In addition to several record labels, they also have a film studio and a television production company. Alicorn is an excellent company as well, but they don't have the deep pockets Hagerman has, and Hagerman knows it. So, my question to you is, what do you want?"

Tonya sighed. "Had I not put myself into the awkward position I've put myself in, I would've jumped at their offer. Do I have to get back with them right away?"

"They would prefer you did, but no, you don't have to."

"Okay, so let's go over the offers and discuss the details."

Kurt handed her copies of both offers as they came out of the printer. "As you can see, they've both made generous offers. You also said you and Shawn would like to remaster Between us Friends, so both have included it in their proposals. Hagerman is also giving you more artistic freedom regarding the remastering, while Alicorn is being very specific about which songs they would like to replace, and what songs you'll replace them with."

"Yeah, I see that," said Tonya..

"What does Shawn have to say?"

"He's okay with making changes. He also said the final decision is up to me."

Kurt went over the remaining details for both offers. After he finished, he once again looked her in the eye. "As I said before, both are well respected companies, and you would do well with either of them. However, when you add it all up, Hagerman is giving you the better deal."

"I know they are. However, with my circumstances being what they are, I'd like to give George an opportunity to match their offer.

"Of course, and let me know what you decide."

George came home earlier than usual that night. He was anxious to know about Tonya's meeting with Kurt. Once again, he opened up his briefcase as they sat down at the kitchen table.

"Kurt and I discussed both offers in detail," said Tonya. "And we both agree Hagerman has made the better offer."

"Have you spoken to Shawn?"

"I have. He would prefer Hagerman because they're giving us more creative control of *Between us Friends*, but he's leaving it up to me."

"Alright then." George started taking notes. "I'll agree to let the two of you decide what to do with your album, but I hope you'll at least consider my suggestions."

"Fair enough. I'll let Shawn know."

"So, did Hagerman offer you a bigger advance?"

"Yes, they did."

"How much more?"

"Twenty-five thousand dollars."

George started laughing, and Tonya suddenly felt confused. "What's so funny?" she asked.

"Tonya, twenty-five thousand is nothing."

"It may be nothing for you, but it's a lot of money to me. I could buy a new car for twenty-five grand."

"As long as you don't mind driving a subcompact or a stripped-down model, so let's get you something nicer. I'll match their twenty-five thousand and give you another ten, which is thirty-five thousand dollars. So, how does that sound?"

"It's certainly very generous, but there's something I want even more."

"And what would that be?"

"My own place."

His response was firm. "Not yet."

"Why?"

"I've told you before. I'm still mentoring you."

"And I appreciate it. I honestly do, but you can still mentor me if I'm living in my own place. I've also told you before I don't want to wear out my welcome."

"You won't." He gave her a firm look. "Tonya, I've invested a lot in you, and I'm not just talking about the money. You're a damn good musician, but you're in a town full of damn good musicians, and while talent goes a long way, you also need luck. You were in the right place at the right time when Ryan's assistant knocked over the light pole, and you were in the right place at the right time when the woman from the Carson agency came to your performance in Dallas. Now, think of where you'd be today if those two events hadn't happened."

"I'd probably be in Texas, working several different jobs while I got my in-state residency so I could finish school without as much student loan debt."

"Exactly," said George. "I didn't have to take you to lunch that day. I could have just as easily said nice meeting you and gone back to my office, but I didn't. Nor did I have to take you into my home and provide for you so you could focus on your music, and your modeling, without having to worry about where your next meal was coming from."

"And I'm very grateful for all you've done."

"Which I very much appreciate. However, the reason I did this was because I saw something extraordinary in you." He looked deeper into her eyes.

"I'm not asking you for a long-term commitment. I already told you I'm not the marrying kind, and everyone knows I'm a rover when it comes to women, but I don't go into a relationship with a predetermined time limit either. I let it run its course, however long it may be."

"You're very special to me as well, and you always will be, but I just don't want to be in Los Angeles for the long-term. I know you love it here, but I'm much happier in Texas."

"I'm not asking you to stay here for the rest of your life. What I am asking is for you to stay long enough to get your career off the ground and be in a position to live wherever you want. It may be a year, two years, perhaps longer. It all remains to be seen. Trust me, Texas will still be there. It's not going anywhere. So, back to the discussion at hand. I'm willing to meet Hagerman's offer and give you an extra ten thousand dollars on top of it. So, what's it going to be?"

She took a deep breath. "I call Kurt's office and leave him a voicemail."

"You can call him later. Tonight. I'm taking you out to celebrate. Anywhere you want." He gave her a playful look. "Then, as soon as we get home, you're going to start returning the favor."

❧FORTY❧

TONYA FELT APPREHENSIVE when she arrived at Wade's studio, but both he, and Carlos, looked the other way when she removed her robe while Jaime, her chaperone, looked bored. Carlos seemed to sense her nervousness.

"Don't worry," he said. "I'll move very carefully, and I promise nothing will happen. Otherwise, my old lady would kill me."

"And she really would too," said Wade. "So, let's get going. The client has a deadline, and so do we."

The shoot was over an hour later. Tonya checked her phone after changing back into her street clothes. Kurt had left a voicemail, while Mike sent a text asking how her day is going. She immediately typed a reply.

"Doing fine. Just finished a photoshoot. Would you like to meet for lunch?"

His response came a moment later. "Wish I could but have another commitment. Let's do it sometime next week."

"Ready to go?" asked Jaime.

"Yeah, I was just responding to a text message." Tonya dropped her phone into her purse and they walked outside together.

"Just so you know," said Jaime, "my car isn't the fanciest ride in town."

"I hear you. I arrived in LA in a twelve-year-old Versa which had seen better days."

"You win. I have an eight-year-old Chevy Impala."

"Hey, as long as it runs." Tonya treated Jaime to a latte at a coffee drive through on the way back to the agency. Once they arrived, Natalie greeted them with her usual warm smile.

"The shoot went well," said Tonya. "I always enjoy working with Wade, and Carlos put me right at ease. I'd work with him again in a heartbeat."

"Carlos is one of our more sought-after models. Everyone loves working with him. So, moving forward. I have another glamour shot coming up for another hair products poster."

"What will I be wearing?"

"The usual bill of fare. A short skirt, a low-fitting top, and a pair of strappy black shoes."

"When do I meet with the client?"

"Two o'clock Tuesday afternoon."

"Okay. I've got it on my calendar. Anything else?"

"Not yet."

"Alright." Tonya took a deep breath. "So, switching gears. My finances have improved considerably, but they could still be better, so George has suggested I look into doing more nude work because it pays more."

"It does, and we can certainly look into it, as long as you're not being pressured into doing something you don't want to do."

"I'm fine," said Tonya. "Although I'd still prefer working with female photographers whenever possible."

"Of course, and not all nude work is for men's magazines, nor does it necessarily show everything. A lot of it is like what you did today. You see backs and shoulders, or a profile, but no nipples. It may not pay as well as the men's magazines, but it's still good money, and I have a feeling you'd be more comfortable doing something like the job you did today."

"Exactly," said a relieved Tonya. "Or like the ad I did in Dallas, where Julianna later airbrushed my thong out."

"Then we'll see what we can do, and have a good weekend."

"You too. I need to make a phone call before I leave. Would you mind if I used the conference room?"

"Help yourself. Just be sure to turn the lights off when you're done."

Tonya hurried down the hall and carefully closed the door behind her. Punching up Kurt's number, she sat down in one of the leather chairs and waited for him to come on the line.

"I got your voicemail," he said. "I've also gone over Alicorn's updated proposal, and while I commend you on your negotiating skills, I still have to ask if this is what you really want."

"George has invested a lot of his own money in me, and he said he wouldn't have taken me in if he didn't think he'd make it back, so I owe him a debt, which I intend to repay."

"I understand, and having you and Mickey on the same label will certainly make it easier for you to contribute to one another's albums. However, Hagerman still would have matched his offer and then some, and my job is to get you the best deal possible."

"Which I appreciate, but as we both know, my situation is complicated."

"Of course. I'll give him a call and we'll start working on your contract, and congratulations on signing on with Alicorn. George is giving you a very good deal."

Tonya felt relieved when they ended their call. She needed to do a little shopping, and once again, a tabloid cover caught her eye at the checkout stand. This time it was a photo of Evan with a headline about Tonya Rose's jilted ex. Rolling her eyes, she tossed a copy into her cart, and on the way home, she sent Shawn a text message.

"Seen the tabloids?"

He soon replied. *"Not yet. What's up?"*

"We now know who leaked the story about my sister."

"Let me guess. Your beloved ex."

"Yep. Now I'm the bitch who tossed him aside for Mickey Lee Janson."

"Figures. I'll check it out later."

Tonya felt relieved as she leaned back in the car seat. Once she arrived home, she turned her attention to the article. It included a few photos of her and Evan in happier times. As expected, Evan claimed to have been completely blindsided when Tonya callously tossed him aside for Mickey Lee Janson. She felt bittersweet after reading it. While their relationship had ended badly, Evan was still her first love. Mike called an hour later. Tonya heard noises in the background.

"Where are you?" she asked.

"Having lunch with Charlie, my tour manager, which is why I couldn't meet you today. He had to step out to take an urgent phone call, so I called Kurt while I was waiting, and he tells me congratulations are in order."

"They are. I'm officially signing on with Alicorn."

"And I'm genuinely happy for you, Ms. Rose, and we'll have to do something special to celebrate. In the meantime, Charlie brought me a copy of one of the tabloids, thinking I'd get a good laugh out of it, and what can I say? My predecessor wasn't bad looking, but good lord."

"I know. Of course, he conveniently forgot about his little indiscretion with Becca, but he's now had his fifteen minutes of fame, so hopefully, we've seen the last of him."

"I'm sure we have. He was a fool to let you go, but his loss is my gain, and I see Charlie heading back to our table so I gotta go. Let's try to get together one day next week."

"You're on."

"I love you, Ms. Rose."

"I love you, too, Mr. Janson."

George looked troubled when he arrived home that evening. Tonya immediately tried to reassure him about the article.

"I'm sorry my ex is creating a stir in the tabloids, but I expect him to disappear soon."

"I'm sure he will, but I actually need to talk to you about something else."

She suddenly felt concerned. "I told Kurt I'd accepted your offer. Didn't he call you?"

"He did, and we'll start working on your contract soon." He motioned for her to take a seat on the sectional.

"I had lunch this afternoon with another Alicorn artist at the Cabana Café, and imagine my surprise when I overheard something about you and Mickey having lunch there the other day."

"He had a meeting with Kurt, and afterwards we met for lunch. End of story."

"No, I'm afraid it isn't the end of the story. As you just mentioned, the tabloids are abuzz with stories of the two of you being an item. I've also told you I want the public to perceive you as single and available, and I want his fans seeing him as single and available as well. Both of you need to lay low until this blows over, and you can start by skipping the lunch meetings."

Tonya bristled while George's tone softened. "You need to step back and look at the bigger picture. You're in an extremely competitive business. You're only as good as your last big hit, and the public can be fickle. What happens if your debut album is a smashing success and *Aquamarine* doesn't do as well as Mickey's first album?"

She started to say something, but he quickly cut her off.

"Tonya, I grew up in the recording industry. I've seen many long-term relationships and marriages fail because of professional jealousy. Both you and Mickey mean the world to me, and I don't want to see either one of you getting hurt."

"But what if we worked together? Other singers have done it, and they've been very successful."

"You have different styles. Mickey's music has a country influence, while you're more into jazz and blues."

"I know," said Tonya, "but we're still recording, "No Where Else on Earth" as a duet."

"I know you are, but it's at least a year away, and a lot can happen between now and then. While we expect Aquamarine to do well, we have no way of knowing how it'll be received, and you have your own music to worry about. So enough with the shop talk. How did your shoot go?"

"It went well. Afterwards, I bought a new outfit for my gig this weekend."

"Good on the shoot, and you needn't look so sad. I know you and Mickey are close friends, but sometimes close friends have to walk away from one another if it's for the greater good. He needs to get ready for his tour, you need to get ready to record your first solo album. I've also told you you're going to be meeting plenty of other men."

❧FORTY-ONE❧

TONYA AND HER MOTHER made a last-minute change of plans for Thanksgiving. Instead of Tonya coming to Tucson, her mother arranged for a substitute teacher the day before Thanksgiving so she and Alberto could drive to Los Angeles.

"Are you sure you'll be okay on your own today?" Tonya asked George.

"I'll be fine. As I said before, we don't celebrate Thanksgiving in the UK, nor am I particularly fond of turkey. I do, however, fancy your American football, so last night I stopped by the deli and stocked up. I'm going to spend the day munching on sandwiches in front of the telly, and enjoying a nice, quiet Thursday away from the office."

Tonya's Uber ride soon arrived, and the driver dropped her off at the motel where her mother and stepfather were staying. After greeting one another with warm hugs, they walked out to Alberto's Chevy Tahoe together, loading Heather's home baked pies and a bottle of wine in the back. Tonya hopped in the backseat and fastened her seatbelt as Alberto fired up the engine.

"Did you get the directions?" asked Tonya.

"I sure did," said Alberto, "so as soon as your mother fastens her seatbelt, we'll be on our way."

It had been years since Heather or Alberto had seen the ocean, so they stopped to take pictures as they made their way up the Pacific Coast Highway. Tonya's spirits rose once they reached Santa Barbara and parked in front of a small, unassuming home in a quiet, residential neighborhood. Mike came out as they exited their vehicle, greeting Tonya with a big hug.

"Okay, that's enough," said Heather.

"Sorry, Mom." Tonya quickly made the introductions, but her mother looked a little star struck. The scent of roasting turkey filled the air as Mike invited them inside and told them to make themselves at home in the living room where Heather presented him with the pies.

"Can I help you with anything?" she asked.

"I'm good."

"Mike's an amazing cook." Tonya's face beamed with pride as she spoke. "He learned how while he was working at his dad's grill."

"Yeah, but they also knew not to serve anything I prepared to the public." He excused himself for a moment, but before stepping away he asked if they liked dogs.

"We love dogs," said Heather.

"Okay, but don't say I didn't warn you."

Tonya grabbed the wine and followed Mike into the kitchen where he greeted her once again, this time with a kiss.

"Happy Thanksgiving, Ms. Rose." He was about to kiss her a second time when Bruno barked loudly from the patio. Both burst out laughing.

"Well, okay, I guess." Mike opened the door and both dogs bounded inside, greeting Tonya with wagging tails while Mike grabbed a few sodas from the refrigerator. Heather still looked a little star struck when they returned to the living room, and she immediately focused her gaze on Tonya.

"So, now that we're all here, I want to talk to you about something. I've been having dreams about your sister again, and she's been saying some interesting things."

"Like what?" asked Tonya.

"She says you need to let it go about Jesse and move on."

"But I—"

"I'm just telling you what she said, and I feel the same, so maybe the dream came from my own subconscious. The point is, you're an up-and-coming musician, and Jesse hosts a nationally syndicated talk radio show. I'm not saying you have to be a guest on his show, and frankly, I'd prefer you weren't. I'm simply saying you could possibly run into him somewhere, and if it were to happen, you need to be gracious. Just give him a nod or a quick hello and go your merry way."

"She's right," said Mike.

Heather turned to Mike. "I've had other dreams in which Annette tells me you have some sort of a plan to get Tonya away from George."

A serious look came over his face. "As we all know, Tonya isn't in a financial position to live on her own. However, I've offered her a room here, and she's saving up her money so she can buy a dependable car. So once she has the means to travel to LA for her modeling gigs, we plan on making some changes."

"What about your advance?" asked Heather.

"I won't have the money until sometime next year."

"I wanted to take her on tour with me," said Mike. "I certainly could have used her on the viola, and it would have given her some nice exposure as well. However, George wants to remaster the album she did with Shawn, so they'll be in the recording studio when I start the first leg of my tour."

"Hold on. Time out." Alberto looked at Tonya. "Have you signed any kind of agreement with him?"

"They're still working on my contract, which my manager will sign for me as my representative."

"Good to know, but I wasn't talking about your record contract. I'm asking about the agreement for you to rent a room in George's home. Did you sign any kind of lease?"

"No. It's a verbal agreement only."

Heather spoke up. "All I can tell you is whenever I have these kinds of dreams about your sister, she's never wrong. She says Mickey will help you break free of George. I have no idea what it means, and it may be nothing more than a concerned mother's worry."

Tonya took a deep breath and swallowed hard. "So did Annette say anything else?"

"No. She just said you need let go of Jesse, and Mickey will help you with George."

The kitchen timer went off. Mike quickly excused himself to check on the turkey. Heather joined him in the kitchen, asking if she could do anything to help.

"As a matter of fact, there is, so hang on a sec." He quickly glanced into the other room. Tonya was busy petting Maize and chatting with her stepfather.

"I've ordered a gold locket for Tonya for Christmas, so would you mind emailing me a photo of her sister to put inside it? She sometimes talks about Annette, and I know they were close."

"They were, and her death really hit Tonya hard. I also know how she feels. I lost my own sister as well. She was killed in a traffic accident, many years ago."

"Tonya has mentioned her aunt a few times, and I'm sorry for your loss. She's also told me about her cousin."

"We're all proud of Emily, and she's been very supportive of Tonya."

Heather began setting the table and everyone pitched in to help with the side dishes. The turkey came out perfectly, much to Mike's relief, and after the dishes were washed and put away, they all hopped into Alberto's Tahoe and drove to a nearby beach for a long after-dinner walk. As they strolled along the shore, Mike pointed out a large beach front house.

"That's where we filmed most of the video for *Aquamarine*."

"It looks like a beautiful home," said Heather.

"It was, and our friend here even thought it was my house." Tonya shrugged while Mike finished his story.

"It's actually a vacation rental and we were only there for the day. I'm just not into big mansions. In fact, I never set out to become famous.

I only auditioned for *American Rockstar* because my friends dared me to. I never expected anything to come of it, and being a so-called famous musician has its drawbacks. It's hard going anywhere in public, especially in the LA area, because everyone's on the lookout for celebrities."

"I'm not surprised," said Alberto, "and my advice to you would be to always be aware of your surroundings."

"You'd better believe I am, and whenever I'm away from LA I find it easier to blend in with the crowd. No one expects to see Mickey Lee Janson filling up his truck at a gas station in Tucson, and if they say anything I just shrug my shoulders and tell them some people think I look like him, but I don't see the resemblance. It ends the conversation pretty quickly."

"So, are you thinking of leaving California?"

"I am. The whole Hollywood scene has gotten old. I was a real party animal when I first came here, but waking up with in strange places with bad hangovers isn't much fun, and there are some real psycho bitches out there."

"As a homicide detective I can certainly vouch for that."

"Which is why I came to Santa Barbara. I wanted to put some distance between me and Hollywood. However, I don't plan on being here for the long term. Tonya keeps saying she wants to go back to Texas, so I guess we'll have to see what happens. In the meantime, we'll see if our mutual staff can arrange for her to join me on tour once her first album is complete."

"So, your sister was right about Mickey getting you away from George," said Heather

"We'll have to wait and see, Mom. Right now, we don't know for certain when I'll be in the recording studio. It may not be until after Mike's tour ends."

The sun was dipping low on the horizon, and it was nearly dark when they returned to Mike's home. He got his guitar while the others made themselves comfortable in the living room.

"I don't know if Tonya mentioned she sang the background in one of the songs on the *Aquamarine* album."

"She did," said Heather, "but she didn't think it would be released as a single."

"It probably won't, but it's still very special song because I wrote it for my mother. It's called, 'My Dear Cordelia.' So, whenever you're ready Tonya."

"Go for it."

They sang the song, and once it was over Heather was nearly moved to tears. "Such a beautiful song," she said. "I had a wonderful relationship with my father, but unfortunately not my mother."

Alberto checked his watch and announced it was time for them to leave. Mike walked outside with them, and as they said their goodbyes, he handed Heather an envelope.

"Can I open it now?" she asked.

"Of course."

Heather eagerly tore the envelope open. Inside were two front-row tickets for Mike's concert in Phoenix, along with backstage passes.

"Oh my god. I can't believe it." She quickly showed them to Alberto. "Thank you so much." She wrapped her arms around him and gave him a big squeeze. "We were planning on coming to the show, but you can never get the good seats through those ticket outlets."

"Because they're reserved for VIPs, such as yourselves. I'll email you a tour schedule, and please let me know if you can make it to any of the other shows." Mike gave Tonya a final hug and kissed her goodnight as her mother and stepfather climbed inside the Tahoe.

"I wish you could have stayed overnight," he said under his breath.

"Me too, and seriously, I want to thank you for giving them those tickets. You didn't have to you know."

"She's your mother." He gave her a final quick kiss. "I love you, Ms. Rose."

"I love you, too, Mr. Janson."

Mike opened the rear door and waited until she was safely inside. Everyone waved goodbye once Alberto put the truck in gear and slowly drove away.

"We'll drop you off at George's house," said Alberto.

"Did you want to come inside?" asked Tonya.

"It's probably best if we don't," said Heather. "The temptation to speak my mind may be too much, and I don't want to jeopardize your record contract."

"He's not a bad person, Mom."

"Maybe not, but I'm still not convinced he has your best interests at heart either. So, moving on. Alberto has to get back to work, so we're leaving in the morning, and I'd like for us to have breakfast together, assuming you don't have a photoshoot."

"I'd like that too, and don't worry, I don't have a photoshoot, although I have a gig tomorrow night and I'm sorry you'll have to miss it."

"Me too, but it's not every day I get to watch my daughter sing with Mickey Lee Janson."

❧FORTY-TWO❧

ALICORN HELD ITS annual Christmas party at the Waldorf Astoria Hotel rwo weeks later. All of their artists, along with other members of the Hollywood elite, were on the guest list. Tonya spent several days shopping for the perfect dress; a sparkly navy-blue floor-length gown with the sides split up to the hips. Mike, however, was unable to attend. He was scheduled to appear on a live television special from the Hollywood Bowl, where he would perform, "Aquamarine" and "Jingle Bell Rock." Tonya planned on watching the show the following morning on YouTube, and she would email him photos of her in the dress. Returning home from the beauty salon, she found George waiting in his tux, and he told her to pack an overnight bag.

"Are we going somewhere after the party?" she asked.

"You are, but I'm not."

She suddenly felt confused. "Come again?"

"As you know, we have an open relationship, and I plan on spending the weekend with an old friend."

"I see."

"So, you'll be staying at the hotel, with a good friend as well."

Tonya's heart leaped for joy. At long last, George was getting ready to cut her loose, and she would be spending the weekend with Mike.

"You need to get ready for the party," he said, "but first I have something for you." George presented her with an extravagant diamond pendant and a matching pair of diamond drop earrings. Tonya could hardly believe what she was seeing.

"I don't know what to say. They're absolutely beautiful, but I planned on wearing the aquamarine pendant I wore on Mickey's album cover, and I bought a pair of earrings to go with it."

"I know the aquamarine pendant has special meaning for you, which is why we wanted you to have it. However, this is a black-tie affair. You're about to become Alicorn's next big star, so you need the proper accessories. Besides, the jewelry isn't from me. It's a gift from one of your admirers."

"Who?"

"You'll find out later."

Tonya felt uneasy as George placed the pendant around her neck. Mike wasn't keen on flashy jewelry, nor would he have asked George to give her such an elaborate gift on his behalf. The diamonds had come from someone else, and she needed to find out who her mystery admirer was.

"There you go." George smiled as he handed her the earrings. "It looks beautiful on you, so go get ready. The limo will be here in an hour."

Tonya hurried down the hallway and jumped into the shower. Once she had her makeup on, she tossed a few items into her suitcase and put on her dress. Her outfit may have looked perfect, but she felt uneasy as she put on the diamond earrings.

Most of the guests had arrived when George escorted Tonya into the ballroom, and he immediately started making introductions. Afterwards excused himself and joined Mandy.

"Well, there you are," said a voice behind her. Tonya turned around and found herself face-to-face with Stanley Klein. He too looked handsome in his tuxedo, and she greeted him with a warm smile.

"You know, I was thinking about you the other day."

His face instantly lit up. "You were? Well, hopefully they were good thoughts."

"They were. We need to get together sometime soon to discuss my advance."

"Of course, but in the meantime, while Mandy's busy with George, I thought I'd keep you company. And by the way, your jewelry looks amazing."

"Thank you. You know my grandmother had an extensive jewelry collection."

"I remember you telling me about your grandmother, and I'm going to see to it you have just as nice of a collection as she had, if not nicer."

George walked up to the head table and announced dinner would soon be served. He took his seat in the center as the other Alicorn executives, along with their spouses and significant others, sat down with him. Stan escorted Tonya to their table and sat down between her and Mandy. Once again, Tonya felt relieved. It was another sign George would soon set her free.

As the waitstaff brought out the appetizers, George stood and thanked everyone for coming. He then raised his glass and toasted to Alicorn's continued success in the coming year. Over the meal, Mandy chatted with some of the other Alicorn artists at their table while Stan and Tonya got better acquainted. Both were the youngest child. Both had overbearing, matriarchal grandmothers, and as the chicken marsala was served, they both reminisced about their family holiday celebrations.

"Of course, we celebrated Hanukah instead of Christmas," said Stan, "but my parents liked to entertain at home on New Year's Eve, and my mother always prepared an elegant meal."

"My grandmother did the same on Christmas Eve, but she either had it catered, or she made reservations at an upscale restaurant. She wasn't big on spending her holiday in the kitchen."

Both Tonya and Mandy skipped dessert, and once the waitstaff cleared the tables The Gyros, one of Alicorn's top selling top rock bands, began playing. Many of the guests went out to the dance floor while Mandy excused herself and said goodnight. She left with George a short time later. Tonya looked at Stan, who seemed unconcerned as he invited Tonya to the dancefloor. Returning to their table, Tonya started searching for something in her evening bag.

"Well, that's strange. George said he reserved a room for me, but he didn't leave me the key."

"Don't worry. I have it."

"What?"

"It's okay, Tonya. If you're ready to call it a night, I'll take you up there."

"Hmm...I guess I must have been in the lady's room when he gave you my key." She grabbed her bag and Stan walked her out to the elevators. The doors opened on the tenth floor. He took her down the hallway and unlocked one of the guest rooms. Inside were two queen beds and a balcony with a stunning view of the city lights. Her bags, along with someone else's bags, had been placed inside.

"So, what's going on, Stan?"

He pulled out a chair at the table and told her to take a seat. "Would you like something to drink?"

"I'm fine. Would you please tell me what's going on?"

He took off his coat and bow tie and sat down in the other chair. "When you first met George, did he by chance tell you he was going to introduce you to his inner circle?"

"I'm not sure. I think he may have said something about introducing me to a whole new world. I assumed he was talking about my becoming a recording star."

"He was, but there's more to it."

Tonya was getting a bad feeling. "What do you mean?"

"I'll begin by saying you're a remarkable singer, but this town is full of remarkable singers."

Tonya was becoming annoyed. "I know. I heard the same line from George, not so long ago. He went on to tell me how he didn't have to do everything he's done for me, but he did, so now I owe him some favors in return."

"You do, and this is one of them. So, how can I put this delicately? Are you by chance familiar with the term, swinger?"

Tonya shook her head. "Not really. I assume it means people who like to party a lot."

"Well, sort of." He looked her in the eye. "It's also a lifestyle choice which George happens to subscribe to. It means partner swapping."

For the moment Tonya was too stunned to speak. Stan tried to reassure her.

"It's okay, Tonya. He's not into threesomes or orgies. He's simply not into monogamy. He believes in, as he puts it, sharing the love. No doubt he's already told you how sex isn't such a big deal in Europe, and we all agree it's something meant to be enjoyed"

Tonya finally found her voice. "He told me we had an open relationship, meaning we were free to see other people if we wished, but he never once said anything about this."

"Well, all I can tell you is I wasn't sure about it either at first, but I gave it a try, and it really is a lot of fun. We're more than happy to introduce it to you slowly, and don't worry. No one will ever force you to do anything against your will. We have our own set of rules, and it's at the top of the list."

"And what if I were to say no, I don't want any part of this? I met George shortly after I'd ended a long-term relationship, and against my better judgement, I agreed to have a rebound relationship with him. However, he assured me it would only be short-term and with no strings attached."

"Unfortunately, Tonya, you've become one of his favorite mistresses, just like Mandy became one of his favorites. And once you become one of his favorites, he expects to have access to you long after you've moved on to other people. So, while he's spending the weekend with my wife, he's arranged for me to spend the weekend with you. This is what is meant by sharing the love."

"I can't believe I'm hearing this."

"It's okay. I'm not going to force myself on you, so I wasn't planning on making love to you tonight, unless of course you really want me to. I also have big plans for us this weekend."

"Such as?"

He smiled. "I don't want to spoil the surprise, so you'll have to wait until tomorrow to find out what it is."

"Stan, I honestly like you, and had we met under different circumstances we could have been an item. However, I'm in love with someone else."

His tone softened and he looked genuinely sad. "Then I'm sorry to be the one who has to tell you this, but you need to let Mickey go. George only loaned you out to him as a reward for his first album's success. The two of you were never supposed to fall for one another."

Tonya's blood turned into ice. "Did Mickey know this?"

"No, he didn't. Mickey isn't in George's inner circle and he never will be. Only a very select few are invited."

"Really? Then why am I so lucky?"

"George bonded with you because you were a virgin, and he's never known anyone like you before. So, like Mandy, you'll be his mistress for many years to come. I also need to warn you that he's become very jealous of your relationship with Mickey."

"I know he has. He's all but forbidden me to have any further contact with him."

"Then I suggest you don't. George Monroe is a very powerful man, and anyone who dares to cross him pays a heavy price. I'm sorry, Tonya, but if you don't end your relationship with Mickey, his career could be in serious jeopardy."

Tonya watched Stan closely as he talked. He was telling her the truth.

"It really is best for all concerned,   and it needs to be done right away. I also hope you'll give me a chance because I'm ready to end it with Mandy. She's head over heels in love with George while you truly are special to me, and I'll see to it you want for nothing."

Tonya undid the diamond pendant and set it on the table. "So, I take it you're the one who gave this to me."

"I did, and it's yours to keep. There's also plenty more where it came from."

"Stan, I can't accept it. It's too much."

"Tonya, I'm a wealthy man, and I'll do whatever it takes to see to it you're taken care of for life. I also meant it when I said you're going to have an even better jewelry collection than your grandmother had, starting with the necklace and earrings." He reached across the table and squeezed her hand.

"It'll get better, I promise, so let's call it a night, and let me know which bed you want. I'll sleep in the other one." He helped her from her chair and carried her bag into the bathroom. She soon returned in her nightshirt and he grabbed a leather pouch.

"Let's see what we have in the pharmacy to help you get a good night's rest." Inside the bag was a collection of prescription drugs. He rifled through the contents and gave her a bottle.

"Here you go. Just take one. I guarantee you won't wake up groggy and you'll feel a whole lot better in the morning."

"Thanks, but no. I have some herbal sleeping remedies with me."

"Suit yourself, and I'll see you in the morning."

❧FORTY-THREE☙

TONYA WOKE UP to a dimly lit room. Somehow, she had managed to get a decent night's sleep. Stan slept soundly in the other bed. The sheets were pulled up to his waist, and his chest was covered with dark hair. She carefully tiptoed into the bathroom, but he began stirring when she returned to her bed.

"Morning sunshine. So, what's with the glasses?"

"I have an astigmatism," said Tonya. "It was time to take my contacts out."

"I understand. I wear contacts myself. So, how are you feeling this morning?"

"Okay, I guess."

He slowly sat up. "I'm glad, and as soon as I find the menu, we'll order room service."

Tonya held her breath as Stan turned on a lamp and pulled down the bed sheets. To her relief, he wore a pair of cotton briefs. The room service menu was next to the phone, and he brought it over to her.

"I think I'll to go with the Denver omelet," she said, "with orange juice and a side of fresh fruit."

"Sounds good. I'll have the same, but without the ham." He picked up the phone and placed their order. Afterwards he gave her a playful look. "It'll be here in thirty minutes, so we have enough time to take a shower. Would you care to join me?"

"I'm fine. I showered last night."

"Okay, but you're welcome to join me if you change your mind." He grabbed a change of clothes and hurried into the bathroom while Tonya quickly put on a pair of jeans with a button-down blouse. Stan returned as she switched on the coffee maker. He too wore jeans. As he took his laptop from his bag he gave her a smile.

"So, would you like to hear some good news?" he asked.

"Sure."

He set the computer on the table and started it up. "You're now in a position to buy a car, as long as you don't go overboard. I know you've been using rideshares, but they really are adding up."

"Must be because I'm getting more modeling work."

"You certainly are. I have a friend who's a manager at a Lexus dealership. We may be able to get you into something new if you don't mind doing without a lot of options. You're also in a town where many people buy a new car every year, so they get some nice trades-ins, and you may get a better deal on something used."

"I'm not into big and flashy. As long as it's dependable, I'm happy."

"Okay, so would you prefer a car or an SUV?"

"Either or. As long as it runs."

"Oh, they run all right, so let's see what we can find." After a few clicks on the mouse several vehicles appeared on the screen. "So, which one do you want to look at first?"

She smiled as something caught her eye. "The red one. Right there. No, not the SUV. The four-door sedan. It looks similar to my old car, but in a prettier color."

"Excellent choice. It's a year-old Honda Accord with some nice options, and it only has twelve thousand miles on it."

"Yeah, but look at the price. Can I afford it?"

He looked her in the eye. "You will by the time I'm done. So, anything else?"

"This little black SUV looks nice."

"Hmm…not bad. It's a Kia, but it doesn't have as many features as the Accord, and it has a lot higher milage."

Their breakfast arrived while they were browsing, and as they enjoyed their meal, Tonya found one more car she liked. After finishing her breakfast, she stepped away to put on her makeup while Stan made a phone call.

"I have good news and bad news," he said when she returned. "The blue Subaru sold last night, but the Accord and Kia are still there."

"I really like the Accord."

"I know you do, so they've put it on hold, which means we need to hurry up and get down there."

Tonya grabbed her purse and they ran out the door. Stan's friend, Julio, greeted them when they entered the showroom.

"Jermaine went to get the Honda," he said. "It's a sweet little car, and it has some really nice extras. A movie producer bought it for his daughter, but she decided to trade it in for something bigger."

Jermaine parked the car in front of the showroom. Tonya's hands were shaking as she slipped behind the wheel and adjusted the seat. Jermaine took the passenger seat while Stan hopped in the back. She took it for a long test drive, and when they returned to the dealership, she gave Stan a nod.

"Just sit tight," he said under his breath. "Let me handle it."

Julio invited them into his office, but once they got down to business Tonya gripped the sides of her chair as the two men haggled over the price. Finally, Julio gave in.

"Stan, you're killing me, but all right. We have a deal. I'll get started on the paperwork." As Julio stepped out to grab some forms, Tonya reached for her phone and started toward the door.

"Where are you going?" asked Stan.

"To take a picture of my new car so I can show it to my mother."

Once the last paper was signed, Julio shook Tonya's hand and presented her with the key fobs. The car, with its temporary license plate, waited at the curb next to the showroom. Stan opened the driver's side door and watched her get behind the wheel.

"I still can't believe this."

"Believe it," he said. "So, where to now?"

"I have no idea. At the moment, I'm completely overwhelmed."

"I'm sure you are. So, if I were to ask you what you'd like to go see, what's the first thing to pop into your head?"

"I don't know. My parents took me to San Diego when I was five. How far it is it from here?"

"Not too far," said Stan. "We should be able to get there in a couple of hours, but first we'll need to drop my car off at the hotel."

She checked her watch. "What about lunch?"

"We can stop somewhere along the way."

Ten minutes later Stan hopped into the passenger seat. As Tonya drove onto the southbound freeway, Stan looked at his phone. "Okay, there are some interesting things to do in San Diego. Would you like to go to SeaWorld or The San Diego Zoo?"

"Neither one. It's Saturday, and by the time we'd get there they'd be way too crowded."

"You're right." He punched a few more buttons. "Okay, there's Belmont Park. It's on the beach, and it has a mini amusement park with a wooden roller coaster."

"You know, that sounds vaguely familiar. I remember something about a roller coaster when my parents took us to the beach, but my dad said I was too little to ride it, which didn't go over well with my sister. He took Annette on the roller coaster while Mom took me on the merry-go-round. Then we spent the rest of the day on the beach."

"So would you like to go back there?"

"Sure," she said. "Maybe this time I'll get to ride the roller coaster."

Stan looked up the directions, but it was cool and breezy when they arrived, and the sky was mostly cloudy. Tonya shivered once they stepped out of the car.

"I'm not sure if my sweater will be warm enough."

"Fortunately, they have plenty of shops," said Stan, "and it looks like everything is open, so let's find you a warmer jacket."

The stores were all decked out with Christmas lights, and they hurried into the nearest one. Tonya soon found a navy-blue sweatshirt with the words, "San Diego," printed on the front. A teenage girl was working the register, and as Tonya set the sweatshirt on the counter, the girl gave her a strange look.

"I know who you are," she said bluntly. "You're Mickey Lee Janson's new girlfriend, and he's way too good for you."

Stan walked up to the counter with a pair of beach blankets and a sweatshirt for himself. "I've got it," he said.

"Are you sure?" asked Tonya.

"Positive." He gave the cashier a stern look as he handed her his credit card. She mumbled an apology and quickly bagged their items. Tonya felt relieved once they were safely outside.

"Thank you for stepping in. I wasn't sure what to do. I've never come across an irate fan before."

"It happens. Mandy's experienced it a few times herself. You really need to be aware of your surroundings."

"I know. Mickey told me the same thing."

Stan quickly changed the subject. "So which beach blanket do you prefer? The red and navy blue? Or the green and purple?"

"I'll take the purple one, but first I want to walk around the amusement park and see if it's like the way I remember it."

The line for the roller coaster was fairly short. Stan bought a pair of tickets, and the operator soon opened the gate and told them to board.

"Where would you like to sit?" asked Stan.

"Somewhere in the middle." Tonya spotted the perfect car, and Stan slid in next to her. She felt anxious as they slowly climbed to the top, and the butterflies roiled through her stomach as they took their first big drop and whipped around the track. Moments later the car came to a stop and they made their exit.

"How was it?" asked.

She smiled as she swept her hair away from her face. "Not bad. Not bad at all."

"Would you like to go again?"

"Maybe later. First, I want to see what else is here." As they wandered through more of the shops, a large pink queen conch seashell caught Tonya's eye.

"My mother would love this. I remember her buying a similar one when we were here before, but later on she had to put it in a yard sale because we needed the money. So, can I afford it?"

"You know, I wish more of my clients were as careful about their spending as you are. Yes, you can afford it. It's not as lavish as you think, and it's also marked down."

"Just checking." She carefully took the shell from the shelf and brought it to the register. This time the cashier was friendly and told her they would be happy to ship it for her.

The sun was peeking out from behind the clouds when they left the store, so Stan suggested they go out to the beach. Tonya pulled on her sweatshirt while Stan spread their blankets out on the sand. It was getting late in the day, and the partly cloudy skies made for a spectacular sunset. Afterwards, they found a restaurant with an oceanfront view. Stan checked his watch when he took care of the check. It was time for them to leave.

"I still can't believe this is my car." Tonya tossed her sweatshirt in the backseat and slipped behind the wheel. "This has been one of the happiest days of my life. Thank you, so much, for making it happen."

"You're welcome, and the pleasure is all mine."

Returning to the hotel, she pulled up to the curb and the valet handed her a claim slip. "Make sure you hang onto it," said Stan. "You'll need it to get your car in the morning.

"I know, Dad."

"Oh, getting sassy, are we?"

Tonya laughed as they entered the lobby, and she plopped herself down on her bed once they returned to their room. "I'm beat. I don't think I can move."

"It was an exciting day, and I'm glad we finally found you a car. You realize, of course, it also means you'll have to watch your spending until you get your advance."

"No problem. I've been watching my spending my entire life, and hopefully my advance will put me in a position to get my own place."

"By the way George is talking, you'll be living with him until well into the new year."

"I know, but I'm still anxious to move out."

Stan took his shoes off and grabbed the remote, channel surfing until he found an action movie. Tonya got up and took her nightclothes from her suitcase.

"Before I head off to the shower, I want to thank you, once again, for an amazing day." She gave him a hug, and afterwards he gently brushed a strand of hair away from her face.

"You're welcome." Looking into her eyes, he gently kissed her, stroking her back and sides, but she pulled away when he squeezed her breast.

"I can't. I'm in love with someone else."

"And I've already told you, you've unwittingly put Mickey in a dangerous place, so you have to end it with him, the sooner, the better. I'm also willing to take my time and court you properly." He gave her a leering grin. "Then, once you're ready, I'm going to make love to you until you're howling at the moon."

❧FORTY-FOUR❧

STAN TOLD TONYA goodbye while he waited for the valet to load his bags in his car. As he drove away another valet brought her car up to the curb. Driving to a nearby shopping center, she shut down the engine in a remote area of the parking lot, where she sat quietly and considered her next move.

She had to get away from George, even if it meant throwing her career away. It was a sacrifice she was willing to make, but not at the expense of ruining Mike's career along with hers. She took a deep breath and let out a long, sad sigh. There had to be a way out, but for the moment it eluded her, so she called Kurt's office and left him a voicemail. Hopefully, he could help. Before leaving, she sent Mike the photo of the car.

* * *

Mandy was curled up on the sofa, busily typing on her phone when Stan came in. "George wants to know when you're bringing Tonya home. So where is she?"

"I have no idea," said Stan. "We said goodbye in front of the hotel."

"Well, it's Sunday, and Christmas is only two weeks away, so I guess Uber must be really busy."

"I suppose." He stopped for a moment and gathered his thoughts before sitting down on a nearby chair.

"You and I need to have a serious talk."

"As soon as I finish my message to George. I'm letting him know Tonya is on her way." She hit the send button and set her phone on the coffee table with a thump.

"All right. So, what's so earth shattering?"

"I'd like for us to start the new year with a clean slate."

"Meaning?"

"Meaning it's time for us to end this sham marriage and go our separate ways."

"Sounds like you and Tonya must have really hit it off."

"Maybe, but it's beside the point," he said. "George got us together because the tabloids were making you and him out to be a serious couple."

"Yeah, but you were willing to go along with it."

"Only because I was getting over a messy divorce, and joining the club sounded like fun. Unfortunately, we're just not a good match. It'd be one thing if we had enough in common to at least be friends, but we don't. We're as different as night and day."

Mandy studied his face for a moment. "Maybe so. However, Tonya is in love with Mickey, and he's in love with her, so I'm trying to convince George to cut her loose. You may recall me talking with Mickey at Tonya's gig. I honestly like him, and I think he and Tonya are good for one another. I know I'm not the nicest person around, but just this once I'd like to do the right thing and help them out."

"As well as get her away from George."

"That too," she said.

"Then I guess we'll have to see how it all works out, but in the meantime, neither of us is happy with our current living arrangements."

"No, we're not. However, George wants us to stay together for appearance's sake, and divorces, as you know, can be costly."

"Yes, they can, but your career is finally taking off, thanks to George. You don't need me to pay the bills, and you can keep the house. I don't want the upkeep, and I'm sure I can find a nice condo somewhere."

"Well, Stan, if it were up to me, I'd say sure, but you know damn well George won't allow anything which could create a scandal, such as you leaving me because he's the other man."

He looked her in the eye. "Which is where Tonya comes in. We drove down to San Diego yesterday, and while were walking around, we noticed people taking pictures of us with their phones. No doubt they're posted all over social media by now. Therefore, you're not leaving me for George. I left you because I found someone else."

"And what about Mickey?"

"He'll soon be out of the picture. George called me the other day about another client, and Tonya's name came up in the conversation. He's going to force her to end it with Mickey."

Mandy's face turned sad. "Then I'm genuinely sorry to hear it, but it doesn't mean you'll end up with her either."

"It all remains to be seen."

"Well, Stan, you're right about one thing. I'm just as unhappy as you are. However, I won't agree to a divorce. They're public record, and I don't want the tabloids sticking their noses into my private affairs. Then again, no one would be the wiser if you were to buy yourself a condo somewhere and move into it when no one's looking, would they?"

Finally, he smiled. "No, they wouldn't. I'll start looking for a new place tomorrow morning, and I'll only take my personal belongings with me when I go. You can keep the dishes and the furniture, and then George can come over whenever he wants. In the meantime, I'm moving into the guest room."

* * *

Tonya took a deep breath as she parked in front of George's house. Grabbing her bags, she rushed inside and said a quick hello as she hurried down the hallway. George stepped into the guestroom as she dropped her bags on the bed.

"I was getting worried," he said.

"I'm fine. I need to bring a few more things inside, then I need to spend some time working on my music. Later on, when you have the time, I need to talk to you about something."

Tonya started toward the doorway, but George blocked her path. "What did you want to talk about?"

"I don't think I can handle being a member of your club."

"Why? Did Stan force you to do something you didn't want to do?"

"No. Quite the opposite. He was a perfect gentleman."

"Then I'm relieved to hear it." George sat down on the bed. "As you know, I like variety. A few years ago, I got together with some likeminded friends, and we created our own private club so we could spend quality time with one another's partners in an open and upfront way."

Tonya was stunned. George had hidden this side of himself remarkably well.

"We also created some strict guidelines. First, when the weekend's over, it's over. We return home, no questions asked. Second, no one can force their visiting partner to do anything they don't want to do."

"I know. Stan explained it all to me, but it still came as a complete shock."

"Tonya, I considered telling you about it, but I knew you wouldn't understand, so I decided I'd let you experience it firsthand for yourself. So, did Stan do anything to make you feel unsafe or uncomfortable?"

"No, he didn't. He asked if—"

"It's okay. There's no need to explain. The point is you had nothing to worry about. If you wanted to make love, you could have made love. No one would have gotten jealous, and there would have been no strings attached. Whatever you choose to do is between the two of you and no one else. However, as a personal favor to me, I would like for you to give it a try the next time. You don't have to have intercourse, but there would certainly be no harm in some heavy petting, would there?"

"And when is the next time?"

"I haven't decided yet. Right now, I want you to focus on your first album. I'll let you know when."

Tonya nodded and started toward the door.

"Where are you going?" he asked.

"To get the rest of my things."

"Then let me help you." George followed her outside. He was surprised to see the little red sedan.

"What do we have here?"

"Stan took me car shopping and he negotiated the deal."

"As well he should have, so I'm giving you the other garage remote. I don't want you parking it out on the street. Does anything else need to go inside?"

"Just this." Tonya handed George her sweatshirt and beach blanket. Once again, he looked surprised.

"You went to San Diego?"

"We did. I haven't been there since I was a kid."

"I see. I haven't spent much time there either, so perhaps we'll go there to celebrate the completion of your first album. We'll make a weekend of it."

George took her things inside, and after she moved her car into the garage, she hurried to the music room where she checked her messages. Mike was thrilled about the new car.

"Now you can finally move out of George's house. We'll talk more about it over Christmas."

She quickly typed a reply. *"Of course. What about the new house?"*

"I flew to Dallas yesterday morning to see it in person. The photos don't do it justice, so check your email. I shot a video. Do you want me to make an offer?"

"Hold on. Let me see the video." She clicked on her email, and a big smile broke out across her face as she watched the video. Mike made jokes and as he showed her around, but the house itself was perfect. She quickly sent him another message.

"I love it, so let's go for it. Did you meet with Shawn?"

He responded a minute later. *"Sure did. He'll call you tomorrow and fill you in."*

"Awesome. Are you back yet?"

"On my way. My flight leaves in about forty-five minutes."

Tonya sighed in relief. It all went according to plan, she would soon be back in Texas for good, and Mike would be waiting for her there. Putting on her headphones, she plugged her guitar into her laptop. It was after sundown when she finally shut down her computer, but George's mood turned serious when she came into the living room.

"Is anything wrong?" she asked.

"We have the early ratings for the live TV special Mickey appeared on. It was number one in all the major markets, and it appears to have given his sales a boost. While we can't be certain just yet, all the signs are indicating that *Aquamarine* will be even more successful than his first album."

"Which is fantastic news. Thanks for letting me know."

"I take it you want him to continue being successful."

She gave him a strange look. "Well, of course I want him to be successful."

"You know, Tonya, sometimes the best way to help someone is to back away from them."

Her heart skipped a beat. "We've already had this discussion. I haven't seen Mike in weeks, but we're still supportive of each other's music. He's also the one who connected me with Kurt and the others."

"I know he did, and while they're all good at what they do, I had other people in mind for you."

"I'm sorry. I had no idea. I don't think he meant to step on anyone's toes."

"You have nothing to apologize for. However, intentional or not, Mickey interfered with my plans." George looked her in the eye. "Are you familiar with the old adage about too many cooks spoiling the broth?"

"Yes, although here we say spoil the soup."

"Either way, it means when too many people are involved with something, the result won't be as good, and in this instance you, my dear, are the something. As you know, Mickey has done quite well with Alicorn, and up to now, he and I have had an excellent business relationship. I'd like very much for him to continue having a good relationship with us, and the best way for it to happen would be for you to walk away from him for good."

Tonya's heart dropped into her stomach. "What do you mean?"

"What I'm saying is I have big plans for you, and they don't include Mickey, so if he continues to interfere, there could be some serious repercussions."

His words chilled Tonya to the bone.

"Of course, it would be a painful decision for me to have to make, but should it become necessary, I'll have no choice." He gave her a cold look. "Mickey has too much influence over you, and I've invested too much in you to allow anyone to interfere with my plans, so what happens next is entirely up to you."

Tonya fought to keep the tremor in her voice down. "What are you trying to tell me?"

His response was blunt. "I just told you. I have big plans for you, but they don't include Mickey, and it would be very sad indeed if his career were to unexpectedly suffer. You're a smart woman. I think you can draw your own conclusions and make the right decision." His mood quickly softened.

"It's like I told you before. Your life is about to change. You're going to be meeting a lot of men, and in all honesty, you haven't had much experience when it comes to men. You were engaged to your first real boyfriend, and Mickey came along right after Evan. There are plenty of men out there for you to pick and choose from, and you need to start meeting them. And in my humble opinion, you'd be wise in pursuing a relationship with Stan."

"He's married," she said, firmly.

"He's also a member of our club, and he intends to do whatever he can to ensure your financial success so you will never, ever have to worry about paying your bills again."

"I know. He already told me, and I'm grateful for everything he's done."

"He's also given you some lavish gifts, and he intends to give you more, so the next time you see him, I expect you to thank him properly, if you know what I mean."

❧FORTY-FIVE☙

SHAWN CALLED TONYA the following morning. "Are you sitting down?" he asked. "Because I have big news. Mike called me, so I invited him over, and we had a long talk. He's impressed with me as a musician and he says I have what it takes to make it in this business. He also wants me to go on tour with him."

"Are you serious?"

"Yes, I'm serious. His people are arranging it as we speak. Don't worry. I'm still coming to LA to record the new tracks for *Between Us Friends,* but as soon as we're done, I'm joining Mike on tour."

"Shawn, this is fantastic news, and I'm genuinely happy for you. Maybe a little jealous too, but what about school?"

"I spoke to one of my professors this morning. He said it's too good of an opportunity to pass up, and I can always come back and finish my degree later. In the meantime, how's everything going with you?"

"I'm working on more material for my album. The one after *Between Us Friends.*"

"I have the file you sent me yesterday and we'll go over it in a minute, but I can tell something's bothering you, so what is it?"

"I'm not sure where to begin," she said. "I got together with Stan. He's my business manager, and we went car shopping."

"What'd you find?"

"A slightly used red Honda Accord. It's sitting in the garage."

"I'm glad. Jacque and I have been concerned for some time about some of the things going on with George, so now you can leave."

"If only I could. As much as I needed the car, buying it has set me back financially, and I won't be getting my advance right away, which means I'm stuck here a little while longer."

Shawn sounded disappointed. "Well, okay, I guess. You've managed to hang on this long, so hopefully you'll be okay for a few more weeks."

"I'm not so sure. George and I had a long talk last night, and I saw a side of him I've never seen before. He's now micromanaging every aspect of my life, including who I can and cannot associate with."

Shawn took an angry tone. "Which is crap. No one can do that."

"Unfortunately, he can. If I don't do what he tells me to, he'll sabotage Mike's career. I also have to cease all contact with him, or else."

"What? That's crazy. George is making a lot of money off of Mike."

"I know he is, but he's also extremely jealous of my relationship with Mike. I've been warned, by people in the know, about just how powerful of a man George Monroe really is. Things don't end well for those who dare to cross him."

"Does Mike know about this?" asked Shawn.

"No. George dropped this little bombshell on me last night. However, I'm seeing Kurt later this afternoon. Hopefully, he can help me find a way to get out of this nightmare."

"I hope so too, but I'm still worried about you, so please keep me posted, and if you have a real emergency, I want you to call me right away."

"I will. I promise."

"I'm also more than happy to be a go between for you and Mike if you need it."

Tonya felt relieved. "Thanks, Shawn. I'm more than happy to accept your offer. Just make sure you text me before you call. We can't talk if George is here."

"Obviously. So, what about the holidays? Will George still be in England?"

"Yes, he will, but unfortunately, all it takes is one person to snap a photo of Mike and me together and post it online, even if we're in Texas, and his career is finished. Alicorn closely monitors social media posts about their artists, so I can't take the chance. This means I'll have to cancel the room at the Weston Galleria. There are no words to describe how heartbroken I am."

"Hey, it's like I told you before. George can't do this, and if it comes down to it, you'll have to hire a lawyer. I'll be more than happy to help chip in on the cost, and I'm sure Jacque will be too."

* * *

Kurt looked concerned as he motioned for Tonya to take a seat. "I don't mean to sound rude, but you look like hell."

"Because I feel like hell," said Tonya.

"Are you okay?"

"Physically, I'm fine. Mentally and emotionally, not so much."

"What happened?"

"I'm not sure where to begin."

"It's okay. Take your time."

Tonya took a moment to gather her thoughts. "It turns out all the rumors and allegations about George Monroe are true, and then some. He's more than just a lady's man. He's into partner swapping, or swinging, or whatever the hell you want to call it. I think of it as glorified pimping myself. Friday night was Alicorn's holiday party and—"

"Yes, I know. My wife and I were there."

"That's right. We even talked a little."

"We did. So did something happen at the party?"

"I'm afraid something did. George told me to pack an overnight bag. I figured we were making a weekend of it, but I was only half right. He took Mandy home with him, while I spent the weekend at the hotel with her husband, Stanley Klein."

For a moment, Kurt looked astonished. "Isn't he also your business manager?"

"He is, and in all fairness, he was a perfect gentleman, but it still came as a total shock. Both he and George assured me no one would ever force me to do anything I didn't want to do. However—"

"However, they still expected you to fully participate, didn't they?"

She looked down at the floor and nodded. "Yes. At least George did."

"Tonya, they can't force you to do anything without your consent. If they did, it would be considered rape, and if I were to find out about it, whoever forced you would be in deep, deep shit."

"Unfortunately, it's not so simple. Next time, I either go along with it, or someone's career gets ruined."

Kurt looked concerned. "Whose career are we talking about?"

"George knew I'd walk away from everything before I allowed him to loan me out to his friends, but he also knows my Achilles heel. I either do as I'm told, or Mike's career comes to a sudden end." She took a deep breath and sighed. "So now my dream has become my biggest nightmare."

"Tonya, I happen to know some pretty good attorneys, so as soon as we're done, I'm making some phone calls. I promise you, we'll take care of Mike, and I'll see to it nothing happens to you either. You have too much going for you to walk away, and Hagerman would still love to sign you on. Mike too, but right now I'm more concerned about your personal safety."

"I'm fine. I'm not in any physical danger. At least not at the moment."

"You're sure about that?"

"I'm positive. George tells me my next, shall we say, club meeting, won't be any time soon. It sounds like it won't be until sometime next spring. What we need to do now is figure out a way to stop him from hurting Mike. Then, I'll leave as soon as it's safe for me to do so. In the meantime, Stanley Klein has taken a personal interest in me, but he also says he intends to court me properly, so he's invited me to lunch on Wednesday."

"Where are you meeting him? And what time?"

"Mr. Chow's. In Beverly Hills. At one o'clock."

"Then I'm coming with you. I know Stanley Klein. He works with some of my other clients, and I need to discuss your advance with him anyway, so I have a legitimate reason to tag along. If George says anything to you later on, you can tell him the same thing. However, starting today, you don't meet with him, or anyone else George knows, unless Bailey or I go with you."

* * *

Kurt walked Tonya out to her car and congratulated her on her purchase. Returning to his desk, he sent Mike an urgent message to call him right away. He didn't have to wait long.

"What's up?" asked Mike.

"I hope you're sitting down, because we have a serious problem regarding Tonya."

"What kind of a problem?"

"We need to get her away from George, as quickly as possible. He's trying to force her into doing sexual favors for other men at his request. If she refuses, he says he'll damage your career."

"If he thinks I'll allow anyone to rape her, then I'll put the son of a bitch out of his misery right here and now."

"Hold up there, Mike, and listen to me. Over the years, George has abruptly broken contracts with other artists, claiming they were too difficult to work with. Some were able to recover, but others weren't so lucky."

"Then let me make myself crystal clear. There are some things which are a hell of a lot more important to me than a damn music career. I'll quit the business right now and go open a bar and grill somewhere."

"Mike, you need to take a deep breath and calm down before you do anything rash. If you quit abruptly, it might make things worse for Tonya. We need to discuss this rationally."

"Okay, give me a moment."

"Take your time. Do you want me to call you back in a few minutes?"

"No, I'm fine." Mike took a deep breath sighed loudly. "You know, deep down, I had a feeling something like this might happen, so I already had a plan in mind. I was just hoping I wouldn't have to use it."

"All right, so would you mind filling me in?" Kurt listened closely as Mike talked. "I like the way you think, and it just may work. And if George says anything, which I know he will, I'll tell him I didn't know anything about it either. However, you may be in for a bumpy ride."

"Yeah, but it's nothing I can't handle. I also need to call Tonya before George gets home."

"Then you'd better do it quickly, and after you're done, I'm your go-between."

"Kurt you will always have my unending gratitude. You have no idea how much I appreciate you going the extra mile for us."

"I have my own reasons too," he said. "If the two of you were to quit the business, I wouldn't make any money."

***

Tonya's phone rang as she was driving home. Pushing the button, a familiar voice came through the car speaker.

"I just got off the phone with Kurt. Are you okay?"

"Not really."

"Remember your mother saying your sister told her in a dream about how I had a plan for getting you away from George?"

"Yes."

"Well, your sister was right. I do have a plan, and the other night I had a weird dream myself. I didn't actually see Annette, but it felt like I was being told the time had come for me to act. I woke up the next morning thinking it was because I was going to Dallas to look at the house, which, by the way, they accepted my offer on."

"They did? Oh, thank goodness. It's the best news I've heard all day."

"It is, but I was about to tell you the reason why I didn't say anything on Thanksgiving was because I didn't want to upset your mother. I was also hoping I'd never have to use it."

Tonya started feeling scared. "No. Please. Whatever it is, I'm begging you. Don't do it."

His reaction was equally firm. "Hell will freeze over before I allow him to turn you into a call girl. I'm going to get you away from him. You have my word on it, and hopefully, it won't take long. So, here's what I want you to do. I want you to tell George we ended it. Then I want you to keep working on your music, and I want you to do whatever you have to do to keep yourself safe."

"I understand."

"Good. If some sort of unexpected emergency comes up, and you need to contact me, call Kurt. He'll relay the message to me, but please, only if it's really urgent."

"I spoke to Shawn this morning. He's also volunteered to be a go-between, and I'm grateful the two of you finally connected."

"Me too. He's a hell of good musician, and he'll be a real asset on the tour, but back to the topic at hand. The less you know about what I'm up to, the better. That way, when George starts questioning you, you can honestly tell him you don't know."

"Okay."

"We're going to get through this. I just don't know how long it will take. So, until then, remember, I love you."

"I love you too, Mike, and I'll do whatever it takes to stop him from ruining your career."

"He won't, and the less you worry about me, the better. Over and out."

The call abruptly ended and the music resumed playing. Tonya felt completely numb when she returned home. To her relief, George believed her when she told him she and Mike had ended things.

❧FORTY-SIX❧

AS PROMISED, KURT came along when Tonya met Stan for lunch. To her surprise, Stan was expecting him, and the three had a productive meeting. Tonya would soon receive her advance, and they both wanted to be sure she remained financially solvent, even if her career only lasted for a short time.

"Somehow, I don't think we have anything to worry about there," said Kurt. "If the public warms up to her the way I expect they will, she'll be a pop star for many years to come."

"She's also doing well as a glamour model," said Stan, "and Tonya, I recommend continuing with it for the foreseeable future. You've built up a following and you're starting to make good money."

"And I enjoy doing it," said Tonya.

"You certainly have sex appeal," said Kurt, "and I mean it in the most respectful way. You're not trashy. You're like the girl next door who's not afraid to go out and get what she wants without apologizing for it."

Stan looked at his watch. "And while I hate to cut things short, I have to go meet another client. Kurt, good seeing you."

"Likewise, and we'll talk soon."

"I call you, Tonya." He gave her a quick wink as he stepped away.

* * *

Tonya's stomach twisted in a knot when she heard George come inside the house. To her relief, he appeared to be in a pleasant mood.

"I hear Kurt joined you and Stan for lunch, and the three of you discussed your advance."

"We did."

"I'm glad. You'll soon be receiving a substantial sum of money, and it was smart thinking to give Stan a head's up on how to best invest it. And speaking of Stan; I just found out he and Mandy have separated. Did you know anything about this?"

"No, I didn't. Are they getting a divorce?"

George shook his head. "No. A divorce would cost both of them a lot of money. However, he and I had a business agreement. He agreed to marry Mandy as a cover for me, and in exchange, I've referred him as a business manager for all of Alicorn's artists."

"I understand, but if he and Mandy aren't happy then they shouldn't be living together, and if they're not getting a divorce then how would the tabloids find out about it?"

He gave her a look. "You'd be surprised."

"Tell me about it, but so far as I know neither of them have a jealous ex stirring up trouble."

"No, but he's out shopping for a condominium."

"Which some people buy as investment properties. My late grandmother owned several. Besides, Stan's not a celebrity. He doesn't have to worry about the paparazzi following him around."

"No, but you do, so be sure to keep an eye out the next time you see him."

"Which won't be until after the holidays. I'm going to Texas next week, remember?"

He suddenly looked sheepish. "You're right, and I'll be in Manchester as well. So, have you started your Christmas shopping yet?"

"A little. I found something for my mother while I was in San Diego, but I haven't had a chance to get anything for Shawn and Jacque, so I'll shop for them when I get to Texas."

"Assuming you'd have time, and I still need to shop for some of my family as well, so why don't we change into something more casual, and we'll take care of our shopping this evening. Then, when we're done, we'll go back to Casa Vega."

* * *

Two days later George carried Tonya's bag out to her car, waiting patiently as she loaded her guitar.

"That's it. Hopefully my car will be okay in the long-term parking lot."

"It'll be fine," said George. "You'll only be gone a few days."

"And you're still leaving tonight?"

"I'm going straight to the airport from the office. So have a safe trip, and Happy Christmas. I'll see you next year." He gave her a goodbye kiss and waved as she drove away.

Shawn met her at their usual rendezvous spot in the baggage claim at the Dallas Fort Worth Airport. To her relief, her guitar arrived safe and sound. Shawn and Jacque were living in the same apartment complex as before, but they now had a bigger apartment. Jacque greeted her with a warm hug as they came inside, and Tonya immediately spotted the Christmas tree. There were a few presents underneath it, and she would add hers as soon as she unpacked. Her old chocolate-colored sofa sleeper was next to the tree, and it appeared to have been well cared for.

"Neither of us has much time for watching TV," said Shawn, "so we don't use your old sofa too often."

"I see," said Tonya, "and Jacque, I'm sorry for cutting your time together short."

"It's okay. Duty calls, and I have to work on New Year's Eve as well. I also know weird hours and separations came with the territory of being with a musician, although it took me some time to accept it."

"I'm glad the two of you were able work it out."

"Us too," said Shawn.

"I hope it works out with me and Mike as well, but I don't want to talk about it. I just want to enjoy Christmas."

Tonya watched as Shawn and Jacque giving each other knowing looks. Perhaps Mike's plan was working. The conversation turned to other topics as Shawn and Jacque brought her up to date on their other friends. Tiffany and Bobby were officially engaged while Justin and Briana had gone their separate ways. Nathan and Rob had new girlfriends, and Rob appeared to be getting serious with his.

"Which pretty much leaves Jacob as the last confirmed bachelor in the group," said Jacque. "He'll be starting law school in Arizona next fall, so he's in no hurry. Briana and I have gotten closer as friends, and it looks like she and Justin may be working things out, so we're all keeping our fingers crossed. She also told me to tell you hello."

"And please tell her I said hello back," said Tonya. "So, I take it no one's heard from the two notorious ex-members."

"Not a word," said Jacque. "So far as I know, Becca is still in Oklahoma."

"And Evan burned whatever bridges he may have had left when he started talking to the tabloids," said Shawn. "I'm sure by now he knows it would be best to avoid all of us, and we're all relieved you got away from him."

"Me too."

Tonya spent the next few days jamming with Shawn and helping Jacque with her last-minute shopping. Christmas Eve was spent baking pies, and on Christmas morning the three drove to Arlington to have breakfast with Shawn's family. Returning to the apartment, Tonya and Jacque prepared a lemon chicken dinner, but both Shawn and Jacque were acting strange over the meal.

"C'mon you guys," said Tonya. "I can tell you're hiding something, so you all can stop acting innocent. What's going on?"

"Nothing," said Shawn.

"Uh-huh," said an unconvinced Tonya. Someone knocked at the door. Shawn quickly hopped up to answer it.

"I see you finally made it."

"Yeah," said a familiar voice. "Although we had a slight delay getting out of Birmingham."

Mike had barely stepped inside when Tonya rushed up to him. As they wrapped their arms around each other she suddenly burst into tears.

"Hmm…this isn't quite the reaction I was hoping for."

"I'm fine." Tonya squeezed him again. "I just wasn't expecting this."

"Don't worry, Mike. It's happened before," said Shawn. "The last time was right after she threw a bra into Becca's soup."

"Say what?"

"The little bitch had it coming," said Tonya. "I'll fill you in later."

Shawn smiled at the memory. "It was an unforgettable moment. We also saved you a chicken leg and there's plenty of other fixings, so go grab yourself a plate while Jacque and I pack our bags."

"What's going on?" asked Tonya.

"Jacque and I booked your room at the Westin Galleria after you cancelled it. She and I are going to enjoy a little quality time together before I leave. You and Mike will be safe from the public here."

"I'll only be here for thirty-six hours," said Mike. "Then I have to leave for New York. I'm appearing on a New Year's Eve special at Times Square."

"I know you are," said Tonya, "and Shawn and I have a gig in Beverly Hills."

Shawn and Jacque excused themselves to pack their bags. Ten minutes later they were out the door.

"Are you okay?" asked Mike.

"I'm doing as well as can be expected. How 'bout you?"

"The same." He stopped and gave her a smug grin. "So, what's this about a bra throwing incident?"

"I was aiming for her face, but my throw was a little short." Mike grabbed a plate and had a good laugh as Tonya told him the story. After dessert, he helped with the cleanup. Once the last pan was dried and put away, they curled up on the sofa.

"This was my bed in my old apartment, and it's surprisingly comfortable. Shawn bought it from me when I went to LA. I was broke at the time and needed the money for gas." She picked up the remaining present from under the tree.

"I was going to leave this here so Shawn could give it to you."

Mike took a small gift box from his bag and handed it to her. "This is for you, Ms. Rose, and Merry Christmas. I want you to open it first."

He handed her the box and she gave it a shake. "Hmm…it rattles."

"Just open it."

"Okay, okay." She carefully tore off the paper and lifted the lid. Inside was a gold, heart-shaped locket.

"Mike, it's beautiful." She took it from the box and gave it a closer look.

"And let me show you something." He opened the locket. Inside was a laser cut portrait of Annette. "Now you'll always have your sister with you."

"Oh my god! I don't know how to thank you. It's the best present anyone's ever given me."

"Want me to help you put it on?"

"Please do, and I'm never taking it off unless I have to for a photo shoot. Then I'm putting it right back on."

"Just remember, if anyone asks, Shawn and Jacque gave it to you."

"Of course."

Once the locket was secure, she handed him his gift. "I'm afraid my gift to you isn't quite as elaborate."

"It doesn't matter. It came from you, which is all I care about."

Unlike Tonya, Mike ripped the paper off. Inside was a framed photo.

"Now that's hot," he said.

"I thought you might like it. Julianna shot it when I first signed on with the agency, and going topless was her idea."

"It's a beautiful shot. However, my mother will be helping me move, so I'll have to hide it where she can't find it."

"Oh c'mon. It's not that bad."

"No, it's not," he said, "but the look on your face right now is priceless. Let's pull out this sofa and make ourselves more comfortable."

"Mike Jablonski, I'm shocked. Shocked I tell you. Are you saying you want to make love to me in front of the Christmas tree?"

"You'd better believe it, because being here with you is the best Christmas present I could have ever wished for."

✤FORTY-SEVEN✤

MIKE HELD TONYA close after they made love for the last time. "This is it," he finally said. "The limo will pick me up in about forty-five minutes."

"I know. The last thirty-six hours came and went much too fast."

"They sure did." He began stroking her hair. "I wish I could tell you when I'll see you again, but I have no crystal ball."

"Neither do I, unfortunately."

"I want it to work out for us, Ms. Rose. I want it more than anything, but at the moment I can't make any promises. I also want you to know I was willing to quit the business, but Kurt thought doing so might make things worse for you."

"It could've made things worse for both of us, and I don't want you quitting your career. You've worked hard to get to the top, and you can't walk away now."

He gazed into her eyes as he stroked her hair. "You're far more important to me. So, while I'm working behind the scenes, I want you to keep working on your own album, and don't worry about me."

"I'll be fine, Mike. I promise."

He gave her a long, lingering squeeze and hurried off to the shower. Once his bag was packed, they cuddled on the sofa until his phone beeped. His limo had arrived, right on time.

"I love you, Ms. Rose. So, until we meet again." He picked up his bag and gave her a farewell kiss. Seconds later he was out the door. Somehow Tonya managed to hold back her tears until after she locked the door behind him. Her eyes were still a little swollen when Shawn and Jacque returned.

"You okay?" asked Shawn.

"Yeah, I'm fine. I'm just a little weepy today." She nodded toward the freshly folded sheets on the sofa. "After Mike left, I got some laundry done. Keeping busy seems to help."

"What a beautiful locket," said Jacque. "Did Mike give it to you?"

"He sure did, and look at this." Tonya opened the locket so her friends could see Annette's portrait inside.

"Now he's definitely a keeper," said Jacque.

"I think so too. I just hope it works out for us."

"It will," said Shawn, firmly. "So, are you ready to go?"

"Yes."

"Then give me a few minutes to repack my bag. When is the shuttle coming?"

"In about thirty minutes, so the three of us have time to have a last cup of coffee together."

* * *

The hotel ballroom was packed with New Year's Eve revelers. Among them were Stanley Klein and Mandy West. No doubt George had insisted they attend, and during a break Mandy approached Tonya in the ladies' room.

"Nice show." Mandy kept her eyes glued to the mirror while she touched up her makeup. "And your dress is stunning. Red is certainly your color, and you and Shawn have a nice chemistry together."

Tonya remained on guard as she grabbed her lipstick. "Shawn and I are old friends. We've been working together for some time."

"So, I hear." Mandy lowered her voice. "Although you and Mike are a great couple."

Tonya also spoke in a hushed tone. "Not anymore. You know who put a stop to it."

"For now, but it won't be for long if I have anything to say about it. I told our mutual friend you'd never fit in with our inner circle, and I'm going to keep reminding him until he realizes it for himself and sets you free. So, hang in there. I'm on your side." She dropped her compact back into her purse and spoke in her normal voice.

"Happy New Year."

Mandy stepped out, but it took Tonya a moment to gather her thoughts and refocus on her gig. Checking her watch, she hurried out of the lady's room.

"Well, you certainly look happier," said Shawn.

"Turns out I have a friend I didn't know I had."

"You'll have to fill me in later. It's going on midnight, so let's make this next set count." They watched the clock as they played. It was less than a minute before midnight when they finished their final song for the year. Shawn took the mic and began leading the countdown. Balloons and confetti were released at the stroke of midnight and he gave Tonya a hug.

"Happy New Year. It's all going to work out. I have it on the highest authority." They began playing, "Auld Lang Syne," and the audience

224

sang along. Afterwards, they resumed their set as a few people began leaving. An hour later they said goodnight. As the last of the partygoers left the room, the hotel staff began clearing the remaining tables. Shawn and Tonya were packing up their gear when one of the servers brought them a take-out bag.

"Happy New Year," he said.

"Happy New Year to you as well," said Tonya, "and thank you for thinking of us."

"My pleasure. By the way, I'm a part-time musician myself, and you guys are fantastic."

Shawn and Tonya had adjoining suites on one of the upper floors. After changing into his sweats, Shawn tapped on Tonya's door and came in with their food.

"They gave us sandwiches and salads," he said. "One is roast beef; the other is turkey."

"You can have the roast beef." Tonya sat down at the table and kicked off her shoes. "What a night. Great gig, but not easy when you're wearing high heels."

"I don't envy you, although I'm glad to be out of the monkey suit" Shawn took out his phone as he sat down. "Jacque says Happy New Year. She had a busy night and she made a boatload of tips."

"Wasn't tonight her last night?"

"It was. She's taking a few days off. Then she starts an office job with regular hours."

"I'll bet she's looking forward to it."

"She is, and we have a message from another mutual friend. It's a short video he shot in his hotel room. Take a look."

"Hey, you guys," said a tired looking Mike. "It's been a long day, but I got the live performance done. So, before I crash, I want to wish you both a Happy New Year, and with any luck, Ms. Rose, we'll be together next New Year's Eve."

"I sure hope so," said Tonya.

"It'll happen." Shawn took a bite of his sandwich. "Wow. This isn't bad, and it sure hits the spot. As soon as I'm done, I'm hitting the rack."

"Me too."

"Maybe tomorrow we can go to the beach. I haven't been to the ocean in years."

She gave him a smile. "I think it can be arranged."

❧FORTY-EIGHT❧

SHAWN AND TONYA recorded the new tracks for *Between Us Friends* the following week. Kurt stopped by during their final session. He, too, wanted to meet Shawn, and afterwards he invited them to dinner.

"It's been a good, productive trip," Shawn said as they took their seats. "Tomorrow morning I'm flying to Miami to join Mike's tour."

"So I hear," said Kurt. "Any chance I could convince you to relocate here?"

"I'm not sure. My girlfriend just landed a really good job in Dallas, and I'm still weighing some of my other career options as well."

"I understand. However, you have it in you to become a studio musician, and I'd like for us to stay in touch. I'd love to have you as a client as well. Let's try to connect next month, after the first leg of Mike's tour is over."

"I look forward to it."

"In the meantime, I'll email George to let him know the new tracks for *Between Us Friends* are complete, and we can check it off our list. Now Tonya can concentrate on her first official album for Alicorn."

"Which, if all goes according to plan," said Tonya, "will be recorded in March."

The following morning Shawn and Tonya said a hasty but heartfelt goodbye at the curb at Los Angeles International Airport. Shawn promised to text her as soon as he landed in Miami, and he would keep her apprised of how Mike was doing. Her next stop was the Carson Agency, where Natalie greeted her with a warm hug.

"So, how were your holidays?" she asked.

"Fantastic," said Tonya. "I went to Texas and hung out with friends, and now I'm ready to go back to work."

"And with you now having a car, I can send you on assignments in Anaheim or San Diego, or maybe even back to Santa Barbara."

Tonya felt a little sad when Natalie mentioned Santa Barbara. Mike had recently sold his Santa Barbara home. "It all sounds exciting, but do you have anything for me?"

"So much so I'm not sure where to start. The agency loved your bodywash ad, and they'd like for you to do another one. Same product line, this time for their foaming bath oil."

"You mean a bubble bath," said Tonya.

"Pretty much, but because the product is for adults, they call it a foaming bath oil. You'll be relaxing in a tub, full of bubbles. However, for the ad they'll be using an entire bottle to get the extra foam, so I hope you like lavender scent."

"I love lavender."

"Sounds good, and you can wear a swimsuit, as long as it's strapless."

"Good. I have the perfect thing."

"Awesome, so let's set up a meeting with the agency. Does ten-thirty Wednesday morning work for you?"

"It does."

"And just so you know, Jordon Canfield is once again the director. I know you like working with him, and he also asked for you."

"Okay, good. What else do you have?"

"I have several glamour pin ups. Some clothed, some nude, but like the shoot with Carlos, nothing inappropriate will be showing. However, you'll still be in the buff in front of the photographer."

"Then I'd prefer working with a female."

"Okay," said Natalie, "let me go through my files and find out who's shooting what. I'll send you an email, then you can decide from there."

Tonya heard from Shawn a few hours later. He had arrived in Miami and was getting ready to rendezvous with Mike. She had barely sent her reply when another message arrived. George was back. She was to check out of the hotel on Friday morning.

* * *

Derrick, George's personal chef, was working in the kitchen when Tonya arrived. He greeted her with his usual warm smile as Tonya took her seat at the kitchen table.

"So, what's my cooking lesson for today?" she asked.

"Right now, I'm preparing chicken parmesan. There's a pork roast in the oven, and as soon as I'm done with the chicken, I'm making beef with portabella mushrooms."

"I remember the beef from before, and I'm happy to help with it."

"I'd rather put you in charge of the risotto, if you don't mind."

"No worries. My Italian grandmother used to make risotto, and my sister and I used to watch while she made it."

"Well then, don't just sit there," he said. "C'mon over and let's get you started."

Tonya went to the music room after Derrick left. She was working on the lyrics for one of her songs but was having trouble finding the right words. As she heard the garage door open, she felt both relieved and apprehensive as she hurried out to the living room.

"How are you, my pet?" George greeted her with a warm embrace and a big kiss.

"Stuck on a lyric. I was hoping you could offer me some suggestions."

"Maybe later. Right now, I'm starving, and I know Derrick was here today."

"He was, and he made us beef and mushrooms."

"Sounds wonderful, so let's get to it." George accompanied her to the kitchen, and over dinner he brought her up to date on his family, as well as the upcoming Grammy Awards.

"What are you planning to wear to the Grammys?" he asked.

"Either the dress I wore to the holiday party, or the red dress I wore on New Year's Eve."

"The dress you wore to the holiday party is out. You're an up-and-coming celebrity, and it's best if you're not seen at big events wearing a dress you've worn before. However, I don't think I've seen your red one."

"You haven't. I found it at a consignment store in Dallas."

"Then if you don't mind, I'd like for you to try it on for me as soon as we're done." He reached for a second helping and offered her another.

"It was delicious, but I don't think I could eat another bite."

"In that case, I'm finishing it off."

Tonya fixed herself a cup of herbal tea while George enjoyed the rest of his meal. Afterwards, he pitched in and stacked the dishwasher, as he always did. Once the last pan was dried and put away he joined her in the guestroom.

"Here it is." Tonya took the red dress from her closest and laid it out across the bed.

"Let's take off the dry-cleaning bag so you can try it on."

"Of course. However, it's off shoulder, so please excuse the bra straps."

He gave her a look. "You can skip the bra altogether, love. I've seen your breasts before. Many times."

Tonya quietly sighed as she stripped down to her panties. After slipping the dress on, George zipped up the back and a big smile came over his face.

"It's absolutely stunning, and you look incredibly sexy. Hopefully there were no photographers at your New Year's Eve gig."

"None. The hotel wouldn't allow the press inside."

"Then you can certainly wear it to the Grammys. Now, let's get you out of it." He unzipped the dress and stood by as she hung it back up. She had barely closed the closet door when he grabbed her by the hand and led her to the master bedroom.

"We can dispense with these as well." He reached for her panties and raised his brow as he pulled them off.

"Well, I see you're a natural brunette. Not that I had any doubts."

"Taking care of my bikini line would have been awkward at Shawn and Jacque's place, and it always was a hassle, so I told Natalie I want to hold off on doing any swimsuit and skimpy lingerie ads for now."

He pulled the coverlet down. Once she was settled in the bed, he laid down next to her and stroked her.

"It feels nice, and for nude work it's better if you have it."

"The only nude work I do are glamour shoots where nothing is actually showing."

"And as I've told you, many times, you have a beautiful body. It's time for you to start showing it off." He reached into the nightstand and removed a magazine.

"I'm part owner of a British gentlemen's magazine called *Sir Maxwell*. It's similar to your American men's magazines, although it's not distributed here." He opened the magazine and presented her with a layout. Tonya was stunned at what she saw.

"Is this Mandy?" she asked.

"As a matter of fact, it is, and, as you can clearly see, she's softly lit and posed in such a way as to enhance the curves and shapes of her body. We consider the female body a form of art, and we treat it accordingly. And as you can see, she's a natural blonde."

"I've never really thought about her being a natural blonde or not." Tonya quickly handed the magazine back to George. Once again, he gave her an odd look as he put it away.

"As you know, you've been living here, rent free, for some time now, so I consider you an investment, and the time has come for me to collect my return."

"I'm working on my new album."

"I know you are, and while I hope it will do well, there is no guarantee, which means you'll be returning the favor to me in other ways."

"What do you mean?"

"First, we're going to properly initiate you into the club. You don't have to have intercourse with the next member if you don't feel you're ready, but there's certainly no harm in hugging or cuddling, or giving one another a backrub or a massage, is there? It's like I've told you, many times. Sex is a gift. It's meant to be enjoyed, and you'll be treated respectfully."

"And what if I were to refuse?"

He gave her a strong look "I think you already know the answer. However, nothing will happen to him as long as you cooperate. In the meantime, you need to welcome me home properly."

Tonya was hardly in the mood, so she gave him the best acting performance she could. To her relief, George seemed to buy it.

"So, what's the other favor?" she asked.

He gave her a lustful look. "You'll be doing a similar layout for *Sir Maxwell.*"

"When?"

"After you've recorded your first album, and remember, Mickey's career depends on it."

* * *

Mike and Shawn were jamming in the motorhome as it rolled down the Interstate. So far, the tour was going well, and they were due to arrive in Charlotte before nightfall. Suddenly, Mike stopped playing.

"What was that?" he asked.

"What was what?"

Mike's phone rang again and he quickly grabbed it. "It's the attorney. I have to take the call."

"Need me to move?" asked Shawn.

"Nah, you're good." Mike quickly accepted the call and went to the back of the motorhome. He returned a few minutes later.

"Everything okay?" asked Shawn.

"My attorney just got off the phone with George's attorney. They still think I'm bluffing. She's going to assure them I'm not. You know, I was really hoping this would end quickly, but it looks like he may fight me every step of the way."

"Tonya's stepfather is a police detective," said Shawn. "Maybe we should let him know what's going on."

"I've thought about it, but I'm not sure we can prove false imprisonment. Right now, Tonya doesn't have the means to move out, and George could simply say they had a misunderstanding and she's free to leave anytime she chooses. Then, once the cops leave, rest assured, he'll take it out on her."

"Yeah, you're right," said Shawn. "She told me the minute she gets her advance she's out of there. She said if she has to, she'll wait for him to leave for work, then she'll pack her bags and go."

"She said the same thing to me as well, but I'm still trying to speed up the process, because if I know George, he'll come up with some excuse to stall on her advance."

❧FORTY-NINE❧

SHANDRA LAUNCHED a major PR campaign once the holidays were over. Her goal was to make Tonya Rose a household name as the sexy glamour model who would soon be releasing her first album. Tonya's world seemed to change overnight. People were approaching her in public. Like Mike, she was having to use service elevators. Her shopping habits had also changed. She was no longer allowed to shop at thrift stores or Walmart. Now she was expected to do her shopping at upscale department stores.

Tonya looked stunning the afternoon George zipped up her red dress, but deep down she was quivering. He had told her to pack her bag. After the Grammys, she would spend the night at a hotel with a club member, but he refused to give her anymore more information.

"So, are you ready to go?" he asked.

"I think so."

"Good. The limo will be here soon, and afterwards we'll drop you off at the hotel. You'll be there for two days, and I'll pick you up Saturday morning."

The press began taking photos as soon as they arrived at the Grammys, and a reporter approached George. As Tonya stepped aside, another reporter walked up to her. Several Alicorn artists were up for awards, and both she and George were optimistic about their chances of winning. When the time came for them to take their seats inside the auditorium, they were seated ten rows from the stage. If one of Alicorn's artists were to win Record of the Year, George could get to the stage in a timely manner. As the evening progressed several Alicorn artists won awards, but in the end, another label won Record of the Year.

The night air felt brisk when they finally made their way outside. Several reporters asked George if he would be attending any of the post award parties.

"Our artists will be attending," he said. "However, some of us have to be back at the office bright and early tomorrow morning." Once their limo arrived Tonya quickly slid into the back seat and George sat down next to her.

"You know, we had a really good evening," he said. "It would have been nice if we could have won Record of the Year, but we were still nominated, and there's always next year." He looked at her and smiled. "And who knows? You may bring us the trophy next year."

"I'll do my best."

He gave her a heartfelt kiss. Perhaps he had changed his mind and would bring her home after all, but her hopes were dashed when the limo turned into the entrance of a posh hotel.

"Have a good time my pet." George reached into his pocket and handed her an envelope with her room key. "I'll text you Saturday morning when I'm on my way to pick you up."

The driver opened the door, and Tonya anxiously stepped out. Her room was on the eleventh floor. She held her breath as she put her key in the slot, but someone on the other side opened the door.

"Oh, thank goodness it's you," she said.

"Well, of course it's me. Hope you don't mind my making myself more comfortable." Stan was wearing a white terrycloth robe with the hotel logo embroidered on the front. "George is spending the next two days with Mandy, and I'll be spending the next two days with you."

"I thought you two had separated."

"We have, but we're still legally married, so our agreement still stands. Whenever Mandy is with a club member, the club member's partner stays with me."

"Of course. However, George didn't tell me who I'd be with, so I'm feeling a little nervous at the moment. Please, bear with me. I'll be okay in a few minutes."

"You don't need to be nervous," he said, reassuringly. "As I said before, I intend to take my time, so I'm not expecting to make love to you tonight. We'll just hang out and enjoy one another's company and see where it goes from there. Then tomorrow we're going to Malibu to meet a jewelry broker, because I really meant it when I said I wanted you to have an even better jewelry collection than your grandmother had. So, in the meantime, why don't you get out of your dress and make yourself comfortable?"

Tonya glanced around their suite and realized there was only one king-sized bed. "They haven't brought my bags up yet."

"No problem."

He stepped into the bathroom, returning a moment later with a white terry cloth robe which matched his.

"Thanks. I'll go change."

"Hang on. Let me at least help you with your zipper."

He unzipped her dress, and Tonya took a deep breath as she slowly stepped out of it, revealing a strapless bra and lacy panties underneath. Stan smiled in approval.

"Very nice."

She handed him the dress, asking him to hang it up for her.

"In a minute." He dropped the dress on the bed and Tonya held her breath. Mike had told her to do whatever she had to do to stay safe, and she prayed he would forgive her for what might happen next.

"If you'll turn around, I'll unhook your locket for you."

"No, thanks," she said firmly. "I don't take it off."

Someone knocked at the door. Tonya's bags had arrived. She quickly snatched up her robe, hastily tying the belt around her waist. Once the bellman left, she grabbed what she needed from her bag and excused herself to take a shower.

* * *

Stan turned on the TV and channel surfed until he found a basketball game. Setting the remote aside, he turned the bedcovers down and made himself comfortable. The bathroom door opened a few minutes later. Tonya was once again in the white terrycloth robe. As she sat down on the bed, he reached for his leather pouch and took out a prescription bottle.

"This will help you feel less nervous, but it won't put you to sleep." He opened the bottle and removed a capsule.

"No, thanks. I'm good."

"You're sure?"

She nodded. "Yeah, I'm sure. Right now, I just want to unwind and maybe have a caffeine-free soft drink. Do you by chance have any Sprite?"

The capsule was concealed in his hand as he closed the bottle. "Sorry, no Sprite, but there's some mineral water in the mini bar."

"Sounds good."

He hopped off the bed and took a bottle of mineral water from the small refrigerator. "Would you like me to open it for you?"

"Sure, if you wouldn't mind."

The mini bar was behind a divider which separated the sleeping area from the rest of the suite. Tonya was unable to see him from where she sat. He carefully set the bottle down and broke the capsule. The contents quickly dissolved as he emptied them into the bottle, and dropped the empty shells in his pocket.

"You know, I think I'll have some mineral water too." He grabbed another bottle and quickly opened it. Returning to the bed, he handed her the drugged bottle and sat down beside her. She set the bottle on her nightstand and slowly took off her robe.

"That's a pretty nightgown," he said. "It's sexy but it's not trashy, unlike some of the stuff Mandy wears."

233

"I prefer plain and simple when it comes to my own wardrobe, although I've worn some pretty crazy stuff in some of my modeling shoots."

"No doubt you have. So, do you like basketball?"

"My stepfather likes it, but I don't really follow it myself."

Tonya slowly sipped her mineral water while Stan wrapped his arm around her waist as he explained what was happening on the court. She appeared to be comfortable with it, and once she finished her drink, she set the empty bottle on the nightstand.

"How are you feeling?" he asked.

"Okay, I guess."

"Good, because my team is losing." Switching off the TV, he smiled as he ran his hands up and down her sides, making sure she wasn't wearing any panties.

"You and I are good friends," he said. "We know and trust one another, and we had fun the last time we were together."

"We certainly did, and I genuinely like you, Stan. As I said before, had we met under different circumstances, who knows? We could have been an item."

He gave her a warm hug. "As you know, our club is about fully embracing our sexuality. It's not about being in love or in a committed relationship. We believe sex is a gift which transcends love and marriage, and it's meant to be enjoyed solely for its own sake. So, starting tonight, I'm going to help you embrace your sexuality and experience one of the greatest pleasures in life."

He patted her pillow and told her to lay down. Once she was settled, he took a bottle of body oil from his bag and sat down at her feet. A lilac scent permeated the air as he poured some into hand and began rubbing it into her shins.

"I'm going to start by massaging your legs. Then we'll take off your nightgown, and I'll give you an all over body message. While I'm doing that, I want you to relax and enjoy it and concentrate on how good it feels."

Tonya groaned loudly as he rubbed the oil into her calves, but she sounded as if she were in pain.

"Are you all right?"

"I don't know." She began rubbing her forehead. "All of a sudden, the room is spinning around me, really bad. I feel like I'm on that roller coaster again."

"It's just nerves. I know you're feeling anxious and you've had an exciting day, going to the Grammys and all, but it's okay. I'm going to make you feel really good."

She shook her head. "No. My entire body feels really weak right now, and I don't know what's wrong. My father had a severe stroke at a young age, and you need to call nine-one-one, because I think I may be having one as well."

Tonya's face had turned pale. Her eyes looked strange as well. She was having an unexpectedly strong reaction to the drug, and Stan desperately hoped nothing was seriously wrong. He watched in horror as her eyes suddenly rolled back and she lost consciousness. Her breathing sounded unusually slow as he felt along her neck for a pulse. It, too, was very low, and he struggled to control his own fear.

"No, no, no. Don't do this. Don't make me call nine-one-one, because I'm not going to jail."

❧FIFTY❧

TONYA CAME TO IN A dense fog. Opening her eyes, she found herself face-to-face with an anxious looking Stan. He was fully clothed, and daylight was streaming in from the balcony.

"Finally," he said. "You're awake. Are you okay?"

"I don't know. What time is it?"

He looked at his watch. "It's two-seventeen in the afternoon."

"What? Are you serious?"

"Yes, I'm serious. You've been asleep for the past fifteen hours. You said you weren't feeling well."

"What the hell happened? I felt fine when I got here." She felt a sudden jolt as she recalled what had occurred the night before.

"Wait a minute. You gave me a bottle of mineral water, and I started feeling dizzy right after I drank it." She gave him a strange look, and he quickly became defensive.

"Hey, I know what this looks like, but it's not what you think. I didn't—"

"Bullshit. I excel at reading people's body language, and you're definitely hiding something. You offered me a prescription drug, which I refused. Then I drank the mineral water, and afterwards I started feeling weak and dizzy. What happened? Did you slip me some sort of date rape drug?" Tonya watched him closely as he struggled to maintain his composure.

"It wasn't a date rape drug. You were really wired up when you got here, and I was trying to help you calm down."

"What was the drug, Stan?"

"It was a mild tranquilizer. It was supposed to help take the edge off, but it shouldn't have made you feel weak or dizzy."

"Okay, so you're admitting you slipped something in my drink without my knowing it. What the hell were you thinking?"

"As I said before, I was trying to help you relax. I had no intention of harming you."

Her voice remained firm. "I asked you what the drug was, Stan."

He took a deep breath and let out a long sigh. "Diazepam."

"A drug which I've never been prescribed." Tonya stumbled out of bed, relieved to still be wearing her nightgown, but she was having trouble keeping her balance. The effects hadn't completely worn off. Once she had her phone, she got back in bed and did a Google search.

"Okay, I found some information about diazepam." She stopped to read through the article. Afterwards, she gave him an angry look.

"Well, I guess I'm lucky you didn't freaking kill me. This drug shouldn't be taken with alcohol." She looked him in the eye. "I had some champagne at the Grammys. Not enough to make me falling down drunk, but I had several glasses over the course of the evening. I've obviously had a bad reaction to this drug, and the alcohol made it much worse. How could you do this to me? I considered you a friend. Someone I could trust, yet you've betrayed me, in the worst way possible."

"I know I should—"

"What you should have done was call the paramedics, but you obviously didn't. So why didn't you?"

"I'm sorry, Tonya. I truly am. I guess I panicked and wasn't thinking clearly. You know I would never ever do anything to intentionally harm you, and I'm going to take care of you. So can I get you anything?"

"Maybe a glass of water, and so help me, if you put anything in it that shouldn't be there, I will rip you from limb to limb."

Tonya napped for much of the afternoon. Stan ordered her a bowl of soup from room service. Afterwards, she felt well enough to take a shower, but she gave him the cold shoulder when she returned to bed.

"I'm sorry, Tonya. I truly am. I was wrong slipping something into your drink. I deeply regret it and I swear, on everything holy, I will never, ever, do it again."

She closed her eyes, pretending to be asleep. To her relief, she felt better the following morning. Once again, Stan apologized.

"Apology accepted," said Tonya, "but you realize you literally could have killed me. I was in desperate need of medical help, but you didn't bother calling nine-one-one."

"I didn't want to risk going to jail."

"You were trying to save yourself. What would have happened if I had died? You would have gone to prison for a whole lot longer."

"I know." He looked her in the eye. "Tonya, I'd give anything if I could go back and undo what happened. You truly are special to me, and the last thing I ever wanted was to do anything to harm you. So can I at least try to make up for it and order you some breakfast?"

"No, thanks. What I want is to go home, but Mandy is at George's place until tomorrow."

"I know she is. Is there anything I can do?"

"I'd like to be alone for a while. I'm feeling pretty traumatized right now, and I need to sort out what happened."

"So, you're saying you'd like for me to leave?"

"If you wouldn't mind."

"Okay, I'll head out if you're sure it's what you want. Are you feeling well enough to be on your own?"

"I'll manage."

Stan quickly packed his bag. Once the door closed behind him, Tonya burst into tears. She took a shower once she calmed down, and her Uber driver arrived an hour later. When she returned, she ordered room service and spent the remainder of the day curled up on the bed watching old movies. George picked her up the following morning, giving her a concerned look as she got into his Mercedes.

"You seem a little off this morning. Are you okay?"

"It remains to be seen."

"What happened?"

She leaned back in her seat and sighed. "Stan slipped a drug into my soft drink shortly after I arrived at the hotel."

"Are you serious?"

"Yes, I'm serious, and I had a really bad reaction to it."

"Did he call nine-one-one or take you to the emergency room?"

"No, he did not. He said he didn't want to go to jail. I was pretty much out of it the following day, then yesterday morning I asked him to leave. Once he was gone, I went to an urgent care clinic. The doctor said I may possibly have a sensitivity to diazepam, but because it may have been illegally obtained, they did a test to see if it was laced with anything else."

"I see. So did they find anything?"

"Yes, they did. It was a real drug cocktail. They found traces of fentanyl in my system, along with some other barbiturates, and they said I'm damn lucky it didn't kill me. We're still waiting on the final results, so at the moment I'm unsure of what lasting effects I may have."

"I'm sorry, Tonya."

"Me too. I also had the doctor check to see if I'd been raped, and it looks like I wasn't."

"My god." A stunned George went silent for several minutes. As they turned onto his street, he finally spoke up.

"According to Mandy, Stan had a problem with prescription drugs, but he claimed he'd gotten help and was in recovery."

"Then it obviously didn't work. He had a leather pouch full of prescription bottles."

"I promise I'll take care of it, and I'm truly sorry. This should have never happened."

"You're right," she sternly said. "It shouldn't have happened, but it did."

Tonya went straight to the music room once they returned home. Music had a way of healing her, and after a few hours she felt a little more like herself. It was late afternoon when George softly tapped on the door and stepped inside.

"What's up?" she asked.

He looked sober as he sat down in one of the other chairs. "The club has been officially disbanded. I don't want to risk anyone else getting hurt. I also spoke to Mandy. She's pretty shaken as well, so she's going to see if she can have him involuntarily placed in a rehab center. He's not a well man, and he's in desperate need of professional help."

"Something needs to be done. Otherwise, he'll do what he did to me to someone else."

"He's also no longer your business manager, and he's not to contact you again. If he does, I'll take care of it. I sent Kurt an email saying you let Stan go due to a conflict of interest. I'm sure he'll call you first thing Monday morning."

"Thanks, George. I appreciate it."

"You're welcome. And speaking of Kurt, have you heard from Mickey lately?"

"Not a word. You told me I had to end it with him, and I did. Why do you ask?"

"No reason, just curious. Go back to what you were doing."

George stepped out, and for the first time in weeks, Tonya felt optimistic. George was lying when he said he was just curious. Mike's plan, whatever it was, appeared to be working.

∾FIFTY-ONE∾

AS EXPECTED, KURT called Tonya on Monday morning, and they met the following day. Taking her seat in his office, he handed her a business card.

. "Russell Cohen is Mike's business manager. He's done an excellent job for him, as well as some of my other clients, so we'll set up a meeting. And by the way, I caught a glimpse of you at the Grammys."

"It was an exciting evening, but it ended badly."

"Really? What happened?"

"George arranged for my next, club meeting, that night, although I didn't know about it being arranged until the very last minute."

"Were you forced to do something you didn't want to do?"

"Actually, it was something much worse."

Kurt's concern turned to anger as Tonya described how Stan had drugged her. "I'm okay, at least physically. The doctor said I hadn't been raped, for which I'll be forever grateful, but I'm still pretty shaken."

"Understandably so," said Kurt.

"It also scared the living hell out of George."

"As well it should have. What the hell was he thinking?"

"It's like we've discussed before. It's all about the power he has over people, only this time it backfired on him."

"At your expense," said Kurt. "You were very lucky. Stan could have easily killed you."

"I know he could have, but thankfully, he didn't. My sister must have been watching out for me. George also disbanded his so-called club, which means he won't be pimping me out anymore. And by the way, whatever Mike's doing seems to be working. George asked me out of the blue if I've heard from him lately."

"And what'd you tell him?"

"The truth. I haven't heard from Mike in weeks. How's he doing?"

"He's doing well, and yes, he's been putting the pressure on George, which reminds me. He sent me something to give to you."

Kurt reached inside his desk drawer and handed Tonya a large envelope. Inside was a house key, along with a printout of a map and a handwritten note. The sale on the house in Dallas was final, and she eagerly put the key on her keyring.

"The first leg of his tour will be over soon," said Kurt. "Then he's officially moving to Texas, so I gather this is your key."

"It is, but I'm putting the other information on my phone. George doesn't know my passcode."

"Good idea, and by the way, I'm still waiting on your contract."

"Really?" Tonya looked surprised. "I figured you'd already signed it by now. Guess I'll have to remind him when he gets home."

Kurt made a phone call after Tonya left. Afterwards, he called Mike. To his relief, Mike answered before it went to voicemail.

"What's up?" asked Mike.

"Are you someplace where we can talk in private?"

"I am. We arrived in Pittsburg about an hour ago, and I'm in my hotel room. Is anything wrong?"

"I'm afraid so, and it concerns Tonya." He quickly filled Mike in on what had happened. Afterwards there was a long silence. "Mike? Are you still there?"

"Yeah, I'm still here. So, where is Mr. Klein?"

"Tonya said Mandy is trying to get him into rehab, but forcing someone into treatment is easier said than done, so he's probably in his office."

"Which means the cops should be able to find him without any problem."

"They should," said Kurt. "However, I don't think Tonya filed a police report. She told me George doesn't want a scandal, and he won't allow her to press charges. He keeps telling her to be patient because Mandy will eventually get him into rehab."

"Assuming he doesn't pack his bags and leave town in the middle of the night, and I'm sure as hell not letting him get away with this. He could have easily killed her. We need to phone in an anonymous tip."

"Already on it. I called the police right before I called you."

"Thanks, Kurt. I knew you'd have her back."

"I'm just as concerned for her safety as you are. So how are things going on your end?"

"We're keeping the pressure on him, but so far, he hasn't budged. He's one stubborn son of a bitch."

"I thought as much," said Kurt, "and I'm still waiting on her contract. She seemed surprised when I told her Alicorn hadn't sent it yet. She said she'd talk to George about it tonight."

"How much do you want to bet he'll give her some lame excuse about the legal department being busier than usual? So is Hagerman's offer still on the table?"

"It is, and I had the same thought as you. However, she's in between business managers at the moment, so we need to wait for her to meet with Russ. Then I'll give George an ultimatum. Either he sends me her contract, or I sign her on with Hagerman."

"And I'll call my attorney," said Mike. "The more pressure we can keep on him, the sooner he'll break."

* * *

Tonya's phone rang as she was driving home. She was surprised at who was calling. "You have no idea how happy I am to hear your voice."

"Kurt told me what happened," said Mike, "so I'm breaking protocol. Are you someplace where it's safe to talk?"

"I'm in the car, and I'm pulling into a parking lot as we speak."

"Good. I just wanted to be sure you're okay."

"Physically, I'm fine. Most of it should be out of my system by now, and don't worry. He didn't rape me."

"I know he didn't. I also want you to know it's being dealt with, but the less you know, the better."

"I understand," said Tonya, "and I'm grateful for your help."

"I love you, Ms. Rose, and I'll do whatever I to in order to keep you safe. So is George planning on letting you go anytime soon?"

"No, he isn't, and until I get my advance, I won't be in a position to leave."

"Which is what I expected, but I don't want you to worry. I'm doing everything I can on my end to get you free, and we're slowly chipping away."

"I can't thank you enough, Mike. Knowing you're out there is what's keeping me going. I also want you to know George disbanded his sex club, so I'm safe, at least for now. Kurt also gave me the house key and the map."

"I know he did, and from here on out, if you feel you're in any kind of danger, I want you to call your stepfather, and then I want you to get to Dallas as quickly as you can."

"I can't call my stepfather. I don't want my mother knowing about anything about this."

"I understand, but they love you, they want to protect you as much as I do. I also know you're getting ready to record your first album, but again, if you're in any kind of danger, you'll have to leave and worry about it later. In the meantime, I love you, Ms. Rose, and please keep Kurt in the loop. Over and out."

Tonya met with Russ the following week. True to his word, Kurt gave George an ultimatum. The following day George presented the contract to Kurt, and he brought Tonya with him. Russ attended the meeting as well.

"Again, I must apologize," said George. "Our staff attorney has a seriously ill family member, so he's running behind. Tonya also wants her friend, Shawn, to play the bass. He's currently on tour with another of our artists and won't be available until the end of the month.

"Thanks for the update," said Kurt. "I'll start scheduling her studio sessions, and we'll see about finding Shawn a place to stay."

"We'll take care of it," said George. "Call Grace as soon as you schedule the dates, she'll take care of the rest." He then presented Russ with a check.

"Here's her advance."

"Thank you." Russ looked at Tonya. "I'll deposit this into your account, and we'll do as we discussed the other day."

Everyone shook hands, and George walked Tonya back to his Mercedes. "You've come a long way since Mickey's photo shoot, and I'm very proud of you. You've worked damn hard, and now it's finally paying off, so I'd like for us to do something special to celebrate."

"What do you have in mind?"

"I'd like for us to take a trip, right after your final recording session, and I have someplace really special in mind. Have you ever been to Colorado?"

"No, I haven't, but I've always wanted to go."

"Then I'm taking you to Aspen. It's beautiful in the spring. It reminds me of Switzerland. You'll love it."

* * *

The police showed up at Stan's condominium in the predawn hours and banged loudly on the door. Stan shouted from the other side.

"I don't know what you think you're trying to pull, but my wife and I have separated and she's been harassing me ever since, so you can tell her to stick it where the sun doesn't shine."

"We have a warrant, so you can either let us in, or we can bust the door down. The choice is yours."

A panicked Stan raced toward the bedroom, but it was too late. The police kicked in the door and tackled him in the hallway. As they cuffed him, another officer emerged from the bedroom, carrying a leather pouch.

"We just hit paydirt." He showed his supervisor the prescription bottles inside. One of the other officers read Stan his Miranda rights and they loaded him into the back of a squad car. Stan called his attorney when they arrived at the station. He posted bail a few hours later and was released on his own recognizance. Convinced Mandy had tipped them off, he vowed to do whatever he could to destroy her. One of his clients was an investigative journalist, and Stan had a quite story to tell about the secret life of George Monroe.

✐FIFTY-TWO✐

THE FIRST LEG OF Mike's tour ended in late February. Shawn was overjoyed to finally be reunited with Jacque. He spent the next two weeks with her while Mike moved into his new home. His mother flew to Dallas to help him unpack while his brother, Marty, brought the Silverado.

"I don't know, son." She sighed as she opened another box. "While I don't mean to sound hypercritical, I have some real concerns about your choices in women. Jodie strung you along for years, and I'm not quite sure what to think of Tonya. For someone who's supposedly level-headed, she's made some very poor choices, and I can't help but wonder if she's playing the same game as Jodie."

"You know I've had other girlfriends beside Jodie."

"I know you have, but you weren't as serious about them as you are about Tonya."

"Tonya is nothing like Jodie. Jodie was daddy's little girl, and he'll always come first. I have a feeling she won't get married until late in life, if she marries at all."

"So, what about Tonya?"

"Tonya was in a vulnerable place when she met a man who promised to make her all dreams come true, and he took full advantage of her. She now realizes she made a big mistake, and while she's doing her best to get away from him, he still has the upper hand."

"How so?"

"It's a long story, but to cut to the chase, he's well known for ruining those who dare to cross him, but don't worry. It's not if, but when, the opportunity comes along for her to break free, and when it does, rest assured, she'll be out of there in a heartbeat. In the meantime, you need to hand me another box so we can finish unpacking."

* * *

Shawn flew to Los Angeles after a two-week rest in Dallas. Tonya's first album was called, *The White Rose*. The title song would also be released as a single. A big smile broke out across his face as they finished their final recording session.

"You did it," he said. "It's hard to believe it's been a year since we drove to Denton from South Padre Island, and now here we are, in the recording studio. So, how does it feel?"

"Surreal," said Tonya, "and I can't help wondering if it hasn't been a dream, and I'll wake up in my apartment in Denton."

"Which makes two of us. So can two people have the same dream at the same time?"

"I don't know, but somehow I doubt it. In the meantime, today is Tuesday, and there's a coffee place just down the road. George also invited us to dinner."

"Yes, on the coffee, but I have to pass on dinner. I'm taking the red eye to St. Louis tonight. We start the second leg of the tour on Thursday, and Mike would love it if you could join us. You can also plug your album."

"You know I'd love it more than anything, but George is insisting I stay with him for the foreseeable future."

"He can't keep you prisoner," said Shawn.

"Maybe not, but he can still damage Mike's career, which is what'll happen if I leave too soon. I know Mike is pressuring him. So is Mandy, but he's a stubborn man. We're flying to Aspen on Thursday to celebrate my new album, so hopefully, he's getting ready to cut me loose."

"Hopefully. If he doesn't, you'll have to take matters into your own hands."

"I will if I have to, but I have a feeling something really big is about to break, so I'm keeping my fingers crossed. In the meantime, do you want me to drop you off at the airport?"

He shook his head. "No. I appreciate the offer, but I've made other arrangements. My flight leaves at eleven-thirty, which is kind of late for you to drive all the way to the airport and back. We'll do our coffee run and call it good."

George was waiting when Tonya arrived home. He would take her to the restaurant of her choice. Wanting to go full circle, Tonya chose Casa Vega, but on the way home the conversation took an uncomfortable turn.

"I'll call Natalie as soon as we get back from Aspen," said George. "I want to schedule the photo shoot for *Sir Maxwell*."

"Do I have to do it?"

His voice was firm. "Yes, you do. You still owe me some favors. This is one of them."

"Then can we do it the way we've done my other nude work? Where we're seeing my back, or my hip?"

"Nope. It's high time you showed off your body to the world, so we'll see everything. Nigel will fly here from London. He shoots all our nude layouts, and I'll be there as well."

"Will there be any women there?"

"Not this time. It'll just be Nigel, his assistant, Bill, and yours truly. It's a job. You'll be paid a considerable sum of money, and they'll treat you every bit as respectfully as everyone else you've worked with. It's also another opportunity for you to help save Mike's career."

"I ended it with Mike some time ago. Can't we just move on?"

George remained silent and Tonya looked out the window and sighed. He no intention of setting her free. She would have to plan her own escape.

❧FIFTY-THREE❧

GEORGE PACKED HIS bag before he left for work. He planned on driving straight to the airport from the office. Tonya would meet him at the charter company at three o'clock.

"Your name is on the itinerary," he said. "If you get there first, tell the front desk you're with me." He gave her a longer than usual goodbye kiss, and a strange feeling came over her as he left. She had experienced it once before; the morning Evan left for South Padre Island. She quickly brushed it off.

"Your mind's playing tricks with you," she said out loud. Entering the guest room, she caught her reflection in the dresser mirror as she tried to figure out what to pack. The black sweater she wore matched her somber mood. As she laid out different outfits on top of the bed and debated back and forth, the garage door opened. George was back, but now he appeared to be deeply troubled.

"Can we talk?" he asked.

"Of course."

They took their seats in the living room and he gave her a serious look. "Mickey and his attorney have been trying to break his contract for some time now. They were trying to pressure me into letting you go. At first, I ignored them. Then I tried offering him more money, but he turned it down."

"George, I swear, I know nothing about this."

"I know you don't. This morning, when I arrived at my office, I had an urgent message from my attorney. They've filed a lawsuit. My attorney tells me that along with costing the company a lot of money, it would also create a lot of bad publicity, which could seriously damage our reputation. Then there's the other matter. Mickey is one of our biggest money-makers. I simply can't afford to let him walk away. So, he wins. I'm setting you free."

"Do I still have to go to Aspen?"

"Yes. I've already paid for the trip, so it'll be our swan song. You'll leave for Texas as soon as we return. They'll withdraw the lawsuit once you've arrived in Dallas."

"What about the *Sir Maxwell* shoot?"

He gave her a defiant look. "Funny you should ask. Mickey knows nothing about *Sir Maxwell*, so it was never on the table. You'll either do the shoot here, or you'll do it in Dallas. We'll work out the details out later, and trust me, you'll be well paid, but right now I have to go back the office. I'll meet you at the airport at three."

George hurried out, but it took a few moments for Tonya to fully comprehend what had happened. Annette was right. Mike had freed her from George. She did a quick calculation in her head. She would be in Aspen for three days, and it would take another three days for her to drive to Dallas. Her hands were shaking as she picked up her phone. Mike was getting ready for his next performance. His phone would be silenced and stashed away in a bag somewhere, so she sent him a text message.

"OMG! You did it! I'm coming home. Taking care of some personal business and I'll be in Dallas on Wednesday. My phone may be turned off so don't worry if I don't reply to your messages right away. I love you and can't wait to see you."

She sent similar messages to her mother and Shawn and went back to her packing. The doorbell rang a few minutes later. Looking through the peephole, she was surprised at who she saw.

"Good morning, Mandy. I'm afraid you missed George, but I'd be happy to give him a message."

"Actually, I came to see you. Do you have a few minutes?"

"Sure. Can I get you some coffee?"

"I'd love some."

Tonya took Mandy into the kitchen and quickly poured her a cup, along with one for herself.

"Stan had a court hearing yesterday afternoon," said Mandy. "I went, but it was just a formality. His attorney got him a plea bargain so he ended up with a fine and probation, but no jail time. I'm really sorry. For what he did to you, he should have served some time."

"I agree, but I didn't want to have to testify in court either. It was a nightmare I'd rather not relive, and at least it's over done with, so now I can move on."

"Which brings me to the other reason for my visit. George called me a little while ago and he told me what happened with Mike. As you know, I've also been trying to convince him to let you go, so let's get you packed."

"I'm leaving as soon as we get back from Aspen."

Mandy smiled and shook her head. "Not if I have anything to do with it. You're leaving today. Besides, I've never been to Aspen."

"Are you serious?"

"Dead serious. Let's get you packed."

Tonya took Mandy the guest room and they began packing. Before long, her suitcases were full.

"Looks like I have a bigger wardrobe than I had when I arrived, but there are a few things I want to get rid of."

"I'd be happy to have my assistant drop them off at a thrift store if you'd like."

"Thanks, and we can start with this." Tonya handed Mandy her red tunic. "I wore this the day George took me to lunch the first time. It was right after Mike's album cover shoot."

Mandy held it up in front of the mirror. "It's a pretty color and it still looks new. Are you sure you don't want to keep it?"

"I'm positive. It's served its purpose."

"Okay, I can take it with me."

Tonya added a few more items to Mandy's pile, including a white straw hat. "I used to wear this out by the pool to help keep the sun off my face. George always liked it, and it's the last item for the thrift store. Everything else goes with me. Maybe I can find some boxes to pack it in."

"Do you have any canvas bags?" asked Mandy.

"Of course. They're in my trunk. I'll go get them." Tonya quickly stepped out, and before long the last remaining items were placed in a bag.

"Looks like you have everything," said Mandy

"I do, and thank you again for helping me. I just hope George won't be angry with you for taking my place on the plane."

"Somehow, I doubt it. George and I are soul mates, although he won't admit it. We've been through many past lives together, and I can't imagine what I'd do if anything were to happen to him in this life. I'm also hoping he won't be so stubborn the next time around."

"I'm not sure if I believe in past lives or not," said Tonya, "but I could tell you were in love with him the night he invited you and Stan over for dinner."

"And I'm sorry I was such a bitch. At the time I didn't know if you were a threat or not. So, enough about him and me. We need to get you on the road."

Both women grabbed as many bags as they could carry, and before long the car was loaded.

"You're sure you have everything?" asked Mandy. "Your clothes, your laptop, your guitars, and viola?"

"It's all here. We even double checked. All I need is for your assistant to take the other stuff to the thrift store, and again, I can't thank you enough."

"I warned George, many times, about how you would never fit in with our club, and I'm sorry you had such a bad experience. You and

Mike are good people. You're nothing like us and you never will be, which is actually for the best. Now, you need to get going. Otherwise, I get all sentimental."

Tonya removed George's key from her keyring and handed it to Mandy, along with her garage opener.

"I'll close the garage door for you," said Mandy, "and give Melissa my best."

"I will." Tonya hugged Mandy goodbye and hopped in her car, glancing in her rearview mirror as she drove away for the last time. Mandy stood at the foot of the driveway, waving goodbye.

Tonya stopped at the bank a few minutes later and withdrew some cash. Hopefully, it was enough to cover the cost of her trip. Her mother called as she was walking back to her car.

"Are you alright?" asked Heather.

"I'm fine. Annette was right all along. Mike got me away from George."

"How?"

"Something about him trying to break his contract with Alicorn. I don't know all the details. All George said was Mike is making them a lot of money, and they would do whatever it took to keep him from leaving."

"Well, thank the Lord. He finally got through to George. When are you going back to Texas?"

"In a few days. I have some other things to take care of first."

"Any chance I could talk you into coming here for a visit? We're leaving for the Grand Canyon with Robin and Dawson on Saturday, and we'd love it if you could come with us."

"I appreciate the offer, Mom, but I can't, so have fun at the Grand Canyon and I'll call you Wednesday, as soon as I arrive in Dallas. I promise."

Tonya stopped for lunch at George's favorite coffeehouse. As expected, Mike hadn't returned her message. However, for the next few days, Tonya didn't want to talk to anyone, not even him. Returning to her car, she put her phone on airplane mode and headed for the freeway. An eastbound exit soon caught her eye, and she worked her way out of town on a state highway. The southern California backcountry was beautiful, and she when she arrived in Lake Elsinore, she found a motel with hiking trails nearby. It would be the perfect place for her to exorcise her inner demons, once and for all.

* * *

George got stuck in traffic and arrived at the airport a few minutes late. Rushing inside the building, he quickly signed the paperwork. The woman behind the counter told him Captain Eddie and his wife were working another flight.

"I know you prefer Captain Eddie, but you still have two excellent pilots. Shirley is waiting in her usual spot, and Ms. Rose has already boarded."

George hurried out the side door and ran up the steps. One of the pilots told him to take his seat, but when he stepped into the cabin he stopped in his tracks.

"What the hell are you doing here?"

Mandy was wearing Tonya's red tunic, and her hair was tucked inside the white straw hat. She gave him a sultry grin.

"Change of plans. I've never been to Aspen before."

"You know, I should tell the pilot to take you off the plane."

She leaned back in her seat. "Yeah, you really should, but we both know you won't. Besides, they've already loaded my bag." The cargo door closed with a loud thump. "And I guess they just loaded yours too."

George rolled his eyes and tried to suppress a smile.

"Too late, I already saw it. Admit it. You could never be angry with me."

"No, I suppose I can't, and you look pretty damn sexy too. So, where's Tonya?"

"Somewhere on the road, heading east. I stopped by after you left and helped her pack. She needs to go home, and it's not like you'll never see her again. She'll be going back and forth between here and Dallas, as will Mickey."

"I see she gave you her hat and tunic."

"Well, sort of. I told her I'd have Jenna take them to the thrift store, but she also mentioned they were your favorites, and somehow I just couldn't bring myself to part with them."

He chuckled to himself as he sat down and fastened his seatbelt. "I don't know what I'm going to do with you."

"Maybe you don't, but I certainly do."

The plane soon began taxiing to the runway. Once they were cleared, they did their take off roll and began climbing. Seconds later the plane began shaking with a series of loud thumps. They had run into a flock of geese. One hit the window next to Mandy, smearing it with blood and feathers. The geese were gone an instant later, but instead of loud thumps there was total silence.

"Oh my god," said Mandy. "I don't hear the engines."

"Try to stay calm," said George. "We've had a serious bird strike, but we'll be okay. They'll get the engines restarted in a minute."

They overheard the pilots frantically making a mayday call. They needed to make an emergency landing, but the engines weren't restarting, and they were falling from the sky. George tried to reassure Mandy, as well as himself.

"We're returning to the airport. Don't worry. We'll be fine." He looked out the window. They were dropping fast. He realized they might not make it, but for some reason he felt strangely calm. He said a quick prayer, asking for forgiveness, and when he asked for an angel to watch over Tonya, he felt another woman's presence and thought he heard a faint feminine voice.

"Of course. I'll always watch over my sister."

He quickly looked around, but other than Mandy, there was no one else in the cabin. They reached out across the aisle, grabbing one another's hands. The plane hit something and began spinning out of control. Seconds later there was a loud bang as everything went dark.

❧FIFTY-FOUR❧

LIKE THEIR EARLIER shows, Mike's performance in St. Louis was a huge success. After their final encore and curtain call, he and the other musicians ran backstage, where their tour manager, along with other concert promoters, greeted them with smiles and warm handshakes. As they mingled, Mike noticed they seemed a little subdued. They soon left, and as he and the other musicians headed for the dressing rooms his tour manager stopped him and took him aside.

"What's up, Charlie? You've been acting strange all evening."

"We need to talk somewhere private." He motioned toward a small group of chairs and told Mike to take a seat.

"All right, so what's going on?"

Charlie's expression turned serious as he took a deep breath and sighed. "There was a plane crash earlier today, Mike. It was a small charter jet, and it happened near the Burbank airport."

Mike's blood turned to ice. "What are you saying?

"Please, Mike, just let me finish. I was about to say no one on the ground was seriously injured, but there were four people onboard the jet. The pilot and copilot, George Monroe, and Tonya Rose. Unfortunately, there were no survivors. I'm sorry, Mike, I truly am. I know Tonya was special to you, and I'm truly sorry for your loss. We've cancelled the tour for the next few weeks, and we're trying to get everyone home as quickly as possible."

Mike felt a chill go down his spine. Suddenly, nothing seemed real. "So, you're saying George Monroe is dead?"

"I'm afraid so, and again, I'm sorry about Tonya."

"Oh my god. Does his family know?"

"Yes. They've been notified, and they're on their way from England as we speak."

Shawn came out from the dressing room with his phone was in his hand. He looked pale and shaken.

"What's wrong?" asked Mike.

"There's a sign up in dressing room about the tour being cancelled for the next few weeks. I also had an urgent voicemail message from Tonya's stepfather. He was calling from the emergency room in Tucson. Her mother collapsed, and he was waiting to talk to the doctor."

"What happened?"

Shawn's voice sounded mechanical, and a tear rolled down his cheek. "He said he got a call from the Los Angeles County Coroner's office. They were asking for Tonya's dental records. They said she'd been in a plane crash earlier today. He doesn't have your phone number, so he asked me to let you know what happened. He thought it would be better if you heard it from me. He also wants me to call him back, as soon as possible."

Mike suddenly started feeling lightheaded. "No, no, no. This is not happening! There has to be a mistake." He stood from his chair and took a few steps, then everything suddenly went dark. He came to a moment later, lying prone on the concrete floor. Shawn and Charlie, and a few security guards surrounded him. He felt a sharp pain in his left temple. He touched it and saw blood on his fingers.

"Take it easy, Mike," said Charlie. "They're calling nine-one-one, and you're going to the hospital."

"No, I'm not."

"Yes, you are."

"Shawn, would you mind bringing me my phone?"

"Sure." Shawn stepped away and returned a moment later with Mike's phone. There was a text message on the screen.

"Oh, thank God. She's okay," said a greatly relieved Mike. "I knew there had to be a mistake somewhere. She sent me a text message. She's on her way to Dallas."

"I know," said Shawn. "I got a similar message. However, she sent it this morning. The plane crash happened this afternoon."

Mike's phone suddenly started vibrating. Kurt was calling, so Mike put the call on speaker. "Thank God it's you. Where's Tonya, and what the hell is going on?"

"I take it you've heard."

"I have."

"Are you okay?"

"It remains to be seen," said Mike. "Where's Tonya?"

Kurt's voice sounded grave. "Someone from Alicorn called me a few hours ago, and here's what we know so far. The plane crashed in a parking lot. Thankfully, no one on the ground was seriously hurt, but it was fully loaded with fuel and it caught fire when crashed. The fire department got there quickly, but it was a really hot fire and it took some time to extinguish it. There's not much left of the jet. Everyone on board was burned beyond recognition."

"I know the plane crashed. I'm asking you where's Tonya."

"I'm sorry, Mike. According to the itinerary, Tonya was onboard, and I'm truly sorry for your loss. I loved her too." Kurt's voice was breaking. He stopped for a moment to compose himself.

"Right now, I'm at the charter company hanger. They've recovered a few personal items from the wreckage. I'm looking at what's left of George's Rolex watch, along with a broken diamond pendant. It has a pretty big stone, at least a karat or more. They also found a diamond earring."

"Which doesn't sound like anything Tonya would wear. Where's her gold watch and heart-shaped locket? She never took her locket off."

"I know, and I don't see either of them here."

"Are they're certain Tonya was on board?"

"There was a woman who identified herself as Tonya Rose, and I saw the security camera footage. She was wearing a red tunic, and I've seen Tonya wearing the same tunic before."

"But what about the locket?"

"I didn't see it. She was also wearing a hat and sunglasses, and she was looking away from the camera, so I couldn't see her face clearly, but it was definitely Tonya's red tunic."

"But no heart-shaped gold locket?"

"No. There was no heart-shaped locket."

"Then it wasn't her," said Mike, firmly. "She would have never taken her locket off, and they would have found at least part of it, along with her gold watch, but they didn't, which means it wasn't Tonya."

"I know you don't want it to be her. I don't want it to be her either, but they were on their way to Aspen, so George may have insisted she wear different jewelry. Until we hear from the coroner, I don't want you getting your hopes up. In the meantime, try to get some rest, and the minute I hear anything, I promise you'll be the first to know."

The paramedics arrived as they were talking, and someone pointed them to Mike. "I gotta go, but I'll call you in the morning."

Mike was quickly loaded into an ambulance, and Shawn and Charlie met him at the hospital. He was discharged in the wee hours of the morning with a bandaged forehead and cold packs for the swelling, but no serious injuries. Returning to their hotel, Charlie headed straight to his room while Shawn offered to camp out in Mike's room.

"I'm fine," said Mike. "Go get some rest, I need to be alone for a while."

"If you're sure. Call me if you need anything."

"Good night, Shawn. Or should I say, good morning? I guess it's now Friday, isn't it?"

"It is," said Shawn. "I'll be in my room if you need anything."

As Mike changed into his sweats, the reality of what had occurred finally caught up with him. While he prayed Tonya wasn't onboard the plane, the fact remained that no one had heard from her since the crash.

He felt a lump in his throat as turned out the light, but once he settled into bed, his pent-up emotions suddenly came to the surface. He wept uncontrollably until he fell into an exhausted sleep.

* * *

Mike woke up when he heard a text alert. The sun was up. He touched his forehead as he stretched. The lump was still there, but it felt less swollen. Squinting at his phone, he read Shawn's text.

"Call me as soon as you're awake. I have the best news ever."

He sent a quick reply. *"I'm awake. What happened?"*

There was a tap on the door a minute later. Mike got out of bed with a loud groan. Shawn waited on the other side. His face was pale and his eyes were bloodshot, but he was also smiling.

"You look like hell," said Mike. "Did you get any sleep?"

"Nope, but you were right. I just heard from Tonya's stepfather. Her dental charts didn't match the woman on the plane. They still don't know who she is, but she definitely wasn't Tonya. The other good news is Tonya's name was never released to the press, so all news reports are saying George Monroe and an unidentified female passenger."

"Who would most likely be Mandy West. She and George have had a thing for one another for years. She was also trying to convince him to let Tonya go." Once again, the realization suddenly dawned on him.

"Wait a minute," he said as his face lit up. "This means Tonya's alive."

"She is," said Shawn. "Her stepfather also saw a bank cam video. It was shot around eleven-thirty yesterday morning, which is about the same time her mother spoke to her on the phone. She was wearing a black sweater, not a red tunic. Tonya told her mother she had to take care of some personal business, and her phone would be turned off, but she would be in Dallas on Wednesday."

"Which is the same thing she texted all of us. Kurt gave her a map and a key to the house, so what are we waiting for? Let's get the hell out of here."

"Charlie said he'd have us on a flight later today," said Shawn, "but there's still a problem. We still don't know where Tonya went. Do you have any idea?"

"No, I'm afraid I don't. So why aren't they out looking for her?"

"From what I understand, it's because there's no reason to suspect foul play, and she told everyone when to expect her Dallas." Shawn shrugged. "I guess it means we'll have to wait."

"And avoid the press," said Mike. "I'll call Kurt and have him call Shandra, and the sooner we're out of here, the better."

❧FIFTY-FIVE❧

TONYA SPENT THE next three days hiking around Lake Elsinore. Whenever she found a peaceful, secluded spot she sat down and either cried or stared into space. Sometimes she did both. At the end of each day, she took long a hot bath. She was trying to cleanse her soul, and once again, she felt her sister's presence with her.

It nearly sundown when she finally stood and dusted herself off for the last time. She had to leave the following morning, whether she was ready or not. Returning to her room, she had some Chinese food delivered, and upon finishing her meal she broke open her fortune cookie.

"Okay, Annette, you've made your point. It says, 'Forgive yourself and love again.'"

She was anxious to get on the road the following morning. Working her way across the desert, she merged onto the Interstate in Indio and continued east. As she drove through Arizona she felt strange not stopping in Tucson, but her mother and stepfather were at the Grand Canyon with Robin and Dawson. She continued east and stayed overnight in the nearby town of Benson.

The remainder of her trip was the reverse of her drive to Los Angeles, and she reached the Dallas-Fort Worth metroplex two days later. The freeway was busy with the early afternoon rush hour, and it felt good to be home. Tonya had memorized the route to Mike's house. As she drove through the mix master, she switched freeways and headed north. Her exit appeared a few minutes later, and after a few traffic lights she turned onto a side road and drove through an upscale residential neighborhood. Turning another corner, a tan masonry house with a nicely landscaped front yard appeared on her left. At long last, she was finally home. She slipped her key into the lock. Bruno and Maize waited on the other side.

"Hi you guys. Remember me?"

They greeted her with cautious sniffs, but their presence was out of place. Mike was still on tour. The dogs were supposed to be in Birmingham with his family. Tonya called out hello as she cautiously stepped over the threshold, but there was no answer. Whoever was staying there was apparently out.

The house looked clean and freshy dusted. Like George's house in Sherman Oaks, it was bigger than it appeared from the street. The floors were covered with a light gray tile, and she recognized the rugs from Mike's home in Santa Barbara. The living room included a brick fireplace, along with a few pieces of new furniture. As she looked around something unexpected caught her eye, her chocolate-colored sofa from her college apartment.

"Seriously?" she said out loud.

She walked into the kitchen. A large island stood in the center and separated the dining area. Sunlight streamed in through the windows. The countertops were a light granite with dark brown shaker cabinets and a cut glass light fixture hung from the ceiling. Looking out the window, she saw the pool and hot tub in the backyard, along with a built-in grill.

Her next stop was the master bedroom, and she gently tapped on the door. Again, there was no answer. She slowly opened it. To her relief, Mike was napping on top of the bed. Coming closer, she saw a large bruise on his forehead. Her heart sank. Something had gone wrong on the tour, and Mike had gotten hurt. She sat down next to him and gently stroked his arm.

"Hey, babe, it's me," she softly said. "Are you okay?"

He moaned and slowly stirred, but wasn't fully awake. "I'm fine. When did you get here?"

"Just now. Would you like me to make you cup of herbal tea?"

"Yeah, that'd be great."

She had barely set the teakettle on the stove when she heard his voice.

"Oh my god. It's really you." His face looked a little pale as he wrapped his arms around her and held her tight.

"Are you all right?" she asked.

"Yeah." He gave her another squeeze. "Where the have you been? No one has seen or heard from you since Thursday, and whenever we tried calling it went straight to voicemail."

"I know, and I'm sorry. George finally cut me loose, and I've had my phone on airplane mode. For the past week I've been on a spiritual detox."

"Which explains why they didn't find any of your belongings in his house."

"What are you talking about?"

Mike briefly stepped away to get his phone. "I'm sending Shawn a text, and we'll fill you in on everything as soon he gets here. We'll go unload your car while we're waiting."

"Are you sure you're okay?"

"I'm fine. It looks worse than it really is, and I'm on the mend."

"What happened?"

"You're asking me too many questions, Ms. Rose." Once again, he wrapped his arms around her and gave her a long, passionate kiss. "We'd better start bringing your things inside. Otherwise, I'll get distracted, and with Shawn on his way, things could get really awkward, so let me grab my shoes."

Mike smiled when they went outside and he gave her car a closer look. "Nice wheels. It may not be a red Mustang, but it's still a really good car."

Tonya popped the trunk open and Mike grabbed her guitars. "If you'll get your viola, I'll show you the music room."

Tonya eagerly followed him down the hallway to one of the other bedrooms. "Did you get another guitar?" she asked.

"Sure did, and you can play it later, but first we need to get rest of your things, and there's plenty of room in the master closet."

"Being a bit presumptuous, aren't you, Mr. Jablonski?"

Mike laughed as they walked back out to the car. Shawn arrived as they were gathering up the last load. He greeted Tonya with a warm hug and grabbed a suitcase while Mike scooped up the remaining garments from the backseat. Tonya followed them inside, but the house now had a different feel.

"Just put it in the bedroom," Mike said to Shawn. "We'll unpack it later."

Tonya felt apprehensive as she and Mike took their seats on the chocolate sofa while Shawn sat down in a nearby chair.

"Shawn and I got your text messages on Thursday," said Mike. "So have you been listening to the radio or watching the news over the past few days?"

"No. As I said, I had my phone on airplane mode. With all I went through on the George Monroe roller coaster, I had to shut the rest of the world off while I figured out how to live with myself again. So no phone, no Internet, no TV, no nothing. The only thing I listened to was the sound of nature and the playlists on my phone."

Mike looked at Shawn. "We figured as much. Can you tell us everything that happened last Thursday? From the beginning."

"George and I were supposed to fly to Aspen. He wanted to celebrate me finishing my first album. I really didn't want to go, but I had no choice. Thursday morning, he left for work, but then he came back about an hour later, and he was like a broken man. I'd never seen him that way before." She looked Mike in the eye.

"He told me you won. He would set me free as soon as we returned from Aspen. I couldn't believe it. I finally had my life back."

"I know. His attorney called my attorney that morning. I've done really well with Alicorn, and they've made damn good money off of me. So, we gave him an ultimatum. Either he set you free, or I was breaking my contract. I knew in the end he would do whatever it took to save his bottom line, but he fought me every step of the way."

"I know he did."

"Is this when you sent us the text messages?"

"Yes," said Tonya. "Then Mandy showed up shortly after George left the second time. She too had been trying to convince him to let me go, and she was as thrilled as I was. She said not to worry about going to Aspen. She wanted to go in my place. I felt so incredibly relieved. She offered to help me pack, and then she helped me load my car. That's when I left."

"What time?" asked Shawn.

"It was around lunchtime."

"What about your red tunic?" asked Mike.

"My red tunic?" Tonya suddenly felt confused. "What does my red tunic have to do with any of this?"

"We'll explain in a minute. What happened to your red tunic?"

"I wanted to get rid of a few things, including the red tunic, so I put it in a separate pile. Mandy said she'd have someone take it to the thrift store for me."

Mike looked at Shawn. "Which explains everything."

"It does."

"What are you guys talking about?"

Mike squeezed her hand. "Tonya, I don't know how else to say this, so I'm just going to come out and say it. George's plane crashed right after it took off. They're still investigating what happened, but they're all dead. George, Mandy, and both of the pilots. None of them survived."

"What?"

"Their plane crashed," said Shawn. "It happened a few minutes after they took off."

"It came as a shock to us as well," said Mike. "The plane caught fire right after it crashed, but the coroner said they were all killed on impact. However, for those first few hours after it happened, we all thought you were on board. Your name was on George's itinerary, and all of the bodies were burned beyond recognition. Kurt went to the charter company a few hours later to claim your belongings, and while he was there, he looked at the security camera footage. Mandy was wearing a hat and sunglasses, so he couldn't her face clearly, but he recognized your red tunic."

"Oh my god. I had no idea. I told her to donate the tunic to charity, but I think I may have also mentioned it was George's favorite."

Mike squeezed her hand. "It's okay. Ms. Rose. You didn't do anything wrong. No one expected anything to like this to happen. Someone called your stepfather to get your dental records. Afterwards, your mother collapsed and ended up in the emergency room."

"Oh my god! She never got over Annette, and if she thought something had happened to me, she would have lost it completely. I need to call her. Right now."

"She's fine. I spoke to her earlier today, and we'll call her in a few minutes, I promise. However, she wasn't the only one who ended up in the emergency room that night."

She looked at him. "Which explains the huge black and blue mark on your forehead. What happened?"

"As you know, we had a show last Thursday night in St. Louis. Someone from Alicorn called Charlie, but he didn't say anything to us until after the show was over."

"Your stepdad also left me a voicemail," said Shawn. "He said the coroner's office had contacted him, but then he called me again the following morning. Your dental records didn't match. That's when we knew for sure you weren't on the plane."

"But we both went through a night of pure, unmitigated hell," said Mike. "Kurt said your watch and locket weren't among the items they'd found."

"Of course not. Because I'm wearing them."

"I can see that, Ms. Rose, and you have no idea how happy it makes me. However, at the time we were all praying you hadn't taken them off for some reason."

"It was pretty traumatic," said Shawn. "Mike collapsed and got this big lump on his head.

"I did not collapse. The floor came up and hit me in the face."

"My bad." Shawn tried to suppress his smile. "So, after the floor came up and hit Mike in the face, someone called the paramedics, and our friend here went to the ER by ambulance. They released him around four-thirty in the morning, and we flew home that afternoon."

"They've cancelled the tour for the next few weeks out of respect for George," said Mike. "Nor do they want me performing until I'm fully recovered."

Tonya burst into tears. "It should have been me. I was supposed to on the plane, not Mandy, but she took my place, and now she's dead because of me."

"Don't got there." Mike's voice was firm. "None of this is your fault. Stan gave Mandy's ashes to George's family so they can be buried together in England. He said their dying together was for the best. Otherwise, she would have died of a broken heart." Mike gave her another squeeze while Shawn went to get her a tissue.

"Are you okay?"

"I don't know. Somehow, in spite of everything, Mandy and I became friends, and there was a time when I cared deeply about George."

"I know there was," said Mike. "There was a time when I thought highly of him as well, and while I would have never wished him any harm, I'm also greatly relieved he can never hurt you again." He gave her another squeeze.

"Go get your phone. You need to call your mother, and Shandra. So far, she's been telling the media to respect your privacy, but she needs to put out a formal statement from you."

"And I need to head out as well. Jacque should be home by now." Shawn handed Tonya some tissues and gave her a hug. "Welcome home, and I'll call you tomorrow."

❧FIFTY-SIX☙

NO SOONER HAD Shawn left when the doorbell rang again. "I guess he must have forgotten something," said Mike. He opened the door, and a blonde woman stood on the other side.

"I brought you your chicken divan, Mike, and oh my god! I don't believe it. Our wayfarer has finally arrived."

Mike quickly grabbed the casserole dish as Emily rushed inside and greeted her cousin with a warm hug. "Where have you been? When we heard about the plane crash it scared the living hell out of all of us."

"I know, and I'm sorry. I needed to get away from everything and everyone for a few days to sort things out. Once I left George's house, I didn't check my messages or turn on a TV. Mike and Shawn just told me about the plane crash, and I'm still in shock."

"Of course, you are." Emily and Tonya joined Mike in the kitchen and they quickly sat down at the table.

"How do you guys know one another?" asked Tonya.

"Your mom got us together," said Emily. "She was concerned about Mike, so she asked me to check on him, and now I'm playing keyboard on his next album."

"Really?"

"She sure is," said Mike, "and she'd love to contribute to your next album as well."

"I appreciate the offer, but who knows what'll happen with Alicorn? I still can't believe George is gone."

"As you might expect, Alicorn is experiencing some challenges at the moment," said Mike. "Several women have now come forward claiming sexual harassment. Stanley Klein has also jumped in. He says he's working on a tell-all book about the long, torrid love affair between his late wife and George Monroe."

"You're kidding," said Tonya. "There was never any love in their marriage, and Stan wasn't exactly a faithful husband either."

"I know, Ms. Rose, and he'll fade from the spotlight soon enough. So, here's what we know so far. George's father, Philip, has announced that Kaitlin Gleason-Young will replace George as the president of Alicorn Records, USA. She was their executive vice-president, and she was in charge whenever George went to England."

"I know who she is," said Tonya. "George introduced us at the Alicorn Christmas party."

"Really? What'd you think of her?"

"I liked her. She struck me as someone who won't put up with any nonsense."

"Which is exactly what they need right now," said Mike. "Philip also released a statement about Alicorn having zero-tolerance for sexual harassment, and while they won't admit any wrongdoing, they're offering to settle out of court with their accusers. No doubt Kurt will be giving you a call about it."

"I'd prefer to talk to him about it later. Right now, I just want to lay low until this all blows over, and I'm sure Shandra will agree."

"I don't blame you," said Emily.

Tonya looked at Mike. "What about our contracts?"

"Yesterday morning Kurt and I had a video conference with Kate and Philip. Neither of them are harboring any ill will toward me over my recent battle with George."

"Which is good," said Tonya.

"They've read all the correspondence between the attorneys, so they understand what happened. Philip also said that while he raised George to respect women, George had some serious abandonment issues after his mother died, and he's deeply sorry for what happened between you and him. So, under the circumstances, they're willing to let us out of our contracts, no questions asked." A big smile broke out across his face.

"However, both Philip and Kate also made a point of saying they really would like for us to stay with Alicorn. They both liked the way we sounded together on 'Cordelia,' and they'd like for us to do more collaborations."

"How so?"

"They're really excited about us doing, "No Where Else on Earth," on my next album. Kate would also like for us to do a song together on your next album, assuming you stay with Alicorn."

"Really?" said Tonya. "When I brought up you and me working together with George, he said absolutely not. He said our styles were too different."

"Because he had an ulterior motive. Our other option, of course, would be to go with Hagerman, but I've done well with Alicorn, and I honestly would rather stay with them."

"And so would I," said Tonya.

"Then it's settled," said Emily, "and I can't wait to work with you guys. So, Tonya, have you called your mother yet?"

"Not yet," said Tonya. "I only got here a short time ago, and I haven't had the chance."

"Then allow me." Emily took her phone from her purse and placed the call. "Hey, Aunt Heather, you'll never guess who's here."

She handed her phone to Tonya, who stepped away so they could talk in private. Her eyes were red and puffy when she returned.

"Are you okay?" asked Mike.

"I'm fine. She said to tell all of you hello. She also said she and Alberto are coming to Dallas next week, and I can't wait to see them."

"I want to introduce you to my family as well," said Mike. "So, while we're on hiatus from the tour, I'd like for us to take a trip to Birmingham, if it's okay with you."

"Of course, but I'd prefer to drive, not fly."

"I was planning on driving, so we can take our time and maybe see some of the back country, like we did when we went to Morro Bay. I also need to get in touch with Charlie. I want to bring you along on the tour, and we'll perform some of your music so you can promote your album as well."

"And while I'm excited for both you, I have a hungry baby waiting at home," said Emily. "I'll call you later, Tonya."

After Emily left, Mike asked Tonya to join him on the chocolate-colored sofa.

"I can't believe this is here," she said.

"I bought it from Shawn because we needed to have something of yours. He and Jacque are moving to a new place here in town, and they plan on buying new furniture."

"He's getting ready to pop the question. He just doesn't know it yet. I'm also glad I got the two of you together."

"Me too." Mike smoothed her hair away from her face. "However, at the moment my main concern is you."

"I'm fine, although I still can't believe Mandy is gone. She was on our side all along, and her taking my place on the plane will haunt me for the rest of my life."

Mike wrapped his arms around her and held her close. "I expect you'll feel some survivor's guilt for a while. You wouldn't be you if you didn't. But I also know Mandy's life would have never been the same without George, and for whatever reason, they were meant to go together."

"She spoke about them being together in past lives while she was helping me pack, and she said she hoped he wouldn't be as stubborn in their next one."

"Then let's hope she gets her wish."

Tonya took a closer look at Mike's forehead. "Wow. You really took a tumble."

"I sure did. For a while there I thought I'd lost you for good."

The dogs were getting restless. Mike got up and fed them while Tonya popped Emily's casserole in the oven. After the dishes were washed, Mike drew her a hot bath and stood by as she stepped into the foaming bubbles.

"You are so beautiful," he said. "I just don't know if I can hold myself back or not."

"Then I guess you'll have to join me, won't you?"

"You don't have to ask me twice." He tore off his clothes and hopped in the tub with her. After a long, hot soak, he carried her off to the bedroom. This time the coverlet was turned down. As they made love, they both felt an intensity they had never experienced before, and afterwards they held each another close in the afterglow.

"It's good to have you home, Ms. Rose."

"It's good to finally be home, Mr. Janson."

ȣFIFTY-SEVENȣ

KURT CALLED MIKE the following morning to confirm Tonya's arrival in Dallas. Mike put the phone on speaker as Tonya poured herself a cup of coffee and joined him at the kitchen table.

"I'm glad you two are staying with Alicorn, so I'll call Kate as soon as we're done. She'll be happy to hear it, and I wouldn't be at all surprised if she were to ask you to do an entire album together."

"We'd love it," said Mike.

"We sure would," said Tonya.

"Then we're all in agreement. In the meantime, George's family is returning to England later today. They plan on having a private service in Manchester, and afterwards his and Mandy's ashes will be buried together. In the meantime, I'll schedule a video conference for the three of us with Kate."

"Do you think Charlie will be open to the idea of bringing Tonya along for the rest of the tour?" asked Mike.

"I don't know why he wouldn't be," said Kurt. "I call him as soon as we're done, and Tonya, welcome home."

"Thanks. It's good to be home," she said.

Charlie called Mike an hour later. "I just got off the phone with Kurt, and bringing Tonya along would certainly help improve moral around here," he said tongue and cheek. "And you're right. We want to help her promote her new album as well, so I'll call Shandra later. Meantime, how's the head?"

"It's looking better, and I've not had any complications."

"Then it sounds like you're on the mend, and I'm looking forward to getting back on the road. I'm rescheduling your cancelled dates for July, so plan on having a busy summer."

"We look forward to it. We love performing."

Tonya's mother and stepfather arrived the following week. They loved Mike and Tonya's new home, and while they too were sorry about Mandy's demise, both were relieved to finally see Tonya happy with Mike. After they left, Mike loaded his truck and they drove to Birmingham so Tonya could meet his family. Mike's mother took an instant liking to Tonya, as did the rest of his family, much to his relief.

Charlie called the week after they returned to Dallas. "So, how are you feeling, Mike?"

"I'm fully recovered. You'd never know I'd gotten hurt."

"Good, because come the first of May we're back on the road, and Tonya's coming with us."

Tonya's twenty-second birthday was at the end of April. She and Mike invited Shawn and Jacque, along with Emily and Kyle, to help celebrate.

"I'm so happy to finally meet you." Shawn extended his hand as he and Emily were introduced. "I've heard a lot of good things about you, and I'd love to work with you someday."

"I've heard good things about you as well," said Emily. "So I'll have my people call your people."

"Wow." Cory's eye's popped as he looked around. "Is this really your house?"

"It sure is," said Tonya.

"So what'd you do? Get married or something?"

"That's enough, Cory," said Emily.

They spent most of the afternoon in the back yard, enjoying the spring weather. Cory wanted to jump in the pool, but after putting his feet in the water he realized it was still a little too cold. Shawn and Mike got their guitars and Tonya soon joined them while Emily and Jacque took turns holding the baby.

"You're really good with kids," said Emily. "I can tell you'll be a good mother someday."

"What was that?" asked a suddenly startled Shawn.

"Relax," Jacque said firmly. "I'm not pregnant. She was only speaking hypothetically."

As the others burst out laughing, Mike looked at his watch. "You know what? I think it's time to light the grill."

Kyle joined Mike at the grill, and once the hot dogs and hamburgers were ready, they took their seats at the dining table. During the meal both Shawn and Jacque seemed unusually happy.

"You two have been acting like a couple of love-struck teenagers all day," said Tonya. "So what's up?" As she was speaking, she noticed a sparkle in the corner of her eye. Her face immediately lit up.

"Wait a minute. What was that?"

"You mean this?" Jacque smiled ear to ear as she presented her diamond engagement ring. "It's about time you all noticed."

"What the hell?" said a surprised Mike.

Tonya stood from her chair and gave Shawn a congratulatory hug. "I knew you were getting ready to pop the question. I just didn't expect it to be this soon."

"The plane crash was a real wakeup call," said Shawn. "Ever since it happened, I've been thinking about how fragile life really is, and how much I've been taking things for granted. So, rather than wait for the right time to somehow magically appear, we decided to make the here and now the right time, and I wanted her to have the ring before we went back on tour."

"Have you set the date?"

"Late September," said Jacque. "We're still waiting for my employer to approve my taking the time off. Then we'll make an official announcement."

"And we'll have the party here," said Mike.

Emily and Kyle said goodnight after the birthday cake was served while Shawn and Jacque stayed and helped with the clean-up. After they left, Mike turned on some classical music and Tonya joined him on the chocolate sofa.

"You know, Ms. Rose, I've been so preoccupied with going back on tour that I keep forgetting to ask you if you were planning on going back to modeling."

"Nah. I had a lot of fun, but I never set out to be a supermodel. I only did it to save money for school."

"Do you regret not graduating?"

"Nope. If I hadn't lost my funding, you and I would have never met. Funny how things have a way of working out for the best in the end."

THE END

❧EPILOGE❧

MIKE AND TONYA were prepping for their performance. The opening band had started the last song in their set, and a crew member was escorting Tonya's mother and stepfather to their front-row seats in the auditorium. After a brief intermission, Mike and Tonya would take the stage.

"So, here we are," said Shawn. "We're finally down to the final two rescheduled shows of the tour, Phoenix and Las Vegas, and we're doing them in July. Couldn't we have done them in May, and moved Seattle and Portland to July?"

"Nope," said Charlie. "I know it's really hot outside, but it could be worse. We could be stranded on a broken-down tour bus somewhere in the middle of a big winter snowstorm, and I'd rather be too hot than too cold."

"I don't know about that," said Mike. "A little ice and snow would feel really good right about now."

Charlie seemed unmoved. "C'mon you guys, it's a dry heat."

"Maybe so," said Tonya, "but when it's a hundred-fifteen degrees it really doesn't matter. Take it from someone who was born and raised here."

"I'll second that," said Shawn, "and I was born and raised in Texas."

"You all are a bunch of wimps." Charlie laughed and rolled his eyes in mock exasperation as he stepped away to talk with one of the promoters.

"Yeah, but heat or no heat, I'm still looking forward to us spending a few extra days for a honeymoon in Vegas once we're done," said Mike.

"Me too," said Tonya, "but since we're not married, it's technically not a honeymoon, although I am looking forward to a nice, romantic, end-of-tour vacation."

Mike gave Shawn a knowing look.

"If she says no," said Shawn, "we're sending her back to Dallas, and I'll hang out with you in Vegas"

"That works. We could go check out some of the acts while we're there, but you'll have to get your own room."

"No problem, boss."

"Okay, you two. What's going on?" asked Tonya.

"I have no idea." Shawn shrugged and stepped away to talk to Charlie while Tonya gave Mike a puzzled look.

"You and Shawn have been acting strange all day. I can tell you're up to something, and whatever it is, Charlie is in on it too. So what is it?"

"Okay, Ms. Rose, you got me." Mike had a twinkle in his eye as he spoke. "I brought something for you, and I thought with your folks being here tonight, it would be the perfect time for me to give it you, although I was planning on giving to you after the show."

"Aha! I knew it." She gave him a satisfied grin. "So don't keep me in suspense. What is it?"

"You'll find out in a minute, but first I wanted you to know that I thought about giving it to you on your birthday, but it was too soon after Mandy."

He gently took her off to the side, where no one would overhear them, and took a small velvet box from his pocket. Inside was an emerald-cut aquamarine ring in a white gold setting with a smaller diamond mounted on each side.

"Oh my god!" Tonya's hands went up to her mouth, and her body started shaking.

"I know a diamond solitaire is the more traditional ring, but aquamarines have a special meaning for us." He looked into her eyes. "Ms. Rose, would you do me the honor of being my wife?"

For the moment, Tonya was too stunned to speak.

"You okay?" asked Mike.

"I'm fine." Tonya's voice sounded breathy as she spoke. "I'm just really, really, surprised, but in a good way. And the answer is yes."

"Is everything okay over there?" asked Shawn.

"We're good." Mike slipped the ring on Tonya's finger. It fit perfectly. As they embraced, he gave her a long, passionate kiss.

"I take it she said yes," said Shawn.

Mike gave him a thumbs up as the others began cheering. Once the applause died down Shawn raised his water bottle.

"Then let me be the first to congratulate the happy couple. You two had to overcome some incredible obstacles to get to where you are, but you made it, and if anyone deserves a lifetime of happiness, it's the two of you."

"We couldn't have done it without you, Shawn," said Mike. "Tonya and I will always be grateful for your help and support."

"And while I hate to break this moment up," said Charlie, "Tonya needs to touch up her lipstick. Your mom and stepdad will be here after the show, and we'll have champagne waiting for you. I'm also happy to book the chapel in Vegas if you'd like me to. In the meantime, congratulations to both of you. Tonya, you're not going to faint, are you?"

"No, I'm not going to faint. I just can't believe you were on in on this."

"It's what you all pay me for, so let's see the ring, and then you need to go fix your makeup. We've got a show to do."

GRANDMA CARLOTTA'S SPAGHETTI AND MEATBALLS

Sauce:

1 medium white or yellow onion, chopped
1 bell pepper, chopped (optional)
3 to 4 cloves garlic, minced or pressed
3 tablespoons olive oil
4 cans diced or chopped tomatoes (15 oz)
2 cans tomato puree (29 oz)
¾ cup red cooking wine (if desired)
3 tablespoons sugar
3 tablespoons dried basil
3 tablespoons parsley
1 tablespoon rosemary or Italian seasoning
I teaspoon oregano
1 teaspoon salt
½ teaspoon black pepper
Dash of crushed red pepper (if desired)

Sauté onions, garlic, and bell pepper, (if desired), in olive oil in large stockpot at medium heat for about 5 minutes. Add tomatoes, tomato puree and red cooking wine, (if desired) Blend tomato mixture thoroughly. Add sugar and seasonings and bring to a slight boil. Reduce heat to lowest setting. Allow sauce to simmer, stirring occasionally, for about 4 to 5 hours. Do not allow sauce to scorch. If necessary, turn heat off, briefly, and allow sauce to cool slightly, then turn heat back on to the lowest setting.

Meatballs:

1 pound lean ground beef
1 pound Italian sausage, hot, mild or sweet*
1 egg
¼ cup breadcrumbs
1 teaspoon salt
¼ teaspoon pepper

Remove sausage from casings and place in a large mixing bowl along with the ground beef. Add egg, breadcrumbs, and seasonings. Mix thoroughly, either kneading by hand or with a large spoon until all ingredients are well blended. Roll into golf ball sized meatballs and set upon a plate until all the meat mixture has been rolled. Gently place meatballs, one at a time, into the sauce mixture with a large spoon, being careful not to break the meatballs. Continue simmering sauce on low for another 2 ½ to 3 hours, again stirring occasionally to prevent sauce from scorching.

Note: Salt may be omitted if desired

*Ground pork may be used instead of Italian sausage.

ABOUT THE AUTHOR

Marina Martindale began her career as a graphic designer and artist. Over time, however, she discovered that writing was her true life's passion.

"I love creating conflicted characters," says Martindale. "They're more like the people we meet in real life. I also like the complexity of romance. It's an opportunity to delve into the human condition and try to understand what motivates us to make the choices we make."

Martindale draws her inspiration from her own life experiences, as well as those of the people around her. The stories, however, are fiction.

"The path to true love is never easy," says Martindale. "Some are haunted by people from their past. Others have been deceived or betrayed by the ones they trusted the most. We all make bad choices, although we may not realize it at the time. My stories are about the unintended consequences of those bad choices, how the characters resolve them, and how they grow and become better people as a result."

Marina Martindale currently resides in Denton, Texas. In her spare time, she enjoys traveling, photography, music, and cooking.

Other Books by Marina Martindale

The Reunion

Gillian Matthews is making a name for herself in the art world. All of her hard work has paid off, and her paintings are being sold in a number of prestigious art galleries. Yet in spite of her success and accomplishments, one thing has eluded her. True love. Then one night, during her opening at a Denver art gallery, a man from her past suddenly and unexpectedly appears. Her long-lost true love. The one man she never forgot, never got over, and never expected to see again.

The Deception

A string of misfortunes has left photographer Carrie Daniels penniless and desperate. When her former mentor, Louise Dickinson, steps forward to offer her a job as an art model, Carrie has no choice but to accept. Things seem to be looking up with she meets Scott Andrews, however, her friends soon realize Scott isn't who he appears to be, while an unknown enemy sets out to destroy her life.

The Journey

Cassie Palmer's world is shattered when a car crash leaves her hospitalized and fighting for her life. Her husband, Jeremy, begins his own frightening journey after he meets Denise, one of Cassie's nurses. He may not remember her, but Denise has never forgotten how he jilted her, years before. Jeremy mysteriously vanishes, leaving a grieving Cassie behind. As she struggles to rebuild her life, Cassie will discover that things are not as they appear.

The Betrayal

Emily St. Claire's world turns upside down when she finds out her husband, Jesse, has been unfaithful to her. Determined to rebuild her life, she returns home to her father to pursue her life-long dream of becoming a concert pianist. As Jesse fights to win Emily back, her life will be shattered once again when an unforeseen tragedy forces him into an alliance with a corrupt police detective to frame her for a crime she didn't commit. While another detective, Kyle Madden, puts his career on the line to prove Emily's innocence, the plot against her turns deadly, and it may be too late to save her.

The Stalker

Rachel Bennett may have attended her ten-year high school reunion on a whim, but fate intervened once she saw Shane MacLeod. No longer the shy, gawky teenager she remembered, Shane has matured into a handsome and successful man, but her perfect evening ends when another man from her past suddenly reappears. Craig Walker had been her mentor until he became jealous of her talent and success. Now he intends to either have her, or destroy her at all costs. As Rachel's family pressures her to take Craig to court, she can no longer ignore her nagging feeling that a tragedy is about to strike.

The Letter

Stephanie Ellis and Danny Woodruff had a happy relationship until Stephanie accidentally discovered a love letter from Martha, a woman from Danny's past. Believing Martha was a lonely ex, Stephanie ignored her letter, until even more compelling evidence surfaced. Convinced that Danny had been cheating on her, she leaves him, and with the start of a new job she meets Josh, who introduces her an exciting new world. Unfortunately for Stephanie, Josh isn't who he appears to be.

The Scandal

After leaving the soap opera that made her famous, Lauren McAllen is offered a role in a major motion picture. However, her dreams of success on the big screen will shatter before the camera starts rolling. When the studio head is accused of wrongdoing, Lauren is unwittingly caught up in a major scandal that rocks Hollywood. Convinced her career is over, Lauren creates a new life for herself in Colorado under a different name, but fate will intervene once again when an old friend unexpectedly appears at her door.